Elizabeth Lord was born
the age of six she moved
since. After the death o
only twenty-six, she went to work as a legal secretary until she remarried in 1968. She has a son and two daughters, all married; her second husband died in 1984. Elizabeth is an ardent traveller and likes to spend her time visiting ever more exotic locations. Her other novels for Piatkus are *The Stolen Years*, *The Angry Heart*, *A Better Life*, *The Turning Tides*, *The Bowmaker Girls*, *Mile End Girl* and *Brenda's Place*.

Also by Elizabeth Lord

The Stolen Years
The Angry Heart
A Better Life
The Turning Tides
The Bowmaker Girls
Mile End Girl
Brenda's Place

For All The Bright Promise

Elizabeth Lord

PIATKUS

Copyright © 1998 by Elizabeth Lord

First published in Great Britain in 1998 by
Judy Piatkus (Publishers) Ltd of
5 Windmill Street, London W1T 2JA
email: info@piatkus.co.uk

This edition published 2001

The moral right of the author has been asserted

*A catalogue record for this book is available
from the British Library*

ISBN 0 7499 3107 8

Printed and bound in Great Britain by
Cox & Wyman Ltd, Reading, Berkshire

Chapter 1

From her bedroom window Margaret Ross could look down into Victoria Park Road, where she lived. Her mother preferred the back bedroom, which was far quieter.

The houses at this end, coming off from the busy Cambridge Heath Road, one of the many arteries serving East London, were modest two-up two-down homes with tiny gardens at the back but none in the front. They weren't exactly poor or slummy – being in the better part of Hackney – but they couldn't match the fine houses further along, those that faced or backed on to Victoria Park itself.

Some were double-fronted, some three-storied. All had long if narrow back gardens. They had front gardens with low brick walls and shrubbery to shield them from the noise of poorer East End children who trooped to the park in hordes for a bit of fresh air with packets of sandwiches and bottles of lemonade, or to swim at the lido, costumes tucked under their arms, or to feed the ducks with stale bread or just to hang around the ornate drinking fountain and clink the dented metal cups on chains against its granite sides as loudly as they could. The sound could sometimes be heard clear across the park's lawns and flower beds and playing fields.

At her dressing table Margaret leaned nearer her window to see better the large houses once occupied by the middle class in a previous era: small business people, shop owners, bank clerks, all waited on by armies of domestic staff as their basements still bore witness. Now, in 1939, domestic staff were a thing of the past except for the occasional charlady who lived out and came and went at set times. Vacuum cleaners had taken over, and white vans that collected laundry once a week, returning everything clean and pressed the same day, and dry cleaners for finer clothes.

Lipstick poised, Margaret wasn't thinking much about these things. She was thinking more about one particular house, the first one in that row of houses which she could see well, almost opposite. It too was large, not as large as some of those further along, though fine enough, but in that house lived Matthew Ward with his mother and father and sister Louise.

Margaret had met him through becoming friends with his sister four years ago when she and her mother had first come to live in this area after her father had died. Mumsy, who had leaned on her husband all her life, had been inconsolable. After his death, unable to face living in their house in Approach Road on the other side of the park, it had been decided she and Margaret leave all their painful memories there and move. They hadn't moved far, but it was smaller, more manageable; it was comfortable and held no sad memories though Margaret suspected Mumsy still carried each and every one of them in her heart like little fetters. But had they not come here she'd never have met Matthew. He had been sixteen then, and she fifteen.

She thought of Matthew now; how her heart raced every time she saw him. She thought of the looming threat of war, as most people were doing. Barrage balloons were already floating in the breeze on the end of their cables like fat floppy silvery fish, soldiers were digging trenches in the parks and anyone with a garden was sinking an Anderson shelter into it. And already children were being evacuated to the country to escape possible air raids. But mostly she thought of Matthew, whether he'd be sent away to fight – if there was a war.

For a moment, she took her eyes off his house, bathed in the golden light of an August evening, the sun still well above the horizon so as to make it still seem afternoon. It was no good watching the house forever. No sign of life from there. He must already have gone while she had been helping Mumsy to clear away the dinner things. Lingering dismay hung heavy inside her but she doggedly applied her lipstick in the dressing-table mirror all the same. Perhaps she could still make it in time.

Her bedside clock stated ten past seven and she was not yet ready. It was a good ten minutes' walk along Cambridge Heath Road to St John's hall. No good getting a bus, she might have to wait ten minutes for that. St John's Friday night dance started at seven thirty, but there was no guarantee that Matthew would even be there, though he'd said he would be.

She had met him closing up his father's electrical shop as she got off the bus from Leadenhall Street where she worked in an accountant's office. He had grinned at her as she passed, totally unaware how her heart had flipped at the sight of him.

'You look a bit hot and bothered, Maggie.'

She hated his shortening of her name. He was the only one among her friends who did. But she smiled. 'So would you be, working in the City. You're lucky. It's been a real baker there today.' She had hastily changed the subject to what had been uppermost in her mind, posing her question as casually as she could. 'Are you going to the hall tonight?'

Most of the young people she knew frequented the events St John's church put on. Matthew was a helper with the Boys' Brigade, she a Girl Guide lieutenant, and both of them, like most of their friends, would help out at bazaars and church fêtes and Sunday school. And there was the Friday dance.

Matthew had lifted his broad shoulders in a gesture of doubt. 'I'll see how I feel come seven o'clock. Bit too hot for dancing. Might think of going to the lido for a swim. Did have a date for tonight. Mare Street Regent, but it was only casual. It's too hot to sit in the pictures.'

So that had been that. She had laughed lightly, nodded and moved off, feeling vaguely sad for the casual date waiting about outside the Regent cinema, golden hopes dying as frustration set in. That was how he was, quite unaware of the hearts he broke, hers included. But then, she'd never registered in his book. She was more certain than ever that he wouldn't be at the dance tonight, since his front door remained firmly closed when she glanced yet again towards his house. But just in case . . .

Hardly had the thought touched her than she saw the door open. And there he was. Her heart that a second before had sunk into her very slippers now rose like a bird leaving a tree's topmost branch.

Mesmerised, she watched the tall, lithe figure stride with an easy grace along the road, crossing it diagonally to pass beneath her window. Gaining Cambridge Heath Road, he turned – and Margaret's heart leaped again for joy – in the direction of St John's.

The second he was out of sight, she jumped into action. Reaching blindly for the pillbox hat that went with her blue flowered summer dress, her unguided fingers caught the small froth of blue net and sent it tumbling to the lino from its already precarious perch on the edge of her dressing table.

'Damn! Bloody, bloody damn!' she burst out. Why was it that the mere sight of him sent her into paroxysms of clumsiness, she who at work was always known for being so calm and collected? One can always rely on Margaret Ross to cope in a crisis – she'd heard it said more than once and even derived a certain modest pride from it. Yet coming anywhere near or even seeing Matthew Ward was enough to make her no longer mistress of her own actions. And now, the mere thought of arriving late for the Friday dance perhaps to find him gone off elsewhere by the time she arrived, perhaps taking most of her friends with him, sent her into a panic she'd rather no one witnessed.

It seemed all the more precious to be near him these days what with the threat of war and young men talking of joining the Territorials, keen as mustard to have a go if the balloon did go up. Nothing their parents said of the Great War seemed to be making any difference to some of them. And if Matthew joined up, it would be goodbye to her secret joy of being near him.

She had no illusions about herself. Even as she crammed the stylish little hat on her head, she tried not to acknowledge the ginger hair, which some called auburn but which to her could be nothing other than ginger, nor the milky complexion that went with it, typical of those of her colouring. She was well aware of Matthew's preference for dark-haired, petite types.

As far as she could see the hat did nothing for her. She smiled grimly at her reflection in the dressing-table mirror, the raging curls swept severely back from a high forehead into a comb at the nape of her neck; her mouth wide, her nose, in

4

keeping with her firm narrow face, very straight. How she would have preferred to have a short retroussé nose like that of Jean Summerfield, Matthew's current girl, even though such a one would have looked incongruous on the face her critical green eyes now studied. A strong reliable face to match a strong reliable body.

Margaret gave a huge sigh. Well, make the best of a bad job. Mirror, mirror on the wall . . .

'I wish I was dark-haired and petite,' she'd remarked to Matthew's sister only a few weeks ago, her thoughts still centred on Jean Summerfield.

'Why?' Louise had said in her blunt, straightforward way. Louise was the type who offended quite a lot of people by her almost epic frankness, rather like her mother, never seeing it as offensive, though people knew where they were with her. Not one to falsely flatter, also like her mother, one could always rely on the truth with Louise Ward. The way she had said 'why' had given Margaret a certain encouragement to open her heart to her.

'It's the sort Matthew usually falls for,' she'd admitted.

'And you'd like my brother to fall for you?'

That had been just a little too candid and Margaret remembered cringing inwardly, wishing she'd bitten off her tongue. 'Of course not. It's just that I hate being ginger and tall. I hate my face and my frame. I'm so ungainly.'

'You're not ungainly,' Louise had said without glancing up from the dusty old church hall bunting they'd been sorting out ready for yet another church fête to raise funds.

When she hadn't answered, Louise, still busy unravelling strings of faded triangular pennants, had gone on: 'I suppose you are tall. What, five foot eight? But you've got a nice figure, and there's nothing wrong with your looks as I can see.' Louise had stopped what she was doing to search her mind for a comparison, 'A bit like Katharine Hepburn . . .'

'For heaven's sake, Louise!' Margaret had broken in with a self-critical laugh. If the girl had been a natural flatterer she could have been forgiven, but this sweeping statement set Margaret, crouching beside her, back on her heels. 'I can't compare with a *film star*.' Hepburn of Hollywood with her high cheekbones and dancing eyes was one thing, Margaret Ross

5

from across the road with her too-curly hair and her wide shoulders was quite another. 'For heaven's sake, Louise, don't be so silly.'

But Louise had looked up from sorting bunting to regard her closely, comparison to screen idols forgotten. 'You haven't got a *thing* about my brother, have you?'

'No.' Margaret had also put aside Katharine Hepburn, her face warm before the younger girl's shrewd smile. Louise never smirked or grinned. She smiled, as she had then, in a lofty way, the way her mother did, making the recipient want to crawl under a stone.

'I think you have. I think you fancy him.'

'No, I don't.'

One couldn't go on denying hotly. She could only appeal to Louise to say nothing to Matthew of what she'd after all merely surmised.

Now she stared in the mirror, wanting so much to believe Louise's unintentional flattery, but the green eyes beneath the flaming hair merely gazed back in disparagement. Beautiful? Striking? What man, and by what man she knew she meant Matthew, would ever throw himself at *her* feet?

Margaret smiled grimly at her reflection, and turning from its cruelty, she snatched up her handbag from the bed and hurried downstairs to kiss her mother before leaving the house.

She found her on hands and knees in the kitchen, sleeves rolled to the elbows, one plump arm wearily describing soapy circles on the linoleum with a scrubbing brush. Disbelief sharpened Margaret's tone.

'Good God, Mumsy, what on earth are you doing?'

The soft rounded face looked up, downy cheeks flushed from her task, apologetic hazel eyes meeting her daughter's. To Margaret, gazing in horror, she looked much older than her fifty-two years as with a tremulous sigh she sank back on to her ankles. 'The floor looked a bit smeary, dear. I . . .'

'But I washed it all over this morning, Mumsy, before I left for work.'

Whatever possessed her mother? She was forever pottering around the house, doing things that never needed to be done, often after Margaret herself had done them. It made a mockery of all the help she gave.

6

'I just thought a small wipe-over.'

'With soap and scrubbing brush?' It was hard to mask irritation, only too aware of what lay behind all this. 'How can I go out while you're tiring yourself out completely, doing things like this?' It was a way to keep her here, and if she wasn't careful, it would.

'Leave it, Mumsy. Go and rest.'

Mrs Ross drew the back of a wet hand limply across her brow. 'I do really feel I must. I'm so hot.'

'I don't wonder.' Margaret moderated her tone, understanding replacing annoyance. Two years was far too short a span to expect her mother to get over losing Daddy. She herself hadn't yet quite got over it. But she had a job to go to, lots of diversion, friends in the evenings. Mummy had nothing. The woman next door was as deaf as a post. The young couple on the other side had their parents, brothers and sisters, a host of friends, all of them visiting and in turn to be visited, too absorbed in their own pursuits to bother with a woman who tended to wrap herself in her self-imposed shroud of isolation. As for those in their big new houses lining the park, they with their bridge parties and their bowling and tennis and their theatres, to them those in the smaller houses were a world away, seldom encountered for long enough to exchange a word or two. Mumsy was a lonely woman. It was cruel to go off and desert her right now, and Margaret would quite readily have given up her evening to keep her company in normal circumstances, but tonight Matthew was drawing her as a lodestone attracts iron.

Relieving her mother of the scrubbing brush, Margaret tipped the pail of suds down the sink. 'Go and sit in the back garden, Mumsy. Take a book with you,' she ordered, feeling a pang of sorrow at the feeble ploy to keep her here. 'It's still lovely and sunny by the back door.'

Installed in a deckchair in front of the small border of bright annuals which Margaret herself had planted, Mrs Ross gazed up at her. 'You won't be too late home, will you, dear?'

'No, Mumsy, I won't.'

She was rarely late home – usually eleven at the latest, knowing her mother's dread of being alone, but the regularity of the query irked a little.

'I wish you didn't have to go out, dear.'

'I always go out on Friday night.'

'I suppose you'll be out tomorrow as well.'

'Just swimming, that's all. I'll have the rest of the weekend with you.'

Mrs Ross heaved a sigh that said how quickly the weekend would go before she must spend the coming week on her own until Margaret came home of an evening. But before the matter could develop further, Margaret dropped a hasty kiss on the flaccid cheek and went back into the kitchen to mop up the suds on the floor.

It hardly seemed worth going out now. Matthew would already be there. What if he'd taken it into his head to go off somewhere else? She'd have no idea where, and without him, the dance would go down for her like a soggy bun.

She had to at least try. Fraught with anxiety she called goodbye to her mother and hurried off. Turning into Cambridge Heath Road, she caught her breath in a huge gulp of relief. Jean Summerfield was just in front of her, sauntering along as though she had all the time in the world to spare. Breaking into a run, Margaret caught her up.

'Gosh, am I glad to see you,' she burst out, falling into step, already flushed from her short spurt on this hot evening. 'I did think I was going to be late. Matthew's already left. You know what he's like. He could go off anywhere without waiting for us.'

'Oh, he'll wait for me.'

Jean was a willowy brunette. Looking cool as a cucumber, she turned an extremely pretty oval face to Margaret, her voice a purr of self-assurance. She'd been going out with Matthew for nearly two months, a long time for any girl where he was concerned.

Margaret wasn't so sure he'd wait. He might be going out with Jean but he'd been seen on two occasions with that blonde Middleton girl from St Anne's Close, a fact Jean shrugged off with affected nonchalance. Margaret reflected that had she been treated like that, she would have given Matthew his marching orders long ago no matter how it broke her heart. Trouble was, Matthew's dreamy brown eyes hardly ever strayed

8

in her direction, not in *that way*, so there'd never be a chance of her putting that valiant promise to the test.

'Marie Middleton told me yesterday she'd be there,' she remarked, more from the need to move Jean along faster than from any sort of spite, but Jean flicked her a look saturated with venom.

'For your information, she's not his sort. He doesn't care for blondes. Or *redheads* for that matter, if you want to know.'

The dig wasn't lost on Margaret and she felt ruffled. She was no competition. 'I just happened to see him eyeing her at the dance last week, that's all.'

She found herself rewarded by another glare, the small pretty face with its retroussé nose and bright red lips waspish. 'You keep your eyes to yourself. Dennis Cox is your partner. Anyway, Matthew told me he thinks I'm the tops. So there!'

Even so, her stride had quickened, past the Council offices, past the Bethnal Green Children's Museum set back from the road, on their right a train travelling the viaduct above the small shabby shops, filling the air with smoke and a sooty smell. They covered the half-mile to their destination far more quickly than Margaret ever guessed a small-built girl could, and she had to hurry to keep up with Jean, who was rattled.

Finally reaching St John's church at the Salmon and Ball crossroads, they were both hot, Jean's cheeks glowing prettily, Margaret's a fiery flush. In the hall, the pianist, drummer and saxophonist on the tiny stage, with its brown curtains hanging limp and dusty with East End smoke, were still sorting out their arrangements. The hall, with its faded religious prints around the walls and its small grimy windows, echoed with the garbled conversation of young people perched on splintery bentwood chairs waiting for the dance to start, girls in bright dresses, boys with hair slicked back with Brylcreme, their suits well pressed, jackets already hanging on chairbacks to reveal well-ironed white shirts.

Early arrivals had already commandeered the few folding tables on which to put their soft drinks and crisps. Margaret's gaze flicked anxiously to each one, knowing that if Matthew was still here, he would certainly have got himself a table. He had, of course – one of the better tables at the far end of the hall, near the band.

9

Sharing the table were Freddy Perry and Eileen Wilcox, who only had eyes for each other these days, and Dennis Cox. The latecomers were immediately spotted by Matthew who was instantly up from his seat, beckoning, his handsome face alive with welcome as they came over, his lips parting in a wide smile that revealed even white teeth.

'Thought you two would never arrive.' It was a full-toned voice that reflected a zest for life and the natural impatience of a soul seldom in need of rest. 'We got our drinks before it got busy.' He eyed the bar at the far end with its two ladies serving a growing queue. 'What would you like?'

Jean dropped into the seat he'd vacated, very sure of herself. 'God, it's hot! A nice long cool lemonade, darling, large as they can make it.'

Margaret hesitated, wondering if she should offer to pay for herself or not. She heard him chuckle wickedly.

'Come on, Maggie, make up your mind.'

His well-spoken accent made the playful quip sound flippant. Those living in such as Victoria Park Road tended not to have the accents of the East End. Matthew had once said that his mother had been a lady's maid before she'd married. Margaret supposed that the mannerisms of her then upper-class employers must have rubbed off on her, though to her mind Mrs Ward boasted just too many airs and graces. Not that it bothered Margaret. She was well spoken too, her family as good as any. And all her friends spoke very much the same, so there was really nothing for his mother to be snobbish about. Thank God Matthew wasn't. He even joked about it, apparently to his mother's face as well as behind her back. Still, the quip took Margaret a little off guard.

Her already bright flush deepened. 'Can I have lemonade too?' Her thin enquiry annoyed her. His ringing laugh made her wince.

'What makes you think you can't?'

It wasn't his fault. She was an idiot. It was being so close to those velvet-brown eyes. Flustered, she hurriedly sat down next to Dennis Cox.

Dennis immediately began to monopolise her with an account of his new job. Coming straight from college armed with diplomas and bags of hope, he had landed himself a

10

position in a firm of London solicitors. Listening to him, Margaret could well imagine him in years to come, bustling from court to court, bundles of legal briefs under his arm, probably having grown much plumper than he was now.

He was still expounding on his future when Matthew returned with two glasses of lemonade for the girls and two of ginger beer for himself and Dennis. Margaret smirked covertly. She'd seen the drill before. He probably had a tiny flask of whisky in the inside pocket of his jacket now hanging over the chairback. The moment the ginger beer was gone, empty glasses would be surreptitiously replenished by the contents of that flask, the same colour as the soft drink. Lots of the boys did it, not enough to get drunk on, but enough to be lively. If St John's vicar were to know, he would have a fit.

Matthew was lifting a mocking eyebrow at Dennis. 'Why don't you give the mouth a rest, Cox, and do some work for your living? There's two more drinks on the counter, and some crisps. Go and get them for us, eh?'

Dennis looked affronted. 'See here – I've been sweltering all day in the City.' The amiable laugh at his protest provoked even more indignation from him. 'All right for some. All you do is drive about in your dad's van all day. So what happened to that smashing job you were offered by Marconi's when you left college last year? I thought you were going to be big in radio communications or something.'

If he had hoped to rattle his opponent, he was disappointed. 'Turned it down in the end, old man. Dad's shop takes priority. His chest plays him up sometimes and there's only him to run it. He's not getting any younger.'

'And of course it'll be yours one day, won't it?'

The remark had an insinuating ring to it and although Matthew's easy grin did not alter, the dark eyes adopted a fractionally harsher glow. 'I don't need to prove I've more brains than you by sweating in some office.'

'You're just plain lazy,' Dennis sneered.

'I probably am.' The good humour had returned. 'Come on, Cox, get cracking. It's on the counter, all paid for.'

Slipping into a spare seat beside Jean, he left the peevish Dennis no option but to do as ordered. Eileen and Freddy, lost in each other, hadn't caught the small note of dissension, their hands hidden under the table.

Matthew grinned. 'Now then, you two. You're in company, remember? There's a time and place for everything, you know.' As their hands came back into sight, the pair looking sheepish, he turned his gaze on Margaret.

'You look nice tonight, Maggie. Blue suits that hair of yours.' The impish grin seemed to her to belie the compliment.

'You mean ginger?' she corrected, but was halted by the unexpected change in his expression.

'Some girls would give their eye teeth for that colour,' he said slowly, his scrutiny of her so deep and personal that she felt her cheeks flush and her heart give a leap. But Jean's brittle voice cut in.

'Matthew, I'm still waiting for my lemonade.'

The glass was within arm's reach, but he must have realised it was the only way she could get his attention at this moment for as he pushed the glass towards her, he treated her to a low 'mee-ow'. Margaret wanted to laugh out loud as Jean tossed her short dark curls in pique, a pout spoiling her pretty face. It was good to know she wasn't alone in getting the raw edge of Matthew's sometimes far too caustic wit.

When Dennis returned with the remaining refreshments, vague hostilities faded. The hall was growing uncomfortably hotter by the minute with so few windows capable of being opened. The band was still warming up, sheet music was being turned, scales on the sax being tentatively tested, the drums tapped at intervals. Dennis turned his attention to studying his already half-drunk ginger beer, eager for the small tot of whisky to liven it up.

'What do you think of this Hitler lark then? Me, I think he'll go into Poland, whatever Chamberlain says. If you ask me, we're being cocked a snook at. I don't relish giving up a brand-new job, but I'd be willing to go and fight him. The RAF for me. What about you, Matthew?'

'Haven't given it much thought.' Matthew's tone was airy.

'You should, old man. Don't want to sit by too long and get roped into any old thing when they start conscripting. Get in quick, I say. We're all officer material, you know, with our education.'

Jean gave a little giggle, pique forgotten, and squeezed her partner's arm. 'You'd make a spiffing officer, darling.'

'Will it be the RAF for you too?' Dennis was looking at him, waiting for a reply. 'It's the only service to be in. Great uniforms.'

His quarry leaned back in his chair, squinting through the shafts of dust-laden sunlight at the yellowed windows. It was as though he hadn't heard a word of anything that had been said.

'Ye gods,' he sighed, his favourite expression. 'It's bloody hot in here.'

'It's been a hot summer all round,' Margaret offered quickly, all she could think to say with an uncomfortable sense of embarrassment at the way he seemed to have neatly evaded Dennis's question.

But Dennis appeared to have forgotten his own question. 'Where's that flask then? You did bring it?'

'Does it matter?' Matthew grimaced as the band at last sprang into action with a ragged tempo that echoed tinnily around the hall. 'Who wants to bother with this rubbish anyway?'

'I do, Matthew,' Jean protested. 'Listen, darling, it's a waltz.'

He was an excellent dancer, as he was excellent at most things, and Jean was aching to show off in his arms. But he continued to frown at the tempo that would fail to allow him full enjoyment of his skill.

'I know.' His face brightened on a flash of inspiration. 'Why don't we go swimming?'

'Swimming?' There was an echo of disbelief from everyone except the couple still locked in each other's gaze.

'Victoria Park Lido. This time of year it's open till late. We could pop home, pick up our togs and be there inside fifteen minutes. Who's game?'

'Me.' If there was a sport Margaret felt happy with, it was swimming. But Jean was pouting again. Water would spoil those tramline Marcel waves of hers, even under a swimming cap. But rather than lose him this evening as she might well do, she grudgingly agreed. Dennis too had little love of water, but he agreed, not wanting to appear soft.

13

Matthew regarded the two lovers. 'A dash of cold water wouldn't do you two any harm. Fancy going for a swim?'

'What?' They looked blank.

'We're going to the lido. You two want to come?'

For a moment they regarded each other, coming to a silent mutual agreement. 'No . . . Not really.'

Matthew's laugh dismissed them. 'Right then, it's us four.'

It was a dash to get swimming costumes and towels, then back to meet at the park gates. Matthew, with one arm around Jean's shoulders, led the way, Margaret and Dennis following behind.

The evening belonged to Margaret, with Jean, eager to preserve her Marcel waves, sitting on the side of the pool, just her feet stirring the water as she posed hopefully for Matthew's attention.

Dennis, after lowering himself tentatively to his well-fleshed waist in the shallow end, pulled himself out again, shivering with the shock of cold water after the heat outside, then went and sat beside Jean. Matthew was unsympathetic.

'Come on, Cox, shut your eyes and jump. There's enough flesh on you to keep you warm on an iceberg!'

He himself had taken a flying header into the deep end, surfacing among the other swimmers to flick water from his dark hair with a brisk toss of his head before making it the length of the baths with a fast crawl to confront the shivering Dennis, his taunting laugh echoing over the surrounding tree tops above the cries and shouts of the other bathers.

Dennis declined to join him so he swam off again, deftly avoiding those around him, Margaret close behind matching stroke for stroke, until he hoisted himself out at the far end and made for the diving boards. Treading water, she watched the lean figure appear on the top board, poised, waiting for a clear space below before launching itself off, piercing the surface like an arrow. The skill and grace took her breath away. At the same time she felt a small sense of foreboding take hold. He took his physical assets so much for granted, that slim tireless body fashioned to perfection, that abundance of health, that quick alert brain. War was coming, unavoidable. Young men like him would be taken to fight for their country. She had heard her own father's account of the last war, the trenches, the mud, death from disease, bullets, shells, gas; men blinded, maimed, the rest of their lives ruined.

As a child she had shuddered from her own imaginings after listening to such talk. Now she shuddered again, seeing perfect bodies reduced to utter wrecks, bodies like Matthew's. She swam slowly now, trying to push away such visions, but they persisted. Men with such bright promise to their lives, so many blessings to look forward to, plucked off the fair tree like ripe fruit. True, there were those who had, and those who had not. Matthew was one to whom everything had been given; it seemed almost unfair that so many blessings should be heaped on one person while another knew little but ill health and hard luck. Yet how much worse would it be for someone like Matthew, with everything, if his happy world should crumble than for another already equipped for adversity? With no experience of how cruel this world could be, couldn't Matthew be more stricken than the already ill-fated should he come face to face with the worst aspects of this world?

Margaret pulled her thoughts up sharply. It was this threat of war. It might even yet be averted and there'd be no more need for morbid reflection. Matthew was climbing the diving board again. This time she turned away, again plunging into her own pool of dejection. War was no respecter of the beautiful and Matthew was indeed . . .

Her feet were suddenly tugged from below and she instinctively gulped air before going under, surfacing again to see him grinning into her face.

'You . . . you . . .' she spluttered at him.

Dejection swept away, she grabbed for his hair, a move he easily evaded. Together they wrestled, spluttered, yelled, laughed. His hands were cool on her body, his arms strong, hoisting her from the water as the whistle sounded for the lido to close. Jean was jealous, purposefully ignoring her. No doubt Matthew would kiss her into a better frame of mind when he took her to her door to caress her in a way Margaret could only dream of. But this evening had been hers. She was content, even to the point of allowing Dennis to drop a kiss on her cheek without shrugging him off, but no more than that.

They dawdled across the park, taking their time with the air still warm, lounging on a bench talking, giggling, Matthew bent on petting Jean into a forgiving mood. Then they went on in the last crimson glow of this midsummer evening which promised another fine day tomorrow. Matthew cocked a weather eye at the darkening red streaks, remarking, 'Red sky at night, shepherds alight!' His humour was whimsical as always, his mind on the rewards Jean would bestow on him for all the attention he intended to shower on her at her door.

When the friends parted company, Margaret glanced at the purpling sky promising its fine tomorrow. How many tomorrows before the sky darkened forever with Matthew far away? She firmed her lips and shrugged away the thought.

Chapter 2

With the metallic voice of Prime Minister Neville Chamberlain fading away, followed by a defiant rendering of 'God Save the King,' Margaret turned her gaze to her mother's face. It was chalk-white.

'What are we going to do?' For some reason the futile question got under Margaret's skin. She got up from the armchair where she had been sitting taking in what the sad, disillusioned, somewhat quavering voice had to say, hardly able to believe its message no matter that they'd seen it coming for weeks and especially these last few days, and switched off the radio.

'Not much we can do, is there? Sit tight, I suppose.'

'It won't be like the last war.' Mrs Ross, still huddled in her armchair, looked like a plump little elf amid the silence that seemed to have closed in around them now the wireless had been turned off. 'That was the first time ordinary English civilians had ever been bombed. We can expect them to do it again. And this time they'll use gas on us. Why were we issued with those horrible gas masks last year if they didn't think it would be used against ordinary people? Evil-smelling rubber thing, it smells like gas itself.'

'For goodness' sake, Mumsy.' She tried to be flippant. 'How would you know how gas smells? Except what comes out of the stove. It's all a storm in a teacup. Everyone says that once England has shown her teeth and stopped appeasing him, Hitler will back down. It's a show of strength, that's all. In a month this will all be behind us. Now I'm going to make a cup of tea. I think we both need it.'

Wishing she felt as certain as she hoped she sounded,

Margaret went into the kitchen to put the kettle on, followed by her mother who had herself into gear at last. She was sure there'd be more alarmist sounds from her, but thankfully she said nothing, going about the task of setting out the teacups and saucers, the clink of china unreal in the odd sort of silence that lay over them. It was far too beautiful a sunny Sunday morning for such news.

She was on the point of emptying the teapot of its dregs from the last brew made just before Chamberlain's awaited announcement when there came a strange sound, a distant wailing, followed by another, much closer. For a second it was unidentifiable. Then Margaret realised.

'Oh, God, Mumsy, it's an air-raid siren.'

They stared at each other, her mother with fingertips bent against her lips as though to stop their sudden trembling, Margaret with the teapot hanging loose by its handle from her momentarily paralysed fingers.

Her flesh had gone cold, the rising goose pimples conveyed an actual sensation, the fear that clutched at Margaret's heart was like cold fingers attempting to restrict its pumping, pumping so heavy that it felt as though it were in her throat.

It was her mother who first came to life, swinging away from her with a cry, making for the hallway and the front door. She had flung it open before Margaret could collect herself enough to chase after her, catching her halfway down the few stone steps to the street.

'No, not that way. We must go down into the Anderson shelter.'

A man's voice was calling to them from across the road. 'Over here – into our shelter.'

It was Mr Ward standing at his gate beckoning to them. After a brief hesitation, Margaret took her mother's arm, hurrying her diagonally across the road. It would be far more comforting and, even though erroneously, it felt safer to be with others than the two of them all alone in the darkness of the newly built shelter put in for them by a paid man, having to sit by candlelight with the dank shelter's earthy smell all around them. Mr Ward would never know the relief with which she hurried towards him.

He was a tall man, in his early fifties she reckoned, who

must have been an extremely handsome man in his youth – still was, she supposed. He looked very much like Matthew except that he was very thin and looked drawn. Matthew said his father had received a touch of mustard gas in the last war, leaving him with a slightly weak chest. He seemed a kindly man, and always nodded to her or her mother when passing them in the street, not like his wife who, though she would always nod too, left one with a feeling of inferiority. However, Margaret was sure she had no idea of the effect she had on others. She struck Margaret as somehow being older than her husband though she probably wasn't: it was just her attitude that made her seem so. Thirty years ago one might have called her a handsome woman and she still carried herself like a duchess. Margaret was sure she had a kind heart for all that but she had never felt at ease meeting her in the street. And now she was being asked to enter her home – or at least her Anderson shelter.

'We do have our own,' she explained as she came up to Mr Ward. 'We had it put in for us last week.'

He held an arm out as though shepherding them. 'Even so, we can't see two women alone down one of them. This is a time for us all to help each other. Come along.'

They followed him nervously through a narrow side gate into a small, neatly laid out town garden surrounded by trees and bushes whose dusty leaves screened it from neighbours' eyes. Mrs Ward liked privacy.

'Will Mrs Ward mind?' Margaret queried behind him.

'Why should she mind? We should all stick together in these times.' He sounded so like Matthew. Margaret fell silent as she followed him to the mound at the end of the garden that now covered the raw corrugated iron structure half sunk into the ground, its straight sides and curved top precisely fitted together, the soil already made a little less unsightly by a transplantation of geraniums and Michaelmas daisies. Her own, so far covered only by bare earth, had more the appearance of a wallowing elephant as it awaited a few plants to disguise its grimly utilitarian purpose.

She watched as he handed her mother down the four wooden steps to below ground, then herself. There was a curtain across the square entrance covering a small door already fitted. Hers so far had just a curtain. The door stood open and as she entered Mr Ward let the curtain fall back to its proper position, to shut out any light that might be seen at night by enemy bombers looking for a target. She was amazed at the light there actually was. An electric bulb in the centre of the curved roof, shaded by a small but beautiful orange lampshade, cast a cosy glow. But then, Mr Ward knew all about electricity, didn't he? The interior, measuring six foot by eight, was made to seem much narrower by double bunks lining either side to accommodate this family of four. At the far end a small table with a red chequered cloth held a decorative oil lamp; a square mirror propped against the back wall reflected everything back to give the illusion of a less cramped space. Above it a shelf bolted to the corrugated iron held provisions for a night's stay. The cold iron was painted pink, and a pink brocade curtain partly shielded the back wall for an extra sense of snugness. Thus a cosy retreat had been fashioned from what could have been an uncomfortable hole in the ground. Even the pervading mustiness of damp earth was allayed somewhat by a large bowl of home-made pot-pourri beside the lamp.

Mrs Ward was standing by the table, her posture very upright, her expression stiff, the unwilling hostess compelled to receive uninvited guests, which Margaret felt she and her mother must be. They were intruders into this extension of her home, which this musty-smelling underground shelter with its effort to appear cosy indeed was. Yet behind the stiffness lay an attempt to hide her fear for the moment, the air-raid warning having now faded away to leave an eerie silence outside.

'Thank you so much for having us,' Mrs Ross began in a small voice, she too feeling the tension, not just because of this impending air raid. In return she received wintry smile but no word of welcome.

Margaret stood uncertain, wishing they hadn't accepted Mr Ward's invitation. In their own damp, half-finished shelter they'd at least have felt at ease, if isolated. She was glad Louise was also there.

Crouched forward on a lower bunk so that her head wouldn't knock against the one above her, her arms clasped about her chest in foreboding, Louise looked as though she were making some sort of obeisance at her mother's feet. But there the impression of humility ended. A younger version of her mother in many ways, Louise at seventeen bore all the hallmarks of becoming a staid, strait-laced woman by her forties. Already she had a tendency to bossiness and certainly a way of managing people whether they liked it or not. She was nevertheless a generous-hearted person, which Margaret imagined she owed to her father, and she had found herself liking Louise from the very start. Mumsy said once, when she had mentioned it, that Louise was rather like a black widow spider! But Margaret considered Louise's way of calling a spade a spade very commendable and people could not be held responsible for who they took after at birth. She was heartily glad, though, that Matthew took after his father rather than his mother.

'Not made a bad job of it, have we?' Mr Ward was saying with pride in his voice. 'Me and Matthew put it up between us, but the titivating bits his mother did, and a great job she's made of it too. Never know how long we might have to stay down here if things get really bad.'

He gestured to the other lower bunk. 'Well, sit down then, both of you. Make yourselves at home.'

'Where is Matthew?' Margaret asked as she sat.

'Out with a friend, apparently.' Mrs Ward's reply was chilly, sharp, it seemed to Margaret, disapproving of her son's absence at such a perilous time. Margaret fell quiet. She might feel safe here, yet in the chill that had descended she wished she could be anywhere but here.

Her mother ventured, 'Young people seldom understand,' only to be met with more bleak silence, and in this vein the five sat facing each other, the Wards on one side, Miss and Mrs Ross on the other, each with their own thoughts, waiting for the first distant roar from swarms of enemy bombers they were sure were coming to annihilate them all.

Every now and again, her mother sighed, 'Oh, dear.' Mr Ward cleared his throat quite a lot, now and again smiling encouragement at them as they waited. Mrs Ward's face remained stony, but Margaret noticed how she twisted her hands together at one or two unguarded moments, and despite her own fear that persisted in clutching at her stomach, she found herself looking on the woman as being capable of human

21

emotions after all. She knew so little about her, wondered how Matthew and his sister could live with such an unapproachable woman, except that she was their mother and they were used to her, she supposed. But over and above her fear of the unknown beyond this shelter, she counted the minutes when she could be away from here.

Relief was a surge of joy in more ways than one when after only ten minutes – though it had seemed like an hour – the sweet single note of the all clear sounded. Everything that a moment before had seemed suspended in a sort of bubble of waiting, sprang back into life. Voices could be heard beyond the shelter. The whole street seemed to be alive with people as Margaret and her mother emerged to go back home.

She had never seen Victoria Park Road like this before, neighbours standing about in groups discussing where they'd been and what they had been doing at the moment of the siren sounding, speculating if it had been just a false alarm or not.

For Margaret it was an event she felt she'd never forget, not so much because of the fright as the camaraderie that appeared after it. Also it had been her first-ever glimpse into Matthew's home, at least as near as she imagined she'd ever be to it. A little like an eavesdropper, she had watched those twisting hands of Mrs Ward as she'd sat on the edge of one of the lower bunks, had been given an ever-so-brief peep behind the barrier she appeared to put up between herself and everyone else. Although Matthew hadn't been there, just being in the Wards' Anderson shelter had made Margaret feel closer to him than she had ever felt before.

Everyone had grown closer that Sunday. Men who would hardly have nodded the time of day to each other on their way to business, their privacy a virtual barbed wire fence, now passed on their observations of what the next few months might have in store for everyone. Women from the larger houses were even nodding more often to those in the smaller ones, snobbery magically put aside. Only on the bus going each day into the City were people still reserved, minding their own business, reading their paper, staring out of the window, perhaps smoking their pipes and cigarettes a little more reflectively, isolated from each other, apart from those riding together, Cockney vowels ringing loud, and of course the cheery voice of the bus or tram conductor calling for fares and pinging his ticket machine.

Everything was changing. The instant blackout extinguished all light but for the dimmest of blueish light in buses and trains. London's main railway stations were alive with men and women in uniform, with loved ones saying goodbye, husbands embracing wives, fathers kissing their children, mothers clinging to their sons, sweethearts interlocked. For some reason public transport became erratic; no one could be sure of getting to their destination on time any more. Not that civilians had many destinations to go to other than to work, since access to the coast just for pleasure was now forbidden unless one had a relation living there or specific reason to go. Seaside holidays stopped.

Everything stopped. On the wireless the BBC closed down its regional services, sticking to just one, the Home Service; schools closed, places of entertainment shut down to dissuade people from gathering in any one place for fear of hundreds being killed at once in an air raid.

St John's Girl Guide and Brownie troop and its Boys' Brigade ceased to meet, most of the children evacuated anyway from the East End to the country, away from bombs expected to fall on the population in a matter of days or weeks. The second wave of children to go since the Munich scare of 1938, they toddled off with their gas masks and their packets of sandwiches for their journey into the safe heart of the countryside, labels fastened to coat collars, mothers anxiously watching them go and wondering if they would ever see them again. Witnessing the scenes at Liverpool Street Station, and the looks on those mothers' faces as she passed on her way to work, Margaret could almost feel the heaviness of their hearts.

'It all seems so strange. I still can't get used to all this.'

Mrs Ross was helping paste strips of gummed brown paper tape in the recommended criss-cross pattern on the window panes, supposedly to help stop flying glass from the effect of a bomb blast.

'It makes the windows look so horrible. I don't like it at all.'

'It doesn't matter if we like it or not.' The gum tasted awful;

23

Margaret pulled a face as she licked. She had tried resorting to a saucer of water to dip the gummed side in, but it was awkward, far quicker to steel herself to licking. 'They say it's safer. They say just one shard of flying glass can kill. I don't fancy being slashed by something like that, not even in a small way.'

Not that there had been any air raids since that first false alarm, a stray French plane at the time unidentified over the Channel, they had been told. But it was better to be safe than sorry.

Mumsy had already complained about the blackout regulations. Their own efforts were still temporary, made with flimsy frames of batten wood and cardboard with black paper pinned to them, and they had draped their shades with thick material for the time being to lessen any light that might escape. The result was having to sit in a dingy room and that in itself lowered the spirits. In time they would get proper heavy material instead of the present light curtains that let out a little too much light.

Of all the deprivations and inconveniences that had arisen, blackout was the worst. Air-raid wardens already knocked on doors ordering erring occupants in superior tones to 'Put out that light!' A lot of things irked, not the least of them, Margaret calculated, the total change in her social life.

With the departure of London's East End children the young men went off too. Of Margaret's little set Dennis Cox said goodbye and joined the RAF. He asked if he could write to her and Margaret had half nodded, rather hoping he might forget once he got out into the wide world and met other girls. She couldn't tell him she felt somewhat relieved to see him go. She had never really fancied him, but had just been naturally thrown together with him, and consequently was sometimes thought of as his partner.

Jean Summerfield's parents, deciding that London was a dangerous place, went to relatives in Devon, to fulfil a long-standing dream of a cottage by the sea.

Jean's going was rather heartening. Although Margaret had never presented any competition for Jean where Matthew was concerned, Jean would nevertheless no longer be around to disconcert her.

Freddy, who'd enlisted as a part-time soldier during the Munich crisis before he had begun going seriously with Eileen, was called up immediately. Hastily, he and Eileen planned a registry office wedding, and leaving her pregnant, though neither knew that, he went off into the Pay Corps.

Of the group only she and Matthew remained. Obviously he was perfect for conscription under the new National Service Act, but unlike the other two he made no move to volunteer, much to Margaret's confusion. She had expected him to be the very first to do so but now she remembered the day when he had hurriedly and so noticeably – at least to her – changed the subject when Dennis had asked what service he had chosen to go into.

Already three weeks into this war, August and that particular Friday dance seemed years away. Yet every time she saw Matthew, that incident became like yesterday and the embarrassment she had felt then burned as acutely as ever, now also coupled with bewilderment. It was her mother, who like most meek souls always managed to extract a confidence from the most private of people, who treated Margaret to Mrs Ward's admission of dismay at her son's odd reluctance to join up.

'She really expected him to apply for a commission by now,' Mrs Ross related to her daughter as she treadled away on her sewing machine, making blackout curtains to replace the black paper they'd had to use as an emergency measure.

'I don't actually expect it's cowardice, but I'm sure she feels a certain embarrassment about it. She's a person who needs to hold her head up in front of others but how can she while young Matthew is still hanging round? He *must* know he'll be called up sooner or later. I imagine he's thinking right now what a pity it was he didn't take that Marconi job as she wanted him to – he would have had a reserved occupation by now and no one to query his remaining at home.'

Margaret was threading tape through a finished curtain. She let it drop on to her lap. 'That's unfair, Mumsy.'

'I don't think so, dear.' Mrs Ross gave an extra push down on the foot treadle and with a final spurt pulled the fabric free of the machine needle, snipping off the cotton. 'If you ask me, I think he's quaking in his shoes in case he's called up.'

'That's not true, Mumsy!'

'True or not, I think he's being rather silly. He'll end up being pushed into any old thing – something quite unsavoury, with all the riffraff. All that education gone to waste. Unless of course he *is* hoping he'll be deferred. He could be, with his father not in good health and needing help with his business. But I think it unlikely. I hear there are some who are applying for deferment *and* getting away with it. Perhaps that is what's on his mind.'

Extracting the last curtain from the machine, she stood up, stretching her back painfully. After she had laid the curtain across the chair she lifted the domed cover of the sewing machine back into place. 'There – that's done.'

'Matthew wouldn't do a thing like that,' Margaret said, even though her mother seemed no longer to be listening, apparently more anxious to measure her finished work against the upstairs windows. But her taciturn departure left behind waves of doubt pounding in Margaret's breast. What if her mother was right? Meek she might be. Indecisive and dependent she might be. Silly she wasn't.

Angrily, Margaret fought to push away the doubts her mother had sown. The curtain destined for this room idle in her lap, she gazed out of the living-room window at the warm blue of a late September sky. Each pane was criss-crossed by gummed strips of brown paper but she hardly noticed.

'He must have his reasons,' she said aloud several times to the blue sky beyond. 'He must have.' But it wasn't enough.

When the doubts her mother had voiced, innocently she was sure, began to bear down on her like a ton weight, she approached Louise. As his sister she must know more of the inner workings of Matthew's mind than anyone. Approaching his mother was unthinkable. His father would probably be very hurt by any reference to his son even being thought suspect; the last thing Margaret wanted to do was to hurt anyone with her prying. But she had to unburden her doubts on someone. Louise was the most likely candidate.

She caught her on Thursday evening in the church hall, sorting out old Brownie uniforms for storing away for the duration. Louise looked up at her approach and smiled, a smile closely resembling that of Mrs Ward. 'Can I help you, Margaret?' Not 'Hello, what are you doing here?'

She smiled – there was no harm in Louise – and launched into her question. 'I was wondering about Matthew. Is he thinking of joining up yet?'

Louise's face went suddenly frosty. She seemed to age ten years, become Margaret's senior. 'Why don't you ask him? It's his business.'

That was all. Incapable of pursuing it, all she could do was say brightly, 'I suppose so – see you then, Louise,' and depart hurriedly, aware of Louise looking after her as she went.

Chapter 3

September twenty-ninth, Friday; Matthew's twenty-first birthday was two days off. He was to have thrown a party on the Saturday in Dennis Cox's home, his own mother declining to open hers to a troop of heavy-footed young people. But Dennis had joined up and so had most of Matthew's friends. So Margaret saw herself as a poor substitute when she accepted his invitation to help him celebrate his majority with a meal at a tiny restaurant by the Salmon and Ball pub in the Bethnal Green Road.

'Why me?' she'd asked, aware that had Jean still been around or the Middleton girl, now engaged to a young soldier, and had not declined, she would not have been so honoured.

'Why not?' he'd countered with a flippancy that didn't quite manage to hide a certain despondency in his voice.

He was missing everyone, that was certain, and again that insidious suspicion her mother had innocently planted plucked at her. Was he really scared behind that façade he'd put up? She kept telling herself that he must have some honourable reason for rejecting his mother's intentions for him to get himself a commission, but the more she tried to convince herself, the harder it was to believe it. What young man would scorn the chance of an officer's uniform? With his education he would certainly become an officer.

Sitting opposite him at a small table in the restaurant, gas masks in their square boxes hanging on the backs of their chairs, she forced herself to smile at him whenever his brown eyes met hers, knowing he was only using her as a bolster against his own loneliness.

It had been a wonderful meal, yet she had felt that every mouthful had to be forced down; Matthew too just picked at his food, although he had done a great job on the wine, even ordering a second bottle only to consume most of it himself.

Margaret fingered her liqueur glass of Tia Maria, gazing at the thick dark liquid in its narrow vessel. 'You're not enjoying this evening one scrap, are you?' she finally burst out.

He glanced up from the brandy he had ordered. 'Are you?'

'I was asking you, Matthew.'

'Me? I'm having a whale of a time.'

The remark, to her ear loaded with sarcasm, full of the implication that in normal circumstances she'd be his very last idea of a companion, struck at the very core of her being. She could find no reply to give him, and felt starkly aware how easily and suddenly adoration can be changed to vague hostility, no matter how temporary, for her heart told her that it could only be a short while before her secret feelings of love returned.

In silence she watched him lift the brandy glass, study the amber liquid, swirling it thickly around the bowl. Bringing it to his lips he threw back his head, draining it in one gulp and coughing a little against its fiery taste. He signalled to the wine waiter for another.

'You'll get yourself plastered,' she warned, finding her voice again as the drink arrived moments later.

'Wouldn't be such a bad idea.'

'It would be a silly idea. You'll spoil your birthday.'

'Some birthday,' he muttered ruefully, taking a long swig.

Ignoring the connotation of her being poor company, Margaret opened her handbag and brought out a small oblong package wrapped in coloured paper. She laid it on the table in front of him.

'It's not much I'm afraid, but – happy birthday, Matthew.'

For a moment he stared at it, then his face lit up. 'You didn't have to do that, Maggie.'

He sounded suddenly like an excited schoolboy and she forgave him his shortened use of her name, her heart lifting as he began tearing off the wrapping with genuine pleasure as though this was the most important gift he had ever received. It was especially flattering as she knew of the presents he'd been given by his family. He had already shown her a mono-grammed silver cigarette case from his sister. In fact Louise had asked Margaret's advice on what to get him.

'Matthew smokes,' she had told Louise. 'Why not get him a cigarette case? He hasn't got one.' So apparently that was what she had done.

He'd also mentioned getting a couple of hundred pounds in bonds from his grandparents, his father's people who lived in Finchley in north London – there were apparently no grand-parents on his mother's side. Then there had been the main present, a Ford Eight from his parents, in which he had proudly driven her the half-mile or so to the Salmon and Ball.

'Well, open it then,' Margaret urged as he paused over the slim blue box she had given him, now stripped of its colourful wrapping. Carefully he lifted the lid to gaze down at the humble pen and pencil set.

'Maggie . . . that's really nice.'

She shrugged. 'It's just ordinary. I mean, it looks silver but it isn't really. I expect you already have a set.'

'No, I haven't.' He glanced up, giving her a long look. 'Thanks Maggie – it's the best present anyone could give me. I'll probably need something like this when . . . Breaking off mid-sentence, leaving her to wonder what it was he had been about to say, he placed the box in his breast pocket with almost reverent care.

'What about your other presents?' she reminded him.

He gave a sardonic chuckle. 'Beware Greeks bearing gifts.'

'How do you mean?'

'I mean I feel I've been put under obligation by some people.'

'What obligation?'

'Oh . . .' He heaved a sigh, playing absently with a box of matches put on the table for smokers' convenience. 'Doesn't matter. Family business. But thanks, Maggie, for the gift.' He reached for his glass. 'Anyway, happy birthday, Matthew! May you have many more – God willing.'

Not waiting for her to lift her own slender glass, he drained his at a gulp, blinked, then grinned across at her. 'I think I'll have another.'

Margaret gnawed at her lip. 'No, don't, Matthew.'

'It's my birthday,' he stated truculently, then grinned again.

'Good old Libra, that's me. Stuck in the balance. Death of summer, birth of darker days. God! I wish I'd been born in spring, years from now.'

He was talking nonsense. He'd definitely had enough. But apparently he wasn't of the same opinion as her. 'I'm going to have another.'

Frowning, he clicked a finger and thumb rudely at a passing waiter. 'I want another brandy.'

'Please, Matthew,' Margaret hissed, embarrassed. 'You mustn't.'

His frown deepened. 'Christ! Not you as well.'

'Me?'

'Telling me what to do. Making decisions for me. Jus' like my mother. She does that, all the time. Louise and I, we jus' laugh, but sometimes . . . Time I was allowed to make decisions for m'self. Where's that waiter? Ah.'

The man stood beside him, polite yet superior, his elderly face lined and wise, his tone conveying the faintest hint of disapproval. 'You ordered another brandy, sir.'

'I did,' snapped Matthew, but the wind had gone out of his sails. He sat slumped a little as the drink was placed before him. Listlessly he pulled out the new cigarette case, offered one to Margaret which she declined, took one himself, lit it from a gold lighter, a present from an uncle, and drew in a deep lungful of smoke.

She had never seen him like this. It was as though she was looking at a totally different person to the buoyant carefree spirit of only a few weeks earlier. It made her heart ache.

'It's getting late,' she urged, and when he shrugged, continuing to smoke, his brandy untouched, she added, 'My mother doesn't like me to be out too late. She gets lonely. She'll be anxious.'

At last he spoke. 'You too?'

'What do you mean, me too?'

'Parent trouble.'

'No, not really. It's just that now there's a war on, she worries.' But a glimmer of his problem had begun to show itself. She leaned towards him. 'Matthew. What's the matter?'

'Who says anything's the matter? I'm fine. Couldn't be better. I've got my future nicely cut and dried, no worries, nothing.

Life's grand. Just sit back and let my dear mother do the worrying for me, the arranging, the thinking. Who cares?'

He cut off abruptly, stared down at his untouched drink as though unsure how it came to be there, then he grimaced and sucked in his breath, pushing the glass from him and stubbing out his cigarette.

'Ye gods! Maggie – let's get out of here.'

Gathering up her coat, her handbag, the unsightly square box on its cord, while he paid the bill, she hurried after him, thankful that he seemed to be walking from the restaurant more steadily than she had dared to hope. But once outside on the pavement the air hit him and he swayed.

She took his arm firmly. 'You can't drive back in this state.'

'It's only a mile.'

'It's so dark. You'll have us hitting a lamppost. We could walk. I've got my torch. So long as we don't collide with a wall of sandbags.' She tried to make a joke of the sandbags surrounding the council offices. 'You can get your car tomorrow. And you must clear your head before you get home.'

'*Must*?'

She realised she had probably sounded slightly domineering. His earlier words spoken against his mother's efforts to sort out his future ought to have warned her. She hurried to repair the damage, giving a light laugh.

'Your mother will hit the roof if she sees you. You'll never hear the last of it.'

'You can say that again.' He chuckled too, his tenseness easing a little as, falling silent, he leaned on her, letting her guide him. Neither spoke as they negotiated the quiet crossroads under the railway bridge.

It was darker than they had anticipated after the restaurant lights, dim as they had been. Not a chink of light shone anywhere. Margaret's small torch, itself covered by black sticky paper with just two tiny holes cut in it, gave hardly a beam and they needed to walk slowly, cautiously, in case they bumped into something hard like a pillar box or a lamppost, none of them lit, all of them obsolete. The bowl of the sky these days was dead-black from horizon to horizon as no one in town had ever seen it; stars looked as large and bright as sequins and the Milky Way stood out like a solid path of frozen mist in the enveloping silence up there.

'Isn't it beautiful?' Margaret breathed, glancing upwards in wonder at it as they felt their way along. Time stretched out in silence between them; she judged that soon they would come upon that unevenly built wall of sandbags round the council chambers, so she moved even slower. Suddenly Matthew came to an abrupt halt, dragging on her arm.

'What is it?'

She heard his sigh. 'It's ... not been a very successful evening, has it?'

There was a slur to his words which she tried to ignore and she attempted to make yet another joke. 'My fault, or yours?'

'Mine.'

'You've not been the jolliest of people tonight,' she admitted candidly.

'And of course, you know why.' Again that sarcastic ring, but at whom she did not know.

'I don't think I do.'

'Yes you do. It's what's been hanging over my head these last few weeks. I know my mother means well, but she rather jumped the gun telling people her son was going to be an officer. Let her down, didn't I? And now everyone thinks I'm scared to join up, yellow, because I've not made any move to do anything. I can see it in their faces. I can see it in yours.'

'Not mine, Matthew! I don't think that.' But she did think that, had battled with her conscience, tried to ignore the thoughts that assailed her. It had to show in her face, in her voice, no matter how she tried to disguise it, even from herself, as she told herself that Matthew was no coward.

She heard his explosive laugh. 'There's blind faith for you! Real true loyalty. No doubts at all.'

He shrugged away from her, supporting himself with one hand against a lamppost. 'Don't you have jus' one small doubt, Maggie, in that great big heart of yours? Aren't you just a little curious to know why I ... why I didn't volunteer, like Dennis and Freddy and half the country?'

His attitude confused her, put her at odds with herself. Her entire evening with him had been spent struggling with that malignant tumour of doubt, not knowing for a moment that

33

he'd perceived the cracks in her armour. Now he was accusing her and she had no defence. She reached out and took his arm. 'I don't know why, Matthew. You're making me feel very unhappy.'

'I'm sorry.' She wasn't sure if the apology was genuine or spoken in anger. 'Seems it's the fashion t'be unhappy.' His body seemed to sag a little against the lamppost.

'All I know is I've got to tell *someone*.' For a moment he fell silent while Margaret waited, then quietly, as though ashamed of himself, he said, 'Someone I can trust. I trust you, Maggie. Above anyone else I know, I trust you. I wish . . . I jus' wish . . . God, I feel a bit sick.'

She waited while he rested his head against the iron post. In the utter darkness, but for the pinprick of light from her torch, she could hardly see him. Standing there, she stared into the black night, the chill of autumn creeping about her shoulders all the more chill for there being no light anywhere. It felt as though they were the only two people in the whole world; East London was preparing for sleep, no buses, no vehicles of any kind drove past them, just a low hum of which she was only just aware could be heard, so low it was, of some distant flicker of life in this darkened city. Silence, the silence of a metropolis waiting for that something it knew would happen eventually.

She shivered, not from cold, but from foreboding, thankful for the presence of Matthew, even if a little the worse for wine and brandy. Yet if she hadn't gone out with him this evening, she wouldn't be here now to feel this fear of the dark, this ominous dark with its low distant rumbling like the warning of a storm yet to break but still unseen. And again she shivered.

Matthew's voice made her jump, even though it was so low that had a breeze ruffled the still air, she would have missed his words.

'All my life . . .' He paused as though thinking it out, then began again. 'All my life Louise and I have been nursed along, protected, pampered. Our parents have always been there to fight our fights, solve our problems, especially my mother. I know she always meant well so I let her get on with it. I even thought it funny. But I took it all for granted. My fault. But there comes a time . . . I've just begun to realise the harm it's done. It's like being smothered by a blanket, warm and safe, but – well, suffocating if it's pulled too close. Throw it off and you realise just how fresh the air can be. D'you know what I'm trying to say, Maggie?'

He didn't wait for her reply. 'I've got to break away. Make my own life. But how the hell do you say to someone you love, someone who loves you: "Thanks for everything, but I'm off"? She does love me, but so, I don't know, so selfishly, and she doesn't even realise it.'

His words trailed off as he became lost in his thoughts while Margaret stood by not knowing what to say.

He began to talk again. 'This war. It seemed my chance to get away without hurting her feelings. But she's cheated me even out of that. And she can't see it. Had it all worked out for me, trying to help, holding my hand yet again, making enquiries to get me into some officer cadet training unit or other. I don't know what she had in mind or thought she could do – I've not been listening that much. All I know is that this time I want to do things for myself. I'm twenty-one. I don't want her to keep holding my hand.'

Margaret found her voice. 'Can't you explain to her how you feel?'

'Explain!' His voice was still slurred. 'Don't think she'd understand. Only hears what she wants to hear. Diff'rent for Louise. She's a girl. She's nat'rally happy to cling to her mother. But me. Got to let go. Let it go on too long. Should've volunteered for the Territorials last year, but she talked me out of it. Scared then at me going off and getting m'self killed. Everyone was panicking a bit at that time. But now she can see it's inev . . . inevitable she's doing her damnedest to see me in the best possible situation, going into an officer cadet training college, getting a safe job. But I don't want a safe job. I'd have liked to become an officer, but *I* wanted to sort it out. *I* wanted to. She's spoiled that for me. Now, Freddy's got married and joined up. Dennis – that soft idiot – is having a go. Suddenly I'm still a boy in a world of men, and it's shaken me. I decided I wouldn't sign on under her rules – thinking she can sort it all out for me. I'm going to wait 'til I'm called up, take my chances.'

'That could be rough on you,' Margaret said. 'You'd just be in the ranks.'

35

'Exactly. I want to rough it, start from the first rung for a change, on my own. If I get a couple of stripes, it'll be on my own merit. If I get as far as a commission, it'll be my own doing. I probably will get a commission – my education – but it won't be my mother getting me there. I want to do it all on my own, and if . . . if . . .'

He broke off. 'Oh, God, I feel sick.'

In sudden urgency, he leaned towards the kerb and retched quietly.

'You see, Mumsy?' Margaret cried first thing next morning at breakfast after relating Matthew's explanation for not apparently leaping headlong into the forces, her faith in his intentions now unshakeable. 'He isn't a coward. He simply wants to do things his way.'

Mrs Ross's smile was one of sad experience. 'Doing things his way could be biting off more than he can chew. He's always been used to the soft life by all accounts. He'll be in for a shock, I should imagine.'

'So will a lot of men,' Margaret said firmly. 'They'll have to get used to it. I can't see why he should be any different. He'll learn to adapt, like most people do when there's no going back. I'm sure we'll be seeing a side of Matthew no one ever saw before.'

'Well, we shall see, I suppose.'

'Yes, we shall,' Margaret stated with conviction, rising from the breakfast table to start clearing away, confident in the eventual fulfilment of her conviction. She didn't have to wait for long.

Two weeks prior to Christmas, the autumn having been so uneventful it hardly seemed they were having a war at all – people were calling it the phoney war, the funny war, even the bore war, and some evacuees were even returning home – Margaret opened the door to a knock. There he stood, one leather-gloved hand clutching a small suitcase, his overcoat collar turned up against the chill wind, the well-cut suit beneath soon to be exchanged for the rough khaki of a private in the Royal Corps of Signals. His smile was wide, his long narrow eyes bright. He looked as though he had been given a birthday present.

36

'Thought I'd pop over to say cheerio.'

Not knowing what to say, all she said was, 'Come in out of the cold for a second,' and all but dragged him across the doorstep as her mother came from the living room to wish him well and invite him to come and sit by the fire for a moment.

'It's warm in there, Matthew. There's such a draught from the door.'

'No thanks, Mrs Ross,' he said as Margaret dutifully closed the door a little. 'Got a train to catch. Just thought I'd say a quick goodbye to Mag . . . Margaret.'

Despite the miserable feeling inside her at Matthew's going, Margaret couldn't help but smile at the hasty correction before her mother as the woman melted discreetly back into the living room, leaving the pair of them to say their goodbyes. She wondered if her mother suspected the feelings she had for Matthew. If she did, she had never betrayed it.

Alone with him, she still couldn't come up with anything wise or clever to say.

'So you're off then.' It was the only thing she could find, obvious, inane, feeble, betraying nothing of the desolation churning in the pit of her stomach.

'Yes.'

'I hope you get by all right.'

'I hope so too.'

'Nice of you to come over to say goodbye.'

At this he gave her one of those searching looks that never failed to set her heart racing with useless hope. 'Well, I would, wouldn't I?'

'Why?'

'Because . . . it's you. My best friend.'

It wrung her heart. She would always be his best friend, no more than that. That was obvious now.

'I'll miss you, Matthew,' was all she could find to say, a catch in her throat that she hadn't wanted to be there, to her annoyance quite audible.

On impulse she reached up and touched his smooth cheek, then with the same spontaneity, leaned forward and planted a kiss where her hand had momentarily touched. The flesh felt cold from the biting wind outside but the spicy fragrance of his skin warmly filled her nostrils. She stood back, alarmed by her own temerity. For fear of ridicule she had never before dared kiss him. What would he think now?

'Take care of yourself, won't you?' she heard herself say.

His smile was not at all taunting. 'Don't worry, I will.'

Some of her composure returned. 'I'm glad you got your own way in the end.'

'Don't know about that,' he laughed, the laugh light and confident in a way she'd never heard before; before it had always been touched by a tinge of defiance. 'It's up to me now to prove myself right. Anyway, if I don't swim, I can only sink.'

The old defiance coming back, the caustic quip.

'Don't say that.' She experienced a shudder of sudden apprehension, a premonition, dread, so light that it went as quickly as it had come. His was a charmed life, bright with promise. He'd be all right. People like him always were. He had to be.

The easy expression had faded to be replaced by a thoughtful, almost affectionate regard. 'I'd like to thank you, Maggie, for making up my mind for me – the night we had that dinner together.'

Her face grew hot. 'I did nothing . . .'

'You listened. It was enough.'

She was startled by his arm coming around her waist, pulling her gently towards him; then he kissed her full on the mouth. It was a long lingering kiss, revealing the passionate core of him that she had always imagined yet thought she would never be invited to probe. Even now she knew it came purely from regret at leaving a dear friend, or perhaps from his trepidation at the unknown into which he was about to step, but no more than that.

Curiously dizzy, she felt herself put gently from him. When she spoke she was annoyed to find that her voice shook. 'Lots of luck, Matthew.'

'You too, Maggie. I'll write, let you know where I am. Although God knows where I . . . where any of us will end up. But things will never be the same again.'

'I suppose not,' she replied lamely, her shaken nerves calming at last.

For a moment he looked searchingly at her. Then he held out his hand, unaware of anything behind her candid grey-green eyes but what she knew she dared convey – a friendly regret of his going. Yet, oh, how she wished it possible to show him how she truly felt as she took the offered hand, the cool slim fingers closing over hers in a firm and steady grip that had the essence of real friendship in it. How she wished it was love rather than friendship, but she wasn't prepared to fool herself.

'I don't know when our paths will cross again,' he said, his tone low and full, 'if they ever do. But whatever happens, Maggie, I want you to know that you'll always be one of my nicer memories.'

'Perhaps we could keep in touch,' she said quickly and he smiled, almost gratefully.

'Perhaps we will. I'll try and write to you, Maggie. Till then, look after yourself.'

Then he was gone, out of the door and down the steps to the street, turning towards Cambridge Heath Road and the nearest bus stop, moving on swiftly with that fast springy step of his.

The fierce wind battered at his trilby on which one hand was keeping a tight hold. Perhaps that was why he didn't turn and wave, she thought as she stood watching him going out of her life.

Whether his own family had stood at their door to see him go on his way, she had no idea. Her eyes had become too misted to see that far, which she blamed on tears caused by the bitter wind. She couldn't recall when she had cried last, apart from when her father had died, of course. She wasn't really crying now, except that the wind touched a little colder against a small part of her cheek where a rivulet had begun to trickle down as finally she turned and came back into the house.

Chapter 4

A few weeks later, as promised, came a letter from Matthew, from Catterick in Yorkshire, full of his traumatic introduction to the regimental sergeant major, to his platoon sergeant, to square bashing and to evil food and hard beds.

> Slowly getting to be a proper soldier – in hot water all the time. Uniform fits where it touches. The chaps in my hut took the mickey out of my accent at first. I never knew I had one. Said I sounded a bloody snob (their words) and damned arrogant, which I didn't like that much. They started to call me College Boy, but after I had a set-to with one of them and duffed him up, and got seven days C.B. – not College Boy, but Confined to Barracks, they have started calling me Matt and sometimes Wardy after my surname because there's another Matthew in the platoon. So I suppose being called that must stand for something. They're not a bad bunch once you get to know them. I still can't get used to being bawled at . . .

There were two pages of cheerful grousing. He seemed quite genuinely happy, a vastly different man to the one who had said goodbye to her that day. If anything, he seemed happier than he had been in his carefree days before war had broken out, despite the restrictions of army life. Margaret could only think poetically of a bird released.

He had concluded his letter by writing that he was off down the local with a few mates for a couple of jars.

Margaret wrote back, heartened by his writing to her, but

he did not reply. In his usual careless fashion he had written as promised and had already forgotten her. She could imagine him skipping through her reply, thinking he'd answer it when he had the time, but with his thoughts on other things he had probably put it away and lost track of it, his promise pushed further back into the corner of his mind, eventually to die altogether.

Taking what struck her as an obvious hint, she didn't write again, so that the only news she gleaned of him was what filtered through from his mother to others and thence now and again to her mother.

The only one left at home out of the old crowd she'd once gone about with, Margaret began to experience a very real dread of being tied to her home forever, staying in night after night after work, keeping her mother company through the long dreary winter days stretching ahead.

Her whole life had become dreary. Coming home on slow buses in the blue glow that enabled the conductor to see the coins he was given, masked headlamps just penetrating a stygian winter evening although street lamps gave out a tiny downward pinprick of light with the slight relaxing of blackout regulations now that no air raids seemed forthcoming, all made for a miserable existence. There was no point her going out for an evening. The West End was no longer lit up like a Christmas tree. And although cinemas, theatres, dance halls and restaurants had all reopened, football stadiums following suit, what fun could be had going anywhere alone?

Even Matthew's sister had gone away to stay with relatives in Surrey. True, Margaret was again helping run the Girl Guides, the vicar of St John's having restarted all its groups, but it wasn't the same any more. There now seemed just her and Mumsy, the two of them even spending their Christmas alone.

She nurtured wild thoughts of joining one of the women's services – anything to escape this purposeless role of companion to a parent who was prone to seeing herself as already approaching old age. Sympathise with her as she did, Margaret longed for something to give her life meaning, to be somewhere where she didn't have to make understanding noises or give her mother comforting pats on the hand. It was unkind to think

41

like that but she couldn't help it. Everyone was off somewhere. She alone was stuck at home. But when it came down to brass tacks, how could she be so cruel as to desert Mumsy who'd always had a need to lean on her as she had leaned on her husband? Yet were circumstances to call on her to stand on her own two feet Mumsy might surprise everyone by coping admirably, as people often do when forced to battle on alone.

She was slowly coming to know the dilemma that had faced Matthew, but it was her mother who solved her problem, quite by chance.

'I wish you didn't have to work in the City,' she said towards the end of May. 'What if they do start bombing London?'

The papers had reported an air raid on industrial Middlesborough and earlier that month bombs had been dropped near Canterbury, without casualties, but too near for comfort; she was alarmed for her daughter's safety.

'Perhaps you could find yourself something local, away from the City.'

Something local? And be even more at her mother's beck and call? Again came that desire to escape.

'I really should be thinking of doing something towards helping the war effort,' she ventured, immediately crushed by the alarm on her mother's face.

'You mean war work? Oh, no, dear, you couldn't go working in a *factory*. Not a nicely brought up young girl like you.'

'Lots of *nicely* brought up young girls are doing heavy, dirty jobs. I don't see why I should be any different.'

She thought again of Matthew, her heart going out to him for that time of his dilemma. But again it was her mother, mind working on possible ways to have her daughter closer to home, who came to the rescue.

'I was wondering, dear. Perhaps you're right about helping with the war effort. What if you applied for a job in some local hospital? They are crying out for help. There's the chest hospital just the other side of the park. All in the open air. You could go along there and make enquiries.'

With mixed feelings, just to appease her mother, Margaret went along to 'make enquiries'. It was even nearer home but at least she'd be meeting people, new people, instead of the same old faces in the same old stuffy Leadenhall Street office.

It would be nice to get out of it and into someone else's world for a while. She had little idea how one went about applying for jobs in hospitals but assumed it to be much the same as anywhere else. The middle-aged, prim-faced woman who had probably never seen any other application to her shiny well-scrubbed cheeks than soap, looked up at Margaret from her desk, her gaze full of disparagement.

'I am afraid there are no places at the moment for untrained girls. If you care to register in the proper manner you can go to a training hospital if you seriously wish to become a nurse.'

She hadn't for a second thought of becoming a nurse. All she'd come for was a job nearer home. The woman seemed to glare at her.

'If you are looking for romance and excitement, young lady, you will be sadly disillusioned. This is a *demanding* profession, physically, mentally, suited only for the most dedicated women and entailing sheer hard slog and long hours for precious little reward other than the satisfaction of seeing a patient recover under quiet, efficient, selfless nursing.'

'That's all the reward one needs,' Margaret said without thinking, carried along on the woman's zeal. She saw the thin lips compress at her audacity in adding her opinion.

'All too often it is not. After giving oneself until one is drained utterly, and then to be required to do extra duty, one begins to wonder. Such doubts can often form in the mind of a nurse pushed beyond endurance when she grows weary. It is those who find that little extra strength to push aside such doubts who make true nurses. I regret they are all too few.'

Rather than risk another comment that would most certainly be ripe for criticism by the look of this woman, Margaret held her tongue, not sure if she actually wanted all this. Yet she felt herself already being absorbed, the idea of hard unrewarding work an answer, even preferable to the boring, barren futility that had lately become her life.

Refusing to give herself time to think, she filled in the application form under the stern, sceptical eye of her interviewer, if only to show her that she wasn't afraid of hard work.

It was not long after, wondering just what she had got herself into, that she was bidding goodbye to a tearful parent to commence training at a hospital in the heart of Hampshire. She had escaped.

'I don't think I'm cut out for this.'

The fair-haired girl's plaintive sigh reached Margaret from the other side of the bed as they removed the soiled bottom sheet from underneath an incontinent elderly patient.

Trying to ignore the smell wafting up from the stained sheet, Margaret smiled across at her fellow student nurse. 'We were told to expect this, you know.'

'One thing bein' told what to expect, another 'aving it right up your nose. I think I'd sooner 'ave joined the WAACs than this.'

'What, with bombs dropping all over the place around London?' The girl was a Londoner and had been glad to be here in Hampshire. 'Sooner or later London will become a target and you could be stuck with a searchlight unit. That's what they go for first, you know, searchlights. I would sooner be here and safe, with all the slops and bedpans, for all the hard work we have to do.'

All too soon after being sent to Hampshire, Margaret had discovered what real mental exhaustion was as she strove to absorb what the demonstrators and lecturers were telling her. Her ankles had ached from endless bed-making, scrubbing miles of floors, interminable polishing of bed springs and scouring what seemed like millions of metal bedpans until they shone again after being emptied down the sluice.

But for all the headaches: trying to cram six months' training into six weeks, a wartime necessity; the drudgery, being saddled with the distasteful chores second-year nurses passed on to student nurses; all the cleaning up of incontinent patients, emptying slops and bedpans, mopping soiled floors, she had discovered that caring for those unable to care for themselves had its rewards. She really did feel she was doing something worthwhile at last. Often Margaret could hardly believe it was really she who now trod the wards in the uniform of a nurse – not that the uniform enhanced her appearance.

In lisle stockings and flat leather lace-ups, a white apron so starched that it practically stood up by itself, and indeed stood out from the blue striped dress like a bell-tent, she spent hours before a mirror battling with the piece of snow-white material that would eventually form her cap – at least once she had mastered the technique of folding it correctly so that the pinched pleats lay flat enough not to flap about over the crown of her head like some wayward seagull.

Like a true nurse she worked hard to aspire to the art of moving swiftly yet quietly, but with all that quantity of starch, quietly was virtually an impossibility. Her starched uniform heralded her approach with all the subtlety of an oncoming express train.

There was scant opportunity for going home. In this she felt a little guilty. Poor Mumsy, all alone because she had been selfish enough to want to get away. Well she *had* got away, and she *would* have gone home, but a train packed to suffocation with servicemen and women could take three times as long as in peacetime, incessantly stopping and starting and then crawling along between times. Too much of a chunk out of one's day off. Such a thing as a whole weekend off hardly existed. And after working twelve hours at a stretch, she was only too glad to 'live in', falling into bed utterly exhausted to sleep away her day off.

With the beautiful early summer of 1940 she spent many a free day in the corner of some field with a friend or two, dozing in the hot sunshine pouring from a cloudless sky, only too glad to think about absolutely nothing, least of all guilt at not going to see Mumsy.

That year she got home twice, the first occasion in August, the second occasion in the autumn when she ran into Matthew Ward on his way back to his unit after a week's leave. She was amazed at the change in him. In one short year he had become more broad-shouldered, more steady-eyed. He looked taller, older, yet the ring of devilment still echoed in his voice as he greeted her.

'Ye gods! Maggie! And every inch a nurse. You look a picture.'

'So do you,' she returned lightly. She wasn't about to upbraid him for not ever writing to her again. The feeling she'd long thought dead now rose again like a bird as she regarded him.

His uniform, although still the rough khaki of rank-and-file, gave him a debonair appearance, and on his sleeve he bore the twin stripes of a corporal. He was making it there, Margaret thought with a small leap of pride in her heart for him, his own way.

'Not yet an officer, I see,' she said with a brave attempt at flippancy and he gave her a grin, crooked and rueful.

'My CO suggested I put in for it. Went up before the Selection Board but got cheesed off with the stupid questions they asked. Afraid I got a bit bolshie with some silly arse of a psychiatrist there and they chucked me out. Not literally, but well, turned me down – at least for the time being.'

As he chatted, Margaret couldn't help but notice how some of the edges of that 'college-boy' accent had blunted. Listening to him now, each word had a rough-and-ready tinge to it. Oddly enough, it rounded off this new Matthew to perfection – a man of action, certain of himself, a man able to fight his own fights without help from anyone. She wondered as he went on talking how his mother viewed this new person. Did it pull at her heartstrings for the boy he had once been? It didn't pull at her own, that was certain, except to make her heart swell with pride and love for this man who stood chatting lightly, without a care in the world because he had been able to surmount each obstacle as it had come his way.

'I expect the Selection Board will have another bash at me before long,' he was saying. 'The CO was damned disappointed, though God knows why. Me – I'm not sure I want to bother now. I've got a great crowd of mates and just now we're too busy playing soldiers on some godforsaken Yorkshire moor for me to worry just yet about trying to become an officer.'

'What do you do?' she asked.

For an answer he placed a finger against his lips in a playful gesture. 'Careless talk costs lives. Really, we just muck about out in the field with walkie-talkies, practise radio relay, get wet and tired and lost. Usually end up in the right place, eventually, then all go back to the schoolroom to learn where we went wrong. Then we all go off to the pub and forget it. It really is a load of old bull. I don't think any of us bother to take it in except enough to keep our sergeant happy. Don't know as I want to start seriously studying again just to be an officer. Had enough of that at college.'

He paused to regard her closely. 'But what about you? I bet

you do enough of it. A nurse, eh? Always thought you were cut out to be something like that. I think that's why I admired you so much, Maggie. Got anyone in tow yet? Some handsome young doctor?' There was a look in his eye that made a spark of hope leap inside her

'No one at the moment,' she said, smiling, then she said something utterly stupid before she could stop herself. 'I don't have the time.'

'Me too.' He gave a low chuckle. Had she disappointed him? 'Having too good a war to get roped in. Women tell you too much what and what not to do. I'm free for the time being. But you never know, do you?'

He broke off and on a sudden thought crooked his arm and tugged back the sleeve of his overcoat to glance down at his wristwatch, the gold one which he had told her last year had been given him by his father's sister for his twenty-first. 'Ye gods! Got to go, Maggie. If I miss my connection I'll get put on a charge for being late. Cheerio then. And take care of yourself.'

'You too.' Dismally, she was aware she had blown the one chance she might have had of his asking her for a date, or even if he could write to her. On sheer impulse born out of desperation she leaned forward and laid a kiss full on his lips. Expecting him to pull away she was surprised by his arm coming around her, the kiss being held, and it was she who broke away in a fluster, taken off guard by the strength of his lips on hers, there in the street.

'Like you said,' she burst out idiotically, 'you'll be late.'

He nodded, seeming to gather his wits. 'Yes, I will. I'll write to you, Maggie.'

He seemed so tremendously happy as he went on his way. Rosy from his promise, the pressure of his lips still felt on hers while her own foolish confusion mocked her, she watched him go, shouldering his small pack, his step jaunty. War hadn't touched him at all. The terrible events of Dunkirk, of desperate men with their backs to the sea until the armada of small boats had come to their rescue, had passed him by. If anything, she had seen more of conflict than he.

A fleeting vision of her part in it passed through her mind, days and weeks compressed into seconds as she watched

47

Matthew's departing figure. A once-quiet, smoothly running hospital suddenly filled with a consignment of casualties from those beaches. A first-year student nurse thrown into the deep end trying to cope with a picture of defeat, the exhausted, the filthy, the torn bodies, her first-ever experience of war at its most vicious, all the worse because her life as a student nurse only the previous day had been so sedate.

Surrounded by that upheaval, she had cooked porridge, cut mounds of bread and butter, helped undress those who passed out into sleep the moment they were left alone, sometimes just where they stood. She had washed the wounded, tried not to weep over the dying or turn away as gangrenous or maggot-infested wounds were uncovered, and had wished to God she had been qualified to do more than just assist and cut bread while those skilled medical teams operated on the suffering. And the June sun had shone on.

She saw Matthew turn, throw her a careless wave. She waved back, smiled. No ghosts of dead and dying comrades, no splattered bodies and shattered limbs haunted his vision. He had continued, as he'd said, to play at soldiers in the safe environs of a Yorkshire moor. Pray God, Margaret thought as she waved, heartened by his promise to write to her, there would never be need for it to be otherwise.

For a week as he took orders, drilled, cleaned his equipment and uniform free of moorland mud and grass knowing that next day they'd need cleaning all over again, Matthew thought of Margaret Ross and the kiss she had given him. No mere friendly one. He'd always had a sneaking suspicion that underneath that touch-me-not exterior she'd always presented, she had been in love with him. That kiss had proved it, but even then she had broken away before it had had a chance to develop, becoming all formal again, telling him he'd be late back.

Each time he thought about it, he found himself shaking his head in disbelief, found himself wondering about the feeling it had promoted, musing about the girl herself.

Her nurse's navy-blue coat had suited her colouring. Hair, burnished to old gold by August sunshine, still flared despite being drawn into a neat roll behind her ears; it made her look pretty really. He'd never noticed before. Probably the uniform? Not as leggy as he'd once thought her, not so overwhelming and always ready to help everyone. That had always been her trouble. She'd seemed more at ease. She'd make someone a wonderful wife one day.

The thought brought an unexpected pang deep inside him, rather like a longing. He'd write to her again, definitely. In the past she'd always been too much of a managing person to be thought of in any other way than as a friend. Back in those careless days he had much preferred girls who liked to lean on a man rather than have a man lean on them. Maggie had never leaned on anyone. Perhaps she'd changed, had grown less independent. Perhaps it would be nice to find out. At the thought a small ripple of excitement made itself felt in the pit of his stomach.

Sitting on his bed cleaning his equipment after a day on some muddy moor, he found himself wanting to find out, thinking about her, her life. Yes, when this bloody training allowed him a moment to himself, he would write. Good to have a girl to write to. He hadn't got her hospital address but her mother could forward it on. And when he next came home on leave . . .

Chapter 5

He had meant to write. But that weekend, with the Army's usual lack of forewarning, his whole unit found itself transferred to a camp just outside Birmingham. With all the excitement that went with it, writing to Margaret had to be put to one side. That week he had a lot to do, settling in, and the following Saturday when he and a few mates wangled an evening pass into Birmingham, it was shelved again. But he would write, he told himself as he picked up his pass. He still felt good about her.

Cadging a lift in the back of an Army truck to save a bus fare, the group split up to find their own way to whatever part of the city they sought for a few hours' pleasure. Matthew found a dance hall near the town centre. Obviously popular, it was packed, the floor crammed with couples, girls in bright dresses, men in uniform, a tight kaleidoscopic mass gyrating slowly to a strict-tempo waltz by a top-quality band.

'We'll slope off then, see what talent there is.' Once the last two mates with him moved away, Matthew found himself alone, already losing interest.

'See you later,' he muttered to himself, for they had already melted into the crowd. He didn't know why he felt so despondent. Maggie crossed his mind briefly, though why, he couldn't say. She had never excelled as a ballroom dancer. She knew how to dance, but she was better at sports like swimming and badminton and tennis. So why this odd pang thinking of her here in this unfamiliar dance hall? Yes, he was feeling at a loose end at this moment. He would write to her when he got back to camp.

What he needed now was someone to take away this unaccustomed loneliness he was experiencing. With an effort he perked himself up and surveyed the crowd, as his mates were doing a little way off.

Not much was here except for one petite dark-haired girl at one of the far tables, visible now that the floor was clearing from the waltz just ended and the lights were coming back up. She was with a Marine. Yet the way they were leaning away from each other, not talking, conveyed that she might not be with the Marine for much longer. Matthew took heart, began to feel better. She'd do.

'Found anyone yet, Matt?' Dave, one of his mates, was back, himself still looking for a likely partner.

Matthew nodded towards the girl and drew a knowing chuckle from Dave as he followed the direction of the nod. With the remark, 'Didn't take you long, then,' the stockily built Dave prowled off on another search.

Alone again, but this time feeling somewhat better, he fished into the breast pocket of his khaki battle blouse and pulled out the silver cigarette case his sister had given him; he had almost forgotten his twenty-first, it seemed so far away. Lighting a cigarette, he leaned against one of the pillars at the entrance to the large hall and inhaled slowly. He needed to summon up some sense of nonchalance, and, surrounded by a protective cloud of smoke which he was exhaling, he found it.

He seldom needed courage to approach any girl, even when she was with a partner. One could soon calculate whether the partner was steady or merely casual and act accordingly. But that pale oval face set in a mass of luxurious dark hair, hair that even from here contrasted startlingly against the simple yellow dress she wore, brought an odd trepidation that he could not shake off. Suddenly it seemed very important that he should. Margaret, with her fiery hair and her straightforward manner, faded a little as he began his slow walk towards the girl with the Marine.

As if sensing his approach, hardly had he taken half a dozen steps than the girl turned her head towards him. Her lips broadened into a tiny smile, its message unmistakable. She had been looking thoroughly bored, but already the bored look had fled, leaving hope in its place. Matthew's heart lifted. It might not be such a bad evening after all. He threw a glance at her partner as he drew nearer. No wonder she was bored. The guy's face sported a mass of ripening acne. Other than that he could probably be classed good-looking, but in his present condition he couldn't be very savoury to her.

Matthew stubbed out his cigarette in an ashtray on one of the tables he passed, bringing a surge of interest from the hopeful ring of girls around it, each young eager face looking up in brief anticipation of being asked for the quickstep now being struck up by the band.

The dark-haired girl had turned away from him, seeing him bend forward towards the table, assuming she hadn't been the object of his desire after all. He saw a small upward-tilted nose and lips carrying just a little too much bright red lipstick but which now possessed a most becoming little pout. Why did he suddenly feel so shaky?

Matthew took a deep breath and walked the last few paces as nonchalantly as he could. It was the fate of all faced with the prospect of asking the girl of their choice for a dance, especially if she struck them as ravishing, to feel at least a fraction nervous, alive to the possibility of an abrupt turn-down, having to walk away as though it hadn't mattered to them in the least. He had hardly ever suffered from that, but this time, inexplicably, he had joined the ranks of the nervous, at the last minute losing his nerve.

Pausing in front of a wide-eyed blonde, her hair dragged into what was currently called a victory roll, he offered her his hand, at the same time executing a casual tilt of his head towards the rapidly filling dance floor. In a trice the blonde was on her feet, almost knocking over her port and lemon in her haste. Seconds later he was winging her away across the floor, choosing one of the gaps that still remained between the fast-moving couples. To his relief the blonde danced well. Conscious of the eyes of the dark-haired girl following his progress, he couldn't have borne someone who might have hampered his steps.

'You're ever such a good dancer,' came the light words whispered into his ear, to which he nodded absently.

He had no need to be told he was a good dancer. He'd always gained pleasure from it, from being watched, stretching his talents to the full. Yet it had become imperative to put his present partner through every intricate movement of the quick-step he knew, so that those dark eyes watching him would know he was good. Though God knows why that should matter.

A disconcerting thought came. What if she were only mediocre? All this weaving and twirling could frighten her off. Immediately he moderated his steps – the floor was becoming too crowded for showing off anyway – and fell to making occasional light-hearted smalltalk with his partner.

The ending of the quickstep came as something of a relief. Escorting the blonde back to her seat, he made for the bar and the safety of those hovering males who, despite the romance of their various uniforms, hadn't yet felt inclined to leave their kind and ask for dances, and couples having already found a partner for the evening – perhaps, he grinned, for life.

Yet for all the press of people, he could still sense the dark-haired girl's eyes watching him, and he found his need to know more about her pushing away that last-minute reluctance he had felt.

For the past half-hour the dark-haired girl had sat out through dance after dance, feet tapping under the table as she watched the couples, uniforms and dresses melting together as one, moving around the floor.

Susan Hopkins cast her escort a contemptuous glance. Apart from one visit to the bar for a pint of black-and-tan for himself and a small port and lemon for her, he hadn't moved out of his seat the entire evening.

He had cut such a dashing figure in his dark blue Marines uniform when she'd first met him last week: tall, broad, the briefest scarring on his face from an old outbreak of acne giving it a certain rugged look. She had felt proud to be on his arm. They had gone to the pictures, the cheapest seats, but he'd explained he hadn't drawn his pay yet and she was ready to forgive him. He had asked to see her again, but this evening instead of his gorgeous dress uniform, he had turned up in this horrid khaki thing. It diminished the aura of romance, of the debonair. Not only that, but the dormant acne had run riot during the past week she hadn't seen him.

She'd never been endowed with a strong stomach for

unsightly things like suppurating pimples or nasty-looking cuts and bruises. Any physical defect aroused squeamish sensations. It was just as well, she thought watching the dancers, that he hadn't taken her on to that floor – being so close to those yellow-headed pimples would have made her positively sick. Most certainly there'd be no goodnight kiss, that's if she could get out of his taking her home at all. Already she was rehearsing a polite farewell, this date definitely their last.

The previous waltz had been in full swing, the lights dimmed, the faceted crystal orb in the centre of the ceiling flicking sensuous rainbow flecks over the dancers. Suddenly, she had felt a inexplicable compulsion to turn her eyes towards the hall entrance.

Among the slick RAF uniforms, the rakish body-hugging navy blue, the officers' smooth attire, the soldier's khaki battle dress was unspectacular. The man it clothed, however, made it look as superior as any officer's as he leaned with casual grace against one of the dance hall's pillars. She saw him reach into his breast pocket, extract a cigarette case; with growing interest watched him light a cigarette, his head bent for a moment over the flame. It was then he looked at her, directly, just as she was sure he'd done earlier, which had caused in her that odd need to turn. It was as though he had actually spoken to her. When their gaze met across the clearing dance floor, she had looked quickly away, filled with embarrassment.

The band had struck up with a quickstep. The man by the entrance stubbed out his cigarette and began walking towards her, making her heart start to pound against her ribs with excited anticipation. But as she composed herself to rise casually at his invitation to dance, ignoring her Marine, the soldier had paused just a few steps away, bending towards a common blonde in a red dress sitting nearby. Seconds later he had whisked her away.

Pique had replaced embarrassment. How dare he? Susan watched him move with supple grace across the filling dance floor with the girl, looking quickly away every time he glanced briefly in her direction. But she didn't miss his expression. What was it? Appraisal? Amusement? Taunting, perhaps. When the quickstep ended with a final flourishing crash of cymbals and a flamboyant twirl of female partners, she pretended not to look as he conducted the blonde back to her friends. But at least, instead of lingering, the soldier turned and sauntered away to the bar.

In that instant, Susan Hopkins made her decision. 'Oh, look!' she burst out to the practically lifeless Jack, 'I've just seen a friend of mine. Must pop over and have a word. Won't be a tick.'

Giving him no time to reply, she was off, skirting the vacated dance floor, timing it perfectly so as to collide with her quarry as if by accident. It worked, even if in the process she trod on his foot, something she had not planned, almost taking herself off balance. Instinctively he caught her, held her steady with firm hands on her shoulders. 'Careful there!'

Deep brown eyes fringed by thick lashes gazed down at her in open amusement. Her embarrassment was more real than she had intended.

'Oh, golly! I'm sorry. I didn't mean to... Did I hurt you, like?'

'You?' He laughed, taking stock of her diminutive figure. 'I don't think you've broken any toes.'

'Oh I'm ever so glad.'

She was instantly conscious of her Birmingham accent against the refined tones of this man. Yes, he was a corporal, but his speech sounded so incongruous with the mere two stripes on his arm. His smile gently mocked her.

'What, that you didn't hurt me, or that you stepped on my foot?'

Susan fell silent. He must have seen through her ruse. Her face felt hot. Whatever possessed her to embark on this silly idea in the first place?

'You came at me like an express train,' he was chuckling. 'A fraction more weight on you and you could really have done me an injury. There have to be subtler ways to start up a conversation.'

Indignation finally rescued her from embarrassment. 'Fancy yourself, don't you?'

The grin diminished a little. A momentary look of sadness, loneliness perhaps, crossed his face, and she had a strong feeling he was about to play it down as if she almost heard his words form in her head: I'd be the only one that does. But instantly he brightened, his tone teasing. 'Don't tell me you've not been watching me right from the moment I came in. Actually, I'm flattered.'

Now she was embarrassed again – that look that had passed so briefly across his eyes had gone. 'Well, I might've looked at you. You're a good dancer. Everybody looks at good dancers, don't they?' She wriggled a little in the grasp he still had on her. 'I've got to go back to my friend.'

He released his grip. 'The chap you were sitting with? Is that all he is – a friend? And there was I thinking, the prettiest girl in the hall and she's already spoken for.'

That was why he hadn't asked her to dance. She felt a surge of anger towards her innocent escort for spoiling her chances.

'I'm not *spoken for*, if that's what you call it. I just came in with him. Just a date, like, for this evening, that's all.'

'So you're free to dance with whoever you please?'

Why did she feel he was mocking her? If it hadn't been for that look that had flicked past his eyes, she'd have walked away now. She had to put up some resistance so as not to look cheap. He mustn't think she had engineered this meeting. 'Not with you,' she said, trying to appear in control.

'Remember it was you who got in touch with me first, to coin a phrase,' he laughed. He *did* think she'd engineered it all. 'Well, you win. Would you care to dance?' He gave an explosive laugh as she tossed her head in sulky refusal. 'Ye gods! How kaleidoscopic can you get?'

She wasn't sure what that meant but it didn't sound very flattering, and in a huff she swung away. He caught her arm lightly.

'I'm sorry. Don't go.' There was genuine contrition in his dark eyes as she turned to look at him, immediately replaced by a look of enthusiasm as the band struck up. 'Listen. It's a foxtrot, the best dance there is, even better than a tango. You foxtrot?'

She loved nothing more. Moreover he seemed to her so like a young boy in his own delight at it that she nodded despite herself; instantly he caught her up and whisked her away on to the dance floor to the delightful slow and regular beat of a rendering of Glenn Miller's 'Moonlight Serenade'.

It was like gliding on clouds. Guided with swaying grace

through each intricate movement, she floated. Small though her limbs were, she followed his long steps without faltering, each change of direction, each smooth turn, each measured pause. He was so easy to dance with it was as though they were one person. He didn't speak, seemed conscious only of the variety of moves, practically turning them into an exhibition with not too many on the floor for this rather specialised number, unlike the popular easy-to-do waltz that always filled the floor to crush proportions.

At first she felt uncomfortably conscious of being seen so on display, especially by her former companion. But there was no need to worry. A glance towards where she had left him revealed him looking as though he'd fallen asleep. She was sure that had her handbag not been in his keeping he'd have left. Well, as soon as the number finished she'd retrieve her bag and leave him to it. If the man she was now with chose not to see her home after the dance, she'd see herself home, though she hoped it would not be that way. But either way, at least she would escape those horrid pimples.

The music ending, a ragged clap came from those who'd attempted the dance. Susan smiled up at her partner, awaiting his next move.

It came as she had hoped. 'Do you fancy a drink?'

Susan thought quickly. 'Have to get me handbag first. I left it on the table. I could see you at the bar if that's okay. Won't be a tick.' Somehow her accent no longer mattered. He smiled.

'I'll see you there, then.'

She was off. 'My friend's asked me to see her home afterwards,' she told her Marine with a play at urgency as he looked up with an apathetic grin. 'She's frightened of going home on her own. Hope you don't mind. I am sorry about that.'

There was little he could do as she whisked up her handbag. After all, he was only a casual date. A one-evening date. No doubt he'd slide off and find himself someone else and no harm done. It happened all the time, had once happened to her, annoyingly. But not tonight, she prayed as she made her way back to the bar.

She found her corporal, slim, tanned fingers curled around a pint of bitter, the other hand holding a small glass which he offered her with a grin. 'Thought you'd be a gin and orange person. Am I right?'

'Ooh, loverly. Thanks.' She smiled up at him, taking the glass and sipping at it carefully. 'I hadn't better get myself sozzled, had I?'

'You've probably never been sozzled in your life,' he said solemnly.

'I've bin a bit woozy, like. A couple of times.'

He produced his cigarette case and flipped it open towards her.

She regarded it with admiration as she shook her head. 'I don't smoke. Real silver, in'it?'

He shrugged as though her comment had touched a raw spot, but she didn't interest herself beyond that. The orchestra had reached an interval after a jive that had jammed the floor to suffocation; it was the bar that was now crowded, the babble deafening. But between her and her new partner an awkward silence had fallen, threatening to drag on if she didn't find something to say soon. She gazed about, racking her brain and sipping her drink far too quickly. It was he who broke the hiatus. She saw his lips move but couldn't make out what he said above the noise.

'What?'

He raised his voice. 'I said I still don't know your name.'

'Sue Hopkins,' she yelled back.

'Sorry?'

'Sue . . . Susan Hopkins.' No one ever called her Susan, but announcing her name in full above the din helped make it clearer.

Quite audibly, in one of those odd pauses that can occur in the midst of a dozen conversations, she heard him repeat her name, savouring it as though he thought it the finest in the world. Had it been Cleopatra it could not have sounded more romantic to her ears, the way he pronounced it.

She looked up at him, shouting over a new wave of babble. 'What's yours?' For a moment she thought he hadn't heard; his head tilted slightly as though considering her, then with a glance around the crush of people he grimaced.

'I've had enough of this. Shall we get out of here – go for a walk?'

58

Just catching the words, not knowing what to say, she nodded. He shouldered his way through the crowd to place her glass together with his own on the bar. Then he was back, tilting his head at her, and she could only follow him, an odd excitement taking hold somewhere deep inside her. The dance didn't matter any more.

Outside, enveloped in the pitch dark of blackout regulations, it was like entering another world. People moving cautiously, heralded by the merest pinprick of torchlight, came at them out of total darkness, to disappear just as totally. Vehicles, few and far between, lights all but obscured by black paint, faintly showed the kerb for a moment to leave it even more dark and dangerous to the pedestrian after they had driven by. Susan huddled close to her companion.

'You've not yet told me your name,' she reminded him as they took their first few steps, slow and measured in the fitful light of the tiny hand torch she'd produced from her handbag. The reminder was whispered, for their surroundings seemed to demand muted voices, muted sounds.

'Do you want all my name?' she heard him chuckle.

'Why not?' she challenged.

There was a pause, then he said, 'Matthew Leonard Ward.'

'Sounds posh,' she breathed, awed, and tucked her arm more firmly through his.

'Not really. Leonard's my father's name. My mates in my unit call me Matt. My mother would have a fit if she heard. She's always insisted on me being called Matthew. She's a stickler for respectability and . . .'

The tale, bordering upon tongue in cheek, was interrupted by a body colliding softly with them and a mumbled apology as it continued on its way through the blackout. But Susan was wondering about this mother – she sounded a right dragon.

'Damned stupid blackout,' Matthew was saying. 'Nothing happening and they black everything out. When there's a raid, they light everything up, switch on all the searchlights. That's what I'm on at present – searchlights. I'm in the Signals and they stick us on searchlights. Now that's what I call great thinking.'

'Got any brothers or sisters?' she asked, changing the subject from what he did in the Army. He was a corporal and that was all that mattered. She wished he'd been an officer but officers didn't look at girls like her. They went to better places than the Troc.

'One sister, Louise. Reminds me of our mother.'

It seemed he said it a little too tersely for comfort and she hurried to put some lightness back in their conversation. Nasty moments, like nasty cuts, even small ones, unnerved her, made her shudder. There were plenty of arguments in her house but she was used to them. Quickly healed, easily got over. It was with strangers that she cringed at moments like this.

'I've got lots,' she said in an effort to sound bright. 'Two sisters and three brothers. It must be funny having a whole bedroom to yourself. Sort of lonely, like.' This she said with a small pang of sadness for him. Perhaps it was the way he had said 'one sister', as though he regretted not having a brother or something. She'd always been told that only children were lonely children, and two wasn't much more than one. He and his sister were probably spoiled, where she'd never been, and it was still probably lonely and quiet. She hated quiet in a house, never having known it.

He didn't reply. They walked on in silence, uncomfortable silence it now seemed to her.

'It's getting late, I think I'm going to have to be going 'ome soon,' she burst out in a fast gabble, far too loudly, her voice sounding high and thin, lacking sophistication. He, the soft-spoken, refined man-of-the-world from down south would be jolted to his senses, seeing her as just a local girl from Birmingham, without education, the product of a crowded family. The spell had been broken.

'It must be nearly eleven,' she ploughed on, hating herself, the way she spoke, the way she acted. She had ruined the evening for herself. 'It's the air raids we've bin havin-g . . .' The accent fell on the 'g'. He didn't sound his at all, the 'ing' soft and alluring. She should have tried to copy it. Too late now. 'Me mum and dad like me home before anything starts. They worry about me, y'see. And I do have to think of them, don't I? It's only right.'

'Yes, it is only right,' he agreed with a deep sigh which dispirited her even more though she didn't know why. 'Do you live far from here?'

'Not far.' She could in fact walk home from here, which appeared now to be what she was going to do. 'Only walking distance.'

That damned 'g' again. Walk*ing*, she said in her head, walk*ing*. 'I sometimes catch a bus if it's raining,' she finished aloud, forgetting again.

'Well, it's not raining, so may I walk you home?'

Susan held back the gasp of joy. He wasn't disapproving of her after all. But she mustn't sound too eager. 'I suppose you could, if y'like. To the top of my road? I can go on from there. But you don't have to.' She had suddenly remembered what her turning would present to him. No doubt he came from a posh part of the south. 'Don't you have to be getting back to where you're stationed?'

'I've enough time to see you home, I'm sure.' How beautifully he spoke, his tone soft, seductive. He took her arm. 'I'll let you show me the way.'

And, she hoped, the picture of the road where she lived fading into obscurity, he'd kiss her goodnight, and ask to see her again. Oh, please, God, let him.

Chapter 6

It took ages to get to sleep for thinking about her evening's success. Lying in bed in the cramped little bedroom she shared with her two younger sisters at the top of the house, she tried to imagine the world Matthew had described to her as he walked her home. How different it was. The bedroom he had all to himself sounded as though it could swallow this one twice over and still have space to spare.

Hers, measuring four long paces each way, held her single bed and one, three and a half foot wide, for Beryl and June. Hers stood tight against the window wall, theirs against the opposite one, with just space enough between the two to shuffle into bed, going sideways. The wall where the door was had a single wardrobe and a three-drawer chest. Not one drawer or the door to the wardrobe could be opened fully because the beds got in the way. What couldn't be got into drawers or wardrobe went under the bed; every morning in this room resembled a public jumble sale, all three girls squeezing past each other to dress.

The only wash basin was downstairs by the back door in a tiny recess. It meant moving aside to let pass anyone wanting the toilet which stood in a block of six in the communal back yard. It all made for hot tempers when three boys, three girls and two adults were trying to manoeuvre around each other to go their separate ways for the day. Their father moreover did not look kindly on a girl trying to put on her make-up when he wanted to get to the mirror to shave.

Across from her bedroom was the room, even smaller, of her three young brothers, still just boys. Below theirs was her parents' bedroom, below that the living room with an area at one end for cooking. This, their only family room, had five doors: one for the recess where they washed, one to the cellar, one to the yard; a fourth to the street was never used because of a settee in the way – the back door served as the only exit in this place – the last leading to the stairs winding up to the upper rooms.

This was her home, each room atop the other. But for the block of exactly similarly designed houses on either side, each propping the other up like something built from a pack of playing cards, Susan was sure it would have fallen over. Built at the turn of the century for factory workers, the houses were dark, dingy, featureless, all looking as if they had been accidentally leaned on at some time by a careless giant who had concertina'd them, squeezing them upwards like toothpaste from a tube.

She had never considered her home this way before. She'd been born here. All her friends lived in similar places. Some day when she married she had expected to move in to something much like them. But tonight she had peeped into an environment Matthew Ward had described as they walked home, and now she saw these surroundings through a veil of angry discontent, for the first time in her life feeling ashamed of where she lived.

His home might be in London but it sat in a tree-lined road. There were no trees in her street. His overlooked a park. Birmingham had its share of parks and open spaces but not where she lived. His house had hot water, and a bathroom. Her bath hung on the back door, her lav was one of a block of six in the communal yard, with doors so warped anyone emptying rubbish in the dustbins alongside could peep through if they felt that nosy.

Filled with resentment, Susan found herself listening for sounds she had never really noticed before: Beryl, sixteen, eighteen months younger than her, sighing in slumber, probably dreaming; June, fourteen and just left school, a restless girl even in her sleep; her father coughing – too many cigarettes made him bronchial. The back door opening then closing gave a little shake to the house – her mother was coming in from the Red Lion at the end of the street where she was barmaid

63

five evenings a week. Soon came the whistling of the kettle, rising rapidly to a thin scream, fading away, like a soul dying, as it was lifted from the gas stove to make her mother's cocoa.

Susan was still awake when the house vibrated to her mother wearily mounting the stairs. The bedroom door below scraped over the lino, then scraped again as it closed. Complaining bedsprings. The intermittent cough ceased. The springs squeaked afresh as Jack Hopkins humped himself over his wife. After urgent whisperings and a giggle, the springs were soon going like a park seesaw, her mother's mounting joy evident. Then, after a while, silence. Later came heavy snoring – there were no secrets in this house.

Outside sounded the small noises of the night: the mewling cat near at hand, a dog barking further off; an urgent click of high heels on the pavement below, the clink of a milk bottle being put out for the morning; a low distant growl of a solitary lorry, perhaps an army truck, passing a few streets away on its way through the city towards some barracks or other. She thought of Matthew, probably asleep in his. Dreaming of her? Or was she forgotten? She didn't think so. He had asked her for a kiss on the corner of her street, hadn't taken it as his right but had asked permission. He'd asked to see her again. He would write to her when he next got a pass. He had even stood watching her go on along her road, given a brief wave as she turned reaching her door, and gone on his way.

At the recollection a tingle passed through her and in a sudden bout of ecstasy, Susan drummed her heels up and down beneath the bedcover and, taking the sheet between her small teeth, bit hard to relieve the pent-up joy. What did he look like in his sleep? Trying to imagine him, the sounds of the sleeping world went unheeded.

From far away came another sound, faint, but its message already understood, tensing the muscles, plucking at nerves. Rigid, Susan lay listening, waiting though instinct told her to get up and run, though where she was not sure.

The thin lone voice was joined by another, slightly nearer, then another, nearer still, each rising and falling in its own time. The first, hardly discernible now with those nearer wails taking up the cry. That first and the second and the third had died away, their message complete, but their relay was still advancing like a relentless tide.

Her parents' door opened. Her mother called up, 'Sue! Get the gals up. Robert! Les! John! Come on!' Her tone was one of piercing urgency. But Susan was already up, shaking the girls awake.

'Warning's gone. Come on – hurry up.' She dared not put on a light. The blackout curtains were a flimsy affair that needed time to check before one could be sure no chink gleamed out into the night. There was no time to check.

Transition from deep sleep to alert wakefulness was immediate, a gift given only to animals and those in peril. They were on their feet feeling for top clothes – like herself, these times they went to bed in their undies, the easier to dress in an air raid.

Beryl was shivering. 'Brr! I'm cold.'

In the darkness, June's voice: 'I think I've got Beryl's dress on.'

'It don't matter – just hurry up.'

'It does. She'll tear the seams.'

'Then hurry up and change over. We've got to get down the cellar.'

The boys were already racing past the door, boots clumping down the stairs. Grabbing handbag and warm coat, Susan pushed the girls ahead of her, hearing the first crump of anti-aircraft guns.

'Where's the gals?' came her mother's anxious call.

'Sod the gals!' came her father's grating voice. 'Where's my fags?'

'Blow your soppy fags – there's some in the cellar.'

'Tailor-made make me cough. I don't like 'em.'

'You'll have to lump 'em! Where're you gals?'

'Coming, Mum.'

The siren on the roof of the police station in the next street broke into its frantic exchange with an ear-splitting wailing. At the same time the ack-ack gun situated on a piece of waste ground at the far end of the road began cracking. The Hopkins family, like every family around them, all but fell down the four concrete steps into the cellar to be cocooned in comparative safety for the next several hours among the junk of a lifetime spent living in one house. The junk was now pushed to one end to accommodate an ancient double bed, a sagging put-u-up, two camp beds, an oil stove for warmth and a portable electric ring to brew tea, the concrete floor sporting a tattered rug to give a semblance of comfort while age-old cobwebs made grey curtains against the walls.

In this underground environment they sorted themselves out a little more calmly but no less tensely beneath the cold glare of a single electric bulb while above them the night began to rage.

As anti-aircraft guns began whacking away at laden German bombers droning above with their deep-throated, throbbing engine note, most likely caught in a web of searchlights, Susan sat thinking of Matthew. He had said he was in a searchlight unit. Was he on duty tonight? Searchlights were always vulnerable to attack. What if . . .

A noise, like the tearing of canvas, made the family start. It seemed to be in the very cellar. The explosion sent them cowering to the floor as the light bulb swung madly on its flex to send the shadows of the camp beds flying wildly across the bare brick walls.

When nothing more happened they got to their feet, their hearts still racing, to sit back on the edge of the beds or on one of the old kitchen chairs long since consigned to the cellar.

'Sounded like it fell right in this street,' Vi Hopkins said. 'Jack, you ought to go and look. They might need some help.'

Shakily Jack reached for a tailor-made cigarette. 'There'll be others helping, I expect. Better not get in the way, like.'

'Long as it wasn't our house.'

'We'd know if it was, with dust and stuff. And the roof would've come in on us.'

'So much for being safe,' Vi remarked, looking up at the still-intact basement ceiling. But even if the house suffered, cellars would stand up to anything so long as it wasn't a direct hit. 'Someone in this street must have got it though,' she mused sadly. 'Hope no one was hurt.'

'We'll know in the morning,' Jack said as the worst of the raid drifted off. The bombers might come back, or they might not. It all depended. But while there was a lull, it was best to sleep. He climbed into the ancient double bed, fully dressed, pulling the blanket over his head.

Susan looked at him, contempt a dull, wordless emotion inside her, and thought of Matthew out there amid falling, jagged-edged, razor-sharp shrapnel from anti-aircraft guns, a tin helmet his only protection as he did whatever people did with searchlights.

With morning and the all clear, the sun shining as though in mockery of last night's devastation, her father returned from his reconnoitre to say the near-miss had flattened two houses at the end of the road opposite the Red Lion.

'Hope it's not put paid to my job,' Vi sighed. 'I need that money.'

'They said one landed in Lile Street.' He worked in Lile Street in a small factory making the springs that went inside the chin straps of steel helmets. War work and his bronchitis had kept him out of the forces.

'Anyone hurt on our street?' Susan asked.

'One of the families was in someone else's basement. But they can't find the woman as lives in the other one. You know, that one with the frizzy hair. Husband's in the Merchant Navy.'

'Mrs Norton. She often comes into the Red Lion for half a pint. Oh, not her.'

'Old Hardwick said he asked her into his basement, but she wanted to stay in her own place, like. She must be under all the rubble. They're digging now.'

'Oh, that's terrible.' Susan rather liked the plump little woman who always smiled at her when they passed each other. To think of her dead, bleeding limbs all broken and crooked ... Shuddering violently, Susan thrust away the horrific injuries her imaginative brain conjured up. She was going to have to pass that house this morning on her way to Cotterels, just off Broad Street where she worked behind the counter selling underwear. What if the broken bleeding body was brought out just as she was passing? She'd be sick there on the spot.

The gap where the two houses had stood towards the end of the long row just like hers struck Susan as she passed as being like two missing teeth in a previously unbroken set, albeit that the set was full of decay, their stumps a pile of rubble. The roofs of the houses on either side were gone, and the windows in all the others were gone too. So were several windows in Susan's own home. She had left her parents clearing up the glass and her father re-hanging the front door, blown off in the blast, leaving the back of the settee and the living room beyond open to the street.

The Red Lion was minus all its windows, doors and most of its tiles. Already men were spreading a tarpaulin over the roof, the publican having erected a hastily painted sign: 'More Open than Usual.'

Susan tried not to look as she passed the ARP and Auxiliary Fire Service men working among the rubble, faces white with dust, their sweat for all the chill of the bright March morning tracing sepia rivulets down their cheeks.

'Watch that wall!' The warning made Susan stop, but the caller was talking to a comrade. 'Looks dodgy. There's a gap down here. Hang on a minute. Listen.'

She wanted to walk on, but found herself standing mesmerised as the man shone a torch into a hole for another to peer in. 'See anything?' He shouted into the hole. 'Anyone there? Are – you – all – right?' Then to the other man, 'What's the old girl's name?' The name supplied, he called, 'Mrs NORTON!'

'There,' he broke off. 'Is that a leg? Can you see?'

'Only a bit of wood.'

'MRS NORTON! It's no good – someone'll have to get down there.'

It was impossible to tear herself away as a slim man began to squeeze himself through the aperture, careful not to dislodge loose bricks, splintered beams, and broken furniture balanced so delicately. What would they bring out? Susan wanted to run but couldn't. It was like being a rabbit hypnotised by a snake's stare. Her stomach churned with a sick feeling.

The AFS man was halfway in when a shout came. 'There she is!'

Heads swivelled. Turning into Calvert Street, the small round figure, seeing her home in ruins, had broken into a run. Old Mr Hardwick caught her in his arms as she came abreast of him. 'Where've you been, love? We thought you were . . .'

Over his shoulder her eyes surveyed the destruction. 'It's all gone. All my nice furniture . . .'

'Never mind your furniture. 'S long as you're safe.'

'All my John's stamp collection. What's he gonna say?'

'He'll be only too glad to know you're safe when you write to him. You come into my house now and I'll make a cup of tea. You probably need it.'

Being guided across the road towards his own windowless home with its patches of missing tiles, ('Thank God it fell at the back of them places, or I'd of had nothing left either,' he'd said earlier) her gaze still clung to the wreckage.

'Sorry I didn't take up your offer,' she was apologising, as though that mattered now. 'I ran round to my daughter's place as soon as the siren went off round here. I had to be with her. She's on her own too – him in the Navy. I didn't want her to be alone. I shouldn't of gone.'

'If you hadn't of, you'd of been down there,' soothed Mr Hardwick as they passed Susan without seeing her.

The diggers were brushing themselves down. Neighbours waiting in the wings had come out with cups of tea for them as Susan went on her way, leaving them standing in groups, sipping gratefully. She had much happier thoughts now, eager to tell Marie who worked with her behind the counter on ladies' and men's underwear all about the new chap she had found.

A week went by. A fortnight. Disappointed, Susan had given up expecting to hear from him. Then came a letter. There was a Hollywood musical on at the Odeon. Would she care to meet him outside at six thirty?

Would she *care*? She took so long with her make-up, getting her long dark hair just right, choosing what dress to wear, that she made herself late, finally arriving to find him pacing up and down outside. But his face brightened as he saw her; taking her arm, he conducted her inside.

It was wonderful walking into the cinema on his arm, her small figure making him seem taller than he was. Wonderful standing in the foyer, its dull blue lights, in recognition of blackout regulations despite the two lots of dense velvet curtains shielding the line of doors, giving the sumptuous decor a strange wan look as she stood aside for him to pay at the kiosk – tickets to the balcony, of all things. Wonderful going up the wide, carpeted stairs that muffled their footsteps and then sitting with his arm about her shoulders in the comfortable plush seats as they watched Eleanor Powell dance across the screen in typical Hollywood splendour. Afterwards they had taken a long saunter while he told her more about himself and she in turn told him something, not too much, of her life. His arm had been about her the whole time and the warm September night had wrapped itself about them both, a light warm breeze playing with her hair and the hem of her summer frock, and they might have been somewhere on a high mountain top rather than a crowded, dirty, smelly, bombed city.

In a quiet dark corner away from homeward-bound cinema and theatre crowds, he had drawn her to him and kissed her, a long lingering kiss that had set her blood tingling. He had asked no more of her than that, but she knew that they would meet again, and again, and she couldn't wait to get to work on the Monday to tell her two workmates there all about it. She was his girl. It was almost too good to be true, unbelievable. Susan prayed that night for this thing to last forever.

Chapter 7

His back against the unlit mobile searchlight, Matthew stood beside the as-yet mute field telephone, his companions waiting, watching. Nothing doing yet but there soon would be. Thin clouds scudding across a full moon would soon disperse, leaving sky and earth bright from what had become known as a bomber's moon – ideal for Jerry who had already checked the weather and knew he could enjoy good hunting tonight.

Which city would Jerry go for? Birmingham? Coventry? Callous to hope it would be Coventry, but Susan lived in Birmingham. What if she suffered a direct hit? It didn't bear thinking about.

They had been writing to each other for two months now. Each time he thought of her, which seemed to him to be every other second, a flood of warmth swept through his insides followed by cold fear for her safety. He'd never felt like this before. If he were to lose her now . . .

The man beside him chuckled. 'What's that great big sigh for, Matt? Not that girl you go to see every time you get a pass?'

Bob Howlett was a close mate, of a similar background to his own. Their accents often drew smirks from the mix of Welsh, Scots, Midlanders and Cockneys, especially their rough-tongued sergeant, Pegg, constantly and vociferously cursing his luck in being saddled with a couple of junior NCOs whose education put them far above him, except for his military dedication, though theirs, according to him, was nil. Both had been before the selection board. Both had been rejected, one for his flippancy, the other for his apathy. Bob possessed no ambition whatsoever. Six feet tall and thin as a pole, propped at the moment against the sandbagged parapet he looked like a loose bag of bones with a stoop that resisted all the Army's attempts to straighten him up. Nose aquiline, chin long and narrow, physically he was the most unprepossessing man Matthew had ever known, yet he displayed the sweetest disposition and an agonisingly mild temper. People didn't come any better than Bob Howlett. Too good ever to become an officer.

Matthew grinned at him, laying aside thoughts of Susan for a little moment to follow this second train of thought. 'I wonder what old Peggy would do if either of us ever did get a commission?'

'Follow us to the ends of the earth probably,' Bob said with lethargic sagacity. 'It won't be me though. I'm no leader of men. Don't want to be. All I want is this war to end and me to be back with Phyllis and the kids.'

'Amen,' Matthew echoed fervently, at the same time hoping that Bob wouldn't suddenly bring out his latest photos of his blonde-haired wife and three children as he was wont to do.

From far away came an almost inaudible eerie wail of a civilian air-raid siren. But for the stillness of the country around, it would not have been detected at all. Their own klaxon had sounded a short while before, sending men running to their stations. As though in obedience to that faint wail, the moonlight poured out from its shielding of cloud to throw every object on the earth beneath into stark relief. From the direction of distant Coventry tiny dull flashes silhouetted the black horizon. Thin cones of light, made squat by distance, began to play back and forth, crossing and re-crossing the sky in slow motion, low down, like flat furtive ghosts. Hardly discernibly came a low and ominous crump-crump, crump-crump-crump of a far-off barrage. Coventry was getting it. Matthew found himself offering up silent prayers of thanks, his radio set still quiet, their own searchlight still in darkness. Not Birmingham tonight, thank God.

The field radio crackled. Suddenly sick at heart, Matthew unhooked the earphones and put them on to note the coordinates they conveyed. A shape materialised from the darkness of the field around to stand beside him.

'Why are we still in darkness, sonny?' Sergeant Pegg's voice filled the night air, making the nearby mobile parabaloid sound indicators tremble.

Matthew sprang to his job. 'They're going on now, Serg.'

To his barked command, the huge disc clonked. A shaft of blinding light pierced the sky, here picking out remnants of ragged cloud in fleeting, flat and fuzzy patches, moving hastily on, there the cone's vortex swallowed up eerily by the immensity of space. But Sergeant Pegg was not happy. Stepping close, he put his lips close to his quarry's ear to be heard over its messages.

''Alf asleep was we, Corp'ral?'

'No, sir.'

'Well, I suggest yer get yer finger out a bit more sharpish, next time, an' stop bloody daydreamin'. Fine example you are. Whatever'd 'appen to us if you ever got a commission? The day you do, my arse'll turn into a bleedin' pumpkin, that's wot. Now keep yer mind on yer job or I'll 'ave them stripes orf yer before yer can say, "Oh bloody my!"'

For twenty minutes Matthew kept his mind on his job, the sound indicator booming and roaring, amplifying every sound of any plane overhead, pinpointing its direction. On one occasion his searchlight trapped a plane, prompting others to sweep over and join it in a perfect star of beams, the ack-ack guns in a nearby sandbagged pit consequently opening up in an energetic earsplitting barrage. The plane swooped east, then north, finally managing to evade the deadly nucleus of light by slipping behind a low cloud and no doubt veering off to rejoin its fellows over Coventry.

One by one the searchlights were doused. Matthew's radio went quiet. Bob and the rest of the crew fell to rolling cigarettes.

'Tell you what,' he said, his tone low and confidential, recalling the sigh Matthew had given earlier and interpreting it correctly as only a gentle, perceptive soul could. 'Why don't you propose to this girl of yours? In a letter. See what she says.'

Matthew looked up with a frown from the cigarette he too was rolling. On a corporal's pay, packet cigarettes ran away with money and he did his best to discourage his parents sending cheques; telling them in no uncertain terms that it

73

made him look bad before his hut-mates and that he was managing adequately enough.

'I've only known her two or three months. I can't go mad.'

'If you feel about her the way you appear to me to, I would say you wouldn't want to lose her to someone else. Better now than never.'

That was true. But marriage. Matthew gave Bob a nod to placate him and told himself he'd have to think about that one. The more he thought about it, the more it seemed it was what he wanted. He remembered having the same feeling about Maggie, strange little twinges of excitement in the pit of his stomach when he thought of her, but Susan had come along and the sensation had transferred itself to her, fourfold. He knew now who he wanted, that it was Susan for whom he would further his career, making her proud of him. Perhaps he'd take Bob's advice, re-apply to the selection board. A man should do all he could to support his intended.

Sitting on his bed, a book on his knee for support, he absorbed himself in putting down on paper all he wanted to say. But reading it back, he cringed. The worst drivel he'd ever read – she'd laugh her head off. Better to tear it up before he did any damage and made a complete fool of himself.

But he didn't tear it up. Instead he folded the flimsy wartime paper and laid it carefully inside his pay book. Finding a fresh sheet of paper he penned another letter, full of the things he normally wrote to her, his hut-mates, their doings, the smelly Eddie Nutt whose socks stank the place out every time he opened his locker, the lecherous clown Taffy Thomas, the foul-mouthed Bert Farrell, Bob and his family, Sergeant Pegg, the rotten food, the hard beds, how much he looked forward to seeing her again and hoped it would be soon, and how was she, and what had she been doing?

'Ward, M.L.C. 092.' Matthew shouldered through the waiting men to receive two letters. Perched on a wall in the weak sunlight of the November morning that threatened rain, he put aside the one from his parents and opened the other with its large childish handwriting.

The letter was short, two small ruled pages, laboriously written, with several words misspelt, which evoked a surge of

74

compassion ... no, more one of tenderness. It was little more than an outline of her activities since he'd last seen her – pictures with a girlfriend, a dance or two. A twinge of panic smote him that she could so easily meet someone else during one of those dances, someone more conveniently to hand than he.

'Damn this bloody war!' he uttered so vehemently that Bob looked up and grinned.

Hastily scanning the second page of writing which didn't quite reach to its foot, it was the last line that brought relief flooding through his chest in a hot glow: 'I've been worried you might get fed up of riting to me. I cant wait to here from you.' A thousand words penned by the world's greatest poet could not have conveyed as much meaning as he read into that one artless sentence.

Life took on new meaning; time was a most precious commodity. But it was one the Army seemed perversely set on spinning out into an eternity of misery, for just as he was settling down after his day's duty to write to her the beefy bulk of Sergeant Pegg appeared to announce that the whole unit was on the morrow being sent to the wilds of Wales on an exercise, duration not divulged, all passes cancelled. Matthew, who had planned on wheedling a few hours' pass for himself, suffered an intense sense of loss hardly to be borne.

'Damn this bloody war!' he uttered for the second time that day as he fought to rush off a letter to Susan.

The Blitz was a tyrant. Begun in September and still going strong, there was no chance for Margaret to be at home for Christmas or New Year. Her mother had either to spend both on her own or go to her sister in Leicester. That she wouldn't do, fearing to travel alone. Daddy had always done everything and she, used to following him around like a small puppy, had still not learned independence.

'Can't you *try* to get away, dear,' she asked when after the sixth or seventh attempt Margaret got through on the telephone to the couple next door – well, the girl next door now that her husband had been called up.

Her mother sounded out of breath from hurrying into the other house, shouting down the mouthpiece as though distance made this obligatory although there'd not been a lot of static crackling over the wires.

'I'm on duty, Mumsy. I can't just get time off. It's terrible here. So many people being brought in injured.'

'I don't like us being apart.' The voice filled with consternation. 'I'll have to spent all night Christmas down the shelter all on my own. We've had a bomb come down near here. Some of the tiles are off. It's only a matter of time before this place is hit. I wish you were here. I feel so . . . so . . . isolated. Can't you come home?'

'They need every nurse they can get here at the moment, Mumsy.'

'Well, it's terrible. They should allow you home for New Year at least.'

'German bombers don't worry about holidays, Mumsy. They'll drop them whatever day it is.'

'I don't think I can stand being here all on my own.'

'Can't Joan next door come into our shelter with you?'

'I couldn't ask her that, dear.' Her mother's voice had dropped to a whisper lest the girl overhear. 'I couldn't open my house to *strangers*.'

'She's not a stranger. You're in her house right now. Now she's on her own too, you could both become quite good friends and help each other. We need to help each other these days.' The Blitz had made everyone conscious of the need for people to help each other.

'She won't be here at Christmas or New Year. She's spending the holiday with her family or her husband's family.'

Margaret tried not to let her sigh echo down the line. 'Well, I can't come home. The hospital's bulging. There are even beds in the corridors. And during an air raid we have to get as many as we can under the beds or down into the basement. It's like another hospital down there.'

'If you asked them nicely, they'd let you have just *one* day?'

'I can't, Mum.' She'd not been listening. 'This line's going funny. I'll have to ring off.'

'But Margaret . . .'

'I'll try to get home for a few nights after New Year, but it's impossible at the moment. You'll be all right, Mumsy.' She wanted to say that her being at home wouldn't stop a bomb dropping on it. 'I'll get time off eventually. I shall need it to get over all that we're going through here.'

'What, dear? What?' The crackling was growing noisier; impossible to hear anything now. And her time was almost up, her money running out. Moreover, she knew she was taking liberties during work time.

'I've got to ring off, Mumsy. Love you.'

'What?'

'Love you, Mumsy. I must go.' A sturdy, starched blue figure was approaching. 'I'm on duty. I'm wanted. Try to get home as soon as I can.'

She replaced the receiver on its hook, goodbyes cut short by the glare from the stone-grey eyes of Miss Grenville, approaching with a few attendant senior staff.

'Have you not enough to do, nurse?' The question was quietly authoritative. Margaret's reply was hasty, unrehearsed.

'My mother, Matron, asking if I'd be spending Christmas with her.'

In truth she had no real wish to go home. Christmas here would be far more exciting if she could believe what the nurses who'd been here last Christmas told her: wards decorated with paperchains fashioned from whatever coloured paper they could get hold of, spending any off-duty hours in each other's rooms to make them; going round the wards on Christmas Eve, their blue capes drawn close around them as they sang carols in muted voices, each nurse holding a lit candle; later sitting in the nurses' quarters all cosy and warm by a fire while others piled in to roast chestnuts and eat the mince pies someone's mother had sent, swapping jokes and stories of latest conquests with junior doctors.

That had been last year's. Margaret looked forward to this year's but wondered if it would have changed since the Blitz started. But anything was better than just sitting at home with Mumsy, even if there was an air raid on Christmas Day itself. She wouldn't even put that past the enemy.

She had been transferred to the London Hospital from her teaching hospital in October, a month after the Blitz had started. Eight weeks on and night bombing was still going on, not a single night free of it, remorseless, dominating all else. As darkness fell, she, like everyone else, merely prepared herself for the wail of sirens, the drone of bombers, and the horrible tearing sound and crash of falling bombs when the very air shook and dust drifted in from everywhere. The sky turned lurid to the mad clanging of fire engines, ambulance bells that heralded another stream of casualties. She and everyone felt it would go on until the war was finally won, all steadfastly refusing to imagine it could be Britain who might lose. Such a prospect remained so preposterous it was unthinkable.

Margaret stood aside for Matron's entourage to pass, waiting to make her escape back to her ward, but the woman halted, eyes fixed on her. 'If you are on duty, nurse, then you should know that telephone calls are not permissible. If you are not on duty, then you are off limits. I shall see you in my office at six thirty.'

'Yes, Matron.' Margaret watched miserably as she and her staff moved on. Six thirty. Well planned. Two days remained before Christmas and the evening had only just grown dark because of the introduction of British Summer Time. Clocks were now kept one hour forward the whole year round to confuse an enemy whose own time remained as it had been prior to hostilities. The bombers would not arrive for a couple of hours yet. Plenty of time was left for civilians to get home from work, eat and get into shelters, and for her to endure a formal and uncomfortable dressing-down from Matron.

She had been through the drill before, standing in the centre of Miss Grenville's office, Miss Grenville walking around her with measured steps, quoting hospital rules to her in quiet tones as measured as her walk. No punishment had been meted out: humiliation constituted punishment enough. Margaret found herself almost wishing the bombers would come early, requiring her duties to take precedence over any visit to Matron. But that would come sooner or later.

The all clear sounded just before dawn; while the people of the East End sank back to pick over lost homes, grieve lost loved ones, or just feel glad that they had escaped unscathed, the doctors and nurses of the hospitals all around toiled on, endeavouring to repair often irreparable injuries. For Margaret, exhausted by morning, her talking-to from Matron was just added torture. She fell thankfully into her bed in the nurses' quarters to forget about everything for a few hours until night came again. A week of that and then it would be days, spent mopping up the dregs from the previous night.

By February, freezing and cheerless, it was a wonder there were any buildings left to be bombed. Even some already flattened received a second direct hit. Yet, emerging for a breather in the cold light of dawn, she was always amazed so many still stood, windowless, battered sentinels. How this hospital had got away with just glancing blows so far seemed a miracle. How those who worked within it kept going *was* a miracle. Exhausted nerves stretched like rubber bands, they remained professional amid unbelievable chaos. As for herself, she was just an efficient puppet in a starched apron; obedient, mechanical, quietening some hysterical parent while nearby a terribly injured child seemed far more in need of her help; a mind trained at last to say, 'Walk, nurse,' when the sight of a woman with broken legs going into labour screamed for her to run, maybe knocking someone over in the process. It was frustrating, while the injured poured in still, covered in dust and blood, to be required to make tea for overstrained doctors. Though often essential, keeping them going, more often than not the tea remained untouched. It was hard at times to be obedient.

She recalled resentment when, wanting to stand by for the injured to arrive, she'd be required instead to help transfer geriatric patients to the basement. Coaxing the frail and sometimes perverse elderly into wheelchairs to be trundled to safety could test obedience to breaking point and struck a poor second to the business of tending victims of bomb-blast and fire.

'I feel more like a maid-of-all-work than a nurse,' she complained in early March, the night bombing still going full blast, as they carried a dear old soul back up a flight of stone stairs after the all clear had sounded. The lift was again out of order. O'Brien gave a tinkling laugh.

'Dear Mother o' God, isn't that what we're here for?'

O'Brien was small, dark and Irish, a bundle of smiles and dedication whose upbringing had endowed her with the unquestioning obedience of a nun. At times Margaret envied as well as admired her. When it seemed impossible the hospital could continue after broken gas mains cut off the cooking facilities and all they had to cope with was a portable paraffin stove, O'Brien's tranquillity as they fought with the thing reduced Margaret to a state of humility. With no running water for days on end, O'Brien took it all in her stride, emptying bottles of disinfectant into basins of cold water for washing hands after each dressing until the liquid turned cloudy grey, all the while praising God for the blessings of disinfectant.

At these times, Margaret yearned for the smooth routine of that teaching hospital in Basingstoke. She had learned her skills there, but East London was the acid test of a nurse's stamina. Here, controlling fatigue meant overcoming not the simple weariness of a few nights' lost sleep but the perfidious wearing down of her mental faculties, creeping up on her like a hooded assassin. The only hint of anything amiss would be a second or two of apparent sleep, yet coming back to herself to find she had accomplished her task as though she had been wide awake all the time.

More alarming were those longer moments of forgetfulness, as when she had taken a pile of bedpans, not to the sluice, but straight through the doors of an operating theatre without any recollection of how she had got there. Beating a hasty retreat, she had felt flustered and very much awake.

Much more recent had been that strange hallucination when she had looked up from taking a blood pressure to see a haggard and terribly emaciated young man standing at her elbow.

She remembered saying, quite loudly, 'I'll be with you in just one minute,' and wondering vaguely at the astonished look from her female patient. She had turned again to find the young man was not there. He never had been. Recognising her mistake for what it was, a figment of total exhaustion, it had taken a while to shake off a belief that it had been a premonition of some sort, for what really alarmed her was that every time she thought of it, the young face hovering before her seemed to be that of Matthew Ward.

It left her wondering for days how he was, where he was. In fact she could hardly wait for her next time off duty and she sacrificed a night out with the girls to pop home instead. The air-raid sirens hadn't yet sounded and after sitting for a while in the back garden with Mumsy in the improving April weather, she wandered down to the shops in Mare Street where Mr Ward had his electrical shop, with the precise aim of casually asking how his son was doing.

'Stationed in Wales at the moment,' she was informed as he handed a customer a repaired radio. Such things these days were either repaired or second-hand, most things not on ration having vanished from sight.

'He was near Birmingham,' Mr Ward went on. 'But like always, being trooped all around the country.'

'He's okay then?' she pressed, still unable to get her hallucination out of her mind. At least he hadn't been sent overseas.

'Fine. Had a letter from him a few days back.' How like Matthew he spoke. 'Found himself a girl. Don't know how serious it is, but he seems smitten by her. That's how it goes. In the forces, you meet all sorts. His mother's not pleased. Says it probably won't last as she's in Birmingham and he's in Wales.'

And Margaret's heart had sunk as she smiled and left, although it had been inevitable he would meet someone. She thought of herself, out of sight and out of mind. She should stop thinking about him and get on with her own life. But at least he was safe.

In no mood to go home just yet to have Mumsy defining the bleakness she knew must show on her face, she wandered down to St John's church. She needed time to think. Of what, she had no real notion, but she had to sort out her thoughts of the future. It was imperative to stop dreaming of Matthew and get on with her own life.

St John's stood closed on this early Saturday evening but did not look quite so isolated and remote as it once had behind its tall iron railings. They had gone now, as had all iron railings, to be melted down into guns and tanks in the fight for victory over the enemy. It now stood amid the open space looking slightly vulnerable, its sooty brick bathed a dirty gold from the slanting sun, its once-proud stained glass windows now war damaged and mostly boarded up, no longer reflecting back the golden glow.

For a while Margaret stood there, contemplating whether she should go back home now, but she let her feet carry her towards the church itself and into the neatly laid out gardens behind it, still known locally as Barmy Park from the asylum for the insane that had once stood there. Sinking down on a bench with the low sun full on her, she watched people wander past, their thoughts most likely on enjoying a little fresh air before consigning themselves to the communal shelters and Bethnal Green Underground to await the arrival of the night bombers. All these people were passing yet she saw herself as quite alone, not because they ignored her but because she wanted it, so that she could think in peace of Matthew, of herself, of how she stood with him and he with her. Once again she decided to stop thinking about him and get on with her own life.

With that in mind, she got up and resolutely turned her face towards home. A voice hailed her as she passed the church again. Louise Ward ran up to her, slightly out of breath, cheeks flushed, her mousy hair rolled up primly in a style known as a victory roll, unflattering for anyone with the broad jaw line which she had inherited from her mother.

She looked excited. 'What're you doing here, Margaret? I thought you were nursing.'

'I've got a day off,' Margaret supplied but Louise could hardly contain herself.

'I'm only home for the weekend. Guess what, Margaret, I've gone and joined the Wrens.'

'You've what?' Margaret stopped walking.

But nothing could diminish the enthusiasm shining on Louise's face. She looked transformed. Gone was the prudish strait-laced mien. This girl glowed, and Margaret recalled the exact look on her brother's face when he'd come to say goodbye that cold winter day. It was like looking at a bird newly released from a cage and she realised that Louise, for all she would never have admitted it, had been as trapped as he had been once she blossomed into her teens. Without warning she had broken loose from all the old ties that had bound her. Because of the war she was suddenly her own person. 'I'm eighteen now, eligible to join up. I signed on and they took me. I had a medical and I passed A-one. I want to see the world.'

See the world. Perhaps dangerously so. Margaret eyed her dubiously. 'Did you tell your parents what you intended to do? What do they think?'

Louise gave a giddy laugh. 'Mother was shocked rigid. Dad hasn't said much. I sprang it on them. If I had told them what I was going to do Mother would have stopped me, I know. It took me being evacuated . . . well, not exactly evacuated but more or less . . . to give me a taste of what could be had. So I signed on for the WRNS. I'm leaving next week for Portsmouth.'

Walking home with Louise chatting incessantly at her side about her medical, how girls were needed to relieve Royal Navy personnel from office duties, how she had been told that they could be sent anywhere in the world and all the countries she might see, Margaret found it impossible to broach the subject of her brother's involvement with the anonymous Birmingham girl and if she thought it could be serious. Yet again she told herself to put it out of her mind, that their lives had gone their seperate ways. But how nice it would be had it been otherwise.

Chapter 8

The coming of spring found Matthew still crouching in ditches in the wet wilderness of Fforest Fawr in the heart of Wales, trying to keep a crackling field radio dry under a gas cape.

'One thing's obvious,' he muttered to Bob Howlett beside him. 'She's no letter writer.'

In four months he had written Susan one letter a week as regularly as clockwork, each one several pages long. In return he had received just five letters from her, each hardly more than two sides of a piece of Woolworth's notepaper. Her bad spelling, he understood, perhaps made her slow to reply, but if she had any feelings for him, surely she'd write more frequently.

'She's lost all interest in me,' he said miserably. 'Bound to happen, she there and me here, and Birmingham full of uniforms.'

'Is that what you think?' Bob asked, scanning the rain-soaked peaty moorland. 'That she's just uniform crazy and nothing else?'

'No, of course I don't. But no girl is going to wait for months.'

'Lots do, in wartime. They'll wait for years.'

'Yes, if they've been going steady long enough. We hardly met above a couple of times. I wouldn't blame her.'

Beside them, Taffy Thomas shifted his uncomfortable position on his haunches. A Welshman he was, but from sunny, civilised Aberystwyth on the coast. This part of the country with its sopping heather wasn't his cup of tea at all.

'What you need is get it out of your system, boyo. A bit of diversion. Two sisters I know of. Real beauties, the pair of 'em.

Met 'em a week or two ago. One for me, one for you, eh? Make you forget your poor broken heart, that will.'

'No thanks, Taff,' Matthew murmured. Taffy looked mildly spurned.

'There's a terrible waste. Just have to do the best I can with both of 'em, then, won't I?' Grinning, he went back to scanning the horizon and misty forms of men scurrying about on manoeuvres, what could be seen of them through fine rain and the smoke of the thunder flashes going off.

Returning to camp, Taffy was off to the farmhouse where the sisters apparently lived; their father was in the Army, their mother working late in some nearby town. He returned later that evening, a little the worse for wear and very triumphant.

'Missed a treat, you did,' he stated, flinging himself on his camp bed in the tent he shared with Matthew and Bob. 'Damned stupid, you, mooning after a girl that don't want to know, as far as I can see.'

Having spent the entire day trying to put Susan out of his mind and annoyed that she refused to go, Matthew allowed his curiosity to arouse itself, if only moderately. 'What's she like then, this sister?'

Taffy let out an odd sound that passed for a knowing laugh, rather like a lion grunting. 'Big. Would eat you for breakfast, boyo. Put the blood back in your veins for you though. I could take you next time, if there is a next time. And if you was to get a letter from your girl, then no need to tell her, is there?'

'Might take you up on that, Taff.' Defiance held him in a vice. Two weeks waiting for a response to his last letter to her, and still nothing.

'You're on then,' said Taffy, and Matthew's mood loosened enough for him to give way to a terse chuckle.

'You're a lecherous swine, Taff.' But at this moment Taffy was a tonic to an aching heart.

A few days later he was glad he hadn't been led into temptation, with fatigues preventing him sneaking out of camp with Taffy to the infamous farmhouse. Handed a letter from Susan, he read what seemed to be the usual dutiful scribble, except for one short badly spelt paragraph:

I hope you don't think I'm not intrested, Matthew. I don't

know how to put my feelings down on paper because when I read it it sounds so silly so I just tare it up. But I do need to tell you that I reelly do . . .

The next two words had been crossed out, obliterated so completely that a diviner couldn't have read them, after which she had continued:

I won't half be glad to see you again so I can tell you how I reelly feel.

All at once it seemed his luck changed. Before he had a chance to reply, the whole unit was returned to Northwood and with a forty-eight-hour pass to boot. On wings of joy he rushed to the phone box on his arrival, finding a lengthening queue of Army personnel eager to tell families of the chance to be with them for the weekend.

In a fever of impatience he tagged on to the end of it, cursing the time the one already in the phone box was taking. At last, the receiver in his grasp, he gave the exchange the telephone number of the shop where Susan worked, having long ago looked it up after she had told him where she was employed.

'Hello?' A high, piercing voice spoke loudly in his ear as he asked for Susan. And then, querulously, 'Who is this?'

'Can I speak to Miss Susan Hopkins?' he repeated.

'I'm sorry,' came the voice, quite tersely. 'Staff aren't allowed to take private calls.'

'But this is urgent.'

'I'm very sorry, sir. This telephone is for customer enquiries only.' She wasn't a bit sorry, in fact she sounded highly pleased to refuse his request. 'Only if the call is from the family of one of our staff with dire news do we allow them to take a call.'

'Then could you give her a message?' he intercepted. 'Could you tell her I'll her tonight – on the corner of her road – at six-thirty?'

The voice had become filled with exasperation. 'Really, sir, I am far too busy to relay messages from every Tom, Dick and Harry arranging dates with members of my staff.'

86

'Please – just this once. We're – we're . . .' He thought quickly. 'We're engaged, and . . .'

He broke off in the act of his lie as the phone-box door was yanked open. The voices outside came instantly loud, the speaker even louder.

'Git a bleedin' move on, mate. There're ovvers out 'ere, y'know.'

Matthew shot out a hand and jerked the phone-box door shut again. 'Please . . . I've been away on a training course.'

'Engaged, you say?' There was now lively curiosity in the voice on the other end of the phone, and for an instant he hesitated. What had he said? Then he came to an instant decision. 'That's right. And I need to speak to Miss Hopkins. It is very important.'

He waited while the faceless one ruminated on this piece of news.

'Well,' it deliberated at length, 'I really cannot alter our rules, but on this occasion I will pass on your message. What name?'

'Matthew Ward.'

'Very well. But I sincerely hope you are not making a fool of me, Mr Ward. And please keep in mind that my staff are *not* allowed to make use of this telephone for private purposes unless in an emergency.'

'I'll remember. And thank you.'

Thoughtfully he replaced the receiver. Engaged, he'd said, in fear of being cut off. Engaged. Well, why not? All that fretting, all that longing, the tone of her last letter – he was sure now that those obliterated words had been 'love you'. And didn't he want this relationship to last? And hadn't he spent these past four months pining, if he really admitted to it? Well then . . .

The prospect of being engaged sent a thrill of excitement through his veins he hadn't expected. Lost in thought, he opened the door of the phone box to be almost pushed against the edge of it by a soldier squeezing by to get in, throwing Matthew a baleful glance as he did so.

''Bout bloody time too, mate! Got *my* missus ter phone too, y'know.'

The stress lay on 'my'. The man assumed he was married.

87

He would be, soon. And again a thrill coursed through his veins.

He hadn't expected Susan to be there on the stroke of six thirty, but not finding her there on the dot, irrational anxieties began instantly to manifest themselves. Had the manageress not passed on his message? Had he in fact frightened her off with his damned silly proposal? Wouldn't any girl be? She'd never said she loved him, apart from that crossed-out bit in her latest letter which could have been anything, just a spelling mistake too bad to let by. That bit in her letter about wanting to tell him how she really felt, one could read all sorts of meaning into such a line. In retrospect he had kidded himself. He was a fool.

It occurred to him as he waited in the damp warmth of this still-light mid-April evening that he didn't really know anything about her. He *felt* that he knew her, but it wasn't the same thing.

Staring along her street that teemed with grubby children at play, their shouts echoing from the flat, scabrous walls on either side set with endless doors and windows, not a tree, a plant, a blade of grass to be seen, he realised how unlike was her life to his. He had to be honest with himself. Because he thought himself in love was he seeing all this and her too through rose-tinted glass? Perhaps, as well as love, did he feel some sadness and pity for her too? Without that he would be viewing these slums with utter distaste, eager only to get away.

Where he stood was a pub, its blown-out windows and frames covered by sheets of waterproof-painted cardboard, its walls, door and sign pockmarked from flying shrapnel. Across the road, a little way down, a gash in the previously unbroken row of terraced houses held a pile of rubble, a result of the bomb Susan had told him about. The slanting evening sun picking out the interior walls that had once been private pitilessly exposed the wallpapers, the poor fireplaces, the smallness of the rooms that had once been, and almost touching the rubble, the houses of the next street, hitherto unseen from here, now peeped through like people surprised at being caught in the open.

He glanced at his watch. Six thirty-five. Was that all? A

breathless voice called his name, light footsteps from behind him came running, and there she was, almost falling into his arms as he turned, her tone gabbling with panic.

'Oh, Matthew. I had to stay behind at work. Stock-taking. I got your message but I only just got away and nearly missed the bus. I was so scared you wouldn't wait. I thought you might think I didn't care and give up and go away . . .'

She was reaching up, kissing him, here in the street for everyone passing by to see. 'Oh, Matthew, did you mean what you said? On the phone? You did mean it, didn't you?'

He nodded, gently stopping her frantic embrace, aware people were grinning as they went past. 'It wasn't a very romantic way to propose . . .'

'Oh, it was!' she broke in, still holding tightly to him. 'I never dreamed I'd get such a romantic proposal. And to think that bitch didn't tell me until it was time to close and then said we had to do stock-taking. She let me go a bit earlier, but I hate her.'

'Doesn't matter. You're here.' She'd never know how relieved he felt. 'I want to take you out, Susan, to celebrate. I can't afford much in the way of a posh restaurant, but . . .'

'I couldn't eat. I'm too excited,' she burst in. 'I want to go somewhere quiet with you, darling. Just us two, and we can talk all about *things*. We've got to discuss things.'

'Yes.' Her closeness was making him feel worked up inside, a sort of churning making it hard to breathe properly. They had to get away from here. 'Where do you want to go?'

At last she broke away, thought for a moment. 'It's still light. It'll stay light for ages yet. Let's get some sandwiches and take them up on Beacon Hill. We can watch the sunset and be all romantic – just you and me. It only takes half an hour to get there.'

On the rounded promontory called Beacon Hill, more or less deserted but for one or two people walking dogs, they reclined on Matthew's greatcoat on the rabbit-nibbled turf to eat a couple of meagrely filled off-ration chicken sandwiches as the sun sank lower.

'On a clear day you can see ten counties from here,' Susan said, huddled inside her coat against the rapidly cooling air. The sun had become a red ball in the smoky haze of the city, outlining the rim of their world. She pointed southwest. 'That's the Malvern Hills.'

Matthew looked, then laughed. 'Clouds.'

'They're hills, Matthew.'

'All right, hills,' he laughed and she turned a petulant face towards him.

'Don't make fun of me.' Her lips were so close that he leaned forward and kissed them, tasting the sweetness that was her lipstick but which he was sure must also be her lips. Forgetting her pique she returned the kiss, nestled against him, lying quiet now and watching the rim of the sun finally sink out of sight, leaving its reflection to tint the clouds orange and pink, that in turn bathed the earth in ruddy glow.

'Matthew,' she said quietly, slowly, relaxing against him. 'You did mean it, about us being engaged? Only it was so casual. It was romantic, being said over the phone, but . . . well, you know, if you said it again now.'

He tightened his arm around her. 'Darling, I'm saying it now. Shall we get engaged?' Yes, this was what he wanted. Couldn't imagine life now without her. She would be his wife. He felt his insides leap with the joy the thought brought. 'Susan, I want to marry you.'

He heard her deep intake of breath, her reply exhaled in a series of long sighs. 'Oh . . . Oh, Matthew. Oh . . .' She seemed incapable of saying anything else. It meant yes, he knew. But there were material things to think about too, unwanted material things. 'I'll have to tell my mom and dad.'

'Will they object?' She was still not twenty-one. She must have their consent. His heart fell a little. But he needn't have been anxious.

'No. They'll be glad to see me go and make a bit more room. I've got three brothers and two sisters and we've only got three bedrooms. They'll be thrilled, especially as you're someone really nice with enough money . . .'

'Hold on,' he curbed her, laughing. 'I'm not Rockefeller, you know. I'm existing on a corporal's pay.'

'But your family's well off, aren't they?'

'They're nothing to do with me.' He hoped he hadn't sounded a bit grim but he didn't want to think about them at this moment. 'You'll be marrying me, not them.'

'I know. Oh, Matthew, of course I know. Married. I'm going to have to pinch myself to make sure this is me.' She had turned, lifting her face to his. 'I shall love you always, Matthew. Always and always.'

And on her cue he kissed her with a pressing need for her bursting inside him like a radiant explosion. Consumed by its heat he let his weight bear her down beneath him and on the warmth of his greatcoat they made love, she in trusting joy of his promise and he in the knowledge that they would be together till all eternity. And it was beautiful.

He wrote home, cramming his letter with Susan's charms, and defiantly told them that he was engaged.

That Sunday he went dutifully to see Susan's family. Susan had already broken the news and her mother, fair, full-bosomed and not a bit like her trim daughter, planted a kiss on his cheek in a cloud of Evening in Paris perfume.

'She's right about you being so good-looking, love, ain't she, Dad?'

'She's right, yeh,' echoed Mr Hopkins.

Susan's two sisters sat on the arms of the settee, the air around them redolent of peardrops from nail varnish being applied as they both regarded Matthew with mute envy of their sister.

Two of her brothers were in the street, the youngest sprawled on a mat in front of an empty firegrate torturing a clockwork train with a screwdriver.

The place smelled of Sunday midday dinner and Matthew was glad he hadn't been invited to eat with them; the lingering odour of overboiled cabbage almost overwhelmed him so that it was difficult to draw a breath without feeling nauseated. Susan, sweet and fastidious Susan, deserved better than this. He would give it to her as soon as this war was over and they could find a place together. Meantime, as soon as they were married she might go to his parents and live in a far more wholesome atmosphere.

Mr Hopkins, a small man who looked as if he had once been handsome, lounged in an armchair rolling a cigarette which he lit. The match was dropped in the empty grate, the matchbox replaced on an already cluttered mantelpiece. 'Wondered who she'd end up with,' he muttered.

'I'm very glad she's found herself a nice lad,' said Mrs Hopkins, handing Matthew a cup of tea while Susan, sitting beside him on the edge of the settee, smiled with satisfaction and cuddled nearer to him. Her teacup was on the floor at her feet, the liquid in it strong and muddy, as was his. He took a sip, tried not to grimace and put it down beside hers. Behind him a mound of well-thumbed magazines kept sliding forward, making his seat uncomfortable.

'When you planning to marry then?' Mr Hopkins asked.

Matthew glanced at Susan, saw her eyes, those deep blue eyes, full of trust. 'As soon as possible,' he answered.

Mr Hopkins coughed, a moist rumbling cough, and flicked the wet butt of his cigarette into the grate. 'Up the spout is she, then?'

'I'm sorry?' Matthew queried at once, hardly believing what he heard and appalled.

'Pregnant is she?'

Susan's two sisters giggled. The boy on the mat looked up, mildly interested. Mrs Hopkins gave a small embarrassed tut.

'No, Mr Hopkins, she isn't,' Matthew said tersely, wanting to be out of here as soon as he possibly could. Love Susan as he now did, beyond measure, he did not want to set foot in her parents' house ever again. This man repelled him. But that Susan was small like her father, it seemed incredible that he was indeed her father. With no way to explain to him, a man who confused love with lust, his feelings for his daughter, he said instead, 'If I'm posted before we can be married, there might not be another chance for a long time.'

Mrs Hopkins was giving him a scrutinising look. She had quite large breasts. They strained at her sturdy white brassiere, the top of which was visible above a blue organdie blouse. Matthew looked quickly away, thinking of Susan's small firm breasts. He longed to be out of here, to be alone with her.

Mrs Hopkins was appraising him slowly. 'I must say, though, it fair took us all by surprise, our Sue telling us last night as you'd asked her to marry you. Came as a bit of a shock, like. No wonder we thought you and her had been up to a few tricks.' She gave a tinkling laugh at his look. 'Come on, love.

We've all done it. But whether she is or she ain't, I'm glad you're serious about her. And if it's all right with her, then it's all right with us.'

The china-blue eyes followed him slowly as somehow he got to his feet, his hand seeking Susan's and holding it firmly. 'I'll have to be going now, Mrs Hopkins.'

She looked surprised. 'You ain't drunk your tea yet.'

'No, I've got to get back to camp. And Susan and I, well we . . .'

She giggled at his awkward pause, her tone full of feminine wisdom. 'Of course. You two want a bit of time alone – to say goodbye, proper like.' She came over and took his hand in her soft one. 'Now you come and see us again as soon as you can. You're always welcome. I'm glad for you both. I know how hard it is for people in love to wait, but meeting you, I know you'll take care of her no matter what you two get up to. I reckon our Sue's a lucky girl and at least you've asked to marry her. So we can look forward to you both setting a proper date, eh? And soon, eh?'

'Well, as soon as the Army lets us.' He looked at Susan and saw her eyes shining. 'I don't know when that will be, but I'll try to get something sorted out. It will probably have to be at short notice, knowing the way they work – probably end up in registry office. The Army doesn't give weddings top priority for leave.'

Again he looked at Susan, expecting to see disappointment in her face at the possible lack of a wedding without the trimmings, but her eyes were still glowing.

Chapter 9

The Blitz was over. The evening following that Saturday the tenth of May, the worst night of any that the enemy had dished out, people went to their places of safety as usual, nurses stood on alert to receive yet another influx of casualties as usual, but the bombers didn't come.

'I wonder what's wrong?' Margaret's question echoed that of many, almost as though they had been robbed of something. Quite silly really. But O'Brien, jolly as always, had an answer.

'Ah well, isn't it Sunday, an' all? And isn't it about time they'd be thinkin' of havin' a day of rest? Holy Mother o' God, I expect they need it.'

'If they don't, then we do,' Margaret said with just a twitch of a smile. 'But I don't think Hitler believes in Sundays or God.'

Like everyone else she was holding her breath. Come Monday, after lulling poor battered Londoners into a false sense of security, they'd be back again – part of Hitler's plan to demoralise them further, it had to be – and she would again form part of a team trying to patch up a new intake of victims. But after a fortnight and everything still quiet, Margaret felt she could at last let out her breath. She was also given her first full weekend off in months.

'Now you'll have the whole weekend with your mother,' O'Brien said, a wistful lilt in her tone that there was no chance of her getting home to see her family, way off in Northern Ireland. She'd have been appalled to know that the prospect of spending the weekend with her own mother didn't fill Margaret with as much joy as she supposed.

All she wanted was to relax a little. Being with her mother, telling her how lonely she felt, was only swapping one tension for another. Of course it was uncharitable to think like that, but now that the worst of the air raids seemed to be over she felt she would have liked to spend this first weekend off in the company of the friends she had made. She needed a bit of fun, a bit of freedom, for who knew what lay around the corner?

The city's ruins had still continued to smoke ten days after the Blitz ended. Victims were still being dug out of the rubble, domestic services were still not working properly, thousands of families remained without homes, and streets still stayed blocked; sometimes a street had to be cordoned off where an unexploded bomb was being defused.

But slowly the intake of casualties was diminishing and this past fortnight had given Margaret a taste for a new freedom that had begun to be felt by her and her colleagues, a sense of adventure as after a night out she and a few others would clamber back into the nurses' home via a window surreptitiously left unlocked. The hospital's notion of keeping an eye on its vulnerable young nurses meant proper curfew being kept, with doors locked at ten thirty prompt. Anyone returning later than that must get past the superintendent's office, and if she didn't have an official pass, issued to very few for special circumstances only, a visit to Matron the next morning would ensue – a fate usually worse than death. But rules were made to be flouted. After months of air raids with hardly a moment for herself except to flop down exhausted on a makeshift bed in the safer basement after duty, Margaret felt happy to flout them with the rest.

'No, not this weekend,' she told O'Brien as they ate after-duty Bovril sandwiches in O'Brien's room. 'My mother's not expecting me. A few of us are going to a dance at the Palais in Hammersmith. I don't want to miss it.'

O'Brien stopped halfway to taking a bite from her sandwich. 'But I heard you once say you were not much of a dancer, did I not?'

'I'm not. But I'd still like to go. Be nice to let my hair down for once. Why don't you come too?'

'Me? Bejesus, I'd be no good. I've two left feet, so I have.'

'Me too. But it'll get us out of ourselves for a while. We'll keep each other company.' She wouldn't feel so out of it with O'Brien as her life raft, someone to talk to while the others were whirled off in the arms of those who picked them for partners.

It was with amazement that Margaret found herself among the chosen at the very first dance, a waltz, something she could do fairly well without falling over her or her partner's feet. She was in fact asked to dance several times and discovered she wasn't half as left-footed as she had once thought herself, so long as she concentrated on what her partner was doing, and so long as it was a waltz or a not-too-fast quickstep. She felt guilty leaving O'Brien, glad to sit out the more difficult dances, the foxtrots, the tangos and the seductive rumbas. O'Brien seemed quite content just to sit and watch, even pushing Margaret to dance with anyone who came up to them.

'I was niver a one for this,' she said brightly, her ready smile hardly leaving her round face. 'Now a good jig is more in my line, so it is.'

But as the evening wore on, she began to fidget and look at the clock high on the white and gold wall above the band.

'If we don't leave soon, Ross, we'll be back too late to get in properly and have to creep past the superintendent's office, so we will, and if we're caught it will be Matron's office in the morning.'

Margaret laughed. 'That's all solved. Bennett left a lavatory window open and a dustbin underneath.'

'And what if someone closes it?'

'They won't. She's given instruction to one of the night staff to keep an eye on it. But it's still early yet.'

Someone coming towards her with a purposeful expression which she was coming to recognise as an invitation – and the dance was a waltz, thank God – stopped her from saying any more. Not only that but she thought she recognised him as one of the young junior doctors from the London. He held his hand out to her and nodded enquiringly.

Whisked away, her feet by now adjusting to one or two of the more intricate waltz steps, she was unsurprised but highly delighted when he said, 'I know your face.'

She leaned back from him to study him. 'I'm a nurse.' The

floral dress she wore would not have betrayed her. 'I work at the London.'

'I thought I'd seen you somewhere. That's where I work.'

'Oh.' She felt him swing her and concentrated on matching the step and not squashing his toe in the process.

'I'm on Dr Farnborough's team. A junior doctor so far. But I hope to qualify next year. My father's a GP. In Bristol. I'm Ronald Whittaker.'

'Margaret Ross,' she reciprocated. 'I'm just a nurse. Studying hard.'

He chuckled as he swung her into a turn. 'Don't ever say just a nurse. You lot have been worth your weight in gold these last months of the Blitz. Couldn't have managed without a single one of you.'

'Not the mess I've been getting into during the worst of it,' she said with a small self-deprecating laugh. 'Dropping basins of water all over the place ... Oops! Sorry.' She'd caught his toe, breaking his turn but he hardly noted it. He was staring at her, slowing his steps down more to a walk.

'I know you,' he burst out in revelation. 'Yes. During an air raid. In the basement.'

The basements had doubled as operating theatres and casualty. And now she definitely recognised him too, and the recollection made her blush. He had been assisting in stemming a haemorrhage. She had knocked into him as she hurried past with a basin of disinfection solution. The liquid had tipped all over the floor so that she had been obliged to mop it all up, getting in the way while all around people cried out for relief from their pain. Later he had come over to ask how she was. All that had been going on around them and he had asked how *she* was.

By the end of the waltz, to her astonishment, he was asking her if he could see her again. 'I know we work in the same hospital, but I would like to see you on a social basis. Perhaps we could go across the road to the pub for a drink, when we're both off duty.'

Before she could stop herself, she said, 'I'd like that.' Seconds later that last kiss Matthew had given her flashed through her mind, a kiss that meant so much at the time. But that was it – *at the time*. Time had gone on. Their ways, which she'd thought

97

might hold promise, had taken their own turnings and she'd vowed to get on with her own life. Maybe this man was her new life, her future. Matthew certainly wasn't. He was the past.

She found she and Ronald had something in common. He knew the Basingstoke teaching hospital where she had been. He had left just before her arrival. It seemed such a coincidence and only natural they should make a second date as soon as their off duty hours again matched. And when on their third date he told her he thought she was quite lovely, the understatement carrying a depth of honesty, she felt uplifted and indeed felt lovely for the first time ever. Even so, old habits tended to die hard; his admiration of her made her scoff.

'Don't be silly, of course I'm not. I wish I'd been born dark-haired.'

'You've got gorgeous hair, Margaret.'

They sat in darkness on one of the few market stalls operating in wartime, manned by older men and some women holding the fort for their own menfolk away at the war. White-chapel's street market, a thriving place before the war, had become sparse, the variety of goods narrowed down to vegetables, second-hand clothing, bike parts, and so on. Perched on the empty stall between a skeleton of rusting tubular uprights, breathing in the dank odour of cabbage leaves trodden underfoot earlier and the sweet waft of beer from the pub they'd just left, he couldn't see her in the blackout, nor she him, but his hand moved up and in the inky blackness felt its way across her short curls. 'I do so love touching your hair, Margaret.' He leaned forward, gave her a kiss. 'I know this sounds sudden, but, Margaret, I love you.'

For a moment she was quiet, then she said softly, 'We've only seen each other three times. You can't. It's too early.'

'It's never too early, darling. I am, I'm in love with you.' He kissed her again, gently, and all she could do was kiss him back, telling herself that Matthew was another world, a closed chapter. She felt a little sad, but this was *her* life. And she had to take it with both hands.

Sitting in the sunshine of her tiny back garden, overlooked by all the other houses around that were beginning to cast lengthening shadows across it, Margaret let her mind move gently over that third date. It had been far too early for him to start professing love. Had she felt the same it would have been fine, but she hadn't. Nice as he was, she became angry with herself that even as he kissed her, Matthew with his quirky smile had floated into her head, making her merely suffer the kiss, thus allowing some past infatuation to spoil what could become something worthwhile.

She found herself telling Ronald that this weekend she had to spend some time with her mother. After all, duty came first. But was it really that there might be a slim chance of bumping into Matthew or at least finding out how he was? She needed time to think – about Ronald, about her life, to shake off this silly longing and grow up. Ronald was a nice person but it was early days yet. A day or two away from him might clear her head and let her see things as they stood. Too easy to end up an old maid in crying after something that couldn't be had when what could be had was maybe staring her right in the face.

'Margaret, dear, come in and have your tea.' Her mother, calling to her, interrupted her reverie.

'I thought we could take a little stroll in the park afterwards,' Mrs Ross continued as they sat together in the small dining room with the sun pouring in through the window. 'It's a lovely afternoon and I don't usually care for going for walks on my own. But now you're here it would be nice for us. They don't give you half enough time off at that hospital.'

Margaret held back a sigh of protest. She didn't want to stroll anywhere. It had been peaceful just sitting in the back garden relaxing in the gentle curve of the deckchair. So long since she'd been able to relax. Resigned, she went to gather up a cardigan.

'No one would dream there was a war on,' her mother murmured as they passed the noisy Victorian drinking fountain with its usual cluster of children around it denying visitors a chance of peace or a sip of water.

'Let's take a walk over to the other end,' Mrs Ross suggested with a grimace towards the raucous, scruffy children. 'It's quieter over there. I like the grottos and rockeries with all the rhododendrons. They should be in bloom.'

It was a long walk; the park was vast. Margaret let her

mother chatter on as they wandered past the wide lake with its twin islands designed as sanctuary for water fowl. There was another lake, an ornamental pond near the main entrance with fish and water lilies. But it was all beginning to look a little sad. Parts of the park had been turned over to allotments rented by local men too old to be called up. Margaret could see some of them hoeing around their spring cabbage, lettuce, onions, carrots, stringing up runner beans, all bent on their work, everything else around them going unnoticed. Men who no doubt had once only ever got their hands in the soil for a hobby, now dug like navvies. Tomorrow, Sunday, they would be at it again, bending their backs and trundling their wheel-barrows home laden with tools or green produce to help supplement the family rations for another week. People who had any sort of garden or back yard now kept chickens for their eggs and flesh – another boost to a larder slimmed by rationing.

The cricket field now had guns on it, multi-barrelled cannons that had made a terrible row during the Blitz. 'I'll be so glad to see the end of this terrible war,' her mother was saying. 'It would be so nice for you to go back to a nine to five thirty job and come home every night like you used to.'

'It can't last forever.' She didn't want to go back to some nine to five thirty job. Nursing, for all its restrictions, its rules and regulations, had given her in its own way a taste for freedom. She wanted more and by the time this war came to an end she hoped she would have moved on, living a life of her own. That could be a long way off; the war, the way it was going, seemed to have no end to it at all. Night bombing had ceased for the time being but that was no guarantee it wouldn't start up again. Everyone, for all they had breathed a sigh of relief, was still on edge. The Germans had all of Europe; only this island was left, with just a strip of water between it and the enemy. German invasion was all the talk. Meanwhile British merchant ships were being sunk, every day another one, tight-ening rationing still more. Even clothing had now gone on ration. The loss of seamen's lives meant it broke the heart to listen to the news. War in North Africa was now going badly, troops had been pulled out from Crete. No one knew what would come next. She could be thirty by the time it all ended.

'I know it won't last forever, dear,' her mother was saying, clinging to her arm as though needing support. 'It's just becoming too much for me, for all of us. Look at the bread we eat. Grainy, grey stuff, going stale almost as soon as it's cooled. Real white bread's a thing of the past. By the way, the tiles on our roof have been mended, by quite an elderly man who came. The bombing did such a lot of damage.'

'We're lucky. People have had it really bad elsewhere.' She thought of the injured brought into casualty, smothered in dust and grime and bits of brick, operated on hardly cleaned up. She thought of the gaping spaces left in blocks of tenements, just rubble now, still uncleared and beginning to settle and weather, greening with fast-growing weeds; places where people had once lived. All their possessions were now gone, perhaps they themselves were gone.

'Yes,' her mother agreed, sobered by much the same thoughts. 'We have been lucky. The times I've put my hands together and . . .'

A voice calling Margaret's name cut her short. They turned to see a fair-haired girl pushing a pram in which a child around a year old sat. At her side was a fresh-faced young man sporting a pencil moustache and wearing an officer's uniform. Instantly Margaret recognised them.

'Eileen! Freddy!' She grasped each in greeting as they came up to her. 'How are you?'

Eileen's voice hadn't changed, the same dreamy one she remembered. 'I thought it was you, Margaret. I said to Freddy, "I'm sure that's Margaret Ross," didn't I, Fred? How are you, Margaret. Are you still nursing?'

'I'm fine,' Margaret returned, formally now the surprise of seeing them had passed. 'Yes. In London now. I'm home for the weekend.'

They nodded without interest. 'Freddy's home on leave,' Eileen said while he smiled rather superciliously. If Eileen hadn't altered, he had, from the soft lovesick youth to a man with a bearing that suggested arrogant confidence.

Margaret turned her attention to the little boy in the pram. 'What's his name?'

'Simon. He'll be a year old in three weeks' time.'

'He's a handsome lad, Eileen.' She cooed at him but the boy

101

merely stared back, solemn round eyes regarding her with that peculiar stare most one-year-olds adopt, their trusting baby smiles long since used up. 'You must be very proud of him.'

Freddy nodded and looked pleased while Eileen bent forward over the top of the pram and touched her offspring's fair head with a fond and possessive hand. But her face had clouded.

'I wonder sometimes if this is a world we should be bringing children into, what with our boys bombing Germany, and the Italians on their side, and the fighting in North Africa, and with all this bombing. My mum and dad's house got a direct hit you know. But they weren't in it at the time.'

'Oh, dear.' She didn't fancy conversing about the Blitz. It was past.

'And after all our RAF boys did last summer, fighting up there all alone in the air. You heard about poor Dennis Cox? Killed in his Spitfire.'

Margaret had heard. She nodded solemnly.

'Damned waste,' Freddy said abruptly.

'You used to be his girl at one time,' Eileen said, looking pityingly at her. 'It must have come as a terrible shock to you especially.'

'It was never serious between us,' Margaret said while her mother gave a sad sigh and murmured something about Dennis Cox being such a nice boy too. 'We were just friends really.'

'Even so . . .' Eileen persisted lugubriously, making Margaret want to laugh. Like many who lead uneventful lives, which was how Eileen struck her, she seemed to need to feed, like a carrion crow, on the tragedy of others. 'It doesn't seem possible, though. Poor Dennis Cox – dead. It's terrible.'

'Yes, terrible,' Margaret echoed. So many people dead. So many lives spoiled by loss, by permanent injury, by sights they should never have seen. Men in battle, civilians who should never have been anywhere near a battle, children too young to be thrown into war, young people just leaving school with all their lives ahead of them, their eager lives consisting of but a few short years after all. They shall not grow old as we who are left grow old . . . Margaret felt tears prickle her nose and sniffed them back, probably sounding as though she was making light of Eileen's pet word, terrible, for the tragedy that

102

hung about so many people. But it was true: having seen so much, tended so many dying and torn bodies, she couldn't find it in her to reserve sorrow for Dennis Cox alone.

'But have you heard about Matthew Ward?' Eileen had perked up.

Margaret's heart gave a sickening leap, fear for him pounding like a hammer in her throat. 'What about him?' It was all she could manage.

'Got himself engaged. To a Birmingham girl. They're getting married soon apparently. Now, he's the last person I'd ever have imagined would settle down. I said to you, Fred, didn't I? "He'll end up a bachelor," I said, didn't I? And you said, "He'll still be chasing skirts at forty." You said, "Men like that who can get their pick of girls usually end up with no one. Far too choosy for their own good." Do you remember saying that, Fred?' And as he nodded, 'So you could have knocked me over with a feather when his father told me in his shop the other day. I don't think his parents are very keen. A girl from Birmingham. So far away, isn't it? He sounded as though Matthew was really in earnest about her.'

Margaret's heart, still reeling from her initial fear, now felt as though it was plummeting slowly, a broken-winged bird, spiralling down and down. 'I didn't know,' she said, trying to sound unconcerned, but her voice trembled.

'And so sudden,' Eileen was saying blithely. 'I wonder if he's had to. I wouldn't be a bit surprised, you know. I bet his parents feel terrible.'

In the lounge Lilian Ward glared at the letter which had arrived only moments ago.

'How could he? He hardly knows the girl. He's only just met her. And bringing her here this weekend. It gives me no time whatsoever to prepare and get some food in. I hope she'll be bringing her ration book. I'm not in the mood to feed strangers. He has no consideration at all. Doesn't even ask if I *want* to see this . . . whoever she is.'

Leonard Ward watched her stalking back and forth between the leather three-piece suite and the coffee table where he sat with his breakfast cup of tea by the open bay window of the front lounge before leaving to open up his shop.

103

In summer it was nice to sit a while here with the morning sunshine slanting in, warming his chest that played him up so in winter, the curtains moving gently in a breeze off the park that brought the sharp scent of cut grass. From here he had a fine vista of the park peeping between the large houses opposite. Even so he looked forward to being in the shop to smoke his pipe. No Lilian there to frown and order him into the back garden. He'd have liked his pipe now, but he could hardly get up and walk out with her so furious about Matthew's letter.

'He's already told us about her,' he reminded gently.

'Yes, absolute volumes in his last letter. Not one word asking how we are. Nothing but this . . . what's her name?' She consulted the letter again, then refrained from using it. 'This . . . girl. Now he wants *us* to meet her. Says he's serious about wanting to marry her. We'll see about that.'

'He's over twenty-one, Lilian. Not much you can do about it.'

She was not to be mollified. It would take quite a bit of patience and understanding, perhaps even firmness, to calm her down. She had always been a dominant person. Perhaps that was why he had married her, a woman who had known her own mind and stuck to it in an age when most women were mostly pliable, soft creatures looking to marriage and security. All that despite being in service when servants were expected to be servile.

Leonard smiled. He could forgive her domineering nature, which concealed a good and caring heart. And at the moment that good and caring heart was being tested to the limit. When all was said and done, Matthew was at fault.

'After all we have done for him,' she continued, still pacing, her back stiff, her indignation solid enough to be cut with a knife. 'This is how he rewards us, telling us he intends marrying some common thing from Birmingham, someone we don't even know, and actually bringing her here for us to meet. No warning whatsoever.'

Leonard allowed a little longer for effrontery to cool before getting up and saying he must be off before his customers began to wonder what had happened to him.

Opening up, his first customer had been Eileen Perry who used to be giggly Eileen Wilcox. In just two years she had now become a plain, staid, contented housewife and mother. Her husband was in the forces, but a quartermaster or something that didn't see combat, so she didn't bear that strained expression many wives had with husbands fighting somewhere far away.

Eileen had asked after Matthew and, glad of someone to talk to about it, he told her perhaps more than he should. Later he wondered if it had not been better kept to himself, for Eileen Perry loved a gossip and nothing displeased Lilian more than her private concerns being aired in public.

Ah, well, the deed was done now, he thought as he served customers with torches and fuse wire and round two-pin plugs and took in the odd wireless for repair, and wondered what this girl, this Susan from Birmingham, would be like. Utterly beautiful, stunning, marvellous, Matthew's earlier letter had gone on among many other things, all of which his mother had dismissed with several sharp and disparaging snorts of disgust.

Chapter 10

Susan stared at the large bay-windowed house as Matthew held open the gate for her. She'd seen such houses in the better parts of Birmingham but had never been in one.

Ahead of her lay a wide gravel area bordered by small flower beds in full bloom, and shrubbery. The bay windows displayed white lace curtains, each so perfectly pleated that they resembled a regiment of soldiers. Susan saw a downstairs curtain twitch slightly and felt observed, rather like a fish in a glass tank. She shivered, hesitating in the gateway.

'Oh Matthew, I hope they'll like me.'

She strove hard to say like, rather than loik; strove to keep her voice from shaking. She'd been practising for this day ever since he had said he was taking her to meet his parents, but it was no less harrowing for all that. But Matthew had told her time and time again that he adored what he called her sing-song accent, so surely they would like it as well and thus her.

'Of course they'll like you,' he laughed, taking her arm supportively as they went towards the door, a gesture for which she felt grateful. 'They'll fall in love with you at first sight, just as I did.'

Reaching the porch he planted a small encouraging kiss on her cheek, but in the state she was beginning to get herself into at the daunting prospect ahead, its message was lost on her, for as though by a given signal she saw an indistinct wavering shape distorted by the fluted glass of the door appear behind it, the door opening almost immediately. A slim, tall, upright woman with vivid blue eyes stood there looking at the two of them. An angular face, still with traces of beauty, topped by short greying hair whose stiff waves looked as regimental at the pleated curtains that had twitched earlier turned now to her, its smile of welcome seemingly chiselled from granite.

Matthew pushed Susan forward a fraction. 'Mum, this is Susan.'

Even in the midst of her fear of the brittle blue eyes, so different to Matthew's soft brown ones, Susan wondered at his use of Mum rather than Mother. Mrs Ward looked as though she should be called 'Mother' or even Mater; certainly not Mum.

The woman extended a hand in formal greeting rather in the manner of a pontiff suffering the touch of some unwashed layman. Obediently Susan took it, finding it stiff and cold. But with etiquette observed, Mrs Ward withdrew her hand and stepped back for them to enter.

'Was it a decent journey, Matthew, dear?' The voice was warm and took Susan completely by surprise. The woman was human after all. 'I did begin to think you were just a little late.'

'You know what travelling's like these days, Mum,' Matthew laughed easily and kissed her offered cheek.

'I never travel far these days,' she said as he put down his kit and Susan's small, slightly battered weekend suitcase in the wood-floored hall, a hall of such width that Susan felt her whole family could have almost lived in it. She thought briefly of her own cluttered living room with its old furniture and with its everlasting noise of argument and laughter. About this place there was a silence that seemed almost tangible, as if a cold ghost lived there.

'Dad home?' Matthew queried easily as he and Susan followed his mother into the lounge. Susan wished she could feel as easy, but then, he would feel easy, wouldn't he? This was his home.

The lounge was huge. The furniture looked lost in it, sparsely and tastefully laid out; a parquet floor bordered a large beautifully patterned carpet that looked sort of Turkish. Through the bay window, the high summer sun cast a minimal vertical strip of gold on to one tiny area of the wood floor, missing the carpet completely, which Susan imagined would never be allowed to be touched and consequently faded by any lengthening shaft

107

of autumn sunshine. Mrs Ward probably had one of those posh blinds that well-off people used to keep damaging sunlight out.

'He'll be home for lunch,' his mother answered. 'As usual. But of course he must go back afterwards to open up for the afternoon, Matthew, whether you're here or not.'

'So you're the Susan we've heard so much about in Matthew's letters. He certainly didn't lie about you.'

Mr Ward's appearance prompted a surge of relief after an hour stiff and fraught with tension. She took to him the moment he came in at the back door to immediately shake her hand and utter his hearty comment before turning to his son to ask how long he would be home.

'We go back Sunday night,' Matthew supplied with a chuckle at the innocent, stock question asked nowadays of every serviceman home on leave.

Mr Ward too gave a low chuckle not unlike his son's, with a touch of mockery in it that could be taken the wrong way if one missed the whimsical gleam in his eyes. They were slightly lighter than his son's, more hazel than brown; she could see who Matthew took after, glad that it wasn't his mother. But if he'd taken after his mother, she knew she wouldn't be here with him now.

'Don't give you long, do they? Well, we've got you for the weekend at least. We promise to send you back all nice and clean.'

She had a feeling that as a young man Mr Ward might have possessed the same caustic humour as Matthew, but that it had mellowed or been mellowed by life. She wasn't usually clever enough to see inside people, but he was so much like Matthew in looks and manner, she felt she could guess at the person he'd once been because Matthew had been a bit like that when she'd first met him.

It came to her that she still knew very little about Matthew as they sat down to a small but beautifully set-out cold lunch of salad and luncheon meat, all she supposed the Wards' food ration would stretch to (dutifully she had handed over her ration book which Mrs Ward had not waved away). They were making conversation from which she began to feel excluded. At ease with his family, he was a stranger to her. Why had she consented to come here, when his way of life was so removed from hers? There came a dull feeling that once back in Birmingham, it would be the end of her and Matthew. She didn't fit in here. She was yet to meet his sister. If she was anything like Mrs Ward . . .

Susan felt most uncomfortable, smiling when she thought she ought to, answering the odd question put to her mostly by the friendly Mr Ward. The afternoon when he would disappear back to his shop loomed before her like a prison sentence. To sit looking at Mrs Ward's chilly expression all afternoon was not to be contemplated. She dreaded the moments when Matthew, quite at home among his own, would blithely wander off on some pursuit and leave her alone with this woman.

Mr Ward left, saying he would see her later that evening. Mrs Ward led them upstairs for Susan to put her case in the room allotted to her and freshen up. Freshen up sounded so posh.

'The bathroom is there.' She indicated a door at the end of a long landing which curved slightly at the end.

Susan nodded wordlessly. She had never seen a bathroom. The sort of people she knew in Birmingham did not have them. At least this would be a small refuge for her where she could escape this woman's penetrating eyes.

The landing had six other doors. Six. Susan had never seen such a thing. Surely, other than the bathroom, the rest couldn't be all bedrooms. Matthew said his was a four-bedroom house, so the one at the opposite end to the bathroom might be a cupboard.

'And this is your room.'

The door she had assumed to be to a cupboard was opened for her to inspect her quarters. And what quarters. Everything became a pink and white blur as, blindly, Susan stepped within as she had been bidden, a faint smell of lavender greeting her. It was neat and modest in size, though not what Susan would have called small by any means, with a single bed, a dressing table with delicate white and pink jars on it, and a mirror, a cupboard and a chair. The walls, curtains, bedspread and a fluffy rug by the bed were pink, all the furniture white, and the linoleum brown, the only contrast. Susan stifled a gasp of awe; tried to behave as though she were used to this sort of room.

'Thank you very much, Mrs Ward,' she managed in a whisper, while Matthew grinned and said loudly:

'My room, of course, is that end, by the bathroom.' In other words he and she would be separated by two doors, but only she was meant to detect the amused connotation he was conveying, his mother quite oblivious as she left them to go into their separate rooms to unpack what they'd brought with them.

He did indeed go to his door and open it, but as his mother went on out of sight down the stairs, he stepped back and came towards Susan, moving silently.

'I'll help you unpack,' he whispered purposefully and instantly she knew what he meant.

A knot of excitement formed deep in her stomach as she went into her room. Matthew followed quietly, no longer the stranger he had seemed during lunch.

For the sake of propriety as he pressed her down on the bed with the sun shining bright through the window, she whispered, 'What if your mother comes up and catches us?'

He was bending over her, his mouth ready to close upon hers. 'She won't. As far as she's aware, you'll be unpacking in your room and I in mine and good manners will prevent her intruding into either.'

'But if she hears . . .' But Matthew's lips closing over hers smothered any further protest as, his weight upon her, her body responded with waves of longing surging through it.

'She doesn't like Susan, does she?'

Matthew leaned with his back against the bench in the work room behind his father's shop. The question was a foregone conclusion, but he had to ask it. Now was the time.

The shop was quiet for the moment. Saturday afternoon shopping took many people up west now that they felt safer with the Blitz failing to return. Not that there was much to buy; coupons, ration books, points, had put paid to casual spending. People were forced to save up a certain amount of points to buy a dress or a pair of shoes, so all the joy had long gone out of buying. But it was an excuse to get out, wander around the main shops, perhaps take in a cinema or theatre afterwards to forget shortages, loved ones overseas, the war itself.

With the shop quiet, the opportunity for a heart to heart with his father presented itself nicely. Susan had popped out to get some sweets with the coupons she had been saving for this weekend. She'd be back within a short while and in that time Matthew intended to tax his father on his mother's reaction to Susan. No good asking her how she felt. She'd merely have given him a blank stare and remarked that it was his business at whom he threw his hat, the remark full of disapproval. And he already knew by her attitude that she disapproved, so why ask? Yet he needed to ask, and now his father leaned back in his creaking swivel chair and, pressing dark, pungent tobacco into the bowl of his pipe with his thumbs, frowned in deep thought.

'You know your mother,' he said after a while, effectively avoiding a direct reply. 'Never been one to show her feelings.'

'That's what I told Susan. She's dead scared of her.' He saw the knowing half-smile his father gave and anger rose up inside him. 'Why the hell can't she be normal, like other people?'

'You mean she doesn't conform to your idea of normal, all sugar and spice.' There was reprimand in the quiet tone. 'Does that mean she should be discredited? She is honest and upright and has always done her best for you and Louise – in her own way, the only way she knows.'

'Yes, I know. I'm sorry.' He felt chastened. No one could accuse his mother of under-handedness or paying lip service to anyone. If she called a spade a spade, everyone could be certain it was nothing else. But if only she had one gentle streak in her, let the rules be bent ever so slightly; if only she was capable of letting people down lightly with a little white lie now and again. Timid people like Susan needed a little gentle understanding.

His intention had been to come out this afternoon to see his father, leaving Susan and his mother together to get to know each other without his having to hold Susan's hand, but she had begged to be allowed to come with him. Looking into the pleading in those blue eyes, he knew that to refuse her would have been like leaving a lamb in a lion's den.

His father lit his pipe, its acrid smell mixing with that of solder and flux and dust. It brought a sense of nostalgia, of belonging, that Matthew had once taken for granted, had

111

thought would last forever, but now made his thoughts keen-edged with the knowledge that at any time he could be sent away to God-knows-where, perhaps never to come back. He felt his heart grow pinched and small with the fear of all this being taken from him.

'Your mother,' Leonard was saying, puffing a cloud of blue smoke into the air. 'She has always had high principles, from the day I first saw her. She frightened the life out of me, you know. Me, who always saw girls as soft, pretty creatures with no brains, whom men could command, to see a young woman come striding into my father's draper's shop as though she owned it, really got up my nose at the time. But I couldn't get my mind off her. She fascinated me. She was a beautiful woman, your mother, beautiful and straight-backed, and she held her head high. I used to look for her coming in. But I couldn't get up the courage to tell her how I felt about her. When I did, she turned me down flat.'

Leonard gave a small quirky grin at the recollection, his pipe gripped firmly between his teeth. 'You could never know what that's like, to open up your heart to a woman when it's not in your nature to do so and be turned down the way she turned me down. But finally we did start walking out together. She's a woman in a million, Matthew, believe me.'

'I didn't mean to discredit her,' Matthew said, shamefaced. 'But she's got to understand that I intend to marry Susan. I don't want her resenting Susan. I know she does already and I don't know why she should. She's only just met her, and Susan's the most likeable person I know. She's sweet-natured and loving. She's not pushy and loud. So why?'

The old chair creaked as Leonard leaned back into it again. 'Maybe she considers you both a little young and hasty. You and Susan have known each other only a few months. You've hardly had much chance to see each other regularly. Perhaps if you both waited a while longer.'

'What's there to wait for?' This was his life. They had theirs to look back on, had been fortunate, but what had he got to look back on so far, and how much future would be allowed to him? 'This isn't peacetime with long, well-arranged white weddings and strings of bridesmaids and a fine honeymoon afterwards. We might not have tomorrow and forever. I could be sent overseas at any time. I might not see her for years. I might even be . . .' He checked the words quickly, then reverted to the hackneyed idiom of defiance: 'We have to have something to cling to in this war.'

'Yes.' The pipe stem clicked audibly against Leonard's teeth. 'This bloody war.'

The shop bell tinkled. To its peremptory summons, he hoisted himself out of the chair, knocking the pipe out on the bench.

Matthew listened to the murmur of voices beyond the opaque glass of the dividing door, the conclusive note of a customer departing. The bell tinkled again, fell silent. Leonard came back into the back room bearing a domed, fretwork-fronted wireless set which he set down on the bench. He chuckled, making a joke against himself.

'Look what I've come down to. My father loved his little drapery shop and said I would inherit, but he died in debt and lost nearly all of it. It was your mother who was my widowed mother's mainstay. She made her sink what little was left into another shop after the last war, saying that electrical goods would be the coming thing. She was right. We did well. That's how we came to live in a nice area like Victoria Park Road. I'm no snob and I know where I came from. But your mother wanted better things for you and your sister. That and her love of the old order of things makes her seem to act above herself, but her heart's in the right place where you and Louise are concerned. I've got a lot to thank your mother for.'

The last words had a ring of finality about them. There was no more to be said on that score. Besides, any minute Susan would come running in, waving her few ounces of sweets in triumph. Matthew changed the subject, nodding towards the wireless come in for repair.

'Bloody ancient thing, that one. Looks a bit beyond it to me.'

Leonard grinned compassionately. 'She's a widow. Can't afford much. Asked if I could do anything with it before Tuesday. Doesn't want to miss ITMA. Tommy Handley's her only bit of pleasure these days. God knows, she needs someone to cheer her up, if only on the wireless. There's little to cheer anyone up lately. Every time you tune in there's another

113

setback – what with Rommel and Tobruk. And Crete, us having to pull out, five thousand killed . . .'

'I heard,' Matthew said tersely.

'Enough to make anyone lose heart. But it comes to something when you hear people say we might have to negotiate peace terms with Germany.'

'Rumours,' Matthew snorted. 'Like the bomb that chases people around corners – the German secret weapon. Some are actually believing it.'

'Everyone's on edge, that's why.' Leonard began unscrewing the casing of the wireless cabinet, lifting it up to reveal coloured wires and oblong valves. 'London blitzed to buggery, Coventry too, then suddenly, silence, everyone wondering what Hitler has up his sleeve next. Invasion probably. I don't know.'

Matthew nodded glumly. He'd seen the scenes of devastation as he and Susan took a bus from Euston railway station to home. He had rejected taking the underground, not wishing to subject Susan to the wretched bits and pieces of the thousands who had used the platforms as shelters during the nightly air raids and who still stubbornly went down there at nightfall, refusing to believe the Blitz would not return.

Above ground had looked just as dismal, pitiful. Through the bus windows they had gazed at acres of blackened ruin still uncleared, walls precariously hanging, charred timbers, twisted girders pointing skyward with accusing fingers, the air still heavy with an acrid effluvium of burning that remained in their nostrils long afterwards, a memento of all London had suffered. And even in his own long road fronting an open park some houses had gone. After those guns and searchlights sited in the park itself, he supposed.

He watched his father extract a valve from the set. Testing it, he shook his head with tacit sympathy, then replaced it with one salvaged from another old set already beyond repair. Plugged in, the set crackled into life with tinny music.

'Ah, she'll be pleased,' he breathed. 'Defeated by a dud valve. I won't charge her for that. Husband died two years ago and she hasn't a soul to turn to. Though she keeps telling me her son is serving on the *Royal Oak*.'

'*Is*?' Matthew queried. 'The *Royal Oak* was sunk at Scapa Flow at the beginning of the war. All hands lost.'

114

'Exactly.' Leonard nodded, replaced the casing. 'Not a soul to turn to. I'll get this back to her this evening. She'll be pleased.'

The shop bell tinkled again. This time the back-room door burst open and there stood Susan, her small oval face brighter and happier than he'd seen it all day, his mother forgotten.

'I bought some toffees,' she announced. 'Do you want one, Mr Ward?'

As his father shook his head congenially, Matthew came over and put an arm around her, his mind on her alone, the poor bereaved woman still living in the past put aside. Her empty life wasn't his problem. Everyone had problems these days.

'So you're really going to get married?'

Louise had come home on a weekend leave, declaring it fortunate to have fallen the same time as her brother's. She, as yet still in her WRNS uniform, sat opposite him and Susan in the front lounge regarding him with the steady critical gaze of a nineteen-year-old who felt she knew the world. Two weeks ago she had just seen one of her comrades break down after hearing the news that her fiancé's ship had been torpedoed; he had gone down with it. Her gaze was now fraught with concern as well.

'Not much joy being in love in wartime, that's my opinion. But I wish you both all the luck in the world. I don't suppose it'll be a white wedding, but the result's just the same I reckon.'

Susan simpered and stood close to Matthew, looking up at him for guidance. He gave his sister a rueful grin. 'I hope to get a twenty-four-hour pass for it if I'm lucky. We'll have to make do with that. It'll have to be in a registry office, I expect.'

'Well, perhaps I might wangle some leave. When's it to be?'

Matthew's smile hovered. 'We're not quite certain yet. Whenever we can. Probably at short notice. You should know what the forces are like. It'll have to be in Birmingham, near where I'm stationed. And with Mum and Dad down here, and Susan's people up there, I don't suppose there'll be many of our side there at all. It's going to be a rush in the end.'

Louise looked distinctly put out. 'You don't want me there, that it?'

'No, that's not it, Sis.' He was looking dark. 'I want you there. I want all our people there. I'd have liked to have a big white wedding, for Susan's sake. I wish we could.'

At which Susan clung closer to him, his arm tightening reassuringly about her. Louise, Susan thought, for all she was only a year older than herself, had a lot of her mother in her. And as Mr and Mrs Ward came in from the dining room where they had been lingering over a leisurely cup of tea Louise, it seemed, wasn't ready to pull her punches.

'Did you know they plan to get married in a registry office? It's going to have to be done on the quick, so he says. No time for me to arrange leave to be there to see him married. Him, my one and only brother.'

'That's unkind, Louise,' Matthew shot at her, but it was evident she was disappointed. 'Of course you're invited if you can make it. You'd be the first one to be invited. My one and only sister.'

That last sounded dangerously like sarcasm and probably was, and Leonard Ward looked at his son while Lilian stood aside, her face tight. But his was benign. 'Where do you plan to live afterwards, Matthew?'

It was a practical question, but one that betokened acceptance of his intentions, and Susan, feeling Matthew's body relax, realised it had become taut as Louise had railed on.

'We'll get ourselves a furnished flat for the time being, where I can get backwards and forwards from with a special pass.'

Leonard frowned. 'Not much of a start, a furnished flat. You'd need something unfurnished. Something to call your own. Your own furniture, not someone else's rubbish. Your mother and I aren't broke . . .'

'No thanks, Dad.' Matthew stopped him sharply. 'We can manage.'

'I want to say something else, son. It's that if you're posted away at any time or, God forbid, sent overseas, Susan will always be welcome to come here and stay with us.'

Susan's face went blank and Matthew hurried to her rescue. 'That's nice of you, Dad, but we'll get by. Lots of married women have to manage on their own these days when their men go away. And I expect her own family will be there to help.'

'Just a suggestion.' Leonard went to sit in one of the armchairs but Lilian remained standing, her hands clasped firmly in front of her.

'This is all very well. No one has any *idea* when this is to happen. All we know is that it is going to happen. We have merely been *told*. It would be nice if you discussed it more fully with us, your parents, Matthew?'

He matched her hard stare. 'I thought that was precisely what we were doing – discussing Susan and me getting married.'

'Would you be discussing it now if Louise hadn't blurted it out a few moments ago?'

'Probably,' he returned succinctly, at bay.

Susan cut in, amazed at her own boldness. 'We want to get married ever so much, Mr Ward.' It was far easier to appeal to him than his wife. 'I know we've not been together very long, but me and Matthew do love each other a lot. It don't have to take years just to know that. It can happen very quickly sometimes.' She paused for breath, anxious now at having said so much, uninvited.

He smiled at her. 'I know. So how soon would you *like* it to be?'

'Could be next month,' Matthew replied for her, his tone easier now. 'It'll have to be in Birmingham. I've exhausted all my leave so I'll only get a special day off, I suppose. I'll have to beg for that, I expect.'

'We'll try to make it up there if we can,' added his father. He gave a small apologetic chuckle. 'That sounds terrible, I know – try. But nothing's easy these days. Send us a telegram the second you know, and we'll be straight on a train. If I can get some extra petrol coupons . . .' again he gave a chuckle, a somewhat knowing one this time, 'we'll get the car out and use that. It's kept in good working order, you know, but we don't use it, at least very seldom these days. It's yours still, Matthew, sitting there, your twenty-first present. It's in a garage near the shop, waiting for the time you can use it again, Matthew. And talking of presents. Wedding presents of any good quality being hard to come by, would money be okay?'

'That'll be fine,' Matthew said a little tersely, making Susan look at him in surprise. 'But I still have that trust Grandfather left me. We won't go short.'

117

'Just a token wedding present.'

Susan felt sorry for Mr Ward, hearing the lame ring in his voice. She even felt faintly annoyed at Matthew. Why should he react so unthankfully to his father's generosity?

As Matthew travelled on the train back to Birmingham the following day to be in camp by Monday morning, Susan taxed him on it.

'You shouldn't have gone off at your dad like that, darling. He was only being kind. You acted as if you were bent on having a row with him.'

Matthew was staring out at the passing scenery beyond the carriage window, 'Did you see my mother's face?' he queried without turning. 'In my family we don't need to row. Never a raised voice, but the result's the same – no winners or losers. In a way, worse than any full blown row – no chance for anyone to release their pent up anger.'

He sounded so dark that Susan quickly changed to a lighter subject. 'Your dad said about some money left to you.'

He remained thoughtful for a moment. 'For when I was twenty-one. About five thousand, but I haven't touched it. Wanted to wait until the war was over and I came out of the Army. I expect many of us will come out without a bean, so it'll come in handy.'

'And it'll have made interest,' she added. At the mention of such an amount her eyes had widened. Five thousand pounds. A fortune. To think, being married to someone really well-off. She could hardly wait.

'Let's get married as soon as we can,' she entreated and had him turn to her to put his arm about her shoulder and cuddle her close, prompting quiet smiles from the others in the carriage with them.

Chapter 11

Margaret gazed through one of the pub windows near which she sat, many of them still damaged by the Blitz and patched up as best as could be until shortages allowed for new windows to be put in. God knows when that would be.

Outside, Whitechapel Road was buzzing with stalls and people this Tuesday lunchtime. Whitechapel Road was exceptionally wide for London. It had apparently been made that way in the days of footpads so that they had no cover from which to spring out on passing horsedrawn mail and passenger coaches. Part of that wide road had, she'd been told, for this last hundred years been railed off for a market which still thrived and the noise of buying and selling came loud through every hole and crack in those of the pub's windows not yet completely repaired.

Despite the war, the market was in full swing; maybe now it evoked the days before the motor car. These days hardly any private cars were being used with petrol rationing the order of the day. Some lorries, though, still tried to make deliveries when they could. But there were a lot more handcarts than in peacetime, and the horsedrawn wagon could be seen in great numbers.

Across the still wide road beyond the hubbub and movement sat the London Hospital, a serene potentate, quieter now that the nightly air raids had passed. The injured were being seen to and sent home with no more being brought in to replace them; the hospital had started getting back now to the normal traffic of poorly children and the ailing elderly, those injured by accident instead of design, pregnant women needing treatment, and the ordinary sick; the outpatients department too had reverted to its normal routine rather than the unending stream of bloodied, bomb-torn bodies. Everyone now had time at last to let out a sigh of relief, Margaret included. She had gone back to work after her first weekend off in ages to find that even in the short time away things at the hospital had quietened still more.

'Penny for them.' Ronald's warm hand closed over her fingers and she quickly withdrew hers.

'Not worth a penny.'

'Ah, well, a ha'penny then.' His light brown eyes were searching her green ones as she looked briefly at him. They were full of adoration. 'No, on second thoughts, Margaret, the smallest thought of yours has to be worth more than a million to me.'

'Don't be silly.' She hated him behaving like this, specially when her inability to return his feelings made her seem hard-hearted and his obvious love for her so pitiful. But one couldn't make love happen. 'I was thinking about the people out there, and the hospital. That's not worth a light.'

'Talking shop isn't. Let's talk about us instead.'

'Not just now, Ronald.' She didn't mean to sound so sharp.

Her thoughts as his hand closed over hers had been dwelling on the news she had received about Matthew while home, and then on the surprise glimpse she'd had of him from her bedroom window on the Sunday, his arm around the dainty dark-haired girl he was intending to marry. From her vantage point, Margaret had seen her lift a pretty face ardently to his as they passed underneath her window, and he had paused and kissed her lips. Margaret had felt the passion of that kiss writhe in her bones. It still did.

Gazing through the pub window she savoured a masochistic urge to retain the memory in a moment of self-torture, utterly futile for all it made her feel nearer to the man she knew she could never have. Matthew would marry his Birmingham girl and Margaret would never see him again.

Then Ronald laid his hand over hers, and instead of her private moment being gently suffered as it needed to be, those precious thoughts had raced through her head like a damned whirlwind, to be swept away.

* * *

They departed the Birmingham registry office in a thin shower of home-made confetti and a host of good wishes. The reception had been short, a modest gathering filling the little room with perfume, cigar smoke and perspiration.

'I just hope he knows what he is doing,' Lilian Ward said, watching the happy pair go off.

'Of course he knows what he's doing.' Leonard's own gaze followed the taxi taking Matthew and his new wife off into the unknown; it softened reflectively at the recollection of his son's departing words to him. 'If anything happens to me, Dad, you two will look after Susan, won't you?'

'Nothing's going to happen to you, son,' he had told him sternly, but who could be that certain?

'But it's wartime,' Lilian's voice cut in. 'They don't know what lies ahead of them.'

'It was wartime when we married,' he reminded her gruffly.

Nothing had happened to him, had it, apart from a dose of mustard gas. Left his chest weak, but he'd survived. And so would Matthew.

The taxi going out of sight, he turned back to the registry office with the others to gather up the few belongings they had left behind when they'd gone to wave the happy pair on their way.

Lilian's lips had tightened. She had no wish to be reminded of that utterly mad escapade of hers when she had been young, leaving service to get married to a man going off to join up. She, who had always kept her emotions in check, doing such a headstrong thing! She hated being reminded of it. 'That was entirely different,' was all she could find to say.

'Absolutely.' Leonard gave a playful laugh. 'But we might not have married had I not swept you off your feet.'

'Fiddlesticks!' she shot at him, leaving him to smile after her as she marched ahead of him up the steps of the registry office to retrieve her hat that went with the smart suit she had bought with almost a year's worth of clothing coupons to see her silly, lovesick son married.

In the taxi, Matthew bent towards his wife and tenderly kissed her. He did it, not just because he was in love with her, but to

121

reassure himself of their future together. He badly needed that reassurance.

In the registry office he had stood beside her, smiling, feeling hot and sticky in his khaki uniform as with one eye on the large round clock on the wall he received the felicitations of those gathered there.

Susan had been dewy-eyed the whole time, overcome by the joy of her new estate, the centre of attraction. Her sisters had wept obligingly, her mother copiously, as though her dear daughter were being whisked away to Devil's Island rather than wedded bliss. Friends and family on both sides had kissed Susan and shaken Matthew's hand before wandering off to try the tiny, practically fruitless wedding cake Susan's mother had made, rations not stretching to anything more. Its much larger, thinly iced cardboard cover was impressively decorated to emulate the fine wedding cakes of pre-war years.

Susan's mother had looked overdressed in fluffy pink beside his own mother in a tasteful beige suit, yet it was for his mother rather than Susan's that he felt somehow more embarrassed; the way she stayed aloof from Susan's mother as though she were a lesser being.

His father had been different again. He stood talking to Mr Hopkins, oblivious of the man's rusty best suit, his tobacco-stained teeth when he smiled, the rolled cigarette hanging wetly from his lips.

There had only been Matthew's parents on his side, and Bob Howlett as his best man, the rest Susan's, relatives, friends, workmates, all laughing and gabbling away in incomprehensible Birmingham accents, filling the tiny room with noise and tobacco smoke. It had been a relief to get away, to be alone with Susan at last, his kiss in the taxi a promise of that to come in the small one-bedroomed flat he had found for them, their own little love nest.

Susan returned his kiss, then broke away, pouting a little. 'I wish we weren't going to have to live in those two tiddly little rooms.'

'Why?' He grinned down at her. Pouting, she looked so pretty, her sweet red lips that he wanted to kiss again pushed out invitingly.

'I was just thinking, Matthew, you coming into that trust

your dad was talking about, I mean, surely, couldn't we have got something better?'

'You liked them when we found them,' he told her, frowning. 'You called them adorable, cosy, our own little love nest.'

'Yes, but that was before . . .'

His frown deepened as she paused. 'Before what, darling?'

'Well, before . . .' She tutted, shrugging. 'Oh, nothing. But we will get something better in time, won't we?'

'Yes, of course.' Matthew's brow cleared. He was being stupid about the money coming to him, having for so long conditioned himself against the help his mother, almost selfishly, tried to give him. Even this trust seemed somehow tainted with her influence although he knew that too was stupid. And why should Susan be the loser because of his ridiculous obsession? Whatever he had was hers as well, and he shouldn't be selfish in his feelings about it.

'As soon as we get sorted out, I'll look for somewhere you really like,' he promised and was rewarded by her instantly snuggling against him, her surge of joy rippling through him as well.

The taxi began to slow to his directions at a row of small terraced houses behind spiked railings, with narrow patches of barren gardens in front. Worn steps led up to the sepia glass-panelled doors with names above each one: Rose Villa, Acacia Villa, Magnolia Villa, the taxi finally drawing up outside the one called Laburnum Villa.

The driver leapt out, opened the taxi door for them and, accepting Matthew's generous tip, called good luck before getting back into his vehicle and rattling away to his next fare.

In the bright sunshine they gazed at their new abode. The owner of the house, a Mrs Robertson, had recently lost her husband. It was the first time, she'd said when Matthew had gone there, that she had ever let rooms, and from her nervousness and the modest rent she'd quoted, he had almost been tempted to offer her more, but a corporal's pay didn't stretch to such gallantry. At the time he had been labouring under his ridiculous aversion to using any of the trust his grandfather had left him. He had kept his mouth shut and guiltily counted his good luck at the poor woman's expense.

Susan's hand tightened convulsively on his arm. He under-

123

stood. It might be a modest start but she was still excited at the prospect of entering their first-ever home, closing their door on the world and being alone together.

He patted her hand encouragingly. 'We'll find something much better later. But today's our wedding day. Tomorrow I have to be back in camp, so let's make the best of today.'

This wasn't how it should have been. There should be a honeymoon, somewhere on the coast, somewhere really nice, Bournemouth or Torquay, a lovely hotel. There should have been a church wedding that had taken at least six months to prepare, and a good reception, with lots of money spent on it. There should have been a nice house awaiting them, the furniture bought and sitting inside to welcome them. Bloody war. Bloody Army. Bloody way of having to live . . .

Mrs Robertson was waiting for them. She had given him a key when he paid the deposit money, but motherly soul that she was, she had been waiting for them and now opened the door as they mounted the five shallow steps.

'Come in, dears. Do come in.' Her voice was high, a little weak, a little weepy; that of a woman in her late sixties still not yet adjusted to the loss of a husband after a long married life.

'Now you must treat this place like your own,' she continued, following them to the narrow flight of stairs, eager for conversation. Her main aim in letting her two upstairs rooms had been to secure a little company. 'Don't ever think you have to stand on ceremony now. Come and go whenever you want. It's nice to know there's someone else in the house besides me. There's a little gas ring and a portable stove upstairs, as you know, and there's a basin in the bedroom. My dear George had it put in when we had the bedroom. But of course, I sleep downstairs now. If you'd like a cup of tea now, my kettle is on the boil . . .'

'It's very nice of you, but no thank you,' Matthew cut in, trying not to sound rude. All he wanted was Susan to himself. They'd have so little time together as it was without sitting in their landlady's kitchen drinking tea and possibly listening to her life with her George, dear as he must have been to her.

He could feel the woman's gaze following them wistfully up the stairs, her thoughts no doubt on when she'd been their age with all her life before her. He felt a surge of bitterness shoot through him. All her life before her – did he and Susan have all theirs before them, say forty years of marriage as she'd had, or would theirs be cut short by war? A quick, easy calculation, done automatically, told him that the woman had been married before the last war, but her husband had been lucky and survived it. Would he be as lucky surviving this one? A shudder passed through him and was gone as, reaching the little landing, he shrugged it away and opened the door to the larger room that had once been a bedroom, now their living room.

Susan paused on the threshold looking in, not attempting to enter. 'It's smaller than I thought it'd be.'

'But it's ours. At least for a while.'

He made his voice sound light and jaunty, needing to brighten up. Flipping open the door next to it, he lifted her and bore her inside, kicking the door closed behind him, with her clinging to him, any dejection she might have had dispersing. In one easy movement he tossed her on to the double bed that almost filled this even tinier room. The bedsprings bounced madly under the impact of their light burden.

'That's your place, Mrs Ward,' he announced firmly, and while she lay breathless and laughing, he sat on the foor of the bed, yanking off boots, then socks, battle blouse, shirt, trousers, leaving the clothes draped untidily over the brass bedrail, one or two items already falling on to the floor in his haste as he flung himself down beside her. 'And this is mine. Now – we'll start on you.'

'Matthew!' she squealed as he made to get her out of her suit jacket. 'You'll rip the buttons off. It's a new suit.'

'Well, you do it.'

'No, I want you to do it. But mind the buttons.'

With her he romped and laughed. With her help he rid her of one garment after another, she making a play at struggling, he at Victorian mastery, until finally she lay naked beneath him, his wife, ready for his demands, but still laughing, the pair of them trying hard to keep the sound down away from the woman below.

'I've one night with you, woman,' Matthew hissed. 'And I intend to make the most of it. So behave yourself and do your duty. Now, lie back.'

After love stolen previously in secret, purported to be all the sweeter for that, this love was the most wonderful thing he had ever known. It must have been for her too, for she complied without any of the earlier tension he had always felt in her, the desperation of her acceptance of him. Together, man and wife, it would be the first of a glorious uniting, quite beautiful and satisfying. What more could either of them, or anyone, want than this?

He opened his eyes. He must have dozed. Sunlight was touching one wall of the bedroom; the sun had moved round just a little, so it was still afternoon. He couldn't have slept long.

Turning his head leisurely to look at Susan, he studied her. She lay with eyes closed, vulnerable to his scrutiny so that he felt vaguely guilty in taking advantage of it. Deep in sleep, her breathing sounded gentle; her dark lashes lay against the pale cheeks, lips just slightly thinned as though in a smile of contentment. Matthew watched the quiet rise and fall of her breasts, small and firm with pale nipples, her flesh stretched taut as she lay full length, legs outstretched, the soft darkness rising between her thighs such that he wanted to bury his face there.

He felt his breath come shuddering with a longing to make love to her again. It wasn't purely a physical need, but it still seemed he hadn't been near enough to her even then – could never be near enough. No man is an island? Bloody hell! Of course he was. Trapped and isolated by thoughts impossible to explain, not even to this girl who had become his very life, whom he had this day married. He might try for a lifetime to describe to her how he felt, but she would never really know what it was he was trying to say. In turn could he ever really know her mind? He could bury himself inside her in a brief moment of love, tell himself they were one, yet he would still not know. They were two people, each with their separate sensations. It was that, he guessed, which really disturbed him, that they couldn't truly ever be one in the sense he wanted – in a sense even he couldn't understand. Suddenly angry at what he could not define, he swore softly and closed his eyes, perhaps the easier to unravel this unsettling need.

Her hand brushing lightly against his thigh brought him

suddenly awake. The sun had moved round, now playing on their naked bodies. He glanced at his watch. He had slept away another hour – another precious hour lost in this one day together, and again he felt angered by the thoughts that had plagued him, by fate, by the powers that would soon tear him away from Susan. If only this moment could last forever, the sun hang in its present position, its light remaining warm and luxurious on their bodies.

Susan's hand moved, caressing, not sensuously but possessively, claiming him as her own, reassuring herself of his nearness. The touch brought him back to reality. In the morning he must leave her, go back to the army that had first claim on him.

He stared up at the ceiling, an intense hatred seething inside him of those who could push him this way and that, a puppet manipulated by the strings pulled by some faceless power that had for this one day allowed the strings to dangle and leave him thinking himself free, only to pluck him up in the midst of his happiness to bend him again to obedience. One small jerk on a thread could tug him from this girl he had made his wife; another thread jerked would send him headlong into battle to fight not for his own life but for a continuance of a way of life. And if he should fall, the strings would be severed and he, like the toy he was, would be cast aside, the war going on without him, the peace when it came not for him to see.

Today he had been shown something so sweet, so wonderful; to have it all snatched away now came like a bitter taste in his mouth.

He sat up abruptly, went over and fumbled in the breast pocket of his battle blouse for a cigarette to calm his thoughts. At least moving about had dulled that sensation of panic he had felt. Susan had gone back to sleep. That was if she had woken at all: her hand on his thigh had likely been a purely instinctive gesture. He sat on the edge of the bed and watched her contented slumber. Susan lived for the day. She bent with the breeze, like a slender sapling and harboured no thoughts she couldn't understand. He envied her contentment.

Lethargically, he stubbed out the butt of his cigarette in the ashtray on the round cane table by the bed. The small stab of heat scorched his finger and thumb, making him draw in a hiss of breath. Susan stirred, rolled over on to her side and laid a loving hand on his arm.

'Happy, darling?'

'Uh-huh.'

His reply was purely automatic. He wasn't happy. Their marriage, hardly off the ground, could be cut short within hours.

Her hand began to travel, conveying its own message. Arresting its journey with his own, he held it in a firm grip for a moment, then casting away the dismal thoughts, fell back on the bed and turned until he lay over her.

'You're a little pig,' he told her, masking that earlier anger with a deep-throated chuckle. 'You're a greedy little pig.'

It made her giggle. She fought him as he took command, but only for a moment or two, and it was really she with her gentle resistance who commanded.

Loving her took away the last of his anger and yet this time he took her as a starving man might devour a morsel of bread lest it be snatched from him. And it was a terrified love that burned in his breast.

Chapter 12

'You're going through with it this time then.'

'I owe it to her.' Matthew stared blankly at the dartboard at which they were playing in one corner of the little hut where the NAAFI served refreshments to the ranks.

Bob Howlett grunted and launched his three darts at the board in quick succession, adding up his score as the last one embedded itself in the cork surface. 'Fifty-six. Leaves me double seven.' Retrieving his darts, he stood back, allowing Matthew to take his turn.

Matthew fixed his sight along the line of flight. 'How can I let her exist on a corporal's pay when I could see her more comfortable on an officer's?'

He sent the first dart on its way as though at an enemy. Twenty. All he needed now was a double six to finish, winning him the game and a free cup of coffee from Bob. But he was keyed up. This morning he'd had an interview with the CO, who promised to put his name forward. He'd hear in a couple of weeks, and depending on the selection board he would be sent off to OCTU for that pip on the shoulder that meant better pay and a lot more allowances for Susan. It meant leaving his best mate behind, but Susan's well-being took precedence over all else.

Ever since their marriage last month she had been worrying about that bloody trust that had come his way. Yes, he could have dipped into it, and yes, they could be living well, but there was after the war to think of. After the war he'd have to get himself a job, and if tales of the last war were anything to go on, getting a job with thousands piling out of the forces could take months, maybe years. That trust would be needed to stand them in good stead while he hunted. Oggle-eyed at the idea of five thousand pounds, Susan naturally hadn't been able to see beyond the end of her nose. It was up to him to think ahead for both of them, and a pip on his shoulder, perhaps two in time, would keep her better contented until the war was over.

Bringing his thoughts back to the game, he licked his lips and took aim for the double six, the narrow area between the twin wire rings looking narrow indeed on the right-hand side of the circular board. With a dull thud the dart landed squarely in the single six. Matthew swore while Bob grinned.

'Double three you want,' he blared in triumph. If the last dart landed in the single three section, one-double-one was the only place left to go, the most awkward of scores well named as being up in the madhouse. Bob would surely make his double seven first, and the buying of the coffee would be down to Matthew instead, though it was the winning that mattered most.

Balancing his weight on the ball of his right foot, he took aim, let fly. The steel point landed neatly between the parallel wires of the double six as though put there by hand.

'Yes!' he exploded, Susan, his interview with his CO, his ambitions for a commission for the moment forgotten. 'A cuppa you owe me, Howlett.'

Gathering up their darts they made their way to the tea bar. Sipping hot camp coffee in a haze of cigarette smoke, Bob asked casually, 'Did your Susan ask you to put in for an interview then?'

'No, it was my idea.' To avoid Bob's eyes, he gazed around the white painted walls of the NAAFI hut, the corner with the dartboard now taken over by others. At a battered old piano, a group of RAOCs were trying hopelessly to harmonise. *I'll be with you in apple blossom time, I'll be with you to change your name to mine* . . . Mouths hung open, cigarettes burned away in tin ashtrays. *Some day in May, I'll come and say, happy the bride the sun shines on today* . . .'

'I'll miss you, y'know, Matt.'

Matthew wrenched his attention back to Bob. 'No you won't.'

'Balls!'

'Well, I suppose I'll miss you too, but I don't think I'll miss any of the others.'

Bob was contemplating the sticky black sludge at the bottom of the thick, straight-sided cup he held as though expecting to see a gold nugget lying there. 'Them too, I expect.'

'Certainly not muck like Farrell.' The man with his coarse turn of phrase had always made a point of taunting Matthew and Bob as snot-nosed college boys, a jumped-up pair of pricks, fairies, a couple of queers, and had more than once referred to Susan, whom he had never seen, as an easy bit of skirt until Matthew once almost punched him. Bob had leapt in and pacified him with the assurance that Farrell wasn't worth wasting the skin of his knuckles for.

Bob gave a small, sagacious smile. 'You'll meet muck wherever you go, in all walks of life. Muck isn't reserved entirely for the ranks, old son.'

They fell silent while across the groups of square tables the singing floated. *Church bells will chime, you will be mine . . .*

'Anyway,' he said as they left the hut, 'Susan will be pleased if I get a commission.'

Monday morning, six thirty, October rain coming down in buckets marking the tag-end of summer. Matthew trudged from the bus stop to the main gate of the camp. 'Ye gods – what a morning.'

The collar of his greatcoat wet against his neck, he thought of the cosy flat he'd left behind as he displayed his pass for inspection. Last night he and Susan had snuggled up together, the curtains drawn while rain spattered unseen on the window panes. She would be getting up now, getting ready for work. Every morning until next Sunday when he, hopefully, would be back with her, granted a sleeping-out pass. He supposed he could count himself lucky. Most could only dream of their wives far away.

She'd been over the moon when he had told her about his name being put forward for a commission. She'd squealed in delight and clasped him to her and they had made ecstatic love. But the weeks had dragged on with nothing more heard. He'd seen his CO, Major Deeks, again, who had said that the wheels of Army protocol turned rather slowly sometimes but he would hear eventually and not to worry. Matthew had nodded and come away, visualising his name lying on some desk at the bottom of a pile of others.

Men were moving about the parade ground. The rain brought up the smell of wet tarmac. Matthew straightened and threw up a salute to a couple of officers as he passed them. They barely glanced at him, swagger sticks in gloved hands half lifted to their caps as they walked on in deep conversation. Elegant, relaxed, the rain seemed hardly to touch them whereas it pelted with malicious glee on other ranks. How long before he would saunter past some poor bloody corporal, hardly noticing him as he returned the stiff salute with a casual lift of a swagger stick? If he was accepted, that was. Depressed by the weather, he couldn't see it ever happening.

Bob was waiting for him inside the mess hall as Matthew pushed his way in. The place echoed to the bass babble of men's conversation, the rattle of crockery and scrape of cutlery across plates. His nostrils were assailed by the clogging odour of cooking grease and the sharp tang of burned bacon over which hung the faint reek of the fish from yesterday's dinner.

Soaked from his own dash to the hall, Bob looked like a very thin Great Dane that had been doused by a bucket of water, his long face drooping. Matthew immediately felt for him. He could only have received some bad news, perhaps from home. Had something evil happened to Bob's wife, his children, his parents? Matthew hurried up to him.

'Something wrong?'

Bob's expression didn't alter. 'Can you stand a shock this time of the morning?'

So it wasn't bad news – not that bad anyway. Matthew grinned with relief for his mate. 'Fire away.'

'We're moving out. The whole unit.'

Matthew gazed up at the pale grey eyes. Dismay had already begun to creep through his stomach. Uprooted after just three short, settled months of marriage. 'You sure? Where to? When?'

'No idea. But soon. Bet your boots on it. Peggy let it out last night.'

They had joined the queue being doled out breakfast. Matthew never had breakfast with Susan, needing to be back

132

at camp on time. He looked with distaste at the congealed mounds of dried egg substitute in the trays, the frizzled bits of bacon, the sticky mass of baked beans, the half-burned slices of toast. A couple were being dumped on his plate with a sound like wooden discs, a dollop of dried egg and a portion of beans unceremoniously plopped on top of each blackened slice, a piece of bacon rattling beside them.

Bob surveyed his breakfast with equal distaste. 'Happy as a bloody sandboy, is our Sergeant Pegg. Said that's just what college queers like us need – a bit of action.'

'Action? What action?'

'It's only rumour so far,' Bob soothed. 'Even though Peggy delighted in telling us it could be overseas. Silly arse! He should know about careless talk. Trouble is, old sweats like him seldom get things wrong. They develop a sixth sense about rumours after twenty-odd years' service.'

They found a table and put down their mugs of strong tea. Matthew sat staring at the cooling mess on his plate, his appetite gone, his earlier dismay at Bob's news already turned to premonitory fear. As Bob said, old sweats were seldom wrong about rumours.

Eddie Nutt, Taffy and Farrell joined them with their own food, Farrell's narrow face buried in his mug as soon as he sat down, his slurps carrying across the table. Matthew regarded him. How the man's wife put up with him beggared the imagination, unless she was similar. Birds of a feather.

'Heard our sergeant's bit of news, have you then?' Taffy asked, seeing Matthew's tight expression. 'Abroad, it looks like.'

'Fink we'll get embarkation leave?' Farrell spat bits of half-chewed bacon in every direction as he spoke.

Bob put down his hard-as-rock toast and sipped his tea. 'Peggy could still have it wrong, you know. Though he shouldn't be babbling on about it.'

Taffy grinned. 'Indeed no. That's all Adolf is waiting for, isn't it, to hear what's going on in B Troop. Turn the tide of the war, that will, knowing B Troop might be going overseas.'

Farrell belched loudly. 'They oughter give us leave. If they do, I'm gonna do my missus every night till I get back, give 'er somfink ter bleedin' fink about – anuvver kid. She's always

133

goin' on abart bein' bleedin' bored.' He guffawed at his own joke.

Ronnie Clark, who had come to sit with them, leaned his heavy young chin on his fist. 'If anyone's bored, I am. A bit of action would be welcome.'

'Speak for yourself,' Bob said. 'All right for single chaps like you.'

Matthew pushed his plate away, untouched. 'I think I'll go and get into something dry.'

'I'll come with you,' said Bob, getting up and trailing after him.

The passing days saw rumours gaining momentum. Someone had seen tropical kit being sorted in the QM stores. Two words from a snippet of conversation had been overheard between two officers from their unit – North Africa.

Suddenly it was official: no destination divulged, for obvious reasons, but an issue of tropical kit; half a dozen painful jabs against those nastier diseases prevalent in hot climates that left every victim stiff and aching, and embarkation leave.

Matthew looked in vain for a summons from the selection board. There could be every chance if he were selected of getting out of being sent overseas, at least for the time being, but word from that direction remained stubbornly silent. He'd left things just that bit too late, had been far too bloody complacent, thinking his luck would last forever.

Susan stood in the passage, suitcases packed. She had tried to be brave, to keep her voice even and not break down in tears; had tried not to give way to that terrible panic that all but overwhelmed her when he had appeared on the doorstep explaining the reason for being laden down with full kit.

She still felt dazed; had spent much of her time weeping in secret in the bathroom they shared with their landlady, hoping Matthew would not hear her or notice her red and swollen eyes when she emerged; had kept her head averted from him as much as possible in case he did notice. If he did, he said nothing, but cuddled her a lot, assuring her it would be all right.

'Have you got everything you need?'

Susan nodded dismally as they stood in the passage saying goodbye to Mrs Robertson who also looked unnecessarily upset, probably because she must now look for new tenants, these having been with her for such a short while.

Receiving a peck on the cheek from Mrs Robertson Susan picked up the two suitcases and followed Matthew out to the waiting taxi. The rest of their bits and pieces, ornaments, the clock, the little square wireless set, wedding gifts, would be stored in her parents' attic. Susan would have liked to go to live there but her mother had looked askance.

'We got no room here now, love, not with your gran having to stay with us an' all. Her place was condemned after that bomb fell nearby. Matthew's people have got lots of room. You can stay with them, love, can't you?'

She loathed the thought of living for God knows how long with the formidable Mrs Ward. The woman frightened her. But there was nothing for it except to go there. Matthew was so sure she'd be well looked after that she felt compelled to keep her thoughts to herself.

But in the taxi she couldn't help herself. Clinging to him, she buried her head in his shoulder. 'What am I going to do, Matthew, when you're gone? I'll be left all alone.'

'No you won't.' His voice shook. 'Mum will look after you as though you were her own daughter. And I'll come back. I'll come back.'

He heard the desperation in his words. Susan clinging to him made him ever more afraid of what lay ahead. Would he end up fighting in North Africa? The papers were full of Britain's new offensive against Rommel out there, but British soldiers were still being killed and who could say Rommel wouldn't turn and push them back again with even more men slaughtered, himself, Matthew Ward, perhaps one of them? Never to see Susan again. She would become a widow when she had scarcely become a wife.

The thought stayed with him throughout the interminable journey to London. Their train stopped and started, which seemed the normal thing these days; the delays got worse still as it hit fog just after Watford.

The thought persisted even as he smiled greeting at his parents, his mother taking Susan up to his old room which would now be hers until his return – if he returned. What would happen to Susan if he didn't? Where would she go? She'd marry again, in time . . . God, he had to stop thinking about it, think positive. Of course he'd come back. Yet a premonition that he might not haunted his troubled sleep that night, even though lovemaking helped him wipe it away for the while.

It wasn't that bad coming home, Margaret told herself firmly as, in scarves and warm coats, she and Mumsy walked down to the shops, her mother hanging on her arm in the jaundiced mist of this October Saturday morning. So long as she didn't have to do it every time she had a couple of hours off.

Mumsy, on the other hand, would have relished every second of her free time. But Margaret needed some time with her friends, and there was Ronald too, their off-duty hours coinciding so seldom. What chance they did have to go out together they usually spent going somewhere to eat. Hospital canteen food tasted disgusting and there was not much of it.

A forty-eight-hour week and sometimes eight weeks of night duty when all she wanted to do was go home to sleep, exhausted, until it was time to catch a bus back, took away any desire to go rushing off to see Ronald if he too was off duty. Time off came seldom enough and if he wasn't available it was fun spending it with friends now and again. While she made her way home, which was only a bus ride away, they, getting back after lights out, evaded the porter at the gate by climbing the railings; whispers and stifled giggles erupted as they clambered back into the nurses' residence through purposely unlocked windows before the night super began her rounds. She missed all that coming home.

If only her mother would make some attempt to join some women's group or other. There were plenty of them: wives whose husbands had been called up, elderly widows, spinsters, all knitting socks and scarves for 'the boys', or planning charity events, all an opportunity for socialising and filling in their lonely lives, but her mother had never been outgoing and that first approach towards a group of virtual strangers was always the hardest step for anyone to take.

'I couldn't go alone. I wouldn't mind if I had a friend to take me.'

'Then find a friend. Mrs Crompton next door. She lives alone. Or your other neighbour. I know she's younger than you, but she's on her own with her husband away.'

It was easy to say, but she wasn't the one having to do it. Her mother had gripped her arm hopefully. 'Perhaps you could come with me.'

'I'm a nurse, Mumsy. I can't have afternoons off whenever I please.'

She had hated the reluctance that made itself felt, wished she didn't feel so glad at having an excuse not to have to sit with those women with little else to do but discuss children, home life and the ever-tightening restrictions on food rationing as they knitted or planned their events.

Her mother would never understand. Hospital was another world, a little kingdom behind whose walls existed a strictly graded society of doctors and nurses, over which, next to the Matron's, the sister's authority was law. The outside world never penetrated that kingdom; even patients became changed creatures once they came in, lying in their beds in stiff rows, obedient to the ward sister. But Margaret loved it.

Soon to be a second-year nurse, at the moment on the men's medical ward, she was slowly climbing the ladder to the day when those magic letters SRN could be put after her name. Her feet had long ago stopped swelling like balloons and her back aching from long hours on her feet. She could take twelve hours on them almost, if not quite as lively as when she'd begun. She could fold counterpane corners to perfect angles; her mistakes were far fewer than they had once been, her intricate cap folded just right, the leg o' mutton sleeves of her uniform perfect. She'd be sitting for her second state examination early next year and after that her Preliminary. Still a long way to go, but she would get there in the end in spite of Mumsy looking towards the day when she'd leave nursing and go back to doing a nine to five job.

They were coming back home, turning into Victoria Park Road, when two young people came towards them out of the mist through which the sun was at last beginning to struggle. Margaret immediately recognised the figure of Matthew Ward and they halted simultaneously, she pulling her mother to a stop just as he did the girl on his arm. His face lit up.

137

'Ye gods, Maggie! Didn't expect to see you!'

'Home on leave then?' she asked, trying to control the joy that leapt inside her at seeing him, angering her in remaining as acute as ever, for all the girl with him.

There was a noticeable tightening of his features but he grinned, she was certain, with forced cheerfulness. When he spoke it was in a similar vein, an effort at banter. 'You're not going to ask me when I'm due back, are you? Everyone asks that, as though they'll be only too glad to see me gone again. But, no, I've been given fourteen days' leave – out of the blue.'

Adding that last on a more intense note, it needed no lecture to know what it meant. The obvious effort he was making to be cheerful helped bear out the message. Her next question, 'Where are they sending you?' sounded stupidly superfluous. How could he know that? He obliged with a shrug, then collected himself and turned to the small, neat girl beside him.

'By the way, this is Susan – my wife. Susan, this is Mag . . . This is Margaret Ross, an old friend from the crowd I used to go around with before the war. Margaret lives nearly opposite my parents.'

His use of her full given name, the first time she could ever recall, now spoken so formally, so neatly severed her from him that she actually felt pain. They'd gone their separate ways, yet even now her heart cried out to be the one on his arm instead of the girl to whom she now cordially smiled, saying it was nice to meet her and politely introducing her mother.

'Me and Matthew's staying at his parents,' the girl supplied in a broad Birmingham accent, her small oval face quite beautiful and full of adoration as she glanced up at him. Margaret could clearly see why he had married her. 'I'm going to live with them while he's away. You living so near then, I might probably see something of you.'

'I expect so,' Margaret obliged, her eyes travelling to Matthew. All she wanted now was to be away from here to suppress the sick thumping in her breast. It wasn't fair. 'Well, I won't keep you. This damp weather is chilly.' On an impulse she took off a glove and held out her hand to him. 'Well, wherever it is they send you, Matthew, keep safe, and . . .'

Words echoed inside her head, a sharp recollection of what he had once said to her: 'And whatever happens, you'll always be one of my nicer memories.' She had once had the audacity to think they might have been words of affection, a prelude to something more. But they had not presaged anything.

She had nearly begun to repeat them word for word. Would he have recalled himself saying them? And if so, would he have thought she was being just a little bitter? No, he'd probably forgotten, had never really meant them in the first place, flippant as he'd been those days. And yet, her mind conjured up the look in his dark eyes at the time. He had meant them when he said them, she was certain, but much water had flowed under the bridge since then, and now he was married and in love with his wife, his Susan – that could be seen with half an eye.

'And come back soon,' she finished instead, hardly realising that her voice had dropped to a whisper, almost a prayer, a secret shared between herself and him. But he hadn't noticed as he too removed his leather glove and took her hand, his warmth on her chill flesh making her senses leap. Was it her imagination or did his hand hold hers just that bit longer than was necessary? Was there a spark remaining of that which she thought she had seen in his eyes that day? Silly fool, it had to be her foolish imagination, nothing more.

After they parted she repeated those last words to herself: 'Come back soon.' Now they had become truly a fervent prayer for his safekeeping as she fought the heavy lump in her heart.

Chapter 13

He had meant to make his last night with Susan memorable. Instead, beset by anxiety, he'd failed her, the first time ever. She had been wonderful about it, told him it didn't matter, but he knew she was tearful when she finally turned over to go to sleep, he with his arms about her, cuddling her close.

Mortified by his inability to fulfil her, and himself, Matthew lay awake listening to her occasional sighs as though she was grieving the loss of something precious, yet he knew she was asleep because when he asked if she felt all right there was no reply. Loath to disturb her he left unsaid the words he needed to say.

Awakening to grey light filtering through the curtains and immediately conscious of a deep anger at sleep itself having robbed him of those last few hours with her, he turned to gaze at her sweet face on the pillow beside him, the full lips in gentle repose. He was about to waken her and would have made perfect love to her but for the knock on the door and his father entering in response to his reluctant bidding with a cup of tea for them.

From then on things took on a sense of urgency, washing, dressing, packing his kit, forcing down the boiled egg and toast his mother insisted would 'keep him going', everyone's conversation stilted, shallow, tense.

It had been agreed they'd say their goodbyes here in the privacy of their own home, the severing made clean, but at the last moment Susan pleaded to be allowed to accompany him the whole way to Charing Cross where he was to board the train for Southampton. The prospect of seeing her standing there, a small isolated figure among the seething crowds in that vast station as his train took him from her, was more than he could bear to contemplate; shattering him as well as her. He took her in his arms.

'No, darling, I want you to stay here. It'll only be dragging things out if you come, and the end will be just the same. On top of that you'll have to come all the way home without me.'

She would not see it. In fact his final goodbyes turned into something like pandemonium. Having said farewell to his parents, his father gripping him firmly in a bear hug, telling him to watch himself, his mother kissing his cheek, assuring him she would look after Susan, charging him to look after himself in that cold, stiff manner which he knew hid emotions she had long ago taught herself never to show, Susan standing away from him with her back pressed against the wall of the hall, her naturally pale face now chalk-white, her small slender body as rigid as the wall that alone seemed to be holding her up, she flew at him as though unseen hands had suddenly propelled her forward.

'Matthew, don't leave me! Oh, don't . . . please don't leave me.'

He had to struggle to extricate himself, physically handing her to his mother who held her in a firm grip, her older face like granite. He'd wanted to crush Susan to him, but her demonstration threatened to undermine his own resolve not to give way to too much emotion, so while her tears flowed shamelessly unchecked, his had to remain unshed as he'd put her from him with futile words. 'It'll be all right, love. I have to go. You've got to be brave.' Though what order he said them in he did not know.

He could still hear her calling his name, her voice echoing down the street after him as he stood now on Southampton docks amid long, snaking, khaki queues waiting to board the ship that would take them to God knows where – no one knew as yet, except that they all carried tropical kit.

A fine drizzle sifted down upon the shoulders of the slowly moving queues, upon the loose piles of kitbags ready to be loaded on board, and on trucks and other equipment to be transported the several thousand miles to, where? North

141

Africa? India? It might be India, Matthew prayed. Far away from any war zone. It could be that those in charge thought there was some need of men in that region or perhaps South or West Africa? There they could expect a life of relative luxury, and in time to come back safely. Matthew crossed his fingers as he took his turn to move up the gangway leading to the ship's dark innards.

As soon as permitted, he would write to reassure Susan how well he was and that there had been no need for her to worry about his safety – fair enough, only that he wished he was back with her instead of here. But one must not think of that. Every man here must have loved ones on his mind but knew better than to give too great a thought to it. Pushing that last sight of Susan's tear-ravaged face from his mind, he looked down at the oily green swell rising and sinking between the troopship and the quayside. It was like some slow-breathing animal waiting to engulf them all. From it rose a reek of decayed seaweed, engine oil and bilge water which he could see gushing in small spurts from an outlet below him amid a wreath of steam.

Gaining a position against the deck rail as he and his platoon made it into the ship, he leaned over to watch the water still heaving and sinking, heaving and sinking below the slow climbing of soldiers up the three sets of gangways.

'Get yer arse away from there,' Sergeant Pegg interrupted his reverie. 'All of yer – this way.'

Following him, Matthew found himself in the place where he and the others were to live out the next few weeks; a place with all its port holes well screwed down so no light could escape across a pitch-dark sea to lurking U-boats, their quarters thus promising to become hot and unbearable as they approached the tropics; a place where narrow wooden bunks had been built almost side by side, forcing men by lack of space to share with their fellows most of their personal functions, including seasickness. The all too few, once-elegant toilet facilities for paying passengers, now to be called latrines, had had all but their basic amenities torn out, even their doors, and were painted overall-grey. They needed to accommodate four times as many troops. A line of convenient buckets fixed nearby to make up for the lack of facilities would soon waft their

142

stink to the quarters as they filled before being emptied by fatigue squads. It was a place where snoring, coughing, farting, scratching, conversation and talking in one's sleep would be no secret from anyone.

In this impending claustrophobic atmosphere, Bob dropped his kit down on to a so-far unclaimed area, once beautifully carpeted, now mere metal deck where he and the rest of them would be expected to share their lives in close harmony with all walks of life.

'Like a bloody cargo of meat,' he observed drily and everyone agreed, finding the quip unfunny.

Settled on a top bunk, Matthew wrote his first letters home, the first a brief one to his parents, the second to Susan pouring out all that he had been unable to say to her face. He'd have given the world to see her read it, see her smile with all the confidence he was instilling in her of his safe return.

He could hardly wait for the letter to be collected along with everyone else's and taken ashore for posting prior to moving off, yet it would go with his mixed feelings. In a couple of days it would reach Susan. By then he'd be nearly a thousand miles away. So he concentrated on visualising her beautiful oval face, her tremulous smile as she read, her expression glowing with love, with the certainty of his coming back to her. He worked on retaining that vision. It was one he must carry with him to whatever ends of the earth he was bound for as with the clanging of bells and the deep rumbling of engines vibrating through his whole body, diminishing, then building up again, the great ship began to slide away from the dockside.

His letters sent on their way, Matthew went up on deck – better than meditating below – to watch the huge one-time P & O liner do its majestic about-turn in the incredibly narrow channel, the deep heavy pulsating of engines finally dying away to a regular thumping that in a while would be hardly noticeable, a rhythm to which its cargo of troops would work, rest and think for weeks to come before again setting foot on terra firma.

Margaret sat on the cold park bench staring down at the ring, a band of three diamonds, sitting snugly in the box he had brought from his pocket. What on earth was she to say to him?

'You gave me no warning of what you intended, Ronald.'

It was almost an accusation. What was she supposed to say – this is so sudden – like in those Hollywood films they turned out, those love-scene dialogues so unreal? Don't ask for the moon, darling, when we have the stars . . . Was that it? It would seem laughable if this wasn't so serious.

She turned her eyes from the surprise engagement ring to the man who now held it up for her inspection, ready to be slipped on to her finger. But she had her gloves on. Was she supposed to take them off, or would he? It all threatened to become a clumsy business, stripping it of any romance there might have been. Romance? Really, she wasn't sure she loved him enough to accept his ring. The thing was, she'd let him make love to her. Well, not actually make love, although he'd seen more of her than she'd intended him to see, for every time they got into a clinch, something stopped her, almost as if she were saving herself for someone else. But what someone else? Well, she knew who that was. But it was silly. He was beyond any hope of hers. Married, overseas, his wife waiting for his return. And yet, to accept this ring, this contract for marriage, would be to finally accept the absurdity of that dream to which she had clung for so long.

'You must have known, Margaret,' he was saying, his eyes full of query, his good-looking face a picture.

She looked back at him. Yes, he was handsome. Any girl would have taken him immediately. He could have his pick, but he had chosen her. What did he see in her? What did he see that Matthew had never seen? Yet handsome as he was, there as something missing. What it was she couldn't say. Whatever it was, it wasn't right to hurt him. Ronald, I don't love you.

'I suppose I should have expected it,' she answered instead.

'Then put it on, my love.'

Grasping the fingertips of the woollen glove with her right hand, she pulled it off carefully, finger by finger, making a meal of it, the damp cold December air touching her exposed hand, and held out the hand for him. She watched him slip the ring over the knuckle of her engagement finger with a sort of ritual reverence. It went on so easily, she wondered how and when he had discovered her fit, pondering over it when she ought to have been gasping with pleasure at his wordless proposal.

Hardly giving her time, sitting there in Green Park, to admire what glitter the stars afforded the diamonds with no other lighting, not even a moon visible, he gathered her into his arms.

'Darling Margaret, you've made me the happiest man. The first moment I get, I'll take you to meet my parents. They'll be so surprised.'

Silently Margaret allowed herself to be held, leaning against him at an awkward angle. Seeing her ring glittering but faintly in the darkness over his shoulder she thought of what lay ahead. His parents lived in Bristol. All she could think of was having to go all that way to meet them, of being introduced into his life, quite expected to leave her own behind her. There was her mother to think of. She had no one else but her. Left behind and lonely. There were all the things she had known. Left behind. And there was Matthew, part of her past. Left behind. Panic seemed to take a great bite out of her heart.

'No!' She pushed him away, so hard and suddenly that he all but fell off the seat, regaining his balance with an effort. 'No, Ronald, I can't.'

He looked so taken aback, she could have cried. But there was no altering what she had said. 'I really can't, Ronald.'

'Why not?' For a moment he looked stupid, then he relaxed a little, even grinned. 'Come on, darling. It is a bit frightening I expect, saying yes. But it'll be all right. Let's just sit here quietly for a while. Let you get used to the idea. I shouldn't have sprung it on you like that. But we don't have to get married immediately. A few weeks, a couple of months perhaps.'

'But there's my mother. She doesn't know.'

'Neither do my parents. We'll tell them as soon as possible. I'll write to mine and you write to your mother, warn them ... no, not warn them, tell them. Oh, Margaret, I've dreamed of this day – me giving you a ring and you accepting. We'll be ...'

'I haven't accepted yet, Ronald.'

'What?'

'I haven't accepted. You put the ring on my finger, then you grabbed me and cuddled me.'

'You let me put it on. You let me cuddle you.'

'I wasn't thinking. You took me by surprise. It all happened too quickly for me to say anything.'

Comprehension was creeping not so much into his expression, which in the dark she could not properly see, but into his voice, the stiffening of his posture. 'You mean, you don't want me? You don't want to marry me?' His consternation mounted as Margaret remained silent, unable to trust her voice. 'But we get on so well.'

'I know.' She had to say something. 'I just don't . . . I don't know.'

'You don't love me enough to marry me.'

'Oh, Ronald.' What was she trying to appeal to? He got up, took her hand and gently pulled her to her feet.

'We should be getting back to the hospital. I'm on call tonight.'

'What about the ring?' It was as though they were discussing work.

'Keep it for now. See how you feel as time goes on. I suppose I did jump the gun a bit. But I do love you.'

'I know you do.' How could he stay so calm? Another man would be ranting and raving at her now, for letting him down, making a fool of him.

'Don't you love me at all?' was all he said.

Her heart went out to him. How could she say to him, 'I like you'? How could she insult him like that? In a way she did love him. If only that other face didn't persist in floating before her eyes. Ronald made her feel good when he was around, feel wanted, feel important. His touch did excite. But when he wasn't there, she didn't think about him at all, had never found herself yearning for the time to come for them to meet. So did she love him or not? It seemed she didn't, yet when she saw him her heart leaped with the pleasure of seeing him. They got on well together, never quarrelled. They could chat until the cows came home. She felt easy with him in a way she had never done with Matthew Ward. But Matthew, though claimed, still haunted her.

'You took me by surprise,' she said miserably for an answer as they began making their way out of the darkened park whose gates stood open all night so people could gain access

146

at a moment's notice to the air-raid shelters built there. 'Don't be annoyed.'

'I'm not annoyed.' No, he wasn't annoyed, just deeply hurt.

'I need time to get used to it. I will keep the ring for a while. And I will think about it, Ronald. I promise.'

After all, she must. Theirs would be a stable marriage, she knew that by just knowing him. She would be a fool not to say yes in the end.

'Good girl,' he breathed, his confidence returning, and gave her a thank-you peck on the cheek as they walked on through the darkened streets.

Bombay had hit the troops newly arrived from the sedate, restrained British Isles, most never having set foot on any foreign soil before, not even France, like a bomb. It was an exotic disturbing place, full of disquiet and unheaval. Fine buildings rubbed shoulders with such squalor as Matthew could never have imagined and made him at first feel sickened. But slowly, confronted by its sights and sounds, its unfamiliar aromas and an atmosphere so indigenous that it seemed there could be no other city in the world like this, his eyes became blinded to all but the worst of sights, and all his prayers were those of gratitude that their final destination had been here and nowhere else.

Amid speculation they had pulled in to Gibraltar, spent a day on the Rock while U-boats reported to be lurking outside the Med were being dealt with by the Royal Navy. They hardly had time to see anything Gib had to offer before the ship sailed onward, not into the Mediteranean as had been expected but south, down the coast of Africa, pausing at Cape Town, then round into the Indian Ocean where they finally disembarked at Bombay.

In the pleasant warmth of an Indian November, Matthew sat on his bed writing letters home to say where he had landed up and thought of the chill sleet of England, and of the commission he'd narrowly missed by being too complacent and seeking it too late. Now he saw it as providential that he had not done so. Had he got a commission, who was to say he might not have ended up on some field of battle instead of here. It *was* providence. He should have known. He had always been pretty lucky in nearly everything.

Leaving her house, Margaret saw Matthew's wife emerge from hers. They caught sight of each other at the same time; she saw the girl hesitate and almost draw back as though about to hurry back indoors. But Margaret wasn't to be avoided. She turned in her direction, her steps rapid. 'Hi, there!'

She had been aching for weeks to have a chat with her, telling herself it was of no consequence to her if she didn't, yet feeling a compulsion to look over to the Wards' house every time she came home. She'd told herself she was only coming home at every opportunity for her mother's sake, yet a tiny voice inside her kept repeating the true reason for her visits. That tiny voice was telling her now of the truth behind the avid eagerness with which she called out, 'Hi, there!'

The girl smiled, nodded briefly, but the ice was broken.

In seconds Margaret was at her side. 'Haven't seen much of you since we were introduced.' She was talking like some schoolgirl, far too fast, far too exuberant.

Susan shook her head rather solemnly. 'I haven't been out a lot.'

'Well, I only get home at odd times. That's a nurse's life for you.' She laughed.

'You're a nurse?'

'Didn't Matthew mention it?'

'No, he didn't.'

They had begun to walk towards the main road, Margaret hiding her disappointment that Matthew hadn't thought of her even enough to mention her job to his wife. But then, he wouldn't, would he?

'Where are are you off to, then?' she asked and saw the girl shrug.

'I don't know really. I just had to get out for a walk somewhere. I was going to the park, but it don't matter much where I go.'

She sounded so down. Margaret took a quick guess at what must have driven the girl out. She herself wouldn't relish being closeted with Mrs Ward for days on end. Her own mother with her constant small complaints of loneliness was enough to

148

endure, but Margaret reckoned Mrs Ward could knock spots off Mumsy for driving a person away.

'It's a bit chilly for walking,' she observed as she fell in beside her. A thin fog was threatening to thicken. It clung with cold fingers around cheeks and lips and penetrated the shoulders of the heaviest coat. In mid November, elsewhere on the Continent, flurries of dry snow probably covered everything in glorious pristine white – she still felt a thrill at new fresh snow for all its inconvenience – but here it only got damp and any snow that might fall would soon melt on this seawashed island. Yet she'd rather have all the peasouper fogs unconquered England could dish out than the dazzling whiteness of an occupied Europe. Nineteen forty-two waited just six weeks away – how much longer would this war would go on and when would Matthew come home again?

'Have you heard from Matthew?'

Susan appeared to brighten up. 'We had his first letters in the week. Airmail. One for me and one for his parents. From India, Bombay.'

A vast surge of relief poured over Margaret. Far far away from any fighting. Thank God, oh, thank God.

'That's good,' she said evenly. 'I bet you're glad.'

Susan nodded. 'I wish he was here instead. I wanted to tell him my news to his face, not in a letter. It won't be the same written in a letter. Oh, if only he'd been able to stay here a few weeks longer, I could've told him to his face and seen it all light up. I'm going to have a baby.'

'Oh, I'm so glad for you.' It was even more of an effort to keep her voice steady. Marriage, now cemented by a forthcoming baby. 'You must be very thrilled.'

Susan didn't look thrilled. 'I would be if it wasn't for her, his mother. She's really pleased of course. But she's started making plans for it already, telling me what I should do and what I shouldn't do. I really feel like I'm in a prison.'

The same as Matthew had felt; his mother's over-eagerness to guide and help had only been instrumental in sending him away from her. She felt suddenly sad for Mrs Ward, only able to express love by managing the lives of those around her, succeeding only in driving them away with their misguided conception of her actions. Even Louise, with that time she had

149

secretly applied for the Wrens. She had confided in Margaret. 'I never told Mummy at that time until I was quite sure I would be accepted,' she'd said. 'But honestly, Margaret, she can be quite suffocating at times.' Exactly as Matthew had felt, and now Susan.

'I don't know how long I'll be able to stand it,' Susan was saying. She had begun to screw up beneath her winter coat, the damp cold eating into her small frame. 'She watches me all the time. Everything I eat, everything I do. I was sick first thing yesterday morning. That confirmed it but she carted me off to the doctor to be sure. I hate doctors. I hate the smell of their waiting rooms, and ill people all round the room.'

She seemed bent on unburdening herself to someone. 'I was sick again this morning and she said I should stay in bed. She kept coming in every half-hour to see how I was. I don't want to stay in bed. She said I wasn't to go out, I'd catch cold, but I came out just the same. I know it'll annoy her. She'll be all stiff and starched with me when I get back, like I was a kid, or something. I wish Matthew was here. He'd stick up for me.'

She was beginning to shiver. She seemed so small; a waif. 'Perhaps some evenings when I'm home,' Margaret offered readily, 'if you want to come over to us for a chat, you're welcome. It'll get you out of that house.'

She felt she had never seen anyone look so grateful. 'Could I?'

'Of course.' Also Susan would keep her abreast of news of Matthew, though Margaret didn't admit to it even to herself, for all the tiny voice inside did.

The following ten days saw Margaret on nights, taking over from a girl who had gone down sick. Sleeping most of the day, she was unable to honour the invitation to Susan. But she had managed to get Christmas off. Ronald, still waiting for her answer, had asked to take her home to see his parents, but it seemed only right to think of her mother first on this, the one special family holiday of the year. On top of that it was a time when Mumsy would be thinking of Daddy, who had died just one month before the festive season, for all the years were stretching on.

She hadn't told her mother about Ronald yet. The first thing

150

she'd do would be to start fretting about the impending loss of her daughter, as if Margaret would forsake her entirely. Maybe all mothers felt that way but most wouldn't make a meal of it. Not that Mumsy meant to drag on her, but Margaret found herself dreading the day when she must tell her.

That she would marry Ronald was in no doubt. He was kind and considerate and steady, and she did love him – not in the silly way she'd felt for Matthew – still did, she was ashamed to realise, constantly telling herself off about this idiotic wishing for something that couldn't be – but in a comfortable way which common sense told her would last and last.

It did seem a shame to keep fobbing him off so. Perhaps she would tell him her decision when the spring came and the spirits rose with the climbing of the sun. These days she had no deep feeling for love or anything approaching it. The weather stayed too cold for strolling in parks, so they went to the Natural History Museum, had tea in its restaurant, talking of this and that. He held her hand and gazed at the ring she'd begun to wear when with him, capitulating at last. He spoke of marriage, their future together, again broached the subject of her coming home with him to see his parents, if not Christmas Day, then Boxing Day.

'I know it sounds churlish,' she told him. 'But my mother's all alone. I couldn't dream of leaving her as soon as Christmas is over. She's made a Christmas pudding too. Saved up her dried fruit coupons all year for the thing. She'd be left to eat the rest all by herself on Boxing Day. They don't keep, you know, not like they used to before the war.'

For some reason he thought that funny, His laughter annoyed her for yet some other unaccountable reason.

'I just couldn't leave her,' she stated huffily. The pudding had been just an excuse. It wasn't funny, at least not all that much. Even less, again for some unknown reason, when she remembered that there would come a time when he would insist on naming the wedding day. Why did her insides crawl with reluctance at that thought? Later as she melted into his arms, she wondered why she had felt so reluctant. This was what she wanted, or what common sense told her she must want. Security, friendship, someone to be with, all of those

151

things. And of course love. She did love Ronald, she told herself severely.

Monday came again, one more week nearer to Christmas. Margaret was working, swotting for her second state examination as she had been doing these past months while Ronald worked and studied towards becoming a GP. She had been nearly two years doing practical work on the wards. A couple of years had to pass yet before she could add SRN after her name, though perhaps in wartime it might come quicker. But would she ever get it, now that she appeared to be Ronald's fiancée?

She was just going on the ward when a nurse came hurrying towards her. 'Telephone call for you, love. Better cut short whoever it is or you'll make yourself late.'

'Did they say who it is?' Margaret called as she made her way to the old-fashioned phone fastened to the wall down the passage. Her heart had begun to beat. It could only be bad news. Her mother? She had been all right when she'd left home an hour ago.

'Didn't say,' came back the answer, but Margaret was already there, her ear to the earpiece.

'Hello? Hello.'

A girl's frantic voice assailed her ears. 'Margaret – oh, thank God it's you. I tried to get you before you left. But you'd already gone. I had to talk to *someone*.'

'Who is it?' Margaret interrupted the tirade, not recognising the voice.

'Susan, across the road. I must speak to you. There's no one else.'

'Susan, what's the matter?' She felt just a little peeved being made late by Susan's trivial need to phone her. Nothing at all to do with her mother.

'Haven't you heard the news on the wireless?' The girl's voice still held a note of panic. 'Japan's just declared war on America, and us. They've bombed a base belonging to America, called Pearl Harbor, in the Pacific. Matthew's out there in India. I'm so worried.'

Margaret's mind flitted over past world atlases of her childhood, the Indian continent marked in pink, Siam and similar countries further east in yellow, then pink again for Malaya,

Borneo, Australia. The Pacific, light blue, dwarfed all else. Where Pearl Harbor was she had no idea but it belonged to the USA and was probably somewhere in the Hawaiian islands. Far away from India. Matthew was safe.

'Susan, if war breaks out there, do you know how far away from it Matthew will be? A good couple of thousand miles at least. If he was still stationed here in England he'd be nearer to a war zone. So there's nothing to worry about. Nothing at all.'

The voice at the other end had calmed a little. 'I've sent off an airmail letter to him to tell him about the baby. He'll get it in a day or two. I know he'll be thrilled. You are sure about him being safe in India?'

'I couldn't be surer,' Margaret said, smiling into the mouth-piece. She was going to be late. 'I must go, Susan. I'm at work. See you soon.'

She replaced the receiver and hurried off. She wouldn't be able to listen to the wireless until she came off duty. Perhaps by then there might be a bit more about this new war so far away. But one thing was certain. Matthew, soon to be a father, was indeed safe and it was best not to let her mind keep dwelling on him.

Chapter 14

Among other things; some of the garrison were staging a panto for Christmas and requests had gone out for anyone with talent wanting to join the chorus to come forward. All the acting roles had of course long since gone to those who'd been stationed there some time.

'Go on, Matt,' Bob urged, hearing about it. 'You've not got a bad voice. How about giving your tonsils an airing?'

Matthew had his pencil poised over a blank air letter. Seventh of December already and he needed to write to Susan again. He was waiting for one from her. It should come any moment but in the meantime . . .

He looked up, gave a small explosive chuckle of self-derision. 'One sound from me and I'd be given the about-turn.'

'Don't be daft. It's not half bad, your voice. Now, me, I'd turn lemons sour. Go on, have a go.'

Again Matthew chuckled, but the idea was tempting. He was bored. Life here was one round of ticking over, being given jobs just to kill time and keep men occupied: in the soporific air of old colonial India they painted flagstaffs, whitewashed stones around brigade HQ, cleaned windows, swept paths, spit-and-polished equipment, attended parades and spent the hotter parts of the day in cool schoolrooms, the strong sunlight thwarted by fretted shutters, the still air stirred by squeaking, slowly revolving fans. With time to laze in the shade, seek somewhere to booze away an evening, what at first seemed delightful had quickly palled.

He was about to say he might think about having a crack at it when Ronnie Clark burst into the barrack room like a tornado.

Unable to take in quite what he was blabbering about, those absorbed in reading tatty paperbacks, writing letters, darning socks, looked up.

'Who's bombed what?'

'The Japanese. They've gone and bombed Pearl Harbor.'

'Where the bloody 'ell's Pearl 'Arbor?'

'It's an American naval base in Hawaii,' Matthew supplied, which had Farrell sneering across at him.

''Ark at bleedin' know-all.' But Matthew ignored him. His heart was already filling with a kind of animal fear, nameless and undefined, having nothing yet to draw on, just an instinct of some threat looming from a totally unexpected direction.

'Where did you hear this?' Bob was demanding.

'Over the radio.' Ronnie Clark had been on duty all morning in the communications room. 'A few minutes ago. They've bombed Singapore too.' He looked significantly towards Jeff Downey whose thick lips had dropped open in awe. 'Bet you're glad we didn't go there as you wanted to.'

'The Yanks'll come inter the war now, won't they?' Eddie Nutt said.

'Bugger the Yanks!' someone snapped. 'What about us? Us fighting bloody Jerries, bloody Ities, and now bloody Nips. It ain't fair! Just as we're getting the best of the Jerries in North Africa an' the battle of the Atlantic's goin' our way and everyone's goin' on about us openin' up a second front, now we're inter another bloody war. Ain't it just fair!'

It was Sergeant Pegg who put it all into perspective for them. 'What you lot worrying about them short-arse little monkeys for? Most of 'em wear glasses. Planes tied up with string, like them bloody toys they export to us. I'd sooner fight an 'undred of them than a dozen of Rommel's lot. The Yanks comin' in, all we'll see of them boss-eyed, bow-legged little yeller bleeders'll be their backsides. The Yanks comin' in'll shorten the war in Germany too.'

It all seemed logical and heartening even when days later they were moved on to the transit camp at Deolali; from Deolali station a horrendous three-day train journey across the Indian continent began, to Calcutta, Assam, and on to Rangoon in Burma to join Burmese and Indian brigades there.

Matthew's letters home had been written in fits and starts.

155

Susan's had been delayed because those to her were always precious and needed thinking about, dreaming over. Now there was no time for dreaming. What he had written would have to be sent off as it was. He hadn't heard from her yet, but with all this sudden moving out, hers must still be catching him up. He would get it sooner or later, but it was hell not hearing.

'Knowing the Army,' Bob said as they strolled through the paved courts of the ancient Shwe Dagon pagoda on their first off-duty sightseeing trip, the hot spicy smells of India now replaced by the milder flowery ones of Burma, 'our mail will all come in one batch.'

'And wait another couple of months for the next lot,' Matthew agreed. Pensively he gazed up at the scores of lesser pagodas that surrounded the great *stupa*, of the Shwe Dagon, its graceful curves clad in pure beaten gold.

His ears filled by the soft slap of bare feet on warm tiles, the low murmur of devotees at prayer, the droning intonation of Buddhist monks, the twitter of birds and the gentle tinkle of tiny bells, he watched a group of Burmese women at their labour of devotion, sweeping the smooth paving with flat, fan-shaped brooms. In crisp, straight blouses over colourful skirts, *longyis*, that wrapped tightly around their legs, their shining black hair pulled into a bun at the back of the head and secured by a gaudy flower, they looked sleek and clean, a far cry from the ragged denizens of Bombay.

'I wish my Susan could see all this,' he murmured.

'Yes, a regular Cook's tour, and not costing us a penny,' said Bob appreciatively. 'Just look where we've been at the expense of the Army. We've stopped off at Gib, West Africa, Cape Town, Bombay, Deolali and now Rangoon. Wonder where we'll end up next?'

'This is as far east as I ever want to go,' Matthew said, his mind on their newest enemy. Short, bow-legged, short-sighted they might be, but they still had guns and shells and mortars, and could kill. He didn't fancy Susan becoming a widow just yet.

Taffy had joined them, coming from a side street with a wide grin of self-satisfaction. Matthew gave him a disparaging look. 'Not in the middle of a Sunday afternoon.'

Taffy's grin widened even more. 'Best time for it, isn't it?

156

Make you pretty thirsty, mind.' He eyed one of the many water-sellers squatting on a corner beneath the shade of a tree, clinking a metal cup against a container with a loud urgent rhythmical clatter.

'Wouldn't risk it,' Matthew warned. 'Wait till you get a beer from the mess instead.'

He paused by an ancient crone squatting under a large spreading tree near some open-fronted shops. Surrounded by several of her family and a few onlookers, she leered up at Matthew, her few remaining teeth stained red by betel-nut juice.

'Tell fortune, soldiya?' she croaked in English. There had been a British garrison here long enough for those like her to have a passing knowledge of their language. Dusty feet splayed from beneath a rusty longyi, the old fortune-teller beckoned with clawed hands. 'You want know of long life, soldiya, love, ha?'

'Go one, give it a go,' Bob urged.

'What about you, Taff?' Matthew asked. 'Might find out you're going to turn over a new leaf and find yourself a decent wife. Put a stop to all that whoring of yours.'

Taffy's handsome face was full of injured pride. 'There's nice! You just leave me be to find me own wife when I'm good and ready.'

Matthew laughed and glanced again at the crone with her vermilion grimace. On impulse he squatted in front of her, extending his hand, but the woman waved it away. 'You pay. You pay.'

A couple of coins dropped in her palm quickly appeased her and the old witch grabbed his hand to scrutinise it. Tracing the lines of his palm with a piece of indelible pencil until most of them were linked in mystical triangles and trapeziums, she studied the results, her voice a cracked sing-song.

'See baby. See lady. Lady has your heart, soldiya.'

'I bet she says that to everyone,' Taffy interrupted with a chortle.

Matthew was about to ask, what baby? But the woman went on: 'One more lady has heart for you.'

'Two?' Taffy gave another chortle. 'And you talk about me, boyo?'

157

'Lady with bright hair,' went on the crone.

'No, dark,' Matthew corrected.

The black eyes like polished jet glittered angrily. She glanced round and pointed at the distant Shwe Dagon pagoda glinting like a gold nugget in the sunshine behind the low buildings.

'Bright.' She waggled her old head lest her prediction be contradicted again. 'Like Shwe Dagon.'

He let her have her way. After all it was only a bit of fun. But the old woman's eyes had gone dark. She regarded him narrowly. 'See bad thing here. Binding rope. Bad thing.'

'The ball and chain, that is,' laughed Taffy. 'Don't need your hand read to know that, do you?'

Matthew resolutely kept his palm upwards. 'What do you mean, bad thing?' Was she referring to Susan? Was everything all right with her? The questions came even as he derided this odd belief in the woman's words.

But the crone had dismissed him, already casting about for other clients. Nor, strangely enough, would she take his offer of any more money.

'A baby! Ye gods, she was right.' Matthew stared at the letter that had at last caught him up. He waved it in Bob's face. 'That old bird who told me my fortune said she saw a baby and Susan says here that she's pregnant.'

For hours last night he had lain beneath his mosquito net studying his palm in the glow of a pale shaft of moonlight through the high barrack-room window, trying to make sense of the marks of the indelible pencil. Now had come Susan's letter. It was uncanny. 'I'm going to be a father.'

Bob, a father of three, regarded him as an old dog might a boisterous puppy. 'Well, if she's pregnant, obviously you will be. You're not unique.'

'I feel unique. God, I feel . . .' There was no way to describe how he felt. Susan, his sweet timid Susan, to be a mother. He thought again of that old crone. Binding ropes she had said. Of course, a baby was binding, tying him and Susan together. Of course. Last night that prediction had worried him, he had been unable to pinpoint any of it. Now it all came plain. 'I'll never doubt a fortune-teller again,' he announced. Bob grinned.

'A shot in the dark. Their stock in trade – make it enigmatic enough and you can read anything you want into what they tell you.'

'Two shots in the dark? No, there is something in it, Bob.'

While Bob chortled, Matthew returned to reading the rest of his letter. It said she was two months' pregnant. The letter was nearly three weeks old, so it had happened on his embarkation leave. She would be having the baby around June or July time.

'We might all be home by then,' he said to Bob, roughly calculating the date. 'With the Yanks in the war now it could shorten it considerably.'

Bob's unprepossessing features were wreathed in smiles of joy for him. 'Could be. One never knows. I tell you what, we'll have a drink tonight to celebrate you being a prospective father, wet the baby's head. Drinks on you of course.'

'Thanks very much!' Matthew chuckled, but Bob corroborating his own certainty of being home by next summer heartened him even more.

In this frame of mind he began on his reply to Susan. But it wasn't easy to put into it all he felt. He was in danger of writing a load of drivel and finally had to put it away until the next morning when he might be able to collect his thoughts better. It was the twenty-second of December, with Christmas and its panto, in which he'd got himself into the chorus, not sure if he even wanted to bother, three days away. The next morning the bombers came.

Throughout Christmas and into the early days of 1942, Rangoon continued to be bombed. Detailed to help supervise hordes of terrified refugees pouring out of the city, helping to fill in at the docks now forsaken by hundreds of Indian dock workers who'd also taken to the road, hoping to get back home to India, Matthew's letter to Susan lay unfinished.

His main concern in that letter now was to allay her fears for his safety as news was relayed to England about the fall of Hong Kong and the air attacks on Rangoon. That city would surely be next to fall. Any time Matthew had he scribbled words of reassurance. Above all else, Susan, pregnant, must not be alarmed. He assured her that the bombing had been minimal no matter what the wireless said, but whether some

159

censor would allow that piece of information in his letter to get through was out of Matthew's hands, though he felt better having put it in.

By the middle of January the Japanese were reported to be already concentrated on the Siam-Burma border, the speed of their movements stunning everyone. Matthew's troop found themselves suddenly attached to an Indian brigade very much in need of a signals unit and ordered forward to establish a line of defence just east of the Sittang River which ran into the Gulf of Martaban some eighty miles away.

Gathering up their kit, boarding trucks, they had no time to send last letters home even if they had been allowed to. By the time Matthew was able to scribble a page to Susan, Moulmein to the south was in enemy hands, so fast had the Japanese moved through what had been thought impenetrable jungle.

Two weeks later the letter still lay in his shirt pocket, darkened by sweat, as he crouched by the side of a dirt road passing on crackling coded messages over his field radio, his nerves jumping, his eyes alert to any movement from the dim jungle on either side of the road.

As yet they had seen no action, the enemy being busy around the Bilin River fifteen miles away. But everyone knew by now just how swiftly that enemy could move through this tangle of rainforest, how adept it was at easing around a battalion, small lightly equipped figures appearing out of the greenery in front of their prey like spectres, cutting off whole battalions without warning. It had happened more than once these last few weeks and no one wanted to be caught napping. Orders had come to withdraw to the railway bridge over the Sittang, to guard it until all transport and equipment was safely across. Then the rest were to cross prior to its demolition to prevent any enemy advance upon Rangoon itself.

As Matthew moved back along the road with his platoon, a staff car passed him, empty but for the Indian corporal driving it. Remembering his letter, Matthew frantically hailed the man and as the car slowed he pulled out the letter and waved urgently at the driver.

A slow gleaming smile split the dark aquiline features. There was no need for any exchange of words; the beseeching look on the taut face of the English corporal brandishing his stained envelope spoke volumes in any language. Stretching out a hand, the driver took it, nodded understandingly, and tucking it into his uniform sped off westward in a cloud of dust.

Three months she had been here. Three months and still a guest, not one bit a part of Matthew's family, and she wondered if in fact she wanted to be.

Yes, of course Mrs Ward looked after her, saw she wanted for nothing and was apparently very happy with the knowledge of her son's wife bearing his child. It was the way she went about it, the way she always conducted herself, that made Susan feel like an outsider.

She yearned for home, for the noise and laughter, for her father's uncouth manner and her mother's brassy warmth, the sharp quarrelling of her sisters and the tormenting of her younger brothers, neighbours coming in and out as free as they liked. Their own doors too were open to anyone who wanted to come in for a chinwag and a cuppa. Three months here and she knew none of the neighbours, except Margaret Ross. But she looked for her in vain to unburden her troubles on. It seemed Margaret Ross was too taken up with her work nursing, her own friends and no doubt some young man, to come home at all the right times. Susan had seen her only once since that time they had spoken together, but it had been cold with a threat of more snow when she had glimpsed her entering her house, head down, glad to be out of the bitter wind and Susan had felt it too much an imposition to go across and make herself free as she might have done at home, especially as it was obvious Margaret Ross was eager to get indoors and relax.

Life, with winter closing in, the sounds of the world deadened by the first snows, was turning into a gaol, her gaoler a well-meaning but dictatorial Mrs Ward whom she couldn't bring herself to call Mum. Susan merely cleared her throat should she need to gain her attention, which was as seldom as she could get away with. Mr Ward, whom she did feel she could happily have called Dad except that she couldn't address one in-law that familiarly without the other, was so different. He had the same way of looking at her as Matthew had, as though concealing some joke. He said little, but possessed a sort of warmth his wife did not have, and for Susan any tiny port in a storm was a haven. When the weather had been more clement she'd been able to take a walk down to his shop and spend her time there helping a bit, making tea or serving customers with small items or talking to him in the back room when things were quiet. Now that the weather had turned foul, she was stuck here with her mother-in-law, yearning desperately for her own mother. But her mother was far away and in no way could Susan find courage enough to make an excuse to leave and go off to live up there.

In her own way Mrs Ward was kind enough, but Susan could not master her awe of her. And when she'd found herself pregnant, she also found herself practically in close confinement, watched over night and day by a woman with the eyes of a hawk watching its prey, or so it seemed.

'You must stay in bed longer in the mornings. Don't go out of the house without first telling me where you are going. Don't try lifting that on your own, it could be too heavy and cause the baby an injury, I'll do it for you. Don't upset yourself so about Matthew – it's not good for you in your condition. Try to content youself more, my dear – there's plenty of books to read. If you need to go to the library, tell me and I will accompany you. Is it not time you started knitting for the baby? That would help you. We could get some wool and you can make a start.'

And this when she'd only been two months gone. No better, in fact worse, now she was four months. What would it be like by the time she was seven or eight months? Life threatened to become unbearable.

Early Sunday morning, the fifteenth of February, came, with little to do but sit indoors all day as with most Sundays, and probably get on with her enforced knitting. Mrs Ward inspected it every now and again, helping her with dropped stitches, advising her on how to keep the knitting even: 'You knit far too tightly, my dear. That's because you're too tense. Then when you relax, you knit looser. The result is an uneven garment. Try to remain relaxed all the time.'

But how could she? She hated Sundays. She wished Matthew was here. But he was thousands of miles away, in a sunny climate, enjoying himself. Margaret Ross had told her, when she'd got into a panic over the news of war opening up in the

Far East, that Pearl Harbor and Singapore which had been bombed at the same time were far far away from him. Mr Ward had confirmed that, adding – she suspected to make her feel better – that Matthew was probably living it up in India. Not that she didn't want him to enjoy himself, wasn't glad he was in no danger from this distant war; she just wanted him back here, a buffer between his mother and herself.

This Sunday she was feeling particularly desperate. It was the baby, beginning to twitch ever so slightly, already seeming to be pushing out the walls of her stomach. She needed to get out of the house without Mrs Ward there to hold her firmly by the arm, like some sergeant major.

That woman, why did she behave as if she had to be responsible for everyone else's well-being? Was it because she herself lacked something, was nursing a sense of inferiority, deep inside, needing to combat it by bossing everyone about? Perhaps it was a way of proving something to herself. But could anyone visualise Lilian Ward as ever having lacked self-confidence? Susan could imagine her at four years old, bossing all the kids about, even then managing everything for them; could imagine her in her crib consciously manipulating her mother with a cry, a squeal, a smile. Lilian Ward had been born managing. But she wasn't going to manage her!

Susan made up her mind. The weather looking passable, Mrs Ward was upstairs clearing out a cupboard in one of the back rooms, which she loved doing on Sunday mornings, Mr Ward looked ready to settle back with his Sunday paper, which he was never allowed to read over breakfast. Susan hastily donned coat, scarf, boots, and gloves and quietly opened the front door to let herself out. Just a short walk. She'd be back before they knew she'd gone. Mrs Ward might even assume she'd gone to lie down in her room for an hour though there was a chance she might look in to see if she was all right. There was never any need. Susan felt her health was magnificent. Gone was all that dreadful morning sickness when Mrs Ward would hurry into the bathroom after her, embarrassing when she was being sick, to wipe her brow and advise on how to prevent morning sickness: drink cold water, eat an apple.

'Is that you, Susan?' Her mother-in-law's bat-hearing had detected the door opening. Now she must answer.

163

'I just thought I'd wander down the road a bit. I need some fresh air.'

'Oh, no.' Already Mrs Ward was coming downstairs. 'The pavement is still a little icy. You'll slip and fall. You must not harm that baby.'

It was all she cared about, Susan thought uncharitably, the baby, the mother just an incubator for her son's child, someone else for her to fuss over, think for, do for, the way Matthew had described on one occasion.

'I just want to go out,' Susan blurted. 'I need to go out.'

'I'll come with you. I think I need a little fresh air myself.'

There was only one thing Mrs Ward really needed, to keep an eye on her. Slumping a little, Susan waited as the spotless flowered apron was taken off and outdoor clothes put on, the lightly greying short hair given a brief tidying pat and a hat put on over it. Mrs Ward had a wonderful clear skin, virtually unlined, and Susan thought as she waited for her that when young she must have been a very handsome woman. She still was, but so forceful. Meekly, Susan allowed herself to be conducted a short way across the icy road, in through the park gates, as far as its nearest bench and then back – a distance of no more than five hundred yards, not really a walk at all, and all the time with the woman's arm stayed tucked through hers, practically holding her up as though she were crippled or something. Susan was glad to get back indoors if only to escape to her room on the pretence of a lie-down after the walk, Mrs Ward approving wholeheartedly.

She had hardly closed her door and gone to her bed than she heard voices slightly raised downstairs. While Mrs Ward's voice had a penetrating quality to it, her husband's was always soft and thoughtful. Now, however, his could be heard above hers. Susan got up and opened the door again, the better to eavesdrop on this mystifying rise of voices.

'I think we should let her sleep on, rest, before we say anything,' he was saying.

'I think she should be told immediately,' came the reply.

'I don't think so, Lilian. You know how quickly she gets herself into a state.'

They had to be talking about her. What had she done to cause an argument? They had a damned cheek discussing her when she wasn't there. Becoming angry, she crept out on to the landing.

'Even so, he is her husband. She has a right to be told and as soon as possible.'

Susan made for the stairs. What had Matthew done that she must be told immediately of it? He hadn't found someone else, all those thousands of miles away? She felt sick as she ran into the living room. The two people were standing, their backs to her.

'What mustn't I be told?'

They had turned, were looking at her with a sort of dumb fear in their eyes. It was Mrs Ward who moved towards her first. Susan noticed that Mr Ward was holding the Sunday paper, half folded, half crumpled.

'My dear . . .' Mrs Ward began.

Her voice broke. She reached out and took Susan's arm in a vice-like grip but which Susan felt had been meant to be comforting. 'My dear, you must be strong. You mustn't allow yourself to become panicky.'

'What is it?' Susan asked, her heart already pumping like a little frightened animal behind her ribs although she had no idea why except the two people before her looked frightened and anxious, lending their anxiety to her.

'It's Matthew . . .' Mr Ward began, then checked himself. 'Well, not exactly Matthew, but it concerns him.' With that, he unfolded the newspaper and held it out for Susan to read. She had read with dismay of the fighting that had broken out in Singapore, how the Japanese had come down from the north through hundreds of miles of tangled jungle hitherto thought impassable for any human being, taking that city by surprise, and she had been mildly worried, but Singapore was still a long way from India.

Taking the paper from him while Mrs Ward turned away to gaze out of the window at the bare trees of the park opposite, Susan stared at the large black headlines:

SINGAPORE FALLS. GENERAL PERCIVAL SURRENDERS ON ORDERS
OF MR CHURCHILL TO PREVENT LOSS OF LIFE.

165

and then a smaller heading:

Susan looked up, imploring the couple as though they might be able to do something to make it all better. 'But they said Singapore could never fall. How could it happen?'

With the Japanese capturing Singapore, would Matthew be with those sent to recapture it? He would have to fight, and she had thought him safe. He could be wounded, killed. She'd never see him again. The thought filled her whole being as though glue was being poured into her body. Susan felt herself beginning to sway. The baby seemed to be jumping about inside her.

'I don't know,' Mr Ward was saying. 'All their defences point out to sea, they were so sure no enemy could ever come from the north. But they did. That's all I can say.'

But she hardly heard anything he said for the buzzing in her head. The room had begun to spin. The floor was coming up to meet her and she felt her body grow limp and lifeless. She vaguely felt someone catch her, felt herself being picked up and carried upwards in a jerky manner, guessed in her faint that this was the stairs. But her faint had become complete before Mr Ward ever laid her on her bed.

166

Chapter 15

It was a day of stifling heat. Vehicles lurching from one bomb crater to the next sent clouds of dust over the sweating shoulders of those trying to clear the road of stricken transport on this twenty-second day of February.

The railway bridge over the Sittang River, hastily converted to allow single-file traffic, was making progress slow and hazardous, on top of which a truck had run off the temporary decking, hopelessly blocking the bridge, the tailback now grinding to a standstill.

They were at the mercy not only of enemy aircraft, but of Allied planes who had been ordered to attack the advancing Japanese but not informed that any troops west of Kyaikto would be British, and thus were strafing the waiting columns out of hand. With more transport being knocked out and more men being killed and wounded, the state of the road became steadily worse.

Beneath a smoking carrier a dozen men lay huddled, heads down, as dive bombers screamed over the muddle of men and machinery. Bullets whining like angry hornets ricocheted off the metal sides of the vehicle, and in the ensuing din Bob Howlett's voice had as much power as the squeak of a mouse, begging that they make a run for it to the safety of the jungle.

Some had already sprinted for the trees looking for an easier way to the river, but orders were to hold the bridge for as long as was needed to get the transport across before they were all cut off.

Matthew held on to Bob's shirt to prevent him from making for the deceptive shelter of tangled greenery each side of the open road. 'Stay put! The Japs could already be there. A whole platoon of 'em would be on top of you before you could see them.'

Scarcely any of his mob was left. Taffy – poor libidinous Taffy – dead. Hadn't known what had hit him. Ronnie Clark with his hankering for the excitement of battle, dead. Eddie Nutt, Lieutenant Grice, dead. Sergeant Pegg, somewhere back there along the road, both legs gone, had grabbed Matthew by the shirt front and pulled him close, his bullet-head unbowed, his eyes still glaring though his pain. 'Yer in charge now, Ward. Yer wanted t'be an officer. Now see if yer c'n make somefing of yerself, prove yer can . . . Now git to it!' Letting go Matthew's shirt he sank back to stare at the bloody earth where his legs should have been and waited for the stretcher bearers, if there were any and if he was still alive by the time any did come for him.

Others of his platoon had been separated; of the survivors lying here beneath the shielding carrier, none of them was worth a light: Jeff Downey with chubby cheeks flabby and pallid with terror and fatigue, one side of his shirt stiff with blackening blood, his or someone else's, Matthew hadn't felt inclined to find out; Farrell nursing a shattered hand wrapped in a piece of his shirt; Bob as yet unscathed but becoming rapidly shell-shocked; a few men he didn't know, and himself, feeling as little like a leader as any could, his eyes sore from dust and lack of sleep, his throat clogged and burning, his cheeks sporting several days' stubble, his shirt and trousers caked with sweat and blood, thankfully not his own apart from digs and scratches collected from the lengthy retreat. But most of all his mind had gone quite blank as to how and whom he should be leading as Sergeant Pegg had demanded.

The rising crescendo of dive bombers seemed to expand inside his brain, smothering all ability to think. A bomb blast threw earth and rock high into the air beside the carrier with an ear-splitting fulmination of blinding light, making the vehicle jerk alarmingly as blast and chunks of white-hot metal slammed into it. One piece hissed past Matthew's cheek. Behind him came a gurgling, high-pitched shriek, a brief threshing about; then warm liquid gushed on to his back and he saw the victim flop and lie still.

Beside him Bob was curled into a tight foetal position. Downey was scrambling forward on all fours in an effort to get out from under the carrier and was screaming at the top of his voice: 'Oh, Jesus! We're gonna die – we're gonna die!'

Matthew threw himself on the man, hung grimly on to the squirming body as another string of explosions rocked the vehicle. 'You'll die all right out there.'

Farrell's voice was high with panic. 'Let the bleeder go, can't yer?'

'Shut your bloody mouth, Farrell!' His own voice sounded demented. So much for wanting to be an officer. He could hardly control himself, much less half a dozen panicking men. He felt utterly helpless.

The aircraft were wheeling off, leaving a strange silence. Ears accustomed to the din felt as though cotton wool had suddenly been stuffed into them. The planes would be back. Or perhaps they had realised they were bombing their own side. Oh, God, he hoped so. The panic under the carrier had melted away into shuddering breaths, trembling grunts, but for the moment it was safe to creep out and take stock.

Slowly, buzzing, deafened eardrums began to pick up sounds: the crackle of burning vehicles, the moans of the wounded, the urgent tone of men calling to each other, the crunch of boots running, the spasmodic revving of a lorry.

Shakily, shoving Bob ahead of him, Matthew crawled out, stood up, his legs feeling like rubber. Shattered transport lay everywhere. A truck with a cargo of wounded under a shredded tarpaulin had slewed across the road, its rear wheels in a bomb crater, gripping nothing while its excited Indian driver was revving the thing like a madman. Beside him an officer was leaning from the cab yelling orders to some Indian soldiers already trying to heave against its rear end without falling into the crater themselves.

Seeing the few men who had scrambled from under the carrier, he screeched, 'You lot, there! Give a hand. Give a hand.'

Matthew stared blankly at him, as yet incapable of a response. 'We've hurt men here.'

'Then get 'em on board and get this damned thing moving.'

The order brought Matthew back to his senses. No longer

needing to be a leader, he could take relief in letting someone else do the leading. He and Bob, Bob now coming back to himself with an apologetic grin for his previous show of weakness, helped get their own wounded aboard. Farrell was the first to climb in.

Men's weight was pitted against machine. 'One – two – three, heave!' the officer shrieked. The vehicle lifted, its back wheels back on firm ground; the driver touched the accelerator. The wheels span, briefly spraying dust over the men, then slipped back.

'Hold it! HOLD IT!' The officer's voice was full of panic. 'Again. One – two – three, heave! For Chrissake, HEAVE!'

From the direction of the crossing came the sudden rapid hammering of Bren-gun fire followed by the staccato crack of rifle fire. Caught by the knowledge that those at the river were having to turn and fight an enemy that had crept up on them, the men struggling with the truck paused.

The unsuspecting driver braked frantically but ineffectually and the vehicle slipped violently backwards. Cries of pain came from the wounded unceremoniously thrown about. Eyes rolling, the Indian soldiers exchanged cries of alarm in their own tongue, but it was Farrell leaning out over the tailboard of the stricken truck who said it explicitly.

'Oh, my bleeding Gawd, we're cut orf. We've 'ad it.' Very agile for one who a moment ago had been counted among the helpless injured, he was over of the tailboard and off, bolting towards the jungle.

'Stop that man!' To the officer's yell, Matthew added the power of his own lungs.

'Farrell – stay where you are!'

Farrell paused, Army training prevailing for all his panic, but his face as he turned twisted in an animal snarl of fear. 'Yer can't stop me. I've got a right ter git back ter me own lines. I'm pissin' orf.'

In one quick movement, Matthew unslung the rifle he still had on his back, levelling it at the man's groin. 'You do and I'll cripple you.'

In that moment he knew himself capable of carrying out the threat. It was as though he were another person, not because of his dislike of Farrell, but cold, clinical, the indurate soldier,

170

Army-crafted, a machine, hating what he had become. But he'd halted Farrell who for a moment stood uncertain, though whether he would have defied his corporal's threat or not was not to be discovered as twin dark shapes roared over the rim of the trees, their shadows passing between the sun and the men below. A clatter of machine-gun fire scattered men in all directions, as though a stone had dropped on a cluster of marbles.

Matthew did a nightmare scramble for the carrier again, it seemingly a mile away as he felt rather than saw a line of dust spurts heading his way. In his own panic, he never even heard the explosion of the direct hit on the truck he had been helping to shove.

The attacks continued into the afternoon. In the centre of the road the truck was ablaze, now interlocked with a ten-tonner that had come from nowhere it seemed. From the smoking cab the officer's body hung amid shreds of burned clothing gently wafting away in the upcurrent of heat from the vehicle. Of Farrell there was no sign. He had legged it to the trees and was gone.

The sun going down saw the waves of planes depart. The bridge was at least still being defended, with the heavy hammering of a Bren-gun which sounded almost dignified against the excited clatter of an enemy machine-gun. Occasionally there came the dull flat detonation of a mortar bomb. At one time he fancied he could hear the hollow cough of a bomb as it left the mortar's barrel, the enemy too close for comfort if he was right. After a while it ceased, the operators perhaps moving closer to their goal, ignoring the broken vehicles nearby, but his uneasiness lingered. Those passing him in the sudden darkness that descends in the tropics trod warily, bent double, weapon held tense as they tried to probe the shadows either side of the road.

It made the flesh creep, this sensation of being watched, imagination magnifying fear tenfold. But fear had no place here. There was work to do, a way to be made for vehicles laden with wounded and supplies to get through to the bridge. In the darkness lit by lurid flashes, Matthew heaved and sweated helping to clear blockages while all around came the incessant chirruping of insects impervious to the racket of men locked in battle. At least while the sound of fighting continued there was hope of getting through. Should it cease, it would mean the enemy had taken control.

It was with relief that he saw a staff car approaching out of the darkness, followed by a lorry full of Indian troops. The staff car held two obvious junior officers, even though they had ripped off their lapels and thrown away their caps, and a burly senior officer also minus his insignia.

With the road narrowed by the shattered ten-tonner, the car stopped. The burly officer got out. 'Where's your officer, corporal?'

Matthew indicated the body hanging from the burned-out truck. The man sighed, surveying the tangled wreckage. 'Not having much luck here.'

As Matthew explained his lack of men and tools, the lips beneath the dusty moustache gave a small, tight, tired smile. 'My men will take over, corporal. Corporal . . .?'

'Ward, sir,' Matthew supplied.

'I'm Captain Weatherill. You and your men get some rest. You may need it.' He nodded towards the flashes around the bridge up ahead. 'By the way, the Japs have cut the road at Mokpalin,' he added as calmly as if announcing a cricket score.

Mokpalin, only three miles back, meant they were virtually caught in a neat pincer movement. For a moment, a feeling of doom spread through Matthew together with an irrational impulse to run towards the bridge, to race across and keep going until he got home to Susan and safety. It came to him that he might very well never see her again.

'Dear God,' prayed the panic within him, 'please; get me out of this. Let it all be a dream.'

Beside him Bob's voice came hollow. 'You mean we're trapped?'

The sound of that voice returned Matthew's sanity to him in a rush.

'We're going to get out okay,' he said, more to still his own fears than to reassure Bob. His mouth sour, he lifted a hand to his eyes and with finger and thumb grubbed out the caked dust that had collected at the inner corners. To ease the ache between his shoulder-blades he straightened his back. It was a gesture Weatherill immediately took as determination.

'Good man,' he grunted and left them to find a hole by the road to creep into and rest for a while.

Beside him Bob was fast asleep. Other men also were sleeping, but his own rest was fitful. For something to keep his imagination at bay he took a sip of the warm metallic water from his canteen, rinsed it around his mouth and spat it out, thick and evil, then took another sip and swallowed it. In the canteen the water slapped hollowly. How grand to have been able to wash, if only his face. To think of millions of gallons of fresh water flowing by just half a mile away. He listened to the spasmodic firing and wondered how much longer the two sides would continue taking pot shots at each other. He thought of Susan, the child she bore. He thought drowsily that if he were to get up now before it got light and go towards the firing, the river, there might be a chance . . .

A hand on his shoulder brought him awake, grabbing for his rifle. The grip tightened.

'Easy, lad.' Weatherill stood over him. 'Be light in a few minutes. Get your men together.'

Firing could still be heard from the bridge, a little more energetic in the fast-brightening tropical morning. The driver of the staff car, a cheeky Cockney, was handing out cubes of corned beef, the tin opened with his bayonet. 'We're orf, mate,' he said to Matthew. ''Ad a dekko darn the road. It ain't so bad furver along. A few obstructions but we can all git fru. Once we're over that bleedin' bridge we'll all 'ave a nice cuppa tea at HQ.'

Matthew grinned at his Cockney optimism and was on the point of helping himself to a greasy cube of the corned beef when a terrific triple explosion rocked the already pink dawn.

For a second or two the firing from both sides stopped as though paralysed by the tremendous paroxysm, and in the lull its echoes rumbled away into the distance with slowly diminishing reverberations.

'Mother of Jesus! What the hell was that?' one of the junior officers called out, running over.

Weatherill's answer was one of incredulity. 'They've blown the bridge.' A pall of smoke was spiralling slowly above the tree-tops.

173

The other man's voice shook. 'Bloody HQ. Couldn't wait for us. Left us in the lurch, thousands of us. They panicked.'

Weatherill didn't dispute him. Headquarters had probably had no alternative if the Japanese had been threatening to swarm across. It had been the plan, to delay the enemy's advance on Rangoon enough to allow Allied reinforcements to arrive.

After the first shock of the explosion, hostilities resumed with even greater ferocity, each man now desperately fighting for his own life, gone all thoughts of saving transport and artillery.

Weatherill lost no time. 'We'll try the river further upstream. Thank God this isn't the monsoon. The river should be low.'

'What about the wounded?' Matthew asked. The enemy, it was rumoured, had its own methods with casualties. Weatherill didn't even look at him.

'If they can walk and if they can be quiet, they come too.'

His words were met by silence, the men around him knowing there was no other suggestion to be made. He waited a moment or two for any there might be, then turned and without a word moved towards the trees. The others followed mutely, the green world closing in barely thirty feet into the trees, hiding the abandoned wounded quickly from guilt-ridden sight.

Here even any continuing rifle fire was muffled, the canopy a hundred feet or more above them cutting out all sunlight in a tangle of vines and parasitic growth, echoing only to the whirring of insects and the bell-like early-morning calls of forest birds. Grey wreathing mists of morning lay in motionless flat layers, but as the sun rose they turned delicate pink and lifted steadily through the ceiling of miniature jungle above to disappear. Within minutes that ceiling was pressing the heat down on the men, saturating them with sweat, the soft and spongy earth under their feet smelling dank.

Progress remained snail-like. In some areas the great mottled tree-trunks stood like dead-straight pillars of some vast cathedral, lianas draped from one to the other with curtains of green moss hanging from them. Sometimes the forest thinned enough to allow shafts of sunlight through and vegetation to become rampant, scrambling for light with vivid colouring, thick clumps of bamboo around which the men must time after time make diversions. In half an hour they had covered just half a mile, bearing northeast as much as those diversions allowed.

Breathing heavily from the now steamy heat which by midday would reach ninety degrees or more, arms aching from pushing aside the tough, woody creepers, legs aching from negotiating a surprisingly undulating terrain, from somewhere to their left came the gurgle of water.

'Should see some open space soon,' Weatherill predicted in a whisper. 'Paddy fields probably. We could be easily spotted. Keep your heads down.'

After ten more minutes pushing through undergrowth, they came upon a proper path, the forest beginning to thin.

In the sudden brilliant sunlight, Weatherill crouched just off the path, beckoning to his men to follow suit. 'I think there's a village ahead. Could be sitting ducks if we blunder in there. We'd best skirt it, find the river and somewhere to swim across. Come on, but quietly.'

He stood up, the rest taking their cue from him. A sudden movement of foliage, the metallic sound of hands on rifles, froze the group. In a strange language, a guttural voice grated out a command.

From nowhere there appeared small men in drab tunics with double belts, short legs bound in puttees to the knee, and split canvas boots that divided the big toes from the rest. Black shoe-button eyes trained on the group from behind levelled rifles with incredibly long bayonets; for all their size each man looked strong, immensely capable and very much a fighting man, utterly at home in this hostile environment.

One by one the surprised men let their rifles fall and lifted their arms in the time-honoured abject signal of surrender as their captors moved closer. There were some twenty-five of them plus their officer – that many moving so silently no one had heard them at all.

With a sickness pounding in his chest, Matthew lifted his arms with the rest, submitted himself to be searched by a soldier reaching only to his shoulder in height. His pockets and ration pack were emptied of all he possessed: silver cigarette case, lighter, a little Burmese money, a photo of Susan. It was the photo that hurt most, seeing it scrutinised then torn into four pieces and flung away. The silver cigarette case and lighter were handed to the Japanese officer who immediately pocketed them with a satisfied smile.

Chapter 16

'We'll get another letter from him very soon. You really must stop fretting, Susan. It isn't good for the baby.'

Susan eyed her mother-in-law, just managing to hold back the tears that threatened and which always annoyed the woman. But every time she thought of Matthew's last letter she couldn't help them rising to the surface.

The one prior to that had said he had been over the moon about her news of the baby, and she'd been so happy that he was happy. It had said they were leaving Bombay though where for, as usual, hush-hush.

His last letter had come two days ago, a single page written in pencil in such an obvious hurry she could hardly read it, the soiled notepaper in an even more soiled envelope telling her not to worry, he was all right, that in itself worrying her more although she wasn't sure why. It bore a military Rangoon postmark. Rangoon was in Burma, Mr Ward had told her, and she had heard fear echoing in his tone.

Her geography never good, she'd quickly consulted an atlas, alarmed how near the fighting Matthew had been sent. News from that part of the world had all been of disaster: the sinking of two large Royal Navy ships, the *Prince of Wales* and the *Repulse*, the fall of Hong Kong on Christmas Day, then Singapore on the fifteenth of February four weeks ago. Now it was March. There was fighting in Burma and Matthew's last letter, grubby and stained, made her shiver with imaginings she daren't voice; none of them dared, though the look on their faces said they were thinking the same as she was.

Why was it, Margaret thought, that when she was with Ronald she could talk without a pause about all sorts of things, completely at ease in his company, yet the very anticipation of going to meet him never failed to fill her with strange reluctance, wishing she didn't have to?

'Have a quick drink in the pub tonight?' he'd whisper as they passed in a corridor, if their off-duty hours coincided. 'Wait for you outside.'

She would nod, smile, aware of a sinking feeling, a wish to be doing anything other than meeting him, even preferring to go home to spend a dull evening with Mumsy. There was none of that excited palpitation a girl in love was supposed to experience – the way she used to feel all those years ago when Matthew Ward came into sight or inadvertently touched her. The touch of Ronald's hand on hers did nothing, though if he kissed her, her body would stir, responding of its own accord. Then her head would start to send messages that this wasn't love, but a natural response to the touch of any man halfway handsome. Yet it made no sense to shy away from the knowledge that marriage to Ronald could be the best thing to happen to her; she would become the wife of a general practitioner.

'It's still early days,' she'd hedged. 'Too many people are rushing into marriage because it seems the right thing to do.'

'Don't you want to marry me?' he had asked only last week, towards the end of February. What could she say?

'Of course I do.'

But was she lying, to him and herself? They had had their very first row, as far as it was possible to row with Ronald, who was always even-tempered.

'Then for God's sake why delay it? It's not as if I've nothing to offer you. My family's pretty well off. My father's a GP. Soon I'll be one as well.'

She knew that. He was taking his finals in a couple of weeks and was more than certain that he'd pass. He had talked often of the day when he too would be a GP expected to go in with his father as a junior partner. Perhaps it was that which made her so reluctant about marriage and the assumption that she would accompany him to Bristol. It meant leaving her mother, who still deemed herself lonely after all this time with Margaret

178

not getting home regularly each night. Her mother was destined to become even more isolated if Margaret went off to live on the other side of the country – the other side of the world as far as she was concerned.

'If you go into your father's practice I shall end up in Bristol,' she argued obstinately and saw his lips tighten a fraction. 'There's my mother to think of. I can't leave her all on her own.'

She could have suggested he find some other practice around here, but some quiet little voice said it would be tempting fate – he might agree and she would then have no option but to say yes to his expectations of their marrying.

He had fallen quiet, had sat away from her, his brow furrowed. She too had sat silent over her mild ale and the evening during which they would normally have chattered away like a couple of monkeys had become long and tense until it was she who said she ought to be going to catch the last bus home. He had nodded, got up, got her coat for her and helped her on with it and had said, 'See you tomorrow then. I'll see you to the bus stop.'

This week, during another quick drink in the pub opposite the hospital, the row that had been simmering, exploded. Quietly, but it exploded just the same.

'I've had enough of this, Margaret.' Ronald's voice was harsher than she had ever heard it. 'What the hell do I have to do to show you how much I love you?'

She had to say it now. 'I don't want to go to live in Bristol all that way away.'

'I can't go without you.'

And now she must add: 'Then can't you try for a practice somewhere local, around here?' There, she had said it, had burned her last bridge.

Ronald looked at her, his brows meeting in anger at her selfishness. 'You want me to scratch around here looking for some half-baked practice that'll take me years to get anywhere with when I've an already made place with my father? You must be mad, Margaret. Don't you want to see me get on?'

'Of course I do.' She felt lame.

'Don't you love me?'

'Yes, Ronald.' She wished he wouldn't keep pushing that question.

'Well, it doesn't sound like it to me.'

A group of American servicemen with smooth smart uniforms and girls on their arms, bustling past, filling the pub with their loud easy twang and high spirits, put paid to the couple's quiet argument. Ronald threw them a frown, and repeated his statement a little more audibly. 'It doesn't sound like it to me.'

'Because I don't want to go traipsing all the way to Bristol, leaving my mother? What is this, Ronald – a demand for self-sacrifice?'

'In a way, yes.'

'But you're not prepared to sacrifice yourself when it comes to you.'

'Look, I shall be the breadwinner. I've got to consider what's best for our future. Can't you see that? If you really loved me, Margaret, it wouldn't seem to you like self-sacrifice – as you call it.'

There came screams of laughter from the GIs' girls. Margaret felt tears come into her eyes. 'If that's what you think of me, Ronald, the little lamb ready to follow its shepherd up hill and down dale, I've got a career too. I've studied hard, and I've still got a lot of studying to do, and I want to get somewhere, not just be a GP's wife, sitting at home, joining nice little ladies' clubs and doing your book work. Eventually I'd have liked to go into the QAs.'

This was the Queen Alexandra's Imperial Military Nursing Service Reserve. She hadn't really thought about going into the QAs before, but she thought of it now, more out of anger than ambition.

Ronald was staring at her. The ruckus from the GIs and their girls was getting worse, but they had good money to spend and the landlord would suffer them. The look on Ronald's face tore at Margaret's whole being.

'I had no idea that was all you cared for me, Margaret. You'd sooner join up than marry me.'

'No, darling, that's not what I meant. I want to marry you.' Now, suddenly, she did, seeing herself throwing away the chance of a lifetime. Did she really think she wanted to go on nursing for the rest of her life, to go off and be a Queen

Alexandra's nurse, to take orders when she could live in comfort with a man who loved her? 'Ronald, I really do love you.'

He sat looking at her for a long while, as she watched him, visualising what was going on in his mind, her protestations fallen short. Then he stood up, and got her coat, as always helping her on with it, for he was a caring man even when hurt and angry. Wordlessly, she let him guide her from the now noisy pub. Outside, he took her in his arms and kissed her.

'Perhaps I have been rushing things,' he said in the quiet night, the sounds from inside muffled by the closure of the pub door. 'What I wanted to tell you, darling, is that I got my results today. I've passed.'

She leaned back from his embrace. 'Why didn't you tell me?'

'I don't know. I was going to, but somehow we ended up discussing something else instead.' He wouldn't say row. Easier to call it discussing. But he wasn't finished yet.

'Margaret, darling, I know now that you're not yet ready to commit yourself – not to me or to anyone. But I love you. And I think, deep down, you love me, but there's something in the way. Maybe it's your mother. But you must break away from the hole you're stuck in. So I think it best I let you consider things before you make up your mind what you want to do. In a week or two I'll be leaving to go home to start up in my father's practice. I'll write to you and if you do change your mind about coming to Bristol, I'll be waiting. I'll keep on loving you, Margaret. I won't give up hope. I just want you think about everything and what we are throwing away.'

Tears were streaming down Margaret's cheeks. Now was the time to burst out that she did love him, that she wanted to go with him. But she didn't. For the most futile of reasons. And the moment vanished.

A bleak spring had followed a bleak new year, that first elation at the United States coming into the war dissipating; everywhere Margaret saw set faces that spoke of grim determination to believe things must only get better.

In the Middle East, Rommel, seemingly invincible, had struck back and recaptured Benghazi. At sea the German battleships *Scharnhorst* and *Gneisenau* slipped their hide-out at Brest under the very noses of the British Navy and in attempting to sink them the RAF lost forty planes. Ceylon was raided by the Japanese, the British Eastern Fleet withdrew to Kenya; Britain had abandoned the Far East.

The London Hospital's outpatient department seemed to be full of women showing the strain of trying not to dwell on loved ones away. Women with drawn faces, complaining of backache, neuralgia, stomach pains, stiff necks, strange agitation, trembling hands. 'I c'n 'ardly keep meself still in the mornin', doctor'; 'I'm fair sick of this bloody back of mine'; 'I've got these legs, doctor, wot keeps on swellin'; and usually as he examined whatever compaint presented itself, came the inevitable self-diagnosis: 'Wiv'art me ole man at 'ome I feel lorst.'

Margaret, helping in outpatients, knew how they felt thinking of those absent faces. Too often she thought of one absent face in particular. Since the fall of Rangoon in Burma, Susan Ward said she'd not had any letters from her husband and the Wards were growing anxious. Lots of wives and mothers were going through that strain, added to which was the constant worry of eking out the rations for those still at home. Shoppers needed to be ever more watchful for opportunities to present themselves in the food line.

It wasn't unusual to see whole streets come to life with hurrying women. Coats, aprons, scarves billowing like schooners in full sail as they converged on some butcher's shop from which whispers had emanated: "E's got offal!' Margaret's mother and even the proud Mrs Ward joined in the hasty advance. Margaret would pass a growing queue of women now waiting patiently and not leaving until every last scap of off-ration meat had gone. Nothing stopped the unending search for something nutritious to fill a plate: horse meat, goat, stringy fishy-tasting whale meat being tried out.

'I got a little bit of goat meat,' Margaret's mum told her on one occasion – succulent, tender meat it was too, except, unused to such rich fare, they were both sick. Margaret stayed off duty all next day much to the displeasure of the ward sister. Otherwise, things went on as normal, the tip-and-run daylight raids on country towns like York and Bath and Exeter (Margaret thought of Jean Summerfield whose family had left

London to escape all that) virtually ignored by Londoners, who had suffered the Blitz.

The evening she came home from the hospital, still a little queasy from the enjoyable meal of goat meat, she met Susan wandering along by herself, her coat tight about her stomach. The early March evening was still light, summer time's extra hour still prevailing. Susan looked wan, and hardly smiled as she saw Margaret coming towards her from the bus stop.

'Have you heard from Matthew yet?' was the first question out of her mouth. Susan shook her head.

'Nothing yet. I hope he's all right.'

'He's bound to be. Otherwise they'd have said. You'd have heard.'

'It's been nearly three weeks. I've not been out of the house in ages. I'm so fed up. I'd like to go to the pictures or something, but his parents don't go. I can't go on my own, so I'm stuck.'

Margaret found herself amazed at how easily the girl had slipped from concern at not hearing anything from Matthew to talking at far greater length of her own boredom. She would have thought the former worry would oust everything else from her mind.

'If you like,' she offered, giving Susan the benefit of any doubts, 'we could go to the pictures together. I'm off next weekend. *Casablanca* is on at the Regent in Mare Street. There are bound to be long queues, but we could go early on Saturday afternoon, if you can stand lining up.'

Susan's face was a picture of eagerness. 'Oh, that's ever so nice of you. I'd love to do that, I really would.'

'Then that's what we'll do.'

In her bedroom Susan stared into the mirror at the hardly noticeable lump. It would get larger and larger and she'd never be able to escape. Going to the Regent with Margaret Ross looked like being her last trip out, with Mrs Ward getting ever more attentive.

Just over four months pregnant, and being slightly built, even that tiniest bulge made her look dreadful. There was no one to reassure her that she still looked beautiful, no one to lay a loving hand on her stomach or to gaze on her with pride in her and himself at what they had achieved, no one to tell her she was a clever girl and that he adored her. When this baby was born there'd be no one there to hold it and gaze down on it in wonder. Only God could say when Matthew would return home. As yet she'd not heard a thing from him since that last letter at the end of February. It was March now. Early March, it was true, but waiting made it seem longer. She trembled for him, dared not think of his never coming back. Whatever would she do without him? The thought made her feel sick.

Hastily, she turned from the mirror, trying to push such dreadful thoughts from her, and feverishly got dressed. They'd get his letter soon. Military mail from that part of the world was a bugger, the time it took.

A ring on the front doorbell swept away all her dismal anxiety. Maybe it was the postman. Hurrying from her room she leaned over the banister in time to see her father-in-law closing the door. Aware of her standing there, he looked up, his eyes wide as though with guilt, but she knew it was fear for she had seen the telegram he held. Even from here the blurred bold black letters OHMS leapt out at her, searing through her brain, sending her rushing headlong down the stairs. 'Matthew! It's about Matthew.'

Leonard caught her as she reached him, took her arm and guided her into the lounge through which the early March sunlight was slanting.

'Lilian,' he called as he sat Susan down in one of the armchairs; she felt struck dumb with growing terror. 'Lilian, come here, dear. It's important.'

As Mrs Ward came hurrying in, Susan found her voice. 'It's Matthew! Oh, God, it's Matthew!'

Neither took any notice of her or seemed to hear her as Leonard tore open the envelope, extracting the buff paper to read. He looked up bleakly.

'It says Matthew's missing.'

'No!' Susan's voice rose to a scream. She leapt up, tore the telegram from his hands, but the words blurred, her brain seemed to be exploding and the scream that came from her lips seemed not to be her own, a hollow screaming that went on and on: 'He's dead . . . Matthew's dead . . .'

The telegram fell from her fingers and she felt herself taken on a blind, headlong rush from the room, though where she was going she had no idea; she found herself clinging on to the newel post of the stairs, unable to let go of it. And still the hollow, terrible screaming continued, consuming her.

What happened next was a vague blur of being picked up, of being carried, of being laid down, then shaken until her head felt it would fall off her shoulders. That irrational fear was what brought her to her senses and she found herself looking into the stern face of her mother-in-law.

'Get a hold of yourself, Susan. You must remember the baby – his baby.'

Damn the baby! Tears squeezed between her eyelids as she screwed them tight. 'Matthew's dead . . .'

The hands holding hers were like stiff, dry claws giving no comfort at all. 'He's not dead, Susan. It says he's missing. They will trace him soon. We must cling to that hope. You must cling to it. For his sake. For the sake of his baby.'

'That's all you care about,' she burst out in her grief. '*His* baby – a baby to take *his* place. You don't care about me at all, how I feel.'

'We do, Susan.' They didn't, but she had no strength left to argue.

'The pain's still there in my stomach,' she complained from her bed. She'd been in bed for two days, ever since the dull ache had started. Now she saw Mrs Ward's expression of sympathetic concern change to one of apprehension.

'The doctor said it isn't what we thought it might be, but that you are upset and probably strained yourself when you lost control of yourself, and that we must just keep an eye on you. But doctors can be wrong and I really think we ought to get you to a hospital if this doesn't improve.'

'No!' Susan's voice rose in terror. She had a naked fear of hospitals; it dated from when she had been a child and had had her tonsils out. It had been an awful experience. The smell of the place, a mixture of antiseptic and ether, its green and cream tiled walls and age-yellowed ceilings, all pressed in on her, and the hush of the ward as night had come down emphasised the feeling of being alone away from her parents, shut away from the cosy world outside as though it was a different place – as hell might be, or death. She'd cried for her mother

185

and a stern-faced nurse had told her to be quiet. Taken on a hard, rumbling trolley along corridors and into a stark white room with horrid glittering steel instruments hanging from the ceilings, an evil-smelling rubber mask had been put over her face until her mind seemed to swirl away into a roaring blackness. The next day her throat had hurt terribly and she wasn't allowed to eat and when she cried another nurse had told her off. And all the time that peculiar rustling hush and muted voices and that horrible disinfectant smell. She'd never been near a hospital since, unable even to bring herself to visit anyone in there. The mere thought of going into one brought back the memories of its smell. It must have done something to her because to this day her whole body would cringe from anything savouring of it, from those with a hacking cough to someone with a cut finger. Even an unsightly scar could make her body tingle with revulsion. How Margaret Ross or anyone could bring herself to be a nurse was beyond her.

Mrs Ward was looking down at her. How could she be expected to understand? 'If the pain gets any worse, you will *have* to go to hospital.'

This left Susan gritting her teeth against the dull ache for fear of the threat being carried out. Bidden by the doctor to lie as still as possible in bed for the next week, she did all that was asked of her, determined no one would get her anywhere near the gates of any hospital.

Mrs Ward wrote to Susan's parents. They came hurrying down from Birmingham; the content of Mrs Ward's letter had frightened them. They found Susan looking much better than they had thought, with the pain almost gone, but she was still confined to bed – just in case, said the doctor.

As soon as Susan saw them, she burst into tears and, when Mrs Ward prudently retired from the room, she threw her arms around her mother to be cuddled and crooned over in privacy. She hadn't realised until then how much she had missed her mother.

'Mum, oh, Mum – take me home. I hate it here.'

Her mother let go of her slightly to gaze around the pretty pink bedroom. 'Whatever for, love? This is really lovely. Matthew's parents look after you so well, better'n like I ever could in our crowded house.'

'Don't talk of Matthew,' Susan pleaded tearfully. 'The telegram said he's missing, but it's only another way of telling us he's bin killed.'

'Don't say things like that, Sue.' Her mother leaned back to look up at her husband, seeking help from him, to which he responded in his usual way, merely repeating what had already been said as though that cemented it all perfectly.

'No, don't say things like that, Sue.'

'You've got to 'ave faith, love. He'll come back, right as rain, you'll see. When this war's all over, love, you and him, you'll both pick up like where you left off, and you'll 'ave a little baby then to look after, like. So you got to be strong and look after yourself, for Matthew and for his baby's sake.'

'I could do, at home,' Susan whimpered as her mother gently broke free of her arms, almost as though she were glad to be released of them. 'If I was home, Mum, with you to look after me, everything'd be all right. I hate it here. With Matthew gone, I don't feel I've got any business here.'

'Sue, love, he ain't gone. He's alive somewhere, waiting to be found by the Army. You make it sound as if you think he'll never come back. And look, love, we couldn't have you home with us. You know there's no room. There was hardly no room when you was single, much less when you've got a baby with you. And honestly, our Sue, look what you've got here. No, love, I do think you're better off staying here with Mr and Mrs Ward. They really are nice people and you're being so well looked after.'

So that was that. Abandoned by her own family. Over the next couple of weeks, she rested, slowly recovering, the baby still firmly entrenched inside her. There had been moments when she would have put her hands together if she had lost the baby. Growing more convinced that Matthew must have been killed, lying unfound somewhere in the jungle with creepers and undergrowth hiding his body and (the mere thought made her weep until her eyes appeared permanently red and swollen) the horrid creeping things slowly devouring it, a baby would only be a painful reminder of the love and happiness they'd once shared. She couldn't give her love to a baby when her love for Matthew was of no use to anyone any more. Then, as she recovered, she wasn't so much glad as relieved that she hadn't lost the baby after all. It hadn't grown so much that she was yet attached to it in her mind, but if Matthew had really been killed and was at this moment actually looking down on her, he'd never forgive her for such thoughts about it as she'd had.

If only she'd been asked to go home, it might all be so different. But now she was being pampered all the more by Mrs Ward, who was nothing to her, this in-law business thrust on her, yet was assuming the role of loving mother. She could see no escape. At home she might for the time being go out and enjoy herself, still go off to dances, perhaps dance with some of the young servicemen, Yanks, Canadian, the Free French, the Polish and the British boys, and still be admired for a while. Here, she was trapped, expected to play the wife when there was no one to play wife to.

To escape the sensation of being smothered and continually watched over, she would spend hours in her room reading the limp, buff-coloured magazines that wartime austerity forbade shiny covers. Sometimes she read increasingly tatty books from the library, love books mostly – easy-to-follow love stories with handsome heroes and violet-eyed heroines. They'd bring back a flood of memories, desolate now, of when she and Matthew had made love, had been in love. She'd pretend he was still making love to her, but it brought such wishing that she tried not to imagine it too much. Then she'd throw the book down and weep with loneliness, stifling her sobs in her pillow in case Mrs Ward came hurrying in to see what was the matter. As if the woman couldn't see why she was crying.

Chapter 17

Halfway through April, when her stomach was really beginning to show and not much chance of going out anywhere presented itself, there was no one to talk to. With Matthew's sister serving as a Wren in Southampton even Louise's company was denied her. She'd have felt even more trapped if it hadn't been for Margaret Ross popping in now and again. She'd become a good friend and confidant.

For Margaret, an hour or two with Susan on those evenings when she wasn't with her friends from the London could be a change from sitting with her mother who seemed to want to lean on her more and more. She often wondered how Mumsy would have coped had she married Ronald.

It had been strange not seeing his face about the hospital. She had found herself looking for him, missing him, but as anyone would miss a face no longer there, she told herself. One didn't have to love the person in order to feel keenly that empty place his going had left. She busied herself and put him from her mind.

As promised, he had written to her, a friendly letter, a little formal perhaps, wondering if she had thought any more about the things he'd last spoken of. He phrased the question itself slightly obliquely – no mention at all about the ring, which she still had tucked away in a box. She had replied, sounding just as friendly, just as formal, skirting the question. She had not meant it to be such a short letter, but there wasn't much to say. Time had gone on too long for that. She had wanted so much to say she'd changed her mind but when it came down to it, couldn't.

As time went on the wish had diminished, the dilemma's sharp edges had blunted somewhat. His departure had left a hole, but had she truly loved him, surely it would have left a much larger hole that would have taken a lot more to fill. And that impulsive statement she had made at the time about joining the QAs, then just a silly idea to get out of a spot, began to take more shape. The more she thought about it, the more attractive it was becoming. She'd be given a chance to travel overseas, to see the world, to meet new people, to expand her life. Mumsy wouldn't be too pleased but she had to get out of the rut that Ronald had accused her of being in. The QAs had such smart uniforms too, grey and scarlet with ties and snappy-brimmed hats, unlike the drab dress of ordinary nurses. She'd be tending fighting men instead of, now the Blitz was over, ordinary civilian ills and ailments. But first she had to pass her remaining exams. Prepared to work hard, she'd thrown herself into her work and looked very like passing her exams with flying colours come summer. All that would remain then would be to sit her finals that would turn her into an SRN. Then it would be off into the QAs in earnest.

She sat now talking to Susan in the living room. Mrs Ward was out at one of her many women's meetings, Mr Ward in the lounge listening to the evening news on the wireless and reading his evening paper.

'The Red Cross hasn't come up with anything at all,' Susan was saying, sitting back in a fireside chair nursing the growing bulge over her stomach. She looked particularly down this evening. 'His parents have made lots of enquiries, but he's never been traced. They can only guess he might be a prisoner of war but the Japanese aren't giving out any lists.'

'But they should,' Margaret said, aghast. She had felt the news of Matthew, or lack of it, as keenly as anyone, and in private had shed tears. 'The Geneva Convention says all sides must declare lists of prisoners.'

'The Japanese apparently think they're exempt because they never signed anything, or whatever. So no one knows if Matthew's been captured or gone missing or been ... you know.' Tears flooded the deep blue eyes.

'You mustn't give up hope,' Margaret said in an effort to console.

'What's the point?' Susan got up and began pacing the room, going to fiddle with the heavy curtains that concealed the blackout material, drawn now with the gathering dusk outside. Margaret watched her.

'If he's been taken prisoner, that has to be better news than it might have been.' Meant to give comfort, it only came out clumsy and tactless. She tried to amend it. 'You've just got to hang on to hope.'

Susan swung round, almost viciously. 'Hope! It's all right for you to talk. You didn't love him like I did, so how do you know what it's like not knowing what's happened to him?'

To combat the pain that retort invoked, Margaret got up and came to stand beside her. When she spoke her voice sounded flat even to her. 'Can you be that sure no one knows how you feel?'

Susan gave a sullen shrug. 'All I know is that if he's a prisoner of war, it'll be years before he ever comes home again, not till the war's over, and that could be God knows how long. And in the meantime, there's me stuck here. If I go on living in this mausoleum much longer, I'll go mad. I've got to get away from here before I get any bigger and can't at all.'

Again came the feeling that Susan wasn't thinking so much of Matthew, possibly in danger if indeed he hadn't been killed, as of herself and the loneliness *she* felt. Everyone was lonely who had a loved one away fighting, not knowing if they'd be killed or captured, but they usually kept it to themselves. Susan was too outspoken for her own good. It made her look bad.

'Where would you go if you left here?' she asked.

'Home. And as soon as I can. Trouble is, there's no room at me mum and dad's with our Robert and Les and our John there, and June and our Beryl. I'd rent a room somewhere nearby, but at least I'd be near my family. I'd have me mum near me. If only I wasn't having this baby . . .'

She broke off, not in shame at what she'd said, but swamped by the injustice of it all; Margaret could hear it in her tone. The girl's next words confirmed it.

'Why did all this have to happen to me? It's not fair! Landed with a baby, and Matthew God knows where.'

She began to pace around the room again while Margaret

followed her with her eyes, the sympathy she had initially felt for the girl draining away.

'Haven't you stopped to think how dreadfully unfair it must be to Matthew?' She couldn't control the anger in her voice. 'Wherever he is, he can't be having much of a time either.'

She refused to think him dead. It was unthinkable. One day he would come home and take up his life again. That was all she ever wanted, to see him come home and be happy. The wish for that caught her like a pain. But not as great a pain as being compelled to keep her feelings for Matthew to herself when all she wanted was to sing them from the rooftops.

A day didn't go by that she didn't pray for his safe return. The notion of never seeing him again tore her to pieces. It was bad enough to know that if and when he did come home he and Susan could go off into the blue, that she would never see them again. But at least he would be in this world, somewhere. Far worse to know that he was gone from this world entirely. How dare this girl, his wife who professed to love him so dearly, take the news of his being missing as though she alone suffered – *her* loneliness, *her* grief, *her* plight, not his plight, not the worry and grief of his family, but hers.

Beneath the anger that welled up in Margaret was a dull ache for Matthew which she was sure would stay with her the rest of her life if he never came home again. And here was Susan thinking of him only in terms of herself.

'Wherever he is?' Susan's voice had risen in near hysteria. 'Wherever he is? Don't you understand? He's dead. Matthew's dead! And here I am trying to be a wife, living with people that mean nothing to me.'

'You're carrying Matthew's child. His parents' grandchild. That's what they should mean to you, Susan.'

'Well, they don't. Everyone keeps saying he's been taken prisoner, but I *know* he's dead, lying out there somewhere in that terrible jungle where no one can find him, his body being...'

'Don't talk like that!' Susan had conjured up visions in her mind too awful to bear. 'There had to be others with him. They'd have reported...'

'I don't care! All I know is he's not here and I am, and I

can't take much more of this living with his parents. They're not *my* family.'

'They're your baby's family.'

'I don't care,' she said again. 'I don't want this baby anyway, not now Matthew's gone. All I want is to get away from here. I have to get away.'

She broke off in a flood of tears and threw herself back into the fireside chair, head twisted into one of its wings, her small body convulsed with weeping.

The door opened. Mrs Ward in hat and coat came hurrying into the room. 'Susan! What is the matter? I could hear you shouting as I came in.'

Mr Ward had followed her in, also alerted by the cries. 'What in God's name is going on?'

'Susan is upset,' Margaret offered but neither of them looked at her.

Mrs Ward came forward and lifted the still-weeping girl from her huddled position in the chair. 'This happens each time someone tries to offer sympathy,' she said sharply, and Margaret might have taken umbrage had she not seen the girl's reaction for herself and heard the things she had said.

'Come on now, Susan,' Mrs Ward was ordering as Margaret stood aside, unsure whether to stay or go, both of which seemed ill-mannered. 'Pull yourself together now. We're all worried and anxious, but it does no good to give way like this. We all have to be strong. We all have to believe he'll be returned to us. You're doing yourself and the baby no good. Matthew wouldn't want that. I'm taking you up to your room and you can rest there.'

Helping the girl to her feet, she looked at Margaret for the first time.

'Having visitors seems to upset her even more,' she said with a small, cold smile which Margaret could only take personally, this time smarting from the rebuff. But the things Susan had said made Margaret herself prefer not to pop in and see her again. Let the girl do what she wanted. It was none of her business. And yet came the thought that in the depths of her, Matthew *was* her business, would always be her business wherever he might be.

193

She had intended to wait until at least after the baby was born. But after one miserable evening in early May, still with no news at all of Matthew, and with Mrs Ward telling her for the umpteenth time that they were all worried and anxious for him, Susan made up her mind. Early next morning, she got up before Mr and Mrs Ward were awake and feverishly packed her suitcase with a few essentials. It mustn't be too heavy. She was nearly seven months and she didn't want to harm herself in any way carrying it.

She had enough money, thank God, something under twenty shillings a week serviceman's wife allowance, and her National Savings book. Mrs Ward had never taken anything from her for her keep and she had been able to save quite a bit.

She left a scribbled note to Mrs Ward on the kitchen table, lacking the courage to face her. Retrieving her ration book from the shelf where they were kept, she silently let herself out.

The sun hadn't yet risen. The horizon of Victoria Park with its trees clad in young green glimpsed between the houses opposite was a mere blush, and seemed to emphasise the quietness. It was Tuesday, just gone four thirty, too early even for workers to be up off to work. She couldn't remember the road feeling so quiet or looking so wide. Lined by trees in new leaf, it was filled with the fresh, clean fragrance of the park and the new day, in May not even tainted by chimney smoke. She mightn't have been in London at all. It was a morning that should have been savoured, but it only made her shiver.

Alone in this empty road, all the large bay windows of the bedrooms looking down at her like empty eye sockets witnessing her flight, for a few seconds Susan stood uncertain, fighting the impulse to run back indoors away from those accusing, silent windows that seemed to be asking what she thought she was doing. At least her mother-in-law's home offered protection and comfort. With no idea exactly where she would go, a strong temptation to run back was growing stronger. Then she thought of the woman becoming even more dictatorial once the baby was born. With a final shiver, not at the silence of the morning, but at the well-intentioned if unwanted help of her mother-in-law, Susan turned her face towards Mare Street and Cambridge Heath Road, the bus stop and freedom. Once she got back to Birmingham and her own family she would be all right. It was her only comforting thought on this lonely morning.

Euston was a mad-house of hurrying people by the time Susan got there. Panting engines, the sudden shriek of released steam, the rumble of trolleys full of mail and parcels, deafened her. The last time she was here had been on Matthew's arm, with him to defend her against all this. Now she was on her own, her figure pulled out of all shape by the baby it carried inside it. She felt lost, conspicuous, but no one took a blind bit of notice of her, being more locked up in themselves: people getting to work; couples saying farewell to each other; the men going back off leave. Uniforms of other countries jostled past her, the ever-attentive Americans alone giving her pretty face a quick appreciative glance until seeing her condition and looking away.

By now her mother-in-law would have been bringing her up a cup of tea, telling her she could get up when she felt like it or could have breakfast in bed if she didn't, coddling her, concerned and managing. Suddenly that managing seemed preferable to standing here not knowing where to find the platform she was supposed to be on. Panic came and went in waves as she tried to gather her thoughts together, attempting desperately to hold back the tears her plight was prompting.

Once she found the right platform, the man at the ticket barrier told her the train would be leaving in five minutes. Hauling her suitcase, five minutes seemed hardly long enough to find a carriage and she worried that the train would pull out to leave her standing helplessly on the platform. So few trains ran these days, she could be stranded for hours. She struggled on, the suitcase banging against her legs, almost ready to turn round and head back to Hackney.

The first four carriages were full of people standing in the corridors. The fifth carriage seemed less full and with a struggle she got herself in. There'd be no seats, not here with the corridor partially occupied by servicemen. How could she face standing all the way to Birmingham? If an empty seat couldn't be found, she would go back home. Home. It seemed odd that she should think of it as that now she was away from it. Her heart seemed to sink down at the realisation. She had no home. Common sense told her there was no room for her with her family, and she had shunned the one she'd left behind. Mr and Mrs Ward would be up by now, would have read her note, devastated, not knowing how to find her and bring her back. And she so desperately wanted to be brought back at this moment.

Just as she was on the verge of turning round and forcing her way off again, a voice with a faint northern accent spoke in her ear.

'Pardon me, my luv.'

She turned to see an elderly man in a cap rising from a seat in the near corner of the apartment beside which she was standing.

'Have my seat, luv,' he said, and taking hold of the suitcase, added, 'Allow me,' and hoisted it up on to the string rack above.

'When you want, I'll get it down for you, like.'

Indecision had been taken neatly out of her hands, and she accepted gratefully. The sailor next to her looked a little crestfallen that he'd not offered his seat as the train gave a jerk, then with several more slowly began to move.

'Ooh, love, what you doing here?'

Her mother, her blonde hair in curlers, stared at her from the back door on which Susan had prudently tapped rather than surprise her mother by walking in on her after all this time away. 'How'd you get here? Is anyone with you? You're not on your own?'

'I've come home, Mum,' was all Susan could gulp.

'Good Lord. You'd best come in, love. How'd you get here?'

'I came on the train.'

It had been a long, drawn-out journey, the train stopping and starting as all trains seemed to do in wartime, sometimes to let a troop train through or one carrying munitions, sometimes for no known reason at all. She'd eaten a Spam sandwich she'd bought at Euston, somewhat stale, its grey corners turned up, but there'd been nothing to drink; that train had not carried

196

refreshments. People going on journeys usually brought their own, just in case.

At New Street station she'd had some baked beans on toast and a much-needed cup of tea, then had come straight here on a bus. She felt tired and a little sick from the rather strong-tasting baked beans that were already repeating on her.

She was glad to follow her mother into the single living room. Nothing had changed, the room still looked worn, shabby, comfortable.

Susan had expected to find no one at home other than her mother, with everyone this afternoon still at work or school. So she was surprised to see her grandparents sitting there, having looked up expectantly at her entrance. Now her grandad was rising on his rickets-curved legs to greet her.

'Now then, there's a surprise, gel. Didn't expect to see you, like. What you doing 'ere?'

'That's what I asked her,' her mother put in as Susan leaned forward to give his lips beneath their bristling grey moustache a kiss.

She went over and kissed her grandmother too, feeling the bristles on her chin dig sharply into her like tiny needles. Her grandmother cut them with scissors.

'Nice to see you, luv. Y'look a bit peaky, love. 'Spect it's the baby. Y'r mam told us, but you ain't never come a-visiting. Is y'r husband with you, love?'

'He's away,' her mother explained quickly as Susan's eyes began to mist. 'An' she will look a bit peaky, like, not getting any news about him. I told you, Mum, they reported him missing, like, and nothing more's been heard. Come one, now, our Sue. Sit down and tell us why you're here and I'll get you a nice cup of tea. And I expect you're hungry an' all. So why're you here then, luv?'

'I couldn't stay with Matthew's people any longer – not now he's not here.'

'They ain't turned you out, have they? I wouldn't think . . .'

'No, Mum, I left there.'

'Whatever for? A nice cosy place there to live, everything you want there.'

'I can't stand it there, Mum. I can't stand being told what to do and when to do it and what I should eat and when I should

197

rest, and when I should go to bed, and I mustn't do this and I must do that. I can't stand it.' The words flowed out of her, all the pent-up things she'd been unable to say to anyone.

'But . . .' Her mother was looking at her, bewildered, a little concerned and, with the truth of her visit dawning on her, a little wary. 'But where d'you think you can go? Look, love, I don't want to appear hard and unkind or not caring or anything. I do care. But there's no room here at all, if you're thinking of coming here. I'd love to look after you, you and the baby, when it comes. I'd love to. My first-ever grandchild. Y'r grandma here'll be a great-grandma. Y'r looking forward to that, ain't you, Mum? But staying here, that's another thing, love. Y'see, last week they was bombed out in one of those daylight tip-and-run raids. House was condemned. Cracked walls and the roof's had it. Until it's repaired they've had to come here to live. That's why they're sleeping down here, don't y'see?'

For the first time Susan noticed the sagging double bed in the corner where the old scratched oak sideboard used to be. The sideboard was probably down in the cellar with all the other junk. Too damp for anyone to sleep down there even though during the night-time raids before she'd met Matthew, all the family had endured its damp conditons for safety's sake.

'I didn't know,' she mumbled. 'What am I going to do now?'

'Well, I think you ought to go back to Mr and Mrs Ward. They won't be cross with you, I'm sure. Just say you wanted so much to come and see us all up here.'

'Like this?' Susan looked down at her small bulging stomach.

'Well, you've got to say something. They'll understand. But you do see you can't stay here.'

But she could find somewhere to live nearby, some cheap room for the time being, until her grandparents could return to their repaired home. Her mother must have read her thoughts.

'The council people said your gran and grandad's place might not be repaired until the war's over. There's so many homes needing repair. Some people've had to be evacuated all over the place for the duration. At least your gran and grandad won't have to do that at their age when we can at least give them a roof over their heads, awkward as it'll be for them. You do see, love, don't you? I don't know what you can do except go back to London and I don't think you'd want to bunk in with any of your aunts and uncles, would you?'

No, she wouldn't. Go begging cap in hand to any of them, asking to foist herself on them, saying her own mother couldn't put her up, and them all knowing she already had a posh roof over her head down south.

Her mother appeared to think the problem solved. 'You can't go back tonight. You look all in. We can make a bit of room for you in with June and Beryl. It'll be a bit awkward for them but it'll only be for one night. But you can see, it couldn't be permanent, not with a baby to look after when it comes – nowhere to put a cot or anything. You do see, our Sue, don't you? Well . . .' She brightened as though everything was solved. 'I better get you this cup of tea and a quick sandwich of something. And when the boys come home and your dad and the girls, we'll all have a nice tea. I've got a nice big stew for us all.' Susan had smelled it as she came in and her mouth had watered and her stomach rumbled at the lovely aroma.

'I can get a better bit of meat with your gran and grandad's ration books added to ours,' her mother went on.

Susan fished into her handbag. 'I've got mine.'

Her mother looked horrified. 'Good Lord, love. I don't want yours, not for one meal. We've got plenty of stew. We won't even know it's been stretched. But, Sue love, you must go back home in the morning. Dad'll see you to the station all right. It won't matter if he's a bit late going into work.'

'I shall be all right, Mum.' It sounded pathetic, her mother using the word 'home'.

'No,' her mother argued as though bequeathing some bountiful gift. 'I won't have you going back to New Street on your own with the workmen. Y'r dad'll take you. He'll see you all right.'

Chapter 18

She hadn't felt so tired in all her life. The suitcase seemed to weigh a ton. Outside Euston station Susan checked the money she had left. There wasn't a lot, not enough to waste on a taxi back to Victoria Park Road and she just couldn't face the bus ride, nor see herself creeping back mollified to face Mrs Ward's wrath or relief, whichever it turned out to be. But where else was there to go? No one here to help her, no one to care for her, she felt as lonely as it was possible to be. She just wanted to sit here on her suitcase and burst into tears.

Nearby a news vendor's raucous voice was calling out: '*Standard*, *Ev'n Standard*! Get y'r *Standard*.'

It was getting late though daylight was still being drawn out. It had taken more than half the day travelling from New Street to Euston. And now she had either to go home to Mrs Ward before it got dark or find somewhere to stay at least for the night, she was so weary. But her remaining money for this week wouldn't stretch to any hotel. Misery rose again in her throat, which she fought to hold back with large gulps. She had been such a fool, it had been such a daft escapade. And now even her brain couldn't think properly. She saw herself sleeping here where she sagged, a policeman moving her on in the night like he might a tramp. She wasn't a tramp. She was a fool and she was seven months' pregnant. If only she could stand here and cry her eyes out.

'Get y'r *Standard*! Fifty farsand at Second Front demonstrashern.'

Of course, buy a paper, look in the rooms-to-let columns, the logical thing to do. Feeling uplifted, Susan bought a paper.

She wasn't going back to Mrs Ward, she would stand on her own two feet. At least for a while.

Half an hour later found her on the doorstep of one of the somewhat shabby-looking houses off Mile End Road whose address was the one she'd selected from the to-let column: 'Two furnished rooms, large family home, shared bath/wc, seven and six pw.' She had to knock twice before anyone answered.

She felt and looked sick, and the woman who finally came to the door took one look at her condition, her suitcase, and said: 'Gawd 'elp us – you orlright, dear?' the Cockney accent closing around Susan like a warm blanket.

'I . . . I saw your ad,' she began, unable to say any more for the sick giddiness that was overwhelming her.

'Better come inside, dear,' the woman was saying. 'You don't look too good, and that's a fact. I'll take yer case for yer. Come on in.'

Taken into a cavern of a room, Susan gratefully allowed herself to be eased down on to a sagging brown leatherette sofa that puffed explosively under her small weight. The suitcase was plonked at her feet. 'You stay there, dear. I'm gonna make yer a cuppa tea. Look as if yer could do wiv one. I won't be a tick.'

Left alone to recover, Susan stared about her. The room had a high ceiling and a huge, stained marble Victorian fireplace but was bare of all ornaments and embellishments, almost as though the family were on the point of moving out and had packed away everything easily movable. All it held was two large armchairs that matched the sofa, half a dozen straight-backed chairs and a scratched oak sideboard with a radio on it. There was only lino on the floor and set in the centre was a circle of linked-up toy railway lines with a couple of Hornby trains, their carriages lying on their sides, and nearby some very battered toy cars.

As she sat looking at it, a boy of about thirteen came in. Staring at her from under a thatch of unkempt tawny hair, he said, ''Ello.' Susan smiled through her tiredness.

'Mum's gorn ter make yer some tea,' he announced gravely. When Susan nodded, he went on, 'I'm Malcolm. I've got two bruvvers. They're Percy an' 'Enry. They're younger'n me.'

Again she nodded, too weary to make conversation with

201

small boys. A silence fell and finally Malcolm wandered off leaving her to continue gazing at the square-patterned lino and the indifferent beige wallpaper. The once-heavy green brocade curtains at the long Victorian bay window were faded at the edges by sunlight. Against the wall were propped makeshift blackout shutters of thick black paper in flimsy wood batten frames. The woman returned with an steaming basin-like cup on a wide saucer which she put into Susan's hands.

'Yer'll feel a lot better after this,' she said and sat on one of the chairs while Susan sipped what was the best cup of tea she'd had in what seemed like ages.

'About the advert,' she said at last.

'Oh, yes,' said the woman as though only just recalling that was why Susan was here. Now Susan felt better enough to take note of her, she saw a smallish woman of about thirty-five with uncurling fair hair roughly cut straight about her ears and forehead. Her hands were rough and she wore a washed-out flowered wrapover pinafore over a green dress.

'Well,' she said now. 'I'm Emma Crawley. Me 'usband's often away fer days on end – works fer the Gas Board, reserved occupation, but 'is job takes 'im all over the place and I get a bit lonely. I need a bit of company. That's why I'm lettin' out the rooms.' She eyed Susan. 'An' your 'usband?'

'In the Army,' Susan obliged quickly. 'Abroad. At least he . . .' She faltered to a stop, then added hastily, 'I've got my marriage certificate.'

Mrs Crawley burst out laughing. 'Lord luv us, I don't disberlieve yer, dear. Where is 'e, or is that 'ush-'ush?'

'He's . . . he's been posted missing.'

'Oh, yer poor duck!' Her earlier hilarity swept away, the woman's face creased with pity. 'An' you wiv a baby on the way. But ain't you got no 'ome or anythink? 'Ave yer bin bombed out, then? Not in London though, dear?' She had taken note of Susan's accent. 'D'yer come from Manchester way?'

'No, Birmingham.' Susan was surprised that tears hadn't flooded her eyes at the mention of Matthew, but guessed she was too tired for that.

'Birmingham. They've 'ad it nasty up there too. 'Ad some of them daylight raids. They've left London alone this time, thank

Gawd. We 'ad enough of our share in the Blitz. Shockin' it was rarnd 'ere, flames . . .'

She pulled herself up sharply. 'Look, come upstairs and take a look at the rooms, see if yer like 'em. Yer can cook up there. I've put in a gas ring but there ain't no place fer an oven. But yer can eat wiv us if yer like. Might save yer a few bob in the meter. Don't s'pose yer get much allowance from the Army. Come on, dear, I'll show yer. Leave yer suitcase there fer the time bein'. What's yer name?'

'Susan. Susan Ward.' She got up, put the cup and saucer on the floor because there was nowhere else to put it and followed Mrs Crawley out and back along the passage, its thin runner rucking up under her tired feet, and up the narrow lino'd stairs.

Opening the door to the large bedroom which had been divided into two at some time to form a sitting room as well, Mrs Crawley stood back for Susan to enter.

'Everythink's nice an' clean,' she said. To someone who had been travelling for much of the day, it looked like heaven, despite the well-worn furnishings and, if one had been finicky, really only being one divided room. 'I 'ope it's suitable for yer.'

Suitable! Susan could have cried at the sight of the large brass bed on which she could have flopped this very second, it looked so inviting and comfortable. She turned to the woman. 'I'd like to take it. But do you mind me being . . . like this?' She nodded towards her midriff.

'Bless yer, no. I like kids. Got free of me own – all boys. Wot I'd like is a gel. Well, yer never know. Ain't too old yet. An' Geoff, that's me 'usband, it's Geoffrey really, but 'e's called Geoff by everyone – when 'e comes 'ome, yer never know, it could 'appen and I could spark again. But it'd be nice 'aving a bit of female comp'ny in this family of boys. Me 'usband too – as much boy as any of the kids, I can tell yer.'

'Well, if it suits you to have me here, Mrs Crawley . . .'

'Call me Emma. An' I'll call yer Sue.'

Susan smiled. The woman was motherly, and she needed someone motherly right now, someone like her own mother. Her mother spoke real Brummy, Emma Crawley spoke Cockney; it was all the same when someone saw no point to putting on airs and graces.

'Emma,' she repeated, already feeling at home.

The first thing she intended to do once she was settled in was be to write to her mother telling her of her good luck. As to writing to Mr and Mrs Ward, she would think about that one, but she supposed, as their son's wife, she really should let them know where she was. This she did and bravely prepared herself for their onslaught. It wasn't long in coming.

'What did you think you were doing, Susan? You had us worried out of our wits. You seem to have no conception of what you have put us through. No consideration. Didn't you ever stop to think how worried we'd be?'

In her room, which she had already made even more cosy, Susan withstood the tirade by keeping her head bowed and saying nothing.

'After all we tried to do for you. I don't think we've been unkind or made you do anything you didn't want to do. We've treated you as though you were our own daughter and done all we can to make you feel at home. Not only for Matthew's sake but your own, a girl away from her parents, her husband . . .' Mrs Ward gulped back a wave of emotion, thankful the landlady Mrs Crawley wasn't present to see it, having decently left this family to its argument. 'Her husband, our son, not with her,' she finished.

Collecting herself, she paused again, this time for some sort of reply. When none came, she pushed on. 'How could you have been so thankless, so unkind, so thoughtless as to cause us all this worry?'

'Don't you think you were being just a bit unfair?' Mr Ward added with a little more calm, saving Susan the awkwardness of answering his wife's angry question. 'God knows, we've done you no harm to have been treated in such a way. What *have* we done to you, Susan, to deserve it?'

This was said in such a heartfelt manner, tears began to surge up in Susan's eyes. She hadn't meant to cry, had even steeled herself against crying. So finding herself on the verge of doing so made anger rise up instead.

'You've never let me lead my own life,' she blurted. 'Watching every move I made, you made me feel like I was a prisoner. I want to lead my own life. I'm not a kid. I can look after myself.'

'It looks like it,' Mrs Ward remarked, gazing about her, exactly as she had done on entering the house. 'This place is disgusting.'

'But it feels more like home to me than your fine house ever did.' It didn't matter that she sounded rude. She felt angry. 'Mrs Crawley's like a mother to me, which you never was.'

'Well, that is the absolute limit . . .'

'Now look here, Susan,' Leonard Ward cut in again. 'There's no call to talk to us like that. We have, truly, tried to do our best for you. If the way we did it wasn't what suited you, I'm sorry, it's the only way we know. You must admit, you wanted for nothing. Did you?' he ended firmly.

'No,' she said in a small voice.

'Then where have we failed?'

She was crying now. 'You haven't failed. I didn't mean to upset anyone. I suppose I should have told you how I felt. But it's done now.'

'It isn't. You can come back with us.'

'It is. I want to live on my own. I'm sorry, but I feel smothered. I just want to live on my own.'

There was a long silence, both of them looking at her, she not daring to look at them.

'But the baby . . .'

'I'm all right,' Susan cut across her mother-in-law's lame words. 'Mrs Crawley's got children. She's made me feel wanted and comfortable here.'

'Meaning we haven't?'

'It's like I said. I don't feel comfortable in your home. I want to be on my own. I need to be on my own. I don't want to be smothered.'

'Well, all credit to you, Susan,' Leonard Ward muttered then turned to his wife. 'I can't see anything we can say altering her mind. I think we'd best go, Lilian.'

'I'm not . . .' she began, but again he interrupted her, firmly raising his hand towards her.

'There's no point us trying to argue any more. I give you credit for wanting to stand on your own two feet, Susan. I didn't think you had it in you, but obviously you have. Well, we're not far away if you need us. If we hear anything from Matthew, we'll let you know immediately. Obviously we have no way of writing to him except through the Red Cross, which we will do, and I expect you will too. You're as anxious as us to hear something, no matter what. I expect it's the strain of all this that's made you do what you did. We're going now. But, Susan, keep in touch. Don't alienate yourself against us, whatever it was we did to displease you. Of course, we want to know when the baby is born and if you're all right. You will do that, won't you?'

Dismally she nodded. He came forward, laid a kiss on her downcast cheek and took hold of her shoulders to give them a small encouraging shake. It was like having Matthew touch her and it was all she could do not to fall into his father's arms to receive his hug. Instead, she stepped back, lifting her tear-streaked face, shaking her dark hair from her eyes, a small defiant gesture, and he too stepped away, defeated. It showed in his eyes, again so like Matthew's though a few shades lighter.

Mrs Ward just stood there, not quite looking at her, her face set like granite.

'Take care, child,' Leonard Ward said and his wife, still without looking at her, gave a stiff nod of concurrence and turned, leading the way out of the room.

Susan stood listening to their footsteps echoing down the uncarpeted stairs. She heard Mrs Crawley saying to them before they left, 'I'll see she keeps in touch. She's in good 'ands 'ere.' Then the door closed and Emma Crawley's footsteps came quickly back up the stairs.

'I'm gonna do yer a nice cup of tea, Sue. Make yer feel better.' It was Emma's way of solving all crises. More often than not it worked a treat, just as it did now as Susan smiled at her through her tears.

A fierce stab somewhere in her stomach awoke Susan with a start and for a moment she lay rigid, frightened by a pain that could bring her out of what had been a deep sleep. There was only a dull ache now that wasn't really an ache at all – she wasn't sure what it was – just a feeling. The clinic had told her she had only a week or two to go now, though no one could say quite when. So was this her time? No, it couldn't be. Probably just wind. The fear began to subside but it had left her wide awake.

Turning over she closed her eyes again and tried to sleep. But sleep had gone and all that were left were thoughts, the sort of reflections that come at night, persistent, refusing to be ignored.

All this time, there had been no news whatsoever of Matthew. But she wouldn't think about that. Once on that track it would persist, plaguing her with memories of those wonderful days with him, thoughts of the days that now stretched ahead of her without him, forever and ever. She would end up crying into her pillow. She mustn't think of him. She would try to think of something else. Something positive. Something happy.

It had been the best move she had ever made getting away from his parents. Emma was such a wonderful, motherly person, she couldn't have wished for a better landlady, more a friend than anything, so free and easy. It was a rough-and-ready-come-and-go-as-you-please sort of home. Meals were never the ritual they'd been at the Wards' home. The only time anyone sat around a table – the big bare table in the back room – was when Geoffrey Crawley was home, and even then everyone came one after the other as each plate was filled, leaving the same way, as soon as the plate was empty – no waiting for anyone else.

Helping around the house, going shopping with Emma who held her arm as she got bigger around the middle, was enjoyable. So were these long July evenings. As the sun went down on kids playing in the street, the drawn-out twilight of double British Summertime fading, the Crawleys' flimsy blackout shutters would go up amid a dozen bits of advice how to make them fit so no light finally showed. With the sounds in the street finally muted by the closing of the thin curtains, they'd all settle down to an evening around the wireless, laughing at ITMA, Arthur Askey and Stinker Merdock, Vic Oliver, Ben Lyon and Bebe Daniels; listening intently to the news read by Alvar Lidell or Bruce Belfrage, hoping to glean a little joyful tidings from the war front. Sometimes she and Emma would have a go at one of the dozens of old jigsaw puzzles that lay around the house, the wireless still blaring to itself, while young Malc sat at the other end painting from a tin paint box on bits of old paper, his brothers playing noisily with some toy or other, Geoffrey in his creaking old fireside chair reading the evening paper or studying his work sheets for the following week. All nice and cosy.

With all this going on around her there was little time for fretting any more, although now and again she did, picturing herself and Matthew together in a little home of their own. But this was the nearest to it, and Emma and Geoffrey were so nice, she should think herself lucky. Geoff was an easygoing man. It wasn't at all difficult to talk to him. Mr Ward had been nice too, but it had not been so easy to talk about things that she liked – films, popular songs, singers, the big bands, her life in Birmingham. Geoff would talk about his life too, telling outrageous tales of the people he met in his work, making them all laugh. He told her how he had met Emma, how she'd caught him on the rebound from a girl who'd given him up for a prizefighter. The girl had been a real wow and Emma hadn't measured up to her, he said, but Emma fell for a baby and they'd hastily married. 'Had to,' he said, 'for her sake.' Susan felt a little sad for him that he'd had to take, as it seemed, second best, though Emma had, he admitted, been a bloody good wife to him, more than the other girl might have been.

If Matthew were to come home now, Susan mused as she lay wide awake, she would make sure no one else could match her ...

A second stab of pain broke into her thoughts, making her gasp. It was not as bad as that first stab had been, but she was consumed by a sense of urgency, an ancient instinct that lies dormant within each women so that she knows instantly what it is without being told.

Swinging her feet out of bed, she hoisted herself up and, holding her stomach in which there was now only a dull grinding feeling, she got to the door and out on to the landing.

'Emma.' Her raised voice sounded small and terrified even to herself. 'Emma, quick. Something's happening.'

Geoff was away. Emma came running out from her room and guided her downstairs to sit her in one of the old armchairs in the cavernous front room, the most comfortable place she could find. 'Stay 'ere,' she ordered. 'I'll go up an' get yer clothes an' fings for yer.'

She was back within seconds with a shopping bag holding a

towel, flannel and soap, hairbrush, a change of nightie, and over her arm, Susan's coat and a scarf, and a pair of shoes dangling from her fingers.

'Can yer put yer coat and shoes on yerself?' she queried anxiously. 'I've got ter get meself dressed. D'yer think yer can walk? We've got ter get yer to the 'orspital. It's only half a mile darn the Mile End. Yer've only just started. Yer'll be able to make it if we walk slow.' To which Susan let out another gasp at a fresh small onslaught of pain.

Lights were on all over the house; the boys wandered out of their bedroom asking, 'What the 'eck's up?' before being told by Emma to go back to bed – it wasn't none of their business.

There came a loud hammering and knocking on the street door, a harsh voice shouted: 'What th'ell are you lot up ter? Yer showin' a bloody great light – like a bloody searchlight art 'ere.'

'Oh, Gawd, the blackout!' Emma rushed in panic to the window to find one corner of the blackout frame leaning inward towards the room, not having been put up properly. Only then did she run to the door, flicking off lights as she went, leaving Susan in pitch-darkness.

Her voice was breathless at the street door. 'Gawd, I'm sorry. We've got an emergency 'ere. Me lodger, she's only young, 'er 'usband's overseas, an' she's just started 'er labour pains. I've got ter get 'er to the 'orspital.'

'Can't yer get an ambulance?'

'It's only 'alf a mile ter the London.'

'Yer can't ast 'er ter walk 'alf a mile, not in labour.'

In pitch-dark, Susan felt the pain returning. In panic she cried out. From the door, the voices grew more animated. 'Can't she 'ave it 'ere, in the 'ouse, save walking all that way in 'er condition at one in the mornin'?'

'It's 'er first. She ought ter be in 'orspital. I told 'er 'usband's people I'd look after 'er. I can't be responsible for anyfink goin' wrong.'

'Well, she can't walk. Tell yer what. I've got a bike. We could put 'er on that and wheel 'er. Save 'er walkin'. It's got a wide saddle. And paddin' as well. I got piles an' I 'ave ter 'ave a wide saddle wiv a lot of paddin' on it.'

Sitting in the dark listening, Susan wasn't sure whether to laugh or cry as the present bout of pain began to fade a little.

The baby, a girl, arrived the next day around three in the afternoon. 'Quick for the first,' a nurse told her, but it had seemed like eternity to her as she writhed in terror and pain, a young mother not knowing what was expected of her, what to expect. Throughout she had been alternately encouraged and scolded, assured that it wouldn't be long now, that she was doing wonderfully, then in the next breath upbraided for making a fuss, getting into a needless panic, yelling when there was no need, not co-operating. And when during easier moments she wept for Matthew, she was told she must be brave for him, that he, a stalwart fighting for his country, wouldn't want to see her less brave, breaking down like this.

She couldn't bring herself to tell them he'd been reported missing. Though his family hung on to the hope of his having been captured, she knew deep inside her that he was dead, that she'd never see him again and would have to bring up his child alone.

Chapter 19

Margaret stood by Susan's bedside. Susan's in-laws had just left and her parents, who had further to come, had yet to see her.

Margaret herself had heard of the birth of Susan's baby by chance, being told at teatime by one of the nurses, creased up with laughter, of a woman in labour having arrived at maternity around one thirty in the morning on a bike. 'What people don't do in wartime,' the nurse had giggled over her bread and jam sandwich.

'You mean she rode herself here on a bike?' Margaret had joined in the general laughter. Odd things happened in hospitals, but that one had taken the biscuit.

'Well, not exactly rode herself. An air-raid warden was pushing her. And her landlady apparently kept helping her off every time she got one of her pains. They had the saddle all padded.' This last brought a fresh gale of laughter.

'I'm not surprised,' Margaret had said over the laughter. 'Where were her parents then?'

'She said they lived in Birmingham. She'd walked out on her in-laws or something and lives about half a mile from here. Seems it was easier to get here on a bike than having to walk. I ask you! Can you just see it – some old air-raid warden wheeling a pregnant woman on a bike all the way to the hospital, her hopping on and off every so often? It must've looked a sight. Lucky for her it wasn't midday. Honestly, some people!'

But Margaret had no longer been laughing.

Now she stood looking down at the girl's face, pale from the hard work of bringing a baby into the world, looking wan and down in the mouth when she should have been glowing with pride at her achievement.

'Have you seen the baby, Susan?' she asked for something to say after having enquired how she was, a question which had been met by a tear being squeezed from between the closed eyelids.

'What did you think of her?' she pressed as Susan merely nodded without speaking.

'I'm too worn out to think anything. Except that Matthew's not here and I'm all on my own. I'll never see him again, and no one cares.'

'Of course they care. His parents care. And your family – they care.'

And Matthew, he'd be over the moon with joy and pride if he was here to know about his baby daughter. But there was no way he could know, no way he could be told, could be contacted. Her mother had relayed what little news she happened to glean from his parents, which was hardly anything. And having for a while lost the run of Susan, all she knew of Matthew was of the ongoing but vain efforts of the Red Cross still to trace him, one way or the other. Wonderful people, but as far as she knew they'd hit a complete blank.

Gazing down at the despairing Susan, Margaret bit her lip, refusing to believe Matthew could be dead. Somewhere he had to be alive. She clung to that hope with all her heart, and inside that heart those feelings she had always had for him beat as strongly as ever.

She had tried to put it away from her, had assumed she had at last conquered it when she had written to Ronald Whittaker, finally confronting the stupidity in letting such a chance go of getting Matthew out of her system once and for all by marrying Ronald as he'd once asked. His parents had replied for him, saying they were sending her letter on to him, that against their wishes he hadn't gone into practice with his father but instead had joined the Army Medical Corps. Slightly dismayed, she had got in touch with him at the address they'd given. Ronald's reply had been kind and friendly but said that he had met a girl to whom he'd be getting engaged on his next leave; that he was sorry Margaret hadn't written earlier because they'd got on well together but it wouldn't be right for him to drop the girl he now loved for the one he had thought at the time he loved. He'd always remember her with affection and hoped that it wouldn't be too long before she too found herself someone to settle down with. She had felt hurt, angry with herself and very aware that her only avenue of escape from the love inside her for Matthew had been cut off.

It made her furious that Susan could lie here lamenting her lot and assuming her husband dead when she should at least be fighting to fill herself with optimism that he would eventually come back to her. She didn't even seem interested in her baby as a mother would normally be.

'What are you going to call her?' Margaret asked and received an apathetic shrug.

'I don't really know. I've not really thought about it.'

'Then don't you think you should? What do Matthew's parents say?'

'They suggested a few names.'

'And?'

Another shrug. 'I can't seem to like any of them. I got confused and said I'd think about it. Mrs Ward said don't take too long about it.'

'You'll have to come up with something.' Margaret herself thought about it for a moment, then said, 'How about Mattie?'

'Mattie?'

Yes, it was a lame sort of name and sounded even more so on Susan's amazed lips. 'It's short for Matilda.' Matthew had always loved shortening names. ' . . . Hi there, Maggie . . .'

Margaret swallowed back the sentimental restriction of her throat. 'Matilda is the feminine of Matthew. It would remind you of him, and . . . when he comes home.' He would come home. 'When he comes home he'll know you were thinking of him. Make it Mattie, Susan. It sounds better.'

She spoke positively. Susan was by nature a malleable person and she was at her most malleable now. 'Well, I hadn't got any name ready for her. I suppose it's as good as any.'

She couldn't care less, Margaret thought angrily, but she smiled. 'I had better go or I'll get into trouble,' she said brightly. 'I'm supposed to be on duty. Another nurse is covering for me, so I could only have a few minutes. I'm glad you're okay and I'm glad the baby, Mattie, is okay. She'll be something for you to cling to until Matthew comes home.'

Giving Susan no opportunity to argue with that, she turned smartly on her heel and with a quick wave went back to work.

Sitting by the lounge window for a better light by which to see her knitting pattern, Lilian Ward glanced out at the dull November weather, her fingers still busy with the clicking needles. She had no real need to look at them; the pattern itself had become partially imprinted on her brain so often had she used it to knit the exquisite little dresses for Matilda. The weather was getting colder. Wool was hard to come by, so second-hand woollen garments were usually found in jumble sales, unravelled and re-knitted, but the child needed some warm clothing. Left to Susan, she'd have nothing warm to wear. It seemed to Lilian the mother had no interest whatsoever in Matilda. She insisted the child's name be spoken in full. None of this silly Mattie business. But in truth the shortened name reminded her too much of Matthew. Where was he?

Nothing, absolutely nothing. The Red Cross were even mentioning the dread word. But she wouldn't have it that Matthew was dead. He was *somewhere*. He had to be. Why *couldn't* they find him? Not trying, too many other missing servicemen to trace. But her son was as important as they. Meanwhile this war was dragging on. So what if on the fourth of this month came the long-awaited tidings that German forces were at last in full retreat in Egypt, the wireless announcer hardly hiding his excitement? So what if the Allies had landed in Algeria? So what if the church bells had rung across the whole country to mark Montgomery's victory? One or two swallows didn't make a summer. Meanwhile Matthew continued to be missing. His daughter was going to grow up not knowing him. Susan, his wife, was gadding about as though she hadn't a care in the world, leaving Matilda in the dubious if willing care of her landlady, just as if her husband, missing or dead, meant nothing to her. No sighing after him or, Lilian was certain, tears, except when she and Leonard went to see her – then she'd weep buckets. Lilian's needles clicked angrily in the dull November daylight.

* * *

Crumpling the brief letter into a ball, Susan threw it across the kitchen.

'She never gives up, does she? Says she's got another cardigan for Mattie. I don't want her making clothes for my child. Anyone'd think I can't dress her myself. She looks all right, don't she, in what I put her in?'

Carving hunks of bread for when the boys trooped in from school for their midday break in half an hour, Emma looked up from the kitchen table. 'She means well, Sue. She knitted you both lovely Christmas presents.'

'Means well? She always means well. It's the way she goes about meaning well that gets my goat. Treating me as though I've not got a clue on how to bring up a baby. I know she doesn't approve of me going out every once in a while. That's all it is, once in a while. I'm not gadding about with soldiers. I just need a break now and then.'

'Of course you do.' Emma continued spreading the doorsteps with the thinnest scrape of margarine, her family's rations dwindling towards the end of this week's allowance. She put a small smear of plum jam on them and pressed the slices together, the resulting sandwiches almost too wide for any child's mouth.

'The way she talks,' Susan went on, 'you'd think I was on the streets. I like going dancing with Edie. And we know how to behave ourselves.'

In September, for a bit of extra money, she'd started a part-time job in the Whitechapel High Street near Aldgate East station in the stockroom of a wholesalers of men's underwear and hosiery, Fishman & Sob. The owner's son had been called up. Edie Barrows, who worked with her, also had a husband in the forces, and like herself needed to get out now and again and see a bit of life rather than be stuck at home – it was easier for her, having no children. There was no harm in it, the way Mrs Ward intimated.

'Neither of us are going to go off the rails, both married. We just need a break now and again, that's all,' Susan repeated.

''Course yer do,' Emma murmured. 'Do yer want jam or a bit of yer cheese ration in this sandwich?'

'Jam'll do.'

She began mixing Mattie's bottle with dried baby milk and

215

a tiny drop of cod-liver oil. Her own milk had dried up earlier. Susan wasn't sorry. Though making bottles was a chore, she wasn't confined to the house or to rushing back home having to breastfeed at inconvenient hours.

She set the bottle in a saucepan of cold water to cool for when Mattie woke up. 'I think I do all right with Mattie's clothes. That exchange shop's a real godsend.'

In the Mile End Road near the old Empire Music Hall, a small derelict shop had been set up with a system whereby mothers could barter clothing their toddlers had outgrown for larger clothes. It saved on clothing coupons and it was cheap. Mattie looked a treat in some of the baby clothes Susan had managed to find.

'Trouble is, she inspects everything I buy for Mattie, as if I'm putting her into something lice-infested. The way she purses her lips if Mattie looks the least bit messy! You can't keep babies clean all the time. She's bound to sick up a bit of food on her clothes, and she always manages to come in when Mattie's messy, never when she's clean. I'm sure she times it.'

Emma laughed and glanced at the battered alarm clock on one of the kitchen shelves. Twelve thirty. The boys'd be home any minute, all three of them bursting into the house as ravenous as if they hadn't eaten for a week.

'Wait till she starts feeding 'erself, then yer'll know what messy is.'

When the post fell lightly through the letter box, Lilian was neatly folding the finished baby dress, ready to take with her tomorrow morning. It looked pretty; the pink and white wool she'd picked up from the WI skeined and washed, almost new. Susan should be pleased, though Lilian could bet she wouldn't show it if she could help, merely look askance at it as though she, Lilian, were interfering. How could she be interfering, the child's own grandmother? More than them up in Birmingham ever bothered themselves – she allowed herself that little grammatical lapse in referring to Susan's people who as far as she knew hardly ever came down to see their daughter, much less sent her presents of clothing. Out of sight out of mind. They probably wrote now and again and thought that good enough.

At the sound of the post, she left the dress on the round

occasional table in the bay window and hurried into the hall to see what had arrived. Always in the back of her mind was that one day the post would contain a letter from the Red Cross or some other authority to say her son had been traced. At the same time there lingered that fear of being informed of his confirmed death, so that she never approached the envelopes lying in the wire cage attached below the letter box without pausing, to carry on more slowly in trepidation at what might be there.

This procedure she followed now. Pray God there was no bad news, bills excluded of course. But what was bad news and what was good if it concerned Matthew? Was missing good news? But surely better than that dread which invariably throbbed in her mind. Whatever it was, it had to be faced.

There were several letters, most of them bills and invoices concerning Leonard's business, two private letters, both face down. What would they contain? One had an official look to it. It was that one which she swept up almost in a single movement, knowing even before she turned it over that it bore the small red cross on it.

Feverishly she ripped open the envelope. Her heart thumping heavily, she pulled out the single sheet of limp recycled notepaper and unfolded it swiftly, hardly daring to breathe, hardly daring to let her eyes scan what it had to say. It took only the first two lines to send a sensation of debility spreading through her limbs so that she had to clutch at the newel post to keep her from falling. The waiting was at an end. At last they knew.

Tears she had kept unshed all this time started to flow and she didn't try to prevent them as she sank down on the stairs and, all alone in the house, gave herself up to weeping, the letter crumpled in her hand. Slowly, though, she gathered her thoughts. She must let Leonard know. Her hand automatically reached for the telephone on the hall stand, she dialled the operator, gave her the number of Leonard's shop and waited. It seemed to take forever before his receiver was lifted, but she felt too drained to think in the interval. Her brain seemed quite dead. She actually gave a small start as Leonard's voice sounded close to her ear.

'Hello? Ward's Electrical Shop.'

'Leonard! We've heard. We've heard from the International

Red Cross – a letter – this morning. Leonard – they've found him. He's a prisoner of war. That's all they know. But, Leonard, he's alive. Our Matthew's alive.'

There was a second or two's silence, then his voice came, trembling, just as hers had. 'I'm coming home. I'm closing up and coming home.'

'But your customers. You can't . . .' It sounded quite inane. News of Matthew traced and she was worrying about customers?

'Sod the customers!' He never swore in her hearing. She wouldn't have it. But today she forgave him.

Chapter 20

The rain had ceased. The flood within the railway cutting had subsided and with it part of the earth wall which must now be shored up. The guards, tempers uncertain at the best of times and now made more vile by the appalling conditions which they and prisoners alike were compelled to share, were calling for more speed. Anxious to return to their dry quarters and some warm food, they backed their demands with stick and stone aimed at any prisoner who flagged at his task.

The cutting rang to their demented yells, to the screech of steel being dragged from antiquated lorries, the clang of hammers on the metal spikes securing the rails in place while the sickly glow of carbide lamps gleamed on the glistening shoulders of those who toiled into the night.

To Matthew's fevered mind the whole thing resembled scenes from Dante's *Inferno* as on hands and knees he groped in the yellow mud for the bolts of the fishplate that would join together the two rails placed there.

His last meal of cold boiled rice diluted by monsoon rain had been eaten at mid-morning, eight hours ago. He would not eat again until their overseer, the shoko, called a halt to measure the day's quota of work sometime just before midnight. His brain felt it was bursting from the most recent attack of malaria; he dared not dwell on how he would get through the remaining hours, but get through them he must.

Evading the prospect, he found himself turning his thoughts inward – a sort of mental escapism he'd long ago learned – a way of withdrawing into the depths of his own brain as into a dark little world secluded from all this misery outside.

Slowly a wonderful phenomenon would occur, though it was only imagination. Inside his head there would appear a bright disc and within the disc he'd visualise Susan's face, smiling, gentle as she reached out to him. The clamour around him would recede and he would seem to float on a tiny island of peace, remote from the violence and hunger that made up the world he now existed in. A figment of a feverish mind, perhaps. What did it matter? It sustained him, and with a fanaticism born of sheer desperation he clung to that wavering disc with an insane – because one could become insane in this place – but obdurate conviction that while he could conjure up that disc of light inside his head, he would survive.

He had never dreamed he would, that day of his being taken prisoner. Hands raised, his pockets being rifled, he'd protested at Susan's photo being torn into pieces, had taken a step forward. One of his captors had sprung at him, bayonet whipping round. It was then he'd thought his life over, but the bayonet just scored his outstretched forearm.

The captives, bound together by their own belts in twos, had been pushed and prodded along jungle tracks with the noise of the river, which had meant safety, receding; they had finally been incarcerated in a small bamboo enclosure, full of Indian and British soldiers, which became filthier as the days passed with no latrines and a constant scramble for water. His arm had swollen to twice its normal size from the shallow bayonet wound bound by a piece of his own shirt.

Rangoon fell a week later. He had joined a lengthening column of POWs, taken back across the Sittang River, by then spanned by a hasty bridge flung up by the Japanese, past shattered metal and unburied bodies and into the city.

The poison from his festering wound had spread and he remembered little of the trek across the Irrawaddy Plain beneath a burning sun, but it was then that the strange disc-like brilliance with Susan's image inside it began to fill his head. Bob, who had been with him, and still was, had said that he was holding whole conversations with her. But he'd been convinced then as now of the telepathic origins of that bright light. Susan's thoughts were encouraging him, spanning the thousands of miles between them.

It had been Bob Howlett who'd practically carried him into

the Rangoon jail from that seventy-mile trek, who had badgered him into putting one foot before the other, holding him up, telling him not to give up, that he had Susan and a baby to get home to; Bob who had fed him with tiny morsels of watery rice and bits of fruit as he lay desperately ill.

Now it was Bob who lay desperately ill with dysentery, so pernicious that Matthew feared he would lose him. So many friends had been parted, they had been fortunate staying together this long. If Bob died, there'd be no panacea of shared comradeship, nights spent in their rotting tent talking quietly of their hopes of what they were going to do when they got back home, their wives, their memories of happier days. If Bob died, he'd be totally alone.

With the wall shored up and this particular group of railway workers at last clear of the cutting, a whistle blasted; work ceased abruptly while the shoko went forward to inspect the quota completed. Silence fell, broken only by the dripping of rainwater from sodden vegetation, the drowned earth sucking and bubbling, the laborious breathing of the men, a cough or two, the idle clink of a metal tool and the sigh of the sick, their mates waiting to help them back to the huddle of tents they called home.

With the shoko signalling permission, each man lined up for his mess-tin of cold rice doled out from an old oil drum positioned under a strip of leaking tarpaulin, afterwards to slither their way along a morass of a path to their tents and sleep. But first there was water from the river to be boiled, to cook the edible lizard he'd caught and killed that morning. Anything caught was supposed to go into the common pot, but he meant to cook it himself and feed the broth to Bob, who would have done the same for him.

Armed with a bent and battered petrol can, he made his way from the tent designed to hold three Japanese schoolboys comfortably but now used by eight men, and headed a quarter of a mile down the slippery path to the stagnant backwater of the river. It had to be the backwater. The torrent of the main river could wash away a man, especially one in a weakened condition. Men were already there scooping up the cloudy liquid, a perfect breeding ground for disease. The last to arrive, Matthew sank down on a decaying log to wait for the pool to clear, his head buzzing from his malaria. He watched each man depart with a full container, slipping, sliding, shambling back up the greasy track, all the spring of youth gone out of their step. Sitting here, he too felt like an old man, trying to summon the will just to raise himself up and fill up his can with the cloudy water.

Holding the petrol can below the surface to fill, he stared across the river into the darkness of the jungle. The roar of the river was deafening. A slow, lethargic thought came. What was the point of it all, squatting here, a half-naked, emaciated travesty of a man, shaken by fever, tongue raw from pellagra that made every mouthful of what food he got an agony? Would he drag on for a few more months in this hopeless corner of the world, or somewhere like it further along this growing railway, lost, forgotten, to succumb and be buried under a bamboo cross, one among all the countless other bamboo crosses that lined the route?

'God! Why in Christ's name did you do this to me? Why in Christ's name won't you help us?'

The roar of the river bore away the insane cry. The buzzing night-jungle swallowed it whole. There was no one to hear, just some unseen monkeys disturbed by the strange man-cry, replying with a distant demented howling while the incessant chirruping of myriads of insects in this primeval tangle of sodden vegetation continued uninterrupted.

There was a reply – voiceless in his own head, the memory of a smile, Susan hovering in his head across thousands of miles of sea and desert and mountain and jungle, waiting for him. He couldn't let her down. He couldn't let Bob down, sitting here nursing his own misery while Bob hovered at the edge of death. Rationality returned. The can was full and he had jobs to do.

It was heaven to close the door, to curl up in one of the the old armchairs in the partitioned-off part of her room upstairs, to be alone.

Emma was a wonderful and supportive friend, but her chatter could get a bit much sometimes. With Mattie being looked after downstairs by a willing Emma, who adored girls, she could relax with the latest paperback romance, identifying with the beautiful heroine in the embrace of the dark handsome hero, who in her imagination was Matthew, until it was Mattie's bedtime.

But all the imagination in the world could never compensate for the real thing. She and Edie spent most Saturday nights being whirled around a dance floor by uniformed worthies, one of them invariably whispering a certain invitation in her ear. It was a source of pride to her that she resisted, loyal still to her married state. But sometimes she envied Edie leaving with a partner's arm around her waist. 'You be orlright goin' 'ome without me?'

She'd nod and watch her leave then go and sit at the side of the hall knowing that the next partner – there always was one – asking her to go for a walk with him, the question heavy with innuendo, would get a short answer. But oh, how she envied Edie.

Once, hurrying to catch her bus home, she'd passed a couple hidden in a dark doorway. In the blackout she would have missed them but for a girlish giggle she recognised as Edie's. She heard the deep drawl of a GI and knew that tomorrow Edie would be displaying a fancy bar of toilet soap, or a bar of chocolate or a pair of nylons, perhaps even, with a brash flourish, bring out a packet of US government-issue contraceptives to shock her friend.

'It's safe as 'ouses, Sue, an' what 'arm are yer doing, keepin' the poor things 'appy, far away from 'ome, making yerself feel better in the bargain?'

But she couldn't do that. What if she did fall by accident? How would she ever face Matthew's parents? Yet it had been so long since a man's hand had touched her, really touched her. Her whole body ached at the thought of it. It was now August. August 1943, seven months since she'd heard Matthew had been made a prisoner of war; almost two years since she had last seen him; at times she couldn't remember his face unless she looked at a photo of him first; Mattie's first birthday had come and gone two weeks ago and he had never seen her. She often thought nowadays of herself and Mattie, never herself, Matthew and Mattie.

'I wish I had your courage,' she said to Edie on the Monday morning, knowing Edie had throughly enjoyed her Saturday night by evidence of yet another handful of Hershey bars and a pair of nylons.

Edie ran the gauzy stockings through her fingers. 'Can't get these in this country,' she tempted.

It wasn't the gifts American boys could dish out that made Susan squirm at Edie's efforts to tempt but the thought of someone's arms around her. It was a terrible thought and made her want to cry. Her first joy at the news of Matthew having been traced had long since dwindled. She had been allowed to send him a message if that was what it could be called. Fifteen words on a form, all the Japanese permitted. Whether Matthew received it who was to say? There had been no reply. It felt for all the world as though her message had been written to a ghost. She had never dared voice those sentiments to his mother, who had sent off her own forlorn fifteen words of encouragement and love that day. She would have been appalled. How much more appalled would she be were she to know how his wife yearned for the feel of a man's hand fondling her even though it wasn't her husband's. No, she couldn't.

All very well for Edie in the arms of some frustrated warrior far from home. Edie had changed a lot this year, voiced a different slant on her husband these days.

'Two years away – and God knows 'ow many more years. I mean, the man's stuck out in the Falklands. When're they goin' ter give 'im leave from there? Meanwhile I could go barmy waiting fer 'im ter come 'ome and make love.'

'But don't you feel some loyalty to him?' Susan asked and received a sceptical chuckle as Edie sorted out men's small from men's large, ready for despatching.

''Ow do I know 'e's not 'aving it off with some Falklands floozie? I do know 'e 'ad a rovin' eye, even when I first married 'im. It didn't matter then, I was there to keep my eye on 'im. But now, miles away. Why shouldn't I 'ave a bit of pleasure too? You must feel the need too, Sue? Keepin' yerself like a nun – it ain't natural. What the ole man don't know won't 'urt 'im. You ain't gonna confess all when 'e comes marchin' 'home, are yer? Fer God's sake, Sue, you'll be a physical wreck by the time 'e does if yer don't let off a bit of steam now and again.'

Frustration had its own way of dealing with things. Alone in

224

her room, her senses keened from reading cheap romances about larger-than-life heroines and handsome forceful heroes, she would furtively turn the key of her door, quietly so no one would hear it. Secure behind the lock, she would slip out of her clothes and survey herself before the mirror, run her hands slowly, slowly, over her body, gently following the curve of her small breasts, still firm; over her flat stomach that child-bearing had not marred at all. Closing her eyes she would imagine her fingers to be those of Matthew, tenderly exploring, growing urgent until her disquietened senses shrieked for relief. Then, throbbing from the lack of fulfilment she would fling herself on to her bed to squirm and weep in self-torment. How tempting it would be at these moments to follow Edie's example, to find herself someone to fondle her, fulfil this emptiness inside her – surely more honest than this pathetic self-pleasure that was no pleasure at all and left only misery in its wake.

'I wish I knew if Matthew was all right,' she confided in Emma. 'It could be years before I ever know. I'm so lonely.'

'At least yer've got Mattie,' Emma said, busily darning one of her Geoffrey's socks. He'd gone away for a day or two as usual.

'You have her most of the time these days,' Susan said.

Emma looked up sharply. 'It's you wot asked me ter look after 'er. You goin' ter work an' all. I'm not keepin' 'er away from yer.'

'I know. I didn't mean anything.' She was glad of Emma's help. She wasn't cut out to be a mother, she didn't think, driven to distraction when Mattie got herself into a temper, shrieking at the top of her voice. A child's shriek could be like a hot iron searing right through a person's eardrum. Smacking only made things worse. Many times Susan had been forced out of sheer frustration to resort to a smack on her legs, finally having to rush her down to Emma to pacify her. Emma was a natural mother. At times Susan felt quite envious of her.

'I'm just a bit down, I suppose,' she excused herself now. 'I hope she don't play you up too much.'

'Good Lord, no. She's a real dear. 'Cos, the only fing is we 'ave ter put everyfink up out of 'er reach now she's 'oisting 'erself up on 'er feet. Got 'er little 'ands inter everyfink. Real explorin' character she is. Quick. An' if she don't get wot she

225

wants, gets a real tantrum on 'er. Strong-minded. It's good. She probably takes after 'er dad. You're more of a pliable person, you are. She don't look as if she's gonna be. She ain't gonna be moved from wot she wants in life.'

'Sounds like she takes after Matthew's mother. Nothing can move her either.' She didn't say it in bitterness, just stated what was the truth. Mrs Ward had never deviated from the certainty that Matthew would come home, even though her poor little message hadn't been answered; had not deviated from continually telling Susan that she must be strong and pray for him to come home and not to give way to 'any temptation that may come along'. Such instructions made Susan shudder. What did the woman know of the feelings she harboured? Probably nothing. She was merely wise to such things, being older and having seen and learned more, for all her primness.

'I miss Matthew so much,' she said in an effort to evade thoughts of those temptations Mrs Ward hinted at with more emphasis than Susan cared to acknowledge. 'I know Geoffrey's not in the forces but he's away a lot too. Don't you miss *him*?'

'Miss 'im!' Emma put away the sock she had darned and picked up another, studying the dangerously thin place on the heel that next week would become a hole. 'I'm glad to see the back of him sometimes.'

Shocked, Susan stared at her. 'You don't mean that.'

'Yes, I do.' Emma gave a good-tempered chuckle. 'So will you when he's bin home fer a few years. Most wives do. Not nasty-like. But it's nice ter 'ave 'em out of the way occasionally and get on wiv yer own fings. Before 'e 'ad this job of 'is, it was, "Wot yer goin' out fer? 'Ow long'll yer be? I don't feel like goin' ter the pictures ternight." So I couldn't go either, could I? Not on me own an' leave 'im 'ere on 'is own. Married people don't do that. An' when yer spend all day mendin' 'is socks an 'ironing 'is shirts, an' bringin' up 'is kids, an' gettin' 'is breakfasts and dinners, an' makin' 'is sandwiches, an' bein' woken up out of a deep sleep because 'e wants a bit of the other . . . well, yer've had enough, ain't yer, an' yer want a bit of time to yerself. Miss 'im? I think this job 'e's got 'as bin a godsend. I know 'e's safe, not overseas somewhere in the fick of it all. But Geoff's the limit sometimes – expecting me ter be runnin' after 'im. The least sneeze and I'm 's nursemaid. Men!'

Her darning needle flew fast but without ill will. 'Babies, most of 'em. I expect they're brave enough amongst themselves, but get near their wives an' they're little babies, straight they are. I'm a bloomin' muvver to Geoff.'

She stopped to tap the hand of her youngest trying to fish into her workbasket for the glass marbles that always got in there. 'Yer'll prick yer fingers, yer silly little bugger! I'll get 'em out for yer after I've done this. Jus' wait!' She directed another laugh towards Susan watching. 'Even at that age. You 'ave ter fink for 'em. Mind, I don't mind Geoff wantin' his rights. I'd love ter 'ave a little daughter, just like your'n, it's just 'im waking me up out of a sleep fer it . . .' Another tolerant laugh. 'My mum use ter say, "Before yer married yer could feel yer could eat it. After yer married, yer wish you 'ad!"'

'I hope I never feel like that,' Susan said fervently.

'You will, luv. You will. Anyway I've got my little remedy – just tell 'im I'm out of bounds fer a week. I've told 'im, if 'e wants more'n I can give 'im, 'e can find it wiv a bit of skirt on 'is travels.'

She glanced up at the domed clock on the mantelshelf and sighed, ignoring Susan's look of horror as she put the rest of her husband's socks back into the workbasket to finish off later. 'Come on, you kids, time fer bed. Yer've got school in the mornin'.' Mattie, just a baby, had been put to bed ages ago. Emma's edict was met with a howl from the younger two, because Malcolm was still out playing.

'It's still light, Mum.'

'This time of year, it's always light. It's still eight o'clock and time fer bed.'

'Malc's not bin called in yet.'

''E will be. Soon as you two are up them stairs. Come on now.' She threw Susan an amused backward glance as she ushered them from the room in front of her. 'I was only jokin', Sue. My Geoff'd never go off wiv anuvver woman. 'E knows only too well where 'is bread is buttered, don' you worry.'

In the flimsy bamboo and attap construction they called the hospital, Matthew eased his way between the low platforms of sick men, some still as death, some tossing and turning in delirium, some bloated by beri-beri or calling for a pan as they strained to the flux of dysentery, or waited to have tropical leg-ulcers attended to.

Bob lay at the far end, a cadaverous figure whose hair had mostly fallen out to leave just a few dry tufts. His dull eyes glowed in the depths of their sockets and his lips parted in a grin at Matthew's approach.

'Hi.' He was unable to say more.

'Hi,' Matthew returned. 'How goes it?'

The thin shoulders hitched a fraction. 'Fine,' croaked the voice.

Kneeling beside him, Matthew recounted the day's news as he gave him a drink and then the soup he'd concocted from rice and a tiny bit of dried fish, but Bob turned away after the first mouthful, appetite destroyed.

'Cream of asparagus,' Matthew made the pathetic joke, 'straight from Harrods.'

But Bob's body had doubled up in pain, and Matthew held the panshaped piece of tin beneath his pal as the bowels evacu-ated the black blood-stained fluid. He felt helpless. How Bob had stayed alive for so long was beyond him. Sheer will-power sustained him and nothing else, for he no longer ate.

There were no drugs and food was his only chance. But rice alone was not food enough. For his friend, Matthew stole, but not well. Bob had always been better at it than he, his cheerful slant on life serving him well in the face of the anger of their conquerors if caught. Even for them food was not all that forthcoming and understandably they were apt to become over-wrought by light-fingered prisoners purloining the tiniest portion of what small comforts they did receive. But stealing was a necessary part of survival. Bartering what inedibles he stole called for patience, and again Bob's stolid approach to life had allowed him to stand the strain of it and the disappoint-ment that often followed. Wily villagers knew they had the edge on British POWs with half a mind on prowling guards. The Nippon cigarettes or stolen truck spares they'd risked their lives for would reap a couple of tiny eggs or a pomelo or two or a scrap of dried fish. But beggars couldn't be choosers.

The watery dawn coming up, Matthew turned his face towards camp with a lighter heart than usual. Under his loincloth hung half a tiny chicken, a bit high but edible. It made him walk oddly but the gait of anyone with a raw scrotum was easily ignored. Once the chicken was made into a soup, Bob must surely find the appetite to take a few mouthfuls.

The night shift had been unusually short. Yamagata, their shoko, had miscalculated the quota and his pleasure at their apparently superhuman efforts to reach the target he'd set showed on his round face, his tone almost pleasant as he'd called out 'Yoroshii,' which meant things were good. 'Orr men finish.'

With the railway growing apace it was a long march back to camp. By the time they reached it, Yamagata would have eaten and been in the arms of Morpheus. It was a surprise then to see him coming back to meet them, his short arms flailing like stubby windmill sails, his face animated. He had obviously discovered his error in judging his quota and intended putting it to rights; no doubt he'd been hauled over the coals himself for the mistake. But instead of marching the men back to the railway, he took them down another narrow path into the jungle to arrive at another camp.

It was empty. It didn't take long to discover why. Every one of the native labourers there was dead. Ordered to burn every corpse, a strong suspicion grew that they were disposing of cholera victims and Matthew thought that no Japanese could ever have seen men work faster. Two hours later they were marching back to their own camp, a very sober, thoughtful bunch. But worse was to come. In their absence three British POWs had died of something also strongly resembling cholera.

Matthew felt his flesh creep, seeing the Japanese running about making ready to flee before it struck them also. He noticed too that the guards with his column had disappeared. Nothing would prevent a man escaping except the jungle itself; thousands of square miles of rainforest; a mapless terrain where he would climb and slither endlessly; inedible plant life, poisonous insects, evil water; he would go round in circles until he died. No iron bars could have made a better prison.

In a steady rain that had again begun, the camp was a nucleus of panic, the sick being transported from the hospital on make-shift stretchers to be unceremoniously dumped on the bare, wet ground. Catching the panic, Matthew grabbed the arm of one of the helpers.

'I'm looking for Bob Howlett.'

The man looked put out. With over a hundred sick to get out of this place at the double, who the hell remembered one man's name? 'Go and ask the bloody MO.'

'Where's the MO?'

The orderly shrugged free of his grip. 'Listen chum. We've got just five minutes to get these poor buggers out before them bastards set fire to the hospital. They're bleedin' terrified. If you can't help us, sod off!'

He had jerked a thumb towards three guards, no doubt ordered by their CO to stand their ground, which they would, more frightened of his wrath than cholera. Two had set up a machine gun, obviously meant for any protesters as the third stood by with several cans of kerosene. Their faces, full of terror, were the colour of putty.

'There's blokes gonna die being moved like this. But they ain't gonna burn. Now leave us alone if you ain't gonna help.'

Matthew found the MO inside the hospital frantically supervising the exodus. 'Bob Howlett,' he enquired urgently. 'Lantern-jawed chap. Has dysentery.'

The distinguishing feature had made an impression. The MO paused in his work, his expression one of commiseration. 'Were you the mate who used to feed and wash him?'

There was no need for the man to say more. Matthew felt numbed.

'When?' he whispered.

'Buried him last night.' The statement was almost callous. The MO had expended his compassion in this direction. Now he must return his attention to the living.

'Where was he buried?' Matthew persisted.

'Cemetery.' The soldier with the kerosene can was coming forward, approaching cautiously as though the dread killer might pounce out on him.

'Where in the cemetery?'

'I don't know where!' The MO pushed past, pointing to his helpers. 'You, over there with that one. Quick now!' His shout was one of exasperation. Two British officers, identifiable by the tattered shirts they still retained, were arguing with the soldier.

'Wait – please – wait.'

But he pushed them aside, shaking his head. '*Iie*! *Dame desu*! *Kirai*! *Hayaku*!' He was demanding they move out of his way. Those with the machine gun had grown tense. Defeated, the officers fell back. The can at arm's length splashed against the hut. Numbed by his own grief, Matthew watched a lighted match thrown into the place, heard the fuel ignite with a soft roar. Flames met rain-soaked material, hissed, spluttered, hesitated. A pall of yellow smoke rolled the length of the hut. Men running in and out, bearing their occupied stretchers, coughed in the smoke, shouting, getting in each other's way. More fuel was splashed on, another match struck. A growl rose up from the rescuers, but the Japanese had the machine gun and were trigger-happy.

Conquering the wet bamboo and palm-leaf roof, the flames leapt, and still the rescuers ran in and out, the sick draped over their shoulders, men, hardly able to stand, clambering over the open sides of the hospital.

His own personal loss dulling his senses, Matthew ran with the others, blindly helping the last of the sick to safety until the heat finally forced him to retreat. With the flames crackling behind him he went towards the cemetery at the far end of the camp where a tangle of jungle prevented any further intrusion. There he stood gazing at the rows of bamboo crosses, each tilted in the sodden mud, each bearing a pathetic attempt to inscribe the name of whoever lay beneath.

It was very still here. Just the sound of pattering rain on the soft earth and the distant cries of those still helping with the rescue and the red glow from the burning hospital flickering on the drunken crosses in the monsoon-dulled morning like something in a weird dream.

Which cross belonged to Bob? Was he yet to have a cross? So many crosses. So many. From some of them a fine rivulet of mud was trickling. By the end of the monsoon many of the markers would be horizontal. As the camp moved on, following the railway, the jungle would return, cover them with vines and roots and fungus, all signs of them obliterated as though they had never been. By that time he and others would be far away, perhaps themselves beneath the mud under a rough bamboo cross out there in this senseless tangle. All were living on borrowed time. All a man could hope for was a mate to hold his hand so he would not die alone.

But Bob had died alone. The man who'd been his friend from almost the beginning of their Army service, who had carried him for two days on the march to Rangoon, who had bathed him so many times when he had been sick and helpless, had been denied the privilege of a companion to ease his last moments. Amid other dying men he had gone unnoticed, alone.

The thought of that loneliness constricted Matthew's throat muscles. He should have been with him, should have been there to put an inscription on his pitiful bamboo cross, to honour Bob's burial with his presence.

Without strength Matthew let his knees buckle, sank down in the mud which, disturbed by his light weight on it, offered up a fulsome stink. And as he had failed to comfort his dying friend, so there was no comfort for him – only the rain mingled with salt dribbling down his cheeks; only the empty silence of the lonely graves, the intermittent calling of the wild things of the rainforest, and, faintly, the shouts of men trying vainly to help each other.

Chapter 21

'I really enjoy these moments of peace and quiet.'

Geoffrey Crawley lounged in one the sagging armchairs in the living half of Susan's partitioned room. 'Between you, me and the gatepost,' he continued, 'Emma's jolliness can go right through one sometimes.'

'She's a very nice person,' Susan defended, handing him the cup of tea she'd made on the small gas ring she seldom used except when he came up here to escape the constant din of wife and kids downstairs.

'Oh, don't get me wrong.' He took an appreciative sip of the tea. 'I'd be the first to challenge anyone who says anything against her. Salt of the earth – Emma. But sometimes . . .'

Susan smiled. He seemed to like her as an audience, to get off his chest the little things that bothered him or to regale her with little anecdotes of his travels which Emma, managing three growing boys and a house, had no time to listen to and had probably heard before. At first it had been a little embarrassing, him coming up here. What if Emma got the wrong idea?

She'd said as much to Emma who had promptly viewed the whole thing with amusement. 'Keeps 'im out of my way while I'm gettin' dinner. S'long as yer don't mind 'im. If yer don't want 'im up there, just send 'im packin' back down 'ere. Yer don't 'ave ter put up wiv 'im. Need yer own privacy sometimes, I expect. Just turn 'im out when yer've 'ad enough.'

But she didn't want to turn him out. It was nice having a man's company all to herself. He made good conversation but his was quiet where Emma's could be so noisy. He brought her little things, sweets he'd got from under the counter, most of them for his children and for Emma and even Mattie, but a few for her. Lately he'd been giving her more and more little presents: a pair of nylons; a length of parachute silk from which she made herself a couple of slips; a lipstick on her birthday – Max Factor – not easy to come by. The ends of previous ones were melted down and poured in to one container to make them go further. Emma didn't wear lipstick since having the boys. 'He knows what I look like,' she'd said when Susan had offered her a touch of hers. ''E'd 'ave a fit, me dolled up. Think I'd got meself some other bloke.'

Susan accepted them all gratefully. At least she didn't have to go with some GI like Edie to get them. On her first Christmas with the Crawleys – she'd refused to spend it with her in-laws – he had brought home a tiny wooden doll for Mattie. At Easter a real chocolate egg, not a cardboard one. On her first birthday a pink dress, and on Susan's birthday, lace hankies. Where he got these things from she never asked; she was just flattered by the attention. And ever since her birthday he'd come up to sit in her armchair and chat for an hour or so, whatever Sunday afternoon he was home. It had become almost a habit.

Christmas came round again, and again she refused to spend any of it with Mr and Mrs Ward, nor, to be fair, with her own family. They were too much of a journey away and the house remained crowded with her grandparents still there, their home still uninhabitable. She sent them a card though, one of those postcard things that now took the place of the fancy pre-war ones.

But Mrs Ward was as put out as she'd been the previous year. 'We never see Matilda unless we come to you. Surely one Christmas with us.'

Susan had remained silent, sullen, but she had her way. Here was fun, she could be herself with an easygoing family. The thought of spending it with the Wards, the long silences, the brooding atmosphere she always sensed there, though it was probably of her own making, made her cringe. She turned from the knowledge that there would be just three people at the Wards' house this Christmas, Mr and Mrs Ward and Louise, home on leave, and they would sit and mourn the absence of their son through the whole festive season. She wanted none of it.

On Christmas Eve came an uproar from below, exactly as last year, when Geoffrey arrived home with presents. As before she remained in her room, not wishing to intrude. But soon footsteps echoed up the stairs and she heard a light tapping on her door.

Opening it she saw Geoff standing there, face flushed from the many whiskies and gins offered by various customers and reps who could still get hold of it. Swaying slightly he held out a large square brown paper parcel with a smaller one on top.

'Happy Christmas!' he burst out, thrusting the packages at her, and, too excited to wait for her to open them when the time came, announced in a slurred voice: 'Dolls house f'r Mattie. Cardboard I'm 'fraid. The small one's f'r you, pair o' gloves.'

Susan felt her face flush with pleasure. 'Geoff, you shouldn't have.'

'Part o'th' family, hey?'

Even tipsy, he spoke much better than Emma. A Cockney twang could still be discerned there but Susan supposed that his work called for better speech. He was the exact opposite of Emma in every way; she bonny, sloppy, talkative, animated, her hair fair and frizzy; he slim, neat and quiet, brown hair slicked back by brilliantine. He was something like eighteen years older than Susan – Emma said he was nearing forty though she hadn't said how near – but he looked younger than that. Although shorter, he resembled Matthew in some way, but was more sleek and not so dark-haired and his eyes looked an indeterminate shade of blue where Matthew's had been brown. (She had used the past tense when that thought had come to her, though it had gone unnoticed.) But Geoff was here, and she had begun to notice him a lot. Not only was he nice to look at but he smelled nice, from lotions she supposed he picked up on his travels.

'I've got everyone something,' he was saying, still swaying in the doorway. As she stood back to let him in, he plonked the packages on a chair.

'I've got something for everyone too,' she said. They were already wrapped and waiting, in brown paper. Christmas wrapping had become a thing of the past. 'Wooden toys for the boys,' she announced. 'Someone I know makes them out of old furniture.' It was a man who worked next door to where she worked. 'I've got a brooch for Emma.' That too was made from wood with a picture painted on it by the same man, making quite a trade out of it, it seemed.

'And this is for you.' She handed him the tiny package.

'What is it?'

'I'm not saying. Wait 'til you open it.'

He giggled. 'I've told you what I got you. Tell me what you've got me.'

'It isn't much.' They were cuff-links, not expensive.

'Ah, th' best things always come in li'l packages?' He was regarding her closely and she felt he was referring to her personally. She felt herself blush.

'Don't be silly.'

'No.' He swayed towards her. 'I mean it.' His breath smelled sweetly of whisky, not at all unpleasant. Leaning forward, he laid a kiss on her cheek. Suddenly all the loneliness she'd been pretending wasn't there whenever Edie regaled her with what she'd been up to the evening before welled up inside her. She lifted both arms and put them around his neck and at the obvious invitation, his lips settled on hers.

Susan felt herself trembling with all the longing that had lain inside her, and she realised that he too harboured a certain loneliness, though why he should, with Emma there for him, she couldn't understand. But at the moment she didn't want to understand. Her whole being was crying out for comfort. For a second, her thoughts flew wildly to the bed behind the partition. Her heart seemed to be pounding through her entire body, her blood throbbing to its thumping. Then suddenly he released her.

'God, I must be more stoned than I thought. God, Sue, I'm sorry.'

How could she cry out, 'Don't go?' How could she make herself look cheaper than she must already look? She stood watching him back away towards the door. It was all she could do. What her expression was like she didn't know, but she hoped it wasn't imploring. He was still apologising, clutching the present she had given him. This would be the end of their moments together up here in this room. She'd driven him away by her own stupid actions and now she'd have no one. There was a dull ache where the throbbing had been while he stood teetering in the doorway, apologies still on his lips.

'If you knew, Sue, what I was thinking just now, you'd throw me out,' he said, and it was then that she found her voice.

'Geoffrey, don't go.'

She waited. Then very slowly he closed the door and came back into the room.

She had got through her finals, she was a State Registered Nurse at last. Margaret telephoned her mother, then armed with a four-hour pass went out to celebrate in a local pub with the others of her group who had passed.

'What d' you plan to do now?' asked mousy-haired Molly Fergusson who'd become her best friend. Everyone was asking the same question of each other.

Sipping her third Sanderman's sherry, Margaret thought about that one. The idea of applying for the QAIMNS/R made itself felt again. This time she would apply. Mumsy would be distressed, but she needed some of that freedom she had always dreamed about, which even becoming a nurse had not as yet fulfilled. It meant she could be sent abroad; she couldn't help it but somehow the idea identified her with Matthew, silly fool that she was. When would she ever grow up?

She knew of course that he was a prisoner of war. Susan walking out on his parents as she had, knowing how things stood, had to her mind been a terrible thing to do. Now she lived with some rough family off Mile End Road rather than the nice home into which she had been so generously accepted. Susan must have been off her head. But it was none of her business. She had to get on with her own life. And how often had she told herself that as soon as Matthew came into mind? As he came to mind now, so she pushed the thought away and told Molly of her plans.

'Watch it,' Molly said ominously. 'They could send you anywhere.'

But she was adamant now. It was what she wanted, to be sent anywhere. It was what had happened to Matthew. And she was thinking of him again. All these years and she still thought of him.

Quickly she stopped thinking of him. Even so, she applied, and soon found herself saying goodbye to all the friends she'd made at the London Whitechapel, except for Molly who having readily told her to watch it, had decided to go with her. It felt good to have someone, not exactly to hold her hand, but to be a support in a corner, to be in the same boat with. Paddling one's own canoe could be all very well, but a lonely business, and Molly had become a good friend. It would have been hard to say goodbye to her.

'I feel a bit guilty leaving here at a time like this,' Margaret confided. Air raids had begun again, this time more concentrated, the bombs heavier and more destructive. Dispirited Londoners who'd thought they'd seen the end of the Blitz called it the little Blitz; almost as many victims were being brought into the London as before. The second front was still being talked about, but this time everyone knew it would come soon. Guilty feelings or not, she was determined nothing should stop her now, visions of being sent overseas filling her mind.

'Adventure at last,' she said, shrugging off feelings of guilt.

'Aye, adventure at last,' Molly Fergusson agreed.

Conditions overseas could be uncomfortable, Margaret was told at her interview. She didn't mind. She could be sent anywhere. She didn't mind. A medical was followed by a lengthy shopping list, with her expected to pay for the items it contained.

'We'll be out of pocket a whole of month at least,' she grumbled. 'I never considered us needing these things.'

They were items that very few of the nursing recruits had considered: folding camp bed and bedroll; a collapsible canvas bath, wash bowl and bucket; gumboots; portable paraffin stove. Even the uniform, grey suit and greatcoat with scarlet facings, a change of grey shirts and ties, hat, a change of grey cotton dresses, cape trimmed with scarlet, a lawn veil, had to be bought. Her mother generously sent her a bit of money to help out along with her laments at her daughter no longer coming home most evenings – not coming home at all. She was in the forces, it hadn't properly registered until now. She'd be called sister. Nursing Officer M. Ross number T/348509. And she and Molly were to be sent off to a military hospital somewhere in England. So much for going abroad.

238

In fact they ended up in Essex, at a large manor called Hamdon Hall, now a military hospital in a village of the same name – far from being hundreds of miles from home, she could have cycled there!

New Year's Eve, like Christmas, had been wonderful, the house filled to overflowing with all the Crawley family: friends, relatives, mostly women and children or men too old to have been called up, a sprinkling of uniforms of those who had been lucky enough to be home on short leave. The New Year seen in, the party had lasted until around one in the morning, until slowly growing stale and dwindling as one after another relatives yawned, remembered their own homes, minds on a cup of cocoa and bed. Now they had all gone. All were living close by and did not need to stay the night.

In the now-quiet kitchen surrounded by the debris of the party while Emma said goodnight to the last of them at the door, loath to see them go, when she would have to come back and face the clearing up, yapping away with them in the silence of the freezing early hours of 1944, Geoffrey gave Susan a long, searching look.

'Fancy a nightcap? There's some whisky left, or a drop of port.'

She shook her head. 'I think I've had enough.'

She started to leave but he took hold of her hand. 'Look, Sue, I'm sorry about the other day.'

She wanted to say, '*I'm* not,' but she wasn't even sure about that. It had been so wonderful, then afterwards so wretched knowing what she'd done, and then she had wanted it to happen all over again. She ended up saying, rather stupidly, 'Emma must have wondered why you was so long delivering the Christmas presents.'

'Probably reckoned I was just chatting,' he mused. He moved nearer to her. 'Are you sorry about what happened?'

It was a direct question, one she couldn't answer except to give a small shrug, her eyes lowered. Taking her silence for collusion, he drew her gently to him. 'I love you, Sue.'

His breath smelled of alcohol. She held herself stiff in his embrace. Any moment Emma would be back in, her goodnights said. Fear made her body grow even more tense. 'You don't,'

239

she whispered. 'You had too much to drink that day. You've had too much to drink tonight. We mustn't . . .'

He put a hand gently over her mouth. 'I love you. I can't remember when it started. All those times I sat in your room I could hardly keep from taking hold of you and kissing you and telling you how I felt. But you gave me no encouragement – no sign. I knew how you felt about your husband so I didn't dare . . . I wouldn't muck you about, Sue. You're too nice for that. But that day, when you asked me not to go, knowing by then how I felt . . .'

He let his words drift off, his hand falling away from her mouth. In his arms she felt limp. 'But I don't love you,' she managed to say. She had to be honest with him. But what was honesty? What was truth? 'I was lonely.'

The strength went out of his clasp on her, his tone took on a touch of harsh disappointment, bitterness. 'And I came in handy.'

'No.' She heard Emma call out a last goodnight, the night air making her call sound flat and far away. She would stand watching her guests until they disappeared into Mile End Road, a woman so full of demonstrative affection that she couldn't bear to let those she was fond of fade from sight until forced to by the intervention of something like a street corner. There were a few more minutes left before she came back indoors. Meanwhile Susan gabbled what she needed to say to Geoffrey.

'That's the trouble, all I could think about was you, you near me and the wonderful feeling it gave me. I should've thought about my husband, but I didn't. He's like a dream – something that never really happened.'

'Then why hold me off?' He too was talking fast, knowing his wife would be back any moment.

'Because,' she said, 'I don't know how I feel – if I was trying to put you in his place . . . Geoffrey, I could let you love me, easy as anything. But I must have time to think.' Any minute now Emma would be back indoors. Susan pulled free of the hand still holding her wrist. 'You must leave me alone, Geoffrey. And don't come upstairs to see me any more, please.'

The street door scraped to and closed with a tortured grating thud. The wood had swollen in the damp winter weather. Susan

240

fled to the kitchen door and stumbled past Emma coming along the unlit passage.

'You all right, Sue?' came the startled voice.

'Just want the lav,' she mumbled, making for the stairs. 'Think I'll go straight to bed.'

'It's all that beer – makes yer run. Wanna nightcap? Tea? Cocoa?'

'No thanks.'

Reaching her door she stumbled into her room. Closing the door she leaned against it. Her body felt like an empty sack as she let herself slide to the floor to give herself over to weeping, ceasing only when Mattie stirred in her cot, dreaming, giving a small whimper.

For three months they hadn't moved from where they had been quartered. In huts erected in the grounds of Hamdon Hall, in the depths of January and February and March, they looked forward earnestly to the warmer spring weather. With the second front still being talked about, they treated cuts and bruises on men returning from training manoeuvres, saw to fingers squashed in lorry bonnets, dosed sore throats, winter colds, caught colds themselves and dosed each other.

'Fun, don' ye think?' Molly said, her nose red and sore from the constant application of unforgiving hankies. Margaret chuckled and wiped her own tender nose. Molly was a tonic. Always jolly, always looking on the bright side, a girl to turn every soldier's eye. She was tall, like Margaret herself, but whip-thin, and looked as though the smallest breeze would knock her sideways. Like all women with such figures she looked wonderful in her smart grey and scarlet uniform, whereas Margaret saw herself as doing her uniform no justice whatsoever despite the appreciative remarks of the soldiers about the colour of her hair and the lovely grey-green of her eyes. She took it with a pinch of salt. They'd pay compliments to any nurse in uniform attending their trivial medical complaints.

So their lives continued, spring sunshine lifting the spirits as they went on occasion to the local pictures in nearby Chelmsford, attended the villege fête at Easter, went to the community hall dance that had once only catered for a sprinkling of villagers but now was crammed with a variety of uniforms, hospital staff, and patients. Molly hardly ever danced with the same man twice; she went into town on the arm of every Tom, Dick and Harry. Margaret did the same but somehow could never allow herself to get close to any one man, so she supposed she too lingered on every Tom, Dick and Harry's arm and it was an ever-changing foursome that marched off into Chelmsford for an evening at the pictures or a better-class dance at the town hall.

The next two months passed like a dream, surrounded by the gentle warmth of the Essex countryside, by contentment, comradeship, and all the while learning ever more of the skills and requirements of her chosen career. At last she was forgetting to think about Matthew. This was a different life, her old life and all its sense of confinement and commitment left far behind. As for the yearning to go overseas, although the QAs were an overseas division of nursing, it seemed this was where they would remain for the duration of the war.

Things, however, were to change. Towards the end of May the whole unit of QAs upped stakes and moved to outside Deal in Kent to meet a mounting stockpile of ammunition, military vehicles and chaos. They got fitted out with sloppy dungaree-like garments, heavy boots, webbing, respirator and haversack, raincape-cum-groundsheet and all the other paraphernalia that was designed to hang around the frame of military personnel.

Miles from anywhere, for the last weeks of May life assumed a state of utter immobility beyond the vast camp site with its growing mass of men and military machinery. The first week of June began wet and windy, the wind at times whipping to gale force, making life under canvas more than miserable.

Emerging from the prefabricated canteen that first Tuesday in June to a newly washed morning after the gales of the previous few days, Margaret became aware of a low and steady distant roar that made every girl look up, wonderingly. Within seconds the distant roar was filling the air.

'Christ! Look at that!' Molly's voice had to screech over the growing racket.

As though being raised on a vast curtain, a cloud of dark shapes had begun to loom over the tree-tops from the west. Bearing down on the awed, open-mouthed watchers below –

the whole hospital had turned out to see what the thunderous noise was all about, the building itself being shaken by the weight of it – wave after wave of planes began to pass overhead. Each bomber towed a glider, Halifaxes, Lancasters, Blenheims, the huge Flying Fortresses, moving almost wingtip to wingtip in steady purposeful majesty, deceptively slow, forming a virtual ceiling above the upturned faces.

'It's the second front,' shrieked Molly, the deafening roar practically carrying her voice away. 'It's started. At last!'

But with the last waves of planes receding into the distance, silence descending strangely upon ears still ringing from the earlier noise, Margaret and Molly looked at each other, as did all the women of their unit.

'We'll probably be following them soon,' Molly said, serious for once.

Chapter 22

Obeying her wishes, Geoffrey hadn't visited her room again. Downstairs he was polite to her as though nothing had ever occurred between them. Weeks stretched to months; for Susan it was a most miserable time. The colder he seemed towards her, the warmer he appeared to become towards his family, playing with his boys far more than she was sure he once did whenever he was home. He was good with Mattie too, bouncing her on his knee until she chuckled fit to burst, but not one warm glance did he cast towards herself. She ached for him to give her just one look that said he too remembered Christmas Eve in her room and yearned to repeat it.

Even Emma noticed. 'You done somefink ter upset Geoff?' she asked. When Susan raised her shoulders sullenly without offering any explanation one way or the other, he laughed, assuring Emma he was being a perfect gentleman to their tenant, the innuendo not escaping Susan who wanted to burst into tears and tell him that if anything he was behaving perfectly rotten to her.

She even contemplated giving up her rooms and moving on, but how could she explain why to a bewildered and hurt Emma? Not only that, the courage she had possessed on that one single escapade when she'd left the Wards now evaded her; she couldn't repeat that, not with a twenty-month-old child in tow with all its attendant toiletries, nappies, clothing. And she'd never find herself another place like this with such wonderful people. She gritted her teeth and forced herself to stick out Geoffrey's horrid attitude, knowing it had really been of her own making.

He had even managed to avoid her during the little Blitz when they'd all huddled in the Morrison shelter in the tiny cluttered basement, the air raids less regular but as devastating as the real Blitz three years before – incredible to think the war had gone on so long.

In April they also had ceased as abruptly as the first Blitz, leaving the big cities in a period of quiet, Hitler foiled again. For Susan, terrified as she had been of a direct hit, the debatable closeness of Geoffrey, who continued virtually to ignore her, was taken away. A month had gone by since then and this weekend was only the second time Geoffrey had come home, she and he, as usual, avoiding each other like the plague.

After putting Mattie to bed, she had stayed up in her room, sick of looking at his averted face as he played with his sons. She'd been up here some time and when a gentle knock came on her door she guessed it was Emma wondering why she hadn't come downstairs again. Emma worried that way. She opened the door ready with an excuse, to find Geoffrey standing there. He looked apologetic.

'I'm sorry, I had to come up. Emma's been asking why I never come up here now. I thought I'd better make it look good – just for half an hour. Do you mind?'

'No,' she answered woodenly and stood back for him to enter.

'I could go if you want.' But he was already sitting in the armchair. She stood near hers, not sure whether to sit down or not and make this seem like the cosy little times that once had been.

'Do you want me to make you a cup of tea?'

'No, I shan't stay long. Fact is, after the boys went to bed, Emma went next door to Mrs Fulham for a chat. She'll be in there about an hour, if I know her.'

'Oh,' her voice sounded flat, neutral. Suddenly he was out of his chair.

'Sue, I can't go on like this. I'm in a state. I can't work, I can't think, I can't think of anything but you. Sue, I'm so bloody unhappy.'

She wanted to say that he looked happy enough to her, but she said nothing. Her heart was racing. This was what she had wanted to hear all those months, and now her heart was going like a steam hammer and her mind was in confusion and she could find nothing to say. The fact was, she had no need to say anything. He was saying it all for her, still in the same place where he had stood up from the chair, as though his feet were nailed to the floor, his pale blue eyes trained on her.

'I really do love you, Sue. I'm not a man of any special talent. I don't know what to say on these occasions. All I know is what I feel for you. I've tried to conquer it, as you'd asked me to.'

'I never . . .' But he was rushing on.

'I *know* it's wrong. I'm a married man, but I've never felt for anyone the way I feel about you. I *know* you said you love your husband, that you were just lonely when I . . . when we . . . I'm married. You're married. But we can't help these things happening.'

'Geoffrey.' She tried to stop the flow of pitiful clichés, but he did not hear her.

'I know you love me – the way you look at me. Sue, darling, if you feel anything for me you can't possibly feel the same for – well, anyone else. Do you still feel anything for . . . anyone else?' She knew who he meant, loath to say the name.

'I – don't know,' she stammered.

'You do feel something for me?'

'I – Geoffrey, I don't know.'

'You must know. If I didn't matter to you, you wouldn't go around looking so downcast. I know you love me. You do, don't you?'

She allowed a glum nod, a half-nod really, but enough for him. He came forward and his arms were about her, the sweetness of his breath flowing across her face, she in turn clinging to him, needing this reality.

She couldn't remember reaching her bed, but she would never not remember the delicious, the overwhelming joy of being made love to, all the more wonderful for the mad snatched affair it was, filled with need and with tension and with fear of time overtaking them. She had never felt so fulfilled as when he came inside her, she rising up to meet him.

Afterwards she didn't feel at all ashamed as she had that first time. Lying in Geoffrey's arms, luxuriating in the contentment that flowed over her, she found herself drawing a veil

246

over the man she had once adored, found herself forming a mental note to put his photo away from its place on the bedside table. What could be gained by staring at the flat, lifeless image of a smiling man that a scrap of paper proclaimed was her husband? How did she know where he was and if he still existed? Nothing was ever heard of those whom the Japanese had captured. They stubbornly recognised no conventional rules of war, were said to be fanatical about dying for their emperor and to see captives of war as unworthy of respect. Fearful tales had come out of the Far East of massacres and terrible deeds done by them. How was she to know what might have happened to Matthew?

In Geoffrey's arms, seeing her vigilance as a waste of effort, she blocked out everything else but the hope that this would be the beginning of a long summer of ecstasy, perhaps a lifetime. Only later when he left, dressed and dapper as always as his wife came in through the front door to get his evening cup of cocoa, did she give some thought to what they'd done and what they intended to go on doing. With Emma suspecting nothing. But one day she would, or would have to be told. And then . . .

A shudder passed over Susan at the misery that awaited Emma, and she felt suddenly sick.

The doorbell, of course, didn't work. It had never worked. Lilian would have liked it to work so that she could have kept her thumb on it indefinitely, displaying her anger until the door was eventually opened. Instead she must use the door knocker which wasn't the same thing for she'd be disturbed by the noise as would the neighbours, whereas a bell upset only those on the other side of the door.

It was Mrs Crawley who answered, but that didn't matter. Lilian's wrath was directed as much to her as to Susan. She'd promised she'd make herself responsible for the girl and she had let the side down.

Susan's letter had completely taken her breath away, shocked her to the very core. Unabashed it was, no matter how shame-facedly worded, the grammar and spelling, bad as ever, adding to the ill grace of it.

. . . I've got to tell you sometime. I feel I've got to be honest, because Emma Crawley's walked out on Mr Crawley as him and me are living together you might say. It all just hapened. We couldn't help ourselfs, and now I've found out I'm pregnant. So I thought it was best to tell you the truth. I know it sounds bad, but it wasn't intended to be like that. It just what hapened. I don't expect you'll forgive me and I know you'll say I should wait for Matthew but I could just be waiting in vane? But now there's Mattie to think of. Mr Crawley don't like her around now Emma's not here to give eye to her. He askd me if I'd ask you if you'd like to have her for a wile, being her grandparents . . .

She'd crumpled the letter up and thrown it from her half-read, only to retrieve and re-read it, still with disbelief. How anyone could be so shameless, so brazen? And to choose now of all times to write such things, three years almost to the day Matthew had gone away, had kissed his wife – his *loyal* wife – goodbye to march off into captivity. *Three years!* How could anyone be so faithless? She couldn't wait, could she?

Her mind again seething with the contents of that letter, Lilian had begun to wonder if there was anyone at home. Her knocking was taking so long to be answered. As if there wasn't enough to put up with, she continued to wait for news of Matthew that never came, clinging desperately to the belief that one day she'd hear, that one day, when the war drew to an end, he'd come home.

But this war was on their doorstep yet again in the shape of the doodlebug. Just as the news of Allied advances had everyone reading the papers as though following the football results, excited by it all, there had come the spluttering-engine roar of those V1s, like black crosses spouting blowlamp fire in their wake. From D-Day and throughout June, July and August they had laboured across the sky. All warily watched their course as they cut out, soughing on ominously, the watchers unsure whether to duck or not. When they finally came plunging to earth they demolished homes in huge explosions that fanned out flying glass and debris, killing scores of people, for no one knew where they'd fall. Sometimes a hundred would come over in a day, several at once so no one knew where to look or run. The old air-raid shelters proved of no help; cowering in them would have halted all normal life, they chewed up a body's nerves. Several had fallen near to her, too near for comfort, and people had again left London in droves.

Yet, as though none of this mattered, Susan had had the audacity to carry on an affair with her landlady's husband, heedless of his wife who'd befriended the girl, of her own husband who was a prisoner of war. She was thinking only of herself, her needs, her pleasures.

Lilian's first thought had been to seek out Leonard and show him the letter. On Saturday the shop stayed open until five thirty, but she had eventually decided against going there and demeaning herself by telling him such news in front of goggle-eyed customers. She had to deal with this herself. Making up her mind in a fit of anger, she had got herself ready and now, half an hour later, was waiting for someone to answer her knock.

But she had not been prepared for it to be Mrs Crawley herself. Even so, she collected herself, fluttering the letter in the woman's face. 'This arrived from my daughter-in-law an hour ago. She gave me to believe you'd left. I hardly expected to find you here, circumstances being what they are.'

Mrs Crawley's face was bleak. No longer the amiable woman, she regarded Lilian with a steady pride in her eyes. 'It's still my 'ome, Mrs Ward. I just come back fer a few fings wot's mine.'

'I see.' For a moment she was stumped. 'Is my daughter-in-law here?'

'Upstairs.'

'Is he . . .'

'Wiv 'er? Yes. 'E's wiv 'er.'

Again she was caught by the simple truth spoken so directly, without inflection. 'I need to see her,' was all she could find to say.

Without a word Mrs Crawley stepped aside, allowing her to enter. Her face lifted briefly towards the top of the stairs, indicating for Lilian to go up. She too said nothing, but nodded her head in Mrs Crawley's direction as she passed, noticing a battered suitcase in the hall with a hat balanced on top.

Mounting the stairs, there was no sound behind her but she

had the feeling that the woman hadn't watched her go, and reaching the door to the room where Susan resided, she heard the front door close quietly and knew that Mrs Crawley had let herself out.

For the first time she felt fear. What would she find on the other side of that door? It took all her reserve of courage to rap on it with her knuckles. Then she remembered the letter, how she'd felt reading it, and her rap became firm.

'I couldn't tell you before. You were at work.' Leonard was visibly upset by her going off like that without a word to him.

'You should have allowed me to be there, Lilian. I'd have been able to lessen the impact rather than you having to deal with it alone.'

'I managed well enough.'

She had managed, facing up to the situation that had confronted her on stepping inside Susan's rooms, seeing the state the girl had allowed it to get into. And that poor little mite, Matilda; she could have cried for her.

Entering, she'd been met by the sight of Geoffrey Crawley. In white shirt, brown trousers, plain brown tie and sleeveless pullover, he presented quite an elegant figure until one noticed the pale stubble on his chin. The man hadn't shaved that morning. Lilian knew immediately that her entrance had been heard downstairs. There must have been an unholy rush to dress, making it seem as though they had been up for hours.

Eyes sharpened by the sight of that stubble saw more telltale things: through the open door in the partition wall, a glimpse of an unmade bed and this at eleven thirty in the morning; clothes left on the floor; breakfast cups unwashed. The two must have been idling around the place in a state of undress. The knowledge brought bile into her throat as she swallowed fastidiously. Worst of all, Matilda, who was standing up in her cot, the covers twisted into a heap, was still in nightclothes, her dark curling hair dishevelled, her little face unwashed and still sticky from a piece of bread and jam that now adhered to the cot rail. She'd been crying, no doubt for attention that wasn't forthcoming as these two indulged in each other – evidence of her distress was visible in the mucus drying around her nose. Lilian had never seen the child in such a mess. Usually

Mattie looked quite presentable at other times when she had visited, but now she knew that had been Emma Crawley's doing, never the mother's. And there had stood Susan in a clean dress and hastily applied lipstick, though her long hair had not been combed quickly enough, for Lilian had seen one or two tangles that had been missed because of this couple's vile goings-on earlier this morning.

It was then she had found her voice. With the letter held at arm's length to the girl, she demanded what was the meaning of it. 'Are you saying that this ... animal has got you pregnant?' she'd asked, quite illogically, for had it not been written there in black and white?

Crawley had stepped forward, full of indignation. 'I say, hold on.'

Lilian had recalled her words all the way home and recalled them now with a mixture of pride in her own self-control – her ability to find the right words about which she was now justly satisfied – and of controlled anger which now struck her as totally correct in the circumstances. 'Yes, animal. That can be the only word to describe the sort of person who leads a young woman with a child away from her true path, loyalty to a husband who is not here to fight for her. I call it despicable. It is nothing less. That you, who have so far kept yourself out of the forces by your job while young men are fighting and dying for you, can find it in yourself to break up my son's marriage, is a despicable act. A different story, I can vouch, if he were here. Then a coward like you would run with your tail between your legs. You are a coward, a traitor, a parasite. And you,' she had turned on the trembling girl, her daughter-in-law, 'you are a harlot. I'd rather see my son dead than take you back!'

That had been a mistake. She shouldn't have said that. On reflection it seemed she was condemning her own son. That was when she had nearly broken down. To combat her weakness, she had gone into the other room to stand over Matilda, the other two following at a distance.

Looking down on the child, averting her eyes from knickers, bras, stockings and men's pants that draped every chairback, she'd been revolted by the musty odour that rose up to meet her from the cot itself, an offensive effluvium of urine, long-

unbathed skin and unwashed bedclothes. She'd half expected
disorder but not this abomination. The cot, like the bed, must
have been crawled in and out of for weeks without any change
of linen, and looking at Crawley with his fresh-looking skin
and his attention to dress, it was unbelievable he would put up
with such squalor as met her eyes. There had been another
smell too in that room. A faint reek that she could not at first
place. Susan and her abominable lover had been crawling all
over each other night after night, filling the room with the reek
of their coition. One word had escaped her as she lifted the
child, who must have witnessed this copulation time after time,
out of her cot: 'Slut!' And again, enlarging on the word: 'You
disgusting slut!'

In a smouldering fury she had commanded Matilda to be
washed and dressed, a process that had involved a great deal
of perseverance to control the miniature tempest at the unaccustomed washing. Susan had told her this was how Mattie
always was and that it was easier not to bother and upset her,
a likely excuse for laziness. Finally, Lilian had borne the child
home with her, as Susan had asked.

It still escaped her how the child's mother had stood by and
watched her being taken away without one word of protest.
The last she had seen of Susan, as she bore Matilda down the
stairs and out of the house, was her standing there leaning
slightly against Crawley, his arm protectively about her, a dec-
laration if ever there was one of her intention never to go back
to her husband when he finally came home. Lilian was still
certain of that.

She now cuddled her granddaughter to her. After a proper
bath, her hair now brushed to a dark sheen, the little body
still convulsed with the occasional sob from screaming at such
mishandling. One would think she'd never seen water in her
life, which must almost be true, sad to say, and Lilian again felt
hatred build up against the mother.

'You should have seen those rooms,' she said to Leonard.
'She was never like that when she lived here. I took her always
for a clean girl, clean-living. You could have knocked me over
with a feather. And her cries when Matthew left, I'd never
have believed she could turn so far the other way.'

'Well, she's here now,' he soothed, his arms opening for

252

Matilda to come to him, which she did readily, to lie against her grandfather, thumb in mouth, dark eyes slewed round towards the grandma who had so handled her. 'She'll be with us until Susan wants her back.'

To which Lilian huffed, 'We'll see about that.' And smiling at the child, added, 'One day, you'll thank Grandma. When Daddy comes home.'

As the year drew to its close, that he would come home she was more than certain. And soon. Of that too she had no doubts, the news being what it was, all good. This year of 1944 marked a turning point if ever there was one; despite buzz-bombs, despite frightening V2s that had come after – in June alone Rome was captured and the landings in Normandy took place, but much more heartening, for her at least, was the defeat of the Japanese invasion of India. For her it was a light at the end of the tunnel. A few more months and they'd be defeated entirely and Matthew would come marching home. In the face of that thought, all other victories had paled, even when Paris was liberated in August, then Brussels. And then on the twentieth of October had come the most wonderful news of all, of the Americans' re-landing in the Philippines. Not long now before she saw her son again. Then another heartache would begin when he learned that the wife he loved so much had been and still was unfaithful. At least they had his child here. A beautiful two-and-a-half-year-old to be intro-duced to him, to call him Daddy, compensation for the loss he did not yet know of. Lilian's heart almost broke for him at what faced him on his return.

Meanwhile it was a new half-forgotten world she and Leonard had entered, taking Matilda into their home. They'd scarcely remembered what it was like to bring up an energetic young child. Louise had been quiet, doing all that was asked of her, never resorting to tantrums, when hurt, running to her parents for it to be kissed better in the stubborn knowledge that all would be well. She could be quite self-willed when the fancy took her, but Lilian had always managed her.

Even Matthew, who had been the harder of the two to bring up, a rebel always wanting to kick over the traces, going into a corner to nurse his hurts, brazening out hurt pride with

253

abrasive flamboyance – even with him she had managed. Until, that is, he'd gone against her advice to go for a commission, instead joining up as a mere private. She still felt he had done it just to spite her, though why, she had never been sure, she with only his well-being at heart. And look where his action had got him.

But all the good and bad in her two children had become a distant memory as they'd grown away from her. Louise was now an independent young woman, hardly ever coming home when on leave and, so her letters said, going out with a young Canadian by the name of Ken Turnbull from Winnipeg. They planned to go steady and, reading between the lines, she was hoping to go back with him to Canada after the war. With Matthew a prisoner far away, Lilian prayed daily, if God were willing, that he would come home, but she knew he would probably be a changed man.

Yes, her memories of bringing up a child had dimmed considerably. Matilda, however, altered all that. Invading her grandparents' stagnant lives, she hounded them, small as she was. Being a demanding child, rather like her mother, but charming with it, she made her grandmother's head spin and sometimes ache with her liveliness. With no idea how to stay neat and clean, her clothing coupons never went far enough, and to keep her prettily dressed, Lilian dragged out her old sewing machine, cutting down her own dresses, unravelling old cardigans and often sacrificing her and Leonard's own coupons. But there were rewards, seeing a child they'd brought home looking and smelling like some workhouse waif transformed into the pretty little thing she was. And so like Matthew that it hurt.

It had pained them at first hearing Matilda's plaintive cries of 'Mummy, Mummy'. She said little else, for she was terribly behind with her talking, not yet chattering as a child that age should. It passed, as she was too young to sustain a memory, but Lilian took care not to take her to see her mother and awaken the child's renewed distress. Susan seemed not to mind.

There was never a word from her unless Lilian made it her business to seek her out.

'Aren't you interested in how your daughter is getting along?'

Susan, displaying sullenness at her insistence in coming, had merely shrugged. 'I know where she is if I want her.'

Come Christmas, heavy with her bastard, off-handed and rude to her mother-in-law, Susan had apparently made up her mind that she had been right about Matthew. Now certain she was a widow, she treated Lilian as an interfering old busybody who no longer had any jurisdiction over her actions. Lilian, keeping to her rigid faith, fostered hatred of the weak-willed girl for it.

The International Red Cross, with so much on their plate, were still working hard tracing prisoners of war, and had said that they'd made contact in certain quarters and the name Matthew Ward had been on a list which the Japanese had reluctantly released just prior to Christmas. It could have been any Matthew Ward, the name was not an uncommon one, but Lilian saw it as too much of a coincidence for it not to be her son. His wife had no such weight of faith, continuing to prefer her life with the abominable Geoffrey Crawley. Her and Matthew's child was slowly becoming Lilian's whole life, a straw to cling to, someone to take the place of her son in the unlikely event of his never coming home. But that thought she put from her.

Chapter 23

Sister Ross moved briskly across a quadrangle of the Shaftes-bury military hospital.

Hard to believe the war was over at last. Having only just returned to England, she'd missed the VE celebrations here, and could only hear about it from her mother and from the nurses here.

From her mother she had gleaned all sorts of news, amazingly detailed for one supposed to be reserved, unless of course Margaret's absence had brought her out at last. She heard how Matthew's wife was living with the husband of her erstwhile landlady. Margaret wasn't a bit surprised by that, only sad. Sad for Matthew who would learn of it when eventually he came home, soon, because the war in the Far East couldn't last much longer for all the tenacity of the Japanese in refusing to surrender to superior forces, their allies in Germany allies no longer. He would discover that while he had been sweating it out in Japanese hands, his wife had been enjoying the comfort of another man's arms.

Margaret learned too that his parents had charge of his child, were bringing her up admirably; that his wife had had a baby by her lover, a boy; that she had nothing now to do with Matthew's parents, considering herself wholly a widow. The war had passed her by.

As she walked on, Margaret thought back over her own war, over all that had happened to her after landing in Normandy. Having crossed the Channel in a full gale that seemed at the time to have been waiting just for them, making the whole unit, herself included, seasick, they'd moved forward with the advancing Allies, tending the wounded as they were brought in. Some were injured so grievously it had taken all her resolve not to show revulsion or pity before the sights that greeted her lest she undermine the brave face the wounded had put on. She marvelled at the resolve of most of them not to be done down by their ghastly, disfiguring wounds before their comrades.

She had seen foreign towns and cities, Bayeux, Caen completely in ruins from Allied bombardment, Rouen which had been let off relatively lightly as the troops went through. The gunfire always ahead of them, their trucks had rumbled along in the wake of the advance, bucking and pitching over the shell craters they'd left. And always the grey-faced wounded, the air filled with their moans, the hospital tents packed with hardly room enough for stretcher-bearers, medics, and nurses to go about their business, usually all under a continuous relentless barrage.

She had learned swear words she had never before known existed. She'd also learned a smattering of German as, success following success, German prisoners began being brought in, wounded prisoners in as much need of attention as Allied wounded. The QAs tended them all.

She'd seen Paris and had been entranced by its beauty, and finally, with the guns falling silent, she had been posted to a town called Rotenburg, not far from Bremen, to a small hospital to help nurse the pitiful victims of Sandbostel, a concentration camp in the north of the country. After all she had seen of the wounded and dying, that place had provided the sights she most wanted to erase from a heart still apt to sink with sickening regularity at the slightest recollection.

Finally home, leave, and transfer here, caring for servicemen who had contracted tuberculosis, mostly ex-prisoners of war, victims of conditions they'd been compelled to live under. She had seen a little of the world. In time she'd return to civilian nursing. But she would never forget.

Shovelling sawdust into sacks wasn't pleasant at most times. Now, as with most things in Japanese hands, the extractors had long ago fallen apart and no longer sucked away the fine dust.

Despite strips of sacking tied over nose and mouth, it got into the lungs to be hawked up later in thick yellow phlegm.

The officers complained regularly. The gaol commandant, Major Tanaka, listened sympathetically and did nothing, just as he did nothing about the diabolical bullying by his men, especially one known as Valentino from his handsome narrow face and the dramatic way he swivelled his eyes.

Having felt the weight of his bullying, Matthew trudged back through the gates of Rangoon gaol at sunset in a black mood. Loading sacks on to a barge, one had slipped, spilling sawdust everywhere. Valentino had pounced, wielding his bamboo stick like a samurai warrior, ending up by booting him headlong into the water, strutting off to leave his victim to be fished out by his workmates.

Showering briefly under the Heath Robinson contraption built by the POWs which the Japs allowed to be turned on for just half an hour each evening, subsequently causing long disappointed queues, Matthew worked to take his mind off his treatment, thinking instead of Susan. She no longer floated in his mind as during the days of the railway. He'd come through it, just, though he still suffered malaria from time to time. Almost callously, he had fought to put behind him thoughts of comrades who had died on the way. He had survived. He was determined to continue to survive, and to this end, he put behind him too today's thrashing, and thought only of Susan, of going home to take up their lives together, when all this would become a thing of the past.

In the midst of thinking that as he soaped himself with the tiniest sliver he'd been handed by an officer – told not to overdo it as others had to use it too – the name Maggie flashed into his mind and for a second he saw her quite clearly through the thin curtain of dripping water: her flaming hair, her wide smile, her well-formed features.

Strange though, he thought a lot of Maggie Ross; she came into his mind at the oddest of moments, like now. Mostly it was to recall that ardent kiss she'd given him in the street, right out in the open, all that time ago. Typical of her to do a thing like that. Never seemed to get it right.

Matthew lifted his face up to the drips falling from the makeshift shower head, a perforated canvas bag being spasmodically filled by a pipe from a tank someone in turn kept refilling as long as the water would last.

Her kiss had been a fleeting thing, leaving him to smile reflectively at the lingering sensation it had brought, one that had stirred him enough to make him want to write to her, perhaps further the relationship she had begun. But then his unit had been transferred to Birmingham and he'd met Susan. From then on *she* had taken up all his thoughts.

Strange he should think of Maggie Ross now, and with a small pang of sadness to go with it that he'd let her down. Where was she now? Was she still a nurse or had she married someone, was she raising a family? Without warning an empty place took up residence inside him, a sudden longing for things to be again as they had once been, carefree, safe, full of fun. He could see them all now. And Maggie, she had been a stunner, hadn't she? Just that she hadn't been his type. But a stunner just the same. He should have told her so. He regretted that now. Pity she hadn't had as much confidence in her looks as some men had in them – that Dennis Cox – he'd been smitten by her but hadn't the nerve to tell her. Someone had said Cox had been killed. Well, lots of blokes had been killed. Women too. Serving abroad, nurses being sent overseas, their ships sunk. Perhaps Maggie had been one of them. He wouldn't know, would he? Not here. A stab of panic gripped him then sank away, leaving a sort of empty grief that had no substance because it was unfounded, all in his mind. He had begun to fall in love with Maggie at one time, he was sure, but then he'd met Susan . . .

'F'Chrissake, y' doughy Pom – get a bloody move on, bloody mooning about. Y'r thirty seconds was up bloody ages ago.'

Shot back to the present, Matthew slipped hastily out from the dribbling shower to receive a basinful of ripe epithets from the Aussie waiting to take his place.

'Keep your hair on,' Matthew growled irritably as the man named Phil shouldered roughly past him. Phil glared at him but Matthew's mind was now taken up with more immediate interests, even above thoughts of Susan and Maggie, as he walked away still dripping wet. So were his ragged shorts, with his time under the shower too brief for them to be taken off.

They would dry as he dried. His thoughts now were on what news there might be, if any, over the grapevine.

Hidden beneath the dirt floor of a low wooden lean-to, once a tool shed belonging to the saw mill, then a makeshift latrine but now just a haven for flies and maggots, was a radio, constructed by some boffin or other. With a look-out squatting idly against the sagging rotting walls, certain chosen men – not himself, thank God, for it was an execution if the Japs ever discovered it – would take it in turns, a couple at a time, to squeeze under the floor of the lean-to, lying flat, and follow the crackling news of Allied invasion in Europe, American successes in the Pacific or how many tons of bombs B.29s had dropped on Japanese-held territory, very little of it accurate, being mainly from Japanese sources rather than Allied.

But the news they most sought was lacking – the Fourteenth Army's penetration into Assam and northern Burma five months ago had gone silent, and along with it any speculation of an early release from captivity.

He turned as an angry snort was heard directly behind him, Phil having caught him up after his own thirty seconds had been apparently cut short by two seconds owing to Matthew's delay in getting out as promptly as was required. Phil, a dismal-face individual who shared the next cell to his with a dozen other Australians, was in a bad mood and obviously wanted to make it plain to the miscreant. Giving him little time to finish his complaint, Matthew turned on him. His own temper was none too good, his shoulders smarting still from Valentino's cane.

'Why don't you put a fucking sock in it?'

The Australian looked hurt. He wasn't a brave man, at least not rash in the face of the other's baleful glare that threatened a punch on the nose.

'Don't bloody take ut out on me because yu've had a bloody blue with some lousy bloody Nip.'

Crisis over, Matthew continued walking in the direction of the three steaming oil drums from which wafted a bland aroma of saltless boiled rice.

'I'm not taking it out on you.' A fit of sawdust-laden coughing prevented him saying any more and gave Phil possession of the argument.

'We've all got bludgers t'put up with. Ain't no sense antagonising 'em, is there?'

Harry Hope, who shared Matthew's cell, once a short, naturally chubby man, but now from whose skeletal back, ribs and hips protruded, unhealthy skin hung fleshless like thin grey rows of pelmets, caught the two up, his brief shower over as well. The last of it dripped off his ridged skin like raindrops off a gutter. His voice was soft, with a West Country accent. 'Stay off our Matt's back, old son. He's been a mite touchy all day.'

'Too right, he's touchy.' But Harry ignored the man as he surveyed Matthew's shoulders.

'It do look bloody zore.'

'It *is* bloody sore.'

'You need to keep that covered. Got a shirt?'

'Flogged it last week for a bag of bran.'

Rice bran, discarded during milling as fit only for animal feed, was a precious commodity, rich in vitamin B, and coveted because it helped avert beri-beri and other deficiency diseases. It was consequently hard to come by. Matthew's haul had amounted to under a quarter of a pound, for which he considered himself fortunate all the same.

'I've got a shirt you can borrow until you've healed a bit.'

Giving Matthew no time to thank him, shirts too being precious commodities, Harry made off towards the queue forming behind drums of steaming rice, their supper, leaving Matthew to stare after him until the small dry cough caught him again and he followed after Harry.

Leaning down from his rickety bunk Harry surveyed him lying directly below. He'd been disturbed by his cough. All those in the cell were disturbed by it. ''Bout time you saw the quack on that, Matt, old son. Don't like the zound of that. Zounds loik a touch o' TB ter me. Don't loik your colour either.'

Matthew raised his eyes to the head hanging upside-down. 'You really know how to cheer up a bloke, don't you?'

'Only an opinion, Matt, only an opinion. But if it be TB I don' wanna catch it.'

From the next cell, divided only by open bars, came Phil's monotone drawl. 'Not as it makes any difference. All gotta go

261

sometime, so what's it matter, hundred years from now, if yuh died at nineteen or ninety? Tryin' to live a long life – you're just a bloody gnat on an elephant's arse. Fifty years after they shove yuh under, forgotten, what's it matter if you lived at all?'

Angered, fighting another cough, Matthew turned away from the would-be philosopher. 'You're just a miserable bugger. You might not have anyone to go home to, but I've a wife and a baby waiting for me.'

On that score, senses heightened to the possibility of tuberculosis, next evening after work found him outside the TB outbuilding transfixed by the sight of those within its open door, chests sunken, eyes unnaturally bright, cheeks with that peculiar transparent flush, as his were.

An orderly, just finishing ministering to a frail stick of what three years ago had been a strong young man, now having to be fed sips of watery rice gruel from a tin cup, looked up at Matthew.

'Looking for someone, chum?'

Feeling suddenly fraudulent, Matthew shook his head; he watched the man gently ease his patient down on the platform that served for a bed and with a piece of khaki rag wipe the residue of gruel from the man's lips. The tenderness of the action touched Matthew more than anything had done in a long time. This man with his gentle hands, these men quietly heroic in their suffering, they humbled him. This endless stream of sufferers, crippled by tropical ulcers, blinded by vitamin deficiency, swollen with beri-beri and withered by dysentery, so many struck down by all the diseases the tropics could throw at them; many died without fuss lest they undermine the will of others to struggle on. None had distinguished themselves in battle but they were heroes just the same in their silent acceptance of death. And here he was shivering in fear of his own miserable life as though he were someone special, as if he were the only man who yearned to make it home to wife and child.

The orderly had stood up and was coming towards him. 'Can ah help ye, laddie?' The soft Scots accent emphasised the hush of this place. He gnawed at his lip. He had no right to waste this man's time.

'It's nothing,' he blurted.

The man was looking at him with the eye of the experienced.

'Ye think ye're tubercular then. Hold on a minute.' Drawing Matthew into the outbuilding with him, he began fishing into a box nearby, drawing out a stethoscope, home-made from rubber tubing and the handles of a metal filing cabinet he'd probably come across at some time. 'Let's have a listen.'

Submitting himself to the examination Matthew breathed, coughed, uttered thirty-three when told to. The stethoscope was put slowly away. When the man looked back at him, his smile was fixed, too reassuring by far.

'Ye was reet to come here. But it's no' too bad. In a cool dry climate, why, it cud be cured in three months, Ah'd say.'

But the look on the man's face told its story. In a cool dry climate with good food and rest, of course recovery would be certain. Here, in this humid heat, watery rice for fare, working without respite, it was a death sentence as surely as if he stood before a firing squad.

These three years he had stared at death. Now it had arrived. He nodded casually at the advice to take it easy. 'At least I know where I stand,' he murmured and received a short nod. As he left, an insane notion went through his head. Why wait for death? Why not go out in a blaze of glory, a heroic act of sabotage, take a few of those sons of Nippon with him? But he knew he would do no such thing. Like those who had gone before him, like Bob Howlett, he would await his time, quietly, patiently, reluctant to make a fuss, and carrying Susan's image in his head, would silently say goodbye to her and hope to find courage and a small semblance of dignity when his time came.

'Ain't no good, the bloody thing's had it.'

He and another man named Derek gazed down at the now silent wireless that had crackled itself to its death. From now on they could receive no news of the outside world, no heartening snippets about Germany herself being overrun by the Allies.

'No chance getting hold of another valve?' It was a valve that had gone. It might as well have been the whole set for all that could be done.

Derek shook his head viciously. 'Just when something good came over. Something about the Fourteenth Army fighting around Mandalay. Mandalay's only just up country. Didn't you hear it?'

The sound had been so faint, Matthew hadn't heard. Within days, however, rumours were going around. And the Japs were looking decidedly jumpy. Perhaps Derek had heard right. But everyone had grown concerned by their captors' attitude. If rumours were correct and their liberators not far away, what would the Japs do?

'Don't look too good,' Harry said. 'They're sayin' if the Fourteenth Army do make it to Rangoon, the Japs'll start usin' us for sandbags.'

'If that's the case,' Matthew said grimly, 'I'd sooner be shot running that being a shield for some . . .'

The rest of his words were drowned in a fit of coughing from which Harry moved hastily away. But it didn't matter. He now had hope to cling to and his spirits lifted of their own accord.

May, the monsoon yet to begin, the weather still as sweet as any tropical climate allowed, Matthew came awake from a sleep already disturbed by the bouts of sweating peculiar to his condition and a wonderful dream about Susan to a hand shaking his shoulders. Phil was standing over him, all his worldly goods draped about his waist like tarnished charms on an old bracelet. Above it all the normally doleful hatchet face looked grim.

'Sorry t' disturb your sleep, Matt. But us lot 're movin' on.'

The Japs had been growing more and more jittery of late, even their interest in forcing their prisoners to work all hours dropping off. The air was still full of rumours, all of which the prisoners believed purely because they needed to feel that soon they must be released by the fabled oncoming Fourteenth Army. Now all the rumours suddenly took substance as Phil went on.

'They say your blokes're just up the road. Nips're movin' out. Taking all us *healthy* buggers with 'em. To Moulmein ready for shipment to Japan. You cripples are stayin' behind.'

It was meant to be witty but the grin was one of sick disappointment. From the courtyard came the bellow of the retreating Japanese assembling their 'fit' prisoners.

'S'long then, sport. Take care of y'self. Yuh gonna make it y'know. Bet y'shirt on it.' The grin widened determinedly, the first time Matthew ever remembered Phil smiling without it being a sneer. 'Send yuh a postcard from Sydney one day.'

Going to the now wide-open door of his wing of cells Matthew watched the long gangling figure, deprived of freedom that was nearly his, shoulders hunched in despondency, go off to join the men assembled. He'd never liked Phil all that much but now it felt he was saying farewell to a comrade in a chain of comrades to whom he'd said farewell, one way or another. He should have been feeling elated by the news he'd been given. Instead he felt he wanted to cry. In fact, he was looking at this gangling bundle of misery through a mist and one of his cheeks was being dampened by a thin rivulet.

He forgave himself the tears; TB made a man over-emotional. But in his way, Phil had been close to him, perhaps by his very dolefulness. Watching him go, Matthew thought of all those he'd known, some closer than others: little Taffy Thomas, the endearingly libidinous Welshman blown apart in the retreat to the Sittang River; Bob Howlett, the gentle man who had succoured him on that long march to Rangoon, himself dying alone; another, Colin Pardoe, a religious man of simple faith who had dragged him back to sanity after Bob's ignominious death – where he was now God only knew, might even be sitting at His feet right now for all Matthew could tell what had happened to him. There had been others, and Harry Hope was still here, but one by one they had all gone. Now he felt only utter loneliness as Phil, the man of misery, turned and waved for the last time.

Dawn broke grey and heavy, announcing the coming monsoon season. The sick awoke to find the prison gates standing open, the guardhouse deserted – a faintly bewildering experience after so long close-confined.

Matthew and a few others wandered through them just to savour the sensation of this new freedom. They found a note in English nailed to one of the gateposts: YOU ARE FREE TO MOVE AS YOU WISH. FOOD AND MEDICAL SUPPLIES HAVE BEEN LEFT FOR YOU. THE BRITISH WILL SOON BE HERE, YOU MAY WAIT FOR THEM OR GO TO MEET THEM AS YOU CHOOSE.

Thus, as the British had fled Rangoon three years earlier, so the Japanese, who'd scorned them for their cowardice, had likewise fled before the conquerors. The wheel had turned full circle. Slowly. But it had turned. He was going home, home to Susan. How she must have wept over him, worried herself silly over his well-being, how lonely she must have been.

And himself? The years spent struggling to survive yet seeing death at every turn waiting to pick him up, were over. Death had been waiting for him to thumb a lift from all the misery and degradation that had almost sucked him down into its depths. Thank God he had resisted that dark presence, even through the worst of times. It was over. It hardly seemed true that soon he'd be going home, picking up the threads of his life.

He felt all in, very near to tears at the enormity of this moment as he stood in the emerging sunlight with all the others waiting for their liberators to appear down that road. When they did he would show them that his head had not been bowed, that his spirit had remained strong, had endured. He would throw them a cheeky wave, perhaps even chuck up a smart salute, and not show the true emotions that were ruling inside him. His throat ached from the effort.

All the good intentions. When the first well-clad, sturdy, full-cheeked soldier came marching up to the gaol gates, he could only stand there staring at the health of the man, who smiled at him with such pity in his expression that Matthew found himself stumbling towards him. And as the soldier held out a hand to him, he laid his emaciated arms about the man's neck and sobbed.

Chapter 24

Matilda was not an easy child. Lilian, with recollections of her own, had been taken by surprise. Her little hands were in everything. She was so quick, and it was all her grandmother could do to run after her, those sturdy little legs going like pistons as she found her feet.

It had taken a while to find them, left as she had been in her cot for days on end where she could come to no harm, Susan had said, from the stairs which she could have fallen down, the gas ring from which she could have pulled a kettle of water over herself, the sharp corners in the room. Excuses. Children came to know these dangers by having an alert parent watching them. No, the real reason was that vile man Crawley who didn't want a child that wasn't his hanging around.

Emma Crawley had taken their boys with her to stay with her sister in Valance Road a couple of streets away so that the boys hadn't had to change schools or anything. And of course, in the quieter house, the cries of Susan's baby to be given more freedom had disrupted his enjoyment with his mistress when he was home.

Let free in her grandmother's large airy house, the child found her feet. Five months later and still she was wearing out her indulgent grandparents.

'She's as energetic and high-spirited as Matthew was,' she said to Leonard one night, once the child finally fell asleep after lying wide-awake and bored in the drawn-out daylight of long May evenings, taking up time they would have preferred to have to themselves.

Leonard looked up from his *Evening Star*. 'We should have known what we were taking on. Do you regret it, Lilian?'

'No, I don't,' she answered emphatically, picking up the embroidery she was doing on a dress for Matilda – when she had the time. 'All I dream is for her father to come home and see the pretty little daughter he has. That's worth all the trials and tribulations we've undergone in taking Matilda on.'

She fell silent, bending her head to the rosebud she was fashioning on the front of the cotton garment. It had been a cream skirt of hers. Now it was a dress, needing just this sprinkling of rosebuds to lift its plain colour. Leonard went back to reading his paper.

A quietness descended on them both; it brought thoughts drifting through Lilian's mind as she worked. The war in Europe was over, Hitler dead by suicide. He had deserved a far worse death. Mussolini too was dead, his body afterwards hung by its feet from a lamppost by a mob, those he'd once ruled as dictator, his face kicked in. Lilian shuddered. That should have happened to Hitler too. The ghastly pictures in the papers revealed the horror of those terrible concentration camps. And poor President Roosevelt, a natural death, but a sad, sad loss.

Now there was peace, but not everywhere. The newspapers, when they weren't reporting about the Nuremberg Trials, now concentrated on the Far East and what the Japanese regime was really like. A statement made in January by Anthony Eden in the House of Commons had described the fearful treatment of prisoners by the Japanese, and later, a Japanese prison ship transporting prisoners of war to Japan, had been sunk. The state of the surviving captives showed them to be in the most appalling state.

What then of Matthew? He could easily have been on that ship, one of those who had not survived. No news, never any news. The war in Europe was over, but they might still find that their son had died perhaps a year ago or more.

Holding her baby in her arms, Susan went to answer the knock on the door. She was not really concerned who stood there, except that whoever it was had interrupted her quiet afternoon nap. Trevor, a good baby, unlike Mattie, slept in the afternoon, allowing her to do likewise until Geoff came home. Since the war had finished he'd applied for a transfer nearer home to be with her more, and now worked at a Gas Board office in London. Wonderful. She saw him every night. Well, almost, because some evenings he went round to see his sons. She hated those evenings.

Casually she opened the door, then gasped. Mr and Mrs Ward stood there with Mattie between them, Mrs Ward holding the child's hand in her usual iron grip. Mattie, now nearly three years old, looked happy, her small face animated at seeing the mother she seldom saw these days, but the look on the faces of her grandparents suggested they had received bad news. Susan's mind flew to Mattie with a stab of dismay. Had they brought her back? What the hell was she going to do with her? She had Trevor now. How could she deal with two children?

'What's the matter?' she blurted, hitching Trevor to a less weighty position in her arms. 'What's she done?' She had to have done something awful for them to look like this. Not angry; strange, strained.

'It isn't Matilda,' Mrs Ward began, but Mr Ward cut in.

'We've had news of Matthew,' he said.

Another stab, this time of dismay. If they'd had news that he was dead, she'd be sorry, thinking back to that glorious time they had spent together making love on Beacon Hill, then their wedding day and the little love nest he had found. She saw again the cramped little room with the sunshine coming through the window lighting everything golden. The cosy silence they had shared, the way he had so masterfully commanded her to make love to him, laughing; the love they had made. They had been such wonderful days, but so brief. So long ago. A blur, a photograph, a faded photograph.

And what if the news was that he was alive . . . She tightened her lips, all the complications it would entail filling her head. Did she love him after all this time? She tried in those few seconds to feel what she once had for him. But it wasn't there, only fond memories that could have been those of someone other than her, someone not her any more, totally different.

And what of Geoffrey? She recalled those twinges of excitement when Matthew had talked of the trust made for him, enough to buy a house, live comfortably. His father of

269

course had a shop, so there was money there too. But Geoff had a house, here. She felt comfortable in it. She could imagine the home Matthew would make for them. His mother would constantly be popping in, criticising, this wasn't right and that wasn't right, looking askance at her for not keeping the place spick and span and sparkling. She almost shuddered at the thought, knew immediately, staring from one to the other of his parents, that if he was alive she'd still have to choose Geoffrey, comfortable, dependable Geoffrey, who treated her like a goddess, and no one to interfere in what they said or did.

She became aware that Mr Ward was saying something to her which she hadn't caught and had to beg his pardon to ask what it was he'd said.

He looked irritated. 'I said . . . Look, Susan, may we come in. I can't stand here on the doorstep explaining news as important as this.'

Automatically she stepped back, allowing them inside. She'd had fish and chips for dinner (she'd get Geoff's tonight when he came home) and the smell of it hung in the house – she knew it did by the offended twitch of Mrs Ward's nose, though she said nothing.

They followed her into the still-cavernous front room, no longer with the old blackout frames stuck in the corner. Letting the two sit on the huge sofa, she positioned herself on one of the upright chairs, laying Trevor in one of the armchairs where he wouldn't roll off while Mattie went exploring the room.

'I'm sorry I wasn't quite listening when you were speaking,' she said looking at Mr Ward, but it was his wife who reacted with a disapproving sniff.

'I would have thought you'd at least be attentive seeing that it concerns your husband.'

Mr Ward raised a mollifying hand. 'I said, Susan, that we'd had good news of our son, your husband. He's still your husband, Susan.'

'Yes, I know.' It sounded fatuous, but he'd said it with such distaste for what she supposed he saw as her carrying-on behind Matthew's back. What did he know of how she felt? No one could turn love on and off like a blessed tap.

'Our news,' he continued, 'if it's worth anything to you now, is that Matthew has been released.'

Susan stared. 'But the war out there's not over yet.'

'You *may* have read,' put in Mrs Ward, her tone intimating that Susan's reading power was limited to say the least, 'that the Fourteenth Army recaptured Burma some weeks ago.' Even so excitement rang in her voice. 'They found Matthew there.'

Responding more to her own churning of feelings than the news itself, Susan wasn't sure how to react. To give herself time to analyse how she felt about all this, she merely said, 'Oh.'

Mrs Ward's eyebrows shot up into her forehead, her controlled joy smothered instantly by exasperation. 'Aren't you going to enquire how he is? Aren't you interested?'

'I'm glad he's safe,' Susan offered automatically, taking it that was what she was expected to say. Uppermost in her mind, however, now she'd had time to sort out her reactions, were the complications this news brought. She saw a line of legal wrangles, divorce courts, three years at least being fettered to a man she'd all but forgotten, never again to feel at ease with her Geoffrey without her husband's mother breathing down her neck. She would be marked as the guilty party. She was the guilty party, true, but how can anyone turn aside natural feelings, the way she felt about Geoffrey? A tiny place in her mind cried, why couldn't he have died, a voice she brushed aside the instant it spoke, shuddering that she could even harbour such an evil thought. She wouldn't wish that on Matthew, on anyone, for a million pounds.

In the nurses' home Margaret opened her mother's letter. The hospital overlooking the Blackmoor Vale had a timeless charm; with its smooth grey stone over which this hot, sunny June day seemed to slide like treacle left the interior cool, placid and airy. The windows stood wide open to the fresh breezes essential for those with half a chance of recovery; tuberculosis was a known killer, fresh air, rest, good food were all they could hope for. There was talk of some drug called streptomycin; the press had called it a miracle cure, promising to make TB a thing of the past, but it was still in its experimental stage. The papers hadn't referred to it again, the headlines bowing out to more important political news. The first peacetime general election was set for the fifth of July. Small things like reporting work on a wonder drug took second place. What a glory if it could be used on the patients she cared for. It was heart-breaking to see those glowing-faced young men, the deceptive transparent bloom a cruel symptom of the disease, slip away. Heart-breaking when they died so young, having come through all the perils of war. It was only when Margaret opened her mother's letter, the usual two closely written pages relaying all the home gossip, that the disease suddenly became a personal thing. Halfway down the letter, her eyes paused over the next words:

> ... You remember Matthew Ward, don't you? He was a prisoner of war and they lost trace of him. Well, they've heard from him at last.

Margaret's heart leapt inside her chest, continuing with a thumping of joy and anticipation as she skipped the observations on how it couldn't have been jolly for them, everyone celebrating VE Day, the other war still going on.

> Matthew's parents had no idea he was in Rangoon. He could have been anywhere. It must have been absolutely marvellous, our boys recapturing Burma like that. Mrs Ward's been telling the whole street about it. He's in hospital in Ceylon. They think he's got TB. Isn't that dreadful, after coming through all he's been through ...

There was more about the bits she'd found out about Matthew's wife. And a part that made Margaret go suddenly cold with anger. Hearing of his release, the girl had written to him telling him about the man she was living with.

> What an awful thing to do. Some people can be so cruel. How he must feel I just don't know. How could anyone do such a thing? She should at least have waited until he came home, I would have thought. But I gather she doesn't have much sense, or so Mrs Ward once said, a long time ago now. But ...

Margaret lifted her eyes from the page of neat, tight little writing, her head a hotchpotch of thoughts, silent prayers touching her lips in a gush of thanks for his safety, of pleading for his health, of joy, of hope for him to be sent back to England very soon and for her to see him again, and the opportunity for her to be at his side should he need someone, anyone.

Quickly she scanned the rest of her mother's letter but there was nothing more about Matthew. He just constituted a passing bit of information among all the other snippets her mother had written, the letter closing with a hope that Margaret could be allowed a holiday soon so she could get home.

I don't know why you want to work so far away. The war is over and there are adequate hospitals around here. But if you must work with TB patients, and I hope to God you don't catch it, tuberculosis is so infectious but I expect you're immune by now, we've one just the other side of the park where you first went to get a job, do you remember? You could find a place there . . .

Yes, she could. But not yet. First she'd set about making enquiries about Matthew, find out where they would send him once in England. A lot of the boys from that area came here after landing, because it was convenient from Southhampton. If she could ask the right people.

Whether her efforts had anything to do with it, there was no way of finding out; a few replies came from different quarters saying it would be looked into in due course but no one could give any promises. Her case, she suspected, was put aside, for the months had gone by and she'd heard no more.

Two weeks earlier the dropping of the atomic bombs on Hiroshima and Nagasaki had brought about Japan's capitulation. Great Britain celebrated VJ Day but, less energetically than VE Day, having done it all once. Her mother's letters no longer mentioned Matthew or his family. Margaret made her way across to the TB wing, under a clearing September dawn which promised to become a fine day after twelve hours of rain, to relieve Staff Nurse Merriman from night duty.

Merriman leaned back on her chair, flexing her stiff shoulder muscles, and yawned widely.

'Ooh-ahh . . . What's it like outside?'

'Beautiful. It's going to be a fine day. What sort of night has it been?'

'Pretty quiet,' came the answer. Merriman was already gathering up her bits and pieces. 'Corporal Douglas haemorrhaged and got a bit panicky. Otherwise all quiet.'

The wards were coming alive. Strident voices of nurses were urging patients not to fall back to sleep after having been aroused at five thirty with tea and wash basins. The clang of bedpans resounded from the sluice, and the corridors echoed to the rattle of crockery-laden trolleys bringing the breakfasts. A nurse going off duty hurried in to deposit an admission file on the desk, gave the incoming sister a brief smile, grabbed her cape off the peg behind the door and departed.

'Oh yes,' said Merriman, pushing the notes across to Margaret. 'I meant to tell you, Admission phoned a few moments ago. He's probably on his way up now. Everything's ready for him, so there's nothing to do.'

Margaret laughed. 'Thanks.'

She took the cup of tea handed to her by a skinny first-year nurse who surveyed Merriman with tired, hopeful eyes.

'Is it all right for me to go off now, please, Staff?'

Merriman was in an authoritative mood, still in charge for the while. 'If you've left the sluices clean, yes.'

'Thank you, Miss Merriman.'

'And charted the temperatures?'

'Yes, Miss Merriman.'

'Is the kitchen tidy?'

The girl nodded vigorously. 'Can Harvey go as well, Miss Merriman?'

'If she has finished everything.'

'Oh, she has. Thank you, Miss Merriman.'

As the girl's flat heels clicked urgently away along the corridor to be joined by Harvey's, Merriman sighed and stood up. 'Time I was off too. I need my bed. And I want to wash my hair.' She made a stack of her notes on the desk, laying the admission file on top. 'There, over to you.'

The day staff were coming in, chattering. Margaret heard

274

Staff Nurse Reid's sharp tones reminding them who and where they were. The chattering ceased abruptly. Margaret reached for the admission folder as Reid burst in, her voice querulous.

'You'd think this was a four-ale bar, not a hospital. To hear those girls, you'd never guess there were sick people here.'

Margaret's gaze was fixed on the now-open folder. She hadn't heard what Reid was saying. Reid leaned over her shoulder to see. 'Oh, no, not an admission this early in the morning. I'll take it.'

The file was snatched up from under Margaret's eyes. 'Why can't they come at a convenient time? And we've a probationer coming on the ward today. All our time will be taken up telling her what to do.'

A porter popped his head around the door, his attitude full of self-importance. 'Where d'yuh want this one?'

'I'll deal with it,' Reid said briskly and clutching the folder waved the porter on, leaving Margaret staring into space. After all those letters she had written, all those enquiries, entreaties. They had paid off. Unbelievable. Quite unbelievable. If she hadn't been on duty she'd have burst into tears.

At first she thought she must have been mistaken, misread the file in that short time before Reid had snatched it so imperiously from under her hand. For a moment it was impossible to associate this patient with the man she had once known, the young man full of laughter and abrasive wit, the khaki-clad soldier she last remembered, so certain of where he was going, carrying himself with all the zest of life.

This man, propped up with pillows, bore no resemblance to that one. Her practised eye already noted that he did not yet have the high colour that went with his disease, which hadn't yet secured such a hard grip on him as it had done on others. It was possible that with care and attention he'd overcome it. But of the man himself? The eyes, deep in their sockets, looked out not on a sunny ward but back in time to an existence that had all but destroyed him as it had so many thousands whose lives he had shared. Everyone now knew of the Burma Railway, the prison ships, the conditions of men incarcerated in jails throughout the Far East, the ghastly massacre of men and women in hospitals as they lay sick and wounded. Some, if not all of that, men like this one must have seen, struggling single-

275

minded to survive. Here was such a man. It glowed from his eyes and Margaret shuddered.

It was only after a moment or so that a slight movement of his head touched her as singularly familiar, at first vague but growing stronger so that all at once she wondered why she hadn't been able to recognise him instantly. Gaunt, cheeks still sunken from years of starvation, eyes that dwelled on the past, it was nevertheless Matthew.

As she spoke his name he looked at her, in those few short seconds his regard blank as hers had been: puzzled, uncertain, trying to pinpoint a memory. A spark of recognition lit up his dark eyes, coupled with disbelief.

'Maggie?'

She tried to laugh. 'Margaret Ross. Sister M. Ross, Q.A.I.M.S.'

It was a poor joke and she felt immediately ashamed, seeing the smile trying to reach his eyes, ridden as they were by dark ghosts. Her own eyes filled with sudden tears she tried hard to keep from showing. The last thing a man wanted was what would appear as a superficial show of sympathy, the giver with no idea what it had been like for him.

Instead, she said simply, 'I'm glad to see you, Matthew.'

'Oh, Maggie.' With a cry from the heart, that bond they'd once known formed itself anew, the way it had done when the promise stretching before them had been bright upon a horizon they hadn't then known concealed the shadows of what was to come. It hadn't been a bond of love then, and now it was more a renewing of a friendship that had flourished briefly only to be interrupted by circumstance. But now he was here, she'd nurse him back to health and for her, for the time being, it was enough.

Thank God the disease was proving less advanced than she'd first feared. Despite the conditions under which he'd lived these last three years he'd retained a strong enough constitution to fight it in its early stages.

For that at least, Margaret offered up prayers of thanks. If only his state of mind showed as much promise. He'd sit in the hospital grounds, wrapped up with a coat against the stiff, health-giving breezes from the Blackmoor Vale which patients were expected to endure daily, staring ahead, seldom glancing around him as people normally do. If she approached him, he'd tense, his gaze averted. Asked how he was – a nurse's question after all – his reply would come back in a monotone. He offered no conversation, no observation of his own, leaving her to maybe lift the wrist, feel the pulse, play the nurse's role. Should she try to further her concern for him she'd inevitably be fobbed off with a terse reply that nothing was the matter and why should there be?

At these times Margaret would feel a blaze of anger against Susan Ward, for it could only be she who was the cause of such anguish. Of course some of his attitude stemmed from what he'd endured as a prisoner of war. But with a loyal woman at his side he'd have surmounted it in time. His wilful, selfish wife had let him down – if her mother had been right, and no reason why she shouldn't be. Susan's letter to him had revealed her adultery while he'd been away and helpless to do anything about it. After all he'd been through, to come home and hear something like that! Worse, he never spoke about it and Margaret felt powerless to alter the situation. Even as she came up to him now, she knew there would be no help she could give him.

To think she'd offered the girl friendship. Had she known what she was like, she'd have had nothing to do with her. Reaching Matthew's side, she found herself hating Susan as she'd never hated anyone in her life before.

As Margaret had anticipated, he did not look up at her as she too let her gaze wander to the trees on the horizon, their billowing of full-leafed heads darkened by distance against the sky with its small lamb-clouds marching in procession across the azure expanse. Matthew had said nothing and she tried not to see herself as an intrusion as he continued to ignore her, his hands curled into tight fists against the arm supports of the hospital Bath chair in which he sat. Yet she couldn't walk away, not with the torment she could see in the tightness around his mouth, the fine brows drawn together, the eyes seeing nothing but what must be seething inside his head.

Unbidden, she sank down on the small bench beside him. This time she didn't go through the motions of taking his wrist ineffectually to feel the pulse. He would know it as only a ruse.

Nor did she speak. Making smalltalk would only reap a sarcastic response and send her away hating herself for having stupidly intruded. The time spun itself out, slowly, the silence between them heightening the faint hum of traffic on the road, the musical trill of a nearby thrush, the soft twitter of a myriad other birds in the grounds, the distant intermittent conversation of people further off, enlarging the silence between them as though they sat within a vacuum. When he did speak, low as his voice was, Margaret's nerves jangled sharply although her body itself did not move.

'I'm trapped here,' was all he said. She remained silent, encouraged for a hopeful moment or two, but he didn't appear to want to say anything more, and her hopefulness died.

She reached out and laid a hand on his clenched one, letting it lie there. He didn't draw away as she had half expected. The fist remained there, unmoving beneath hers, the warmth of the skin penetrating hers, her nurse's enquiring mind immediately registering that he might be feverish. A little maybe, nothing to be concerned by; temperature could go up and down. It was expected, so long as it did not flare. She did note something else, that the fist began slightly to relax. He moved his head a fraction and let his gaze fall on to her consoling hand. Did it seem to be a consoling hand to him?

A nurse's voice nearby startled them both. Then the nurse and her charge moved on, the voice fading. Margaret followed their departure with her eyes, so it was a second or two before she became aware of Matthew speaking, of what he was saying, his voice halting and so low as to be hardly audible except for the sibilant sounds.

'Places like that – you need someone. Something. To cling to. In my head. She was in my head. Fever. Does weird things to you. But she *was* real. Thinking of me. Far away. Thinking of me.'

He was talking about Susan. 'But for her I'd have gone under. She kept me going. Once – a mouth full of ulcers – vitamin deficiency – couldn't eat . . .' There came a low mirthless chuckle. 'Starving, and I couldn't eat . . . She kept me going. In my head. And all the time I didn't know. Had no idea she was . . .'

He broke off this time with an intake of breath that sounded more like a sob caught in his throat.

Margaret had said nothing, letting him talk. She hadn't expected this. His need to talk had come out of nowhere, unprompted, unless it had been the way she had lain her hand on his. But she'd done that before only to have him snatch his hand away. There was no reason for her to congratulate herself, nor did she try to probe what had prompted him. She merely sat saying nothing, letting him get it all out of himself, or praying that he would.

He hadn't looked at her once. He seemed to be trying to fight the emptiness that was consuming him, but she was glad he hadn't given way to tears which she knew instinctively would have destroyed his dignity in his own mind. All she could do as he lapsed into silence was to wait and listen if he chose to say more, and if he didn't then she must let it go at that and keep her platitudes to herself. But the emptiness he nursed proved too strong for him. Startling her, he suddenly pulled his hand from under hers and she thought he was about to reject her. Instead, he took her hand and lifted it to his forehead as though in dire need of her comfort. No sound came from him, though she could feel his silent grief as a faint vibration on her arm. When again he spoke, the words were muffled by the cuff of her uniform. 'I love her, Maggie. I should hate her. But I can't.'

Margaret nodded, stifling emotions of her own. The comfort she'd thought he sought from her, was merely what he would have sought from anyone. He still loved Susan.

Chapter 25

People were putting the war years behind them; forgetting was perhaps another matter. Rationing still gripped hard, so Christmas had still been frugal, but it had felt more relaxed than for six years. New Year 1946, this first full year of peace, held out fresh promise for the future.

Spring, welcomed in with open arms, saw hoardings going up around bombed areas, cranes being ferried in to shift the rubble in preparation for rebuilding. Soon, the damage covered over with new buildings, no one who hadn't been here would know there had been any. The old raw fear for one's life was giving way to all the petty concerns of peacetime – politics, nuisance neighbours, making ends meet, keeping children clean. Demobbed men, this time in orderly fashion unlike the mad release of the First World War, were going back to old jobs to demand the sort of wages enjoyed by those essential workers who'd been kept out of the forces. For some the way ahead looked rosy. For those still nursing grief, remembering loved ones never to return, it hardly glimmered.

Watching Matthew's slow progress, Margaret knew it wasn't glowing for him either. He had at last been told the whole truth about Susan by his well-meaning parents: how she'd walked out of the house while heavily pregnant, not a word of warning, not a word of thanks for all they'd done for her; how she had treated them when they'd found where she was living, was still living (they told him the address); the affair she'd had, still on-going, with her landlady's husband, Geoffrey Crawley; Mrs Crawley finally leaving him; how distant and rude Susan had been to them when they had called on her to persuade her to go back home with them; how they had found her and this Crawley fellow living together, but how without a qualm she had let them take her daughter – Matthew's daughter – away from her, the child in a terrible neglected state, as though she had no care or love for Matilda at all; how not once from that day to this had Susan asked after her. (They brought photos of Matilda, now a bonny three-year-old, but they hadn't brought her in person, for fear of infection.)

He had listened to it all without comment, but afterwards Margaret had found him abstracted and unresponsive, his expression frozen, his lips a tight white line in his narrow, set face. Margaret had wondered if now had been the best time to tell him everything. Of course he would have had to know at some time, would have known soon enough once he went home. The drug Streptomycin was now helping to save sufferers from the old resort to surgery. Matthew had escaped the trauma of the knife, and was declared fit to go home and attend check-ups at a local hospital. But how would he face going home, knowing what he did? Not only from his parents but from Susan herself. She had not once visited him or written to him, but she did that Christmas.

It was just after Christmas when Margaret came upon him asleep on his bed one cold afternoon. The windows as ever stayed open to admit draughts of vital fresh air against which patients must huddle under blankets and wool cardigans.

For a moment Margaret allowed herself the luxury, or perhaps the imposition, of watching him asleep, an intrusion upon his privacy she knew, but he looked so peaceful that she needed to take more than a brief glance at him. It was then she noted that his sleep wasn't as peaceful as it first appeared. Nothing specific, just something about the expression, even with his eyes closed, caught her attention and made her frown.

Her gaze travelled to the hand lying limp above the coverlet where she saw that his fingers, that had been curled about a sheet of notepaper, had loosened their hold. Without touching the letter she bent forward, conscious of the cruelty of her intrusion into an unsuspecting person's privacy, to read what she could see of it, a few words only. But they were enough. In fact one word had been enough: divorce. The childish handwriting was that of Susan.

Compressing her lips to stem the seething anger that rose up in her, she could only hurry away, knowing there was nothing she could do to help him. She could not know, not until he told her, and he would not do that. He would keep his pain to himself as he'd learned to do all through his three hard years of suffering while Susan, the treacherous little bitch, had been having a good time with some other man.

All this time, Margaret felt instinctively that her presence had been a bolster for him; she sensed that he clung to her as a friend who would hold his hand should he need it. Now he was leaving. Who would he have to hold his hand against the onslaught of Susan's infidelity? Not his mother, who meant well but who found it impossible to unbend. His father? Perhaps. What he needed was someone who loved him as she loved him. Yet what right had she to presume that her silent love, which would always be there for him although he wasn't aware of it, was what he needed?

On the day of his leaving, he took her hand, grinned up into her face and said, in the same way as he had once told her she would be one of the nicer of his memories, 'I'll miss you, Maggie. Keep in touch.'

He had needed her throughout his time here, sometimes desperately. But love? There were all kinds of love. Maybe he did feel something towards her, something deeper than just friendship, and perhaps such a relationship could grow into something more meaningful given time, but it would never be what people called being in love. And for all Susan had done to him, Margaret knew he still loved her with a desperation that pulled him apart.

So she smiled at him as he got into his parents' car, and said with cheery encouragement, 'Of course I'll keep in touch.'

Mrs Ward smiled her wintry smile at her and nodded her gratitude for all the nursing she had given Matthew, and Margaret, returning the acknowledgement, knew the woman was grateful, although her nature was unable to allow her to express how she really felt.

Mr Ward, coming round the car to take Margaret's hand, was more open and forthcoming. 'He wrote, you know, to tell us all about you. You mean more to him than I think even he realises. You've been a tower of strength to him and I don't think he'd have got this far, little as it is, but for you. I wish . . .' He paused and his eyes studied hers. 'I wish you and he . . .'

Margaret knew what he was trying to say but felt it right that he shouldn't be urged to further it. She broke in quickly. 'Matthew and I are very good friends, Mr Ward. Have always been that. He needs friends.'

'Yes, of course.' The relief that he hadn't had to say what was on his mind was apparent, that and a depth of understanding between them in the significant way he added before going back round to the driver's side of the car, 'Don't lose touch with us, Margaret.'

Watching them go, Matthew appearing wretched and somehow defeated, looking neither right nor left, not even waving to her, she thought about his father's parting words. 'Don't lose touch.' An ordinary saying, but expressed so earnestly that she knew it carried a totally different meaning to the normally light-hearted one. Yet her heart did not rise with hope. It was up to Matthew, not his father, how far their friendship progressed, and Matthew would never let go of Susan. His love for her would forever haunt him, fill his heart, and Margaret Ross would have no chance to squeeze into whatever minute portion of his heart might be left free.

Matthew's going was a signal for her to leave the QAs. She had no more use for them, nor they for her. But it was impossible to see herself as leaving the profession. The mere idea of going back into office work after all she had experienced made her feel like a deflated balloon. She would stay a nurse to the end of her working life. She'd become a civilian nurse. Ignoring the vision of the years stretching on, while she, unmarried, dedicated herself to moving steadily up the ladder one day to become a matron, she applied for a post of nursing sister at the London Chest Hospital, and got it. That she was back near to Matthew's home and would still see him from time to time, she chose to ignore. She had come back for her mother's sake and nothing else. Except for her mother she might possibly have applied for a place elsewhere in any of the distant counties, pastures new, Matthew a closed book. This she told herself, almost convincing herself that he had nothing at all to do with her return home.

But it was good to be home again, with her mother cooking for her in the evenings, seeing the pleasure and contentment in her face. It was good to spend her days off with her, pick up where she'd left off. But that part of it wasn't quite true. The threads of that old life before the war had been well and truly cut. The friends she had known had gone their own ways: Matthew's sister Louise had married and gone to Canada; Jean Summerfield's people were still living wherever they'd gone to (she could no longer recall where it was) and Jean no doubt was married by now; Freddy and Eileen Perry, with their two children, lived in Romford, Essex – she had their address but probably wouldn't bother writing to them; Dennis Cox, poor Dennis, was dead . . . she felt sad for a young life lost, so many young lives lost. But for the war she might have ended up marrying Dennis, settled down to being the wife of a successful solicitor, perhaps with one or two children, attending social events. But there *had* been a war and it *had* altered all their lives, their once carefree, happy lives. Now this was her life and she must settle for that.

'It's nice knowing I don't have to be sent anywhere and everywhere,' she told her mother who, at last convinced that her daughter would be home almost as regularly as if she had gone back to office work, was happily setting the table for this, their first evening meal together for some considerable time. 'Though all the friends I used to know around here are all gone now.'

'There's still the church, dear. You might find someone there.'

'I think I've got a bit old for that, Mumsy.'

Her mother shrugged as they sat themselves down to the table. 'Well, I expect you'll soon make new ones, dear. Perhaps from the hospital. And there's still young Matthew Ward across the road. Now he's home again, I expect he'll be attending there for check-ups. It's the nearest place, easy for him to get to. You'll probably see him now and again.'

Blithely she prattled on this new tack, how ill he was looking, as she began on the stew she'd prepared. 'To think how he once was, poor dear.'

Margaret too remembered.

She had an old photo somewhere around the house of them all, her old friends, all of them happy and unsuspecting of what lay ahead, snapped in the act of fits of laughter. She remembered it being taken by Louise, then a girl of sixteen. Matthew had made a quip in his usual mocking manner: 'Look at her, worst photographer this side of Lower Wallop and west of Katmandu!' Coming unexpectedly, it had them all falling about so that the snap was slightly blurred. It still lay in her dressing-table drawer. He'd been so debonair then, and now looked so thin and ill and haunted.

'His mother looks worried lately,' her mother was saying, chewing on a piece of the precious still-rationed scrag end of lamb. 'For him I suppose, him and his so-called wife. I think I said something about it in one of my letters to you, that they were more or less separated? She really let him down while he was away, poor boy, a prisoner of the Japanese, and nothing he could do about her so far away. His mother looks after their little girl now, you know. That's a comfort to him at least.'

Margaret nodded obligingly as she ate. She had never divulged her secret feelings to her mother, to anyone. She vowed to find an excuse to pop across the road at some time or other and see how he was.

It was with some surprise one bright Sunday afternoon to be welcomed in by his mother on her first tentative visit. Much of what she had always considered the woman's frigid mien melted at the sight of her.

'Of course, my dear, come in,' she said readily. And then, her voice dropping to a whisper, 'He certainly needs someone else's company than just ours. It's hard for him, going nowhere, doing so little. He sits in the garden doing nothing. It was suggested he go to Southend sanatorium for a while. Sea air. Good for his chest. But he won't go. It's a good job we have the park nearby, the air's fresher here than most places in London. Mr Ward thought we should move to the country for his health, but Matthew got himself into such a state about it, we've dropped the idea. He's in the garden.'

All this she relayed as she conducted Margaret along the bright, neat hallway and through the spotless kitchen to where Matthew was sitting in a deckchair on a narrow paved patio which the sun at its summer height could just about touch for a couple of hours.

His head was bent over a photograph but as he looked up at her emerging from the house with his mother he quickly slipped it out of sight between himself and the deckchair fabric, but not before Margaret glimpsed the glossy black and white image of a young woman. That and his reaction to her coming upon him could only mean it was of his wife.

Margaret pretended she hadn't noticed. 'Hope you don't mind me popping in. I just wanted to see how you were.'

He was trying to smile. Watching the effort it was obvious he'd been tormented by the now-hidden photo. Now he must look at this visitor as though nothing had happened, and Margaret felt the weight of guilt at her intrusion, wishing she hadn't so blithely taken it into her head to come over here. His mother having gone back into the house, leaving them to it, she could hardly depart the second she had arrived. Best to brazen it out and make an exit as soon as decently possible.

'See you're taking advantage of the sunshine,' she said brightly. He nodded and she gazed about the long, narrow garden for some inspiration. 'This garden's bigger than ours, but then, your house is larger too. These are nice houses. I see your dad's already taken out the old air-raid shelter. I think ours will stay there permanently if we're not careful, though I suppose in time we'll get a man to take it out for us and grass it over.'

She was talking rubbish, anything to fill the threatening silence.

He was saying nothing. She wondered if he was even listening. What was he thinking? It was hard to tell and she was beginning to feel a virtual idiot standing here talking nonsense about gardens and air-raid shelters.

She stopped, regarding him. What had she come here for? To cheer him up? To give him a pep talk? To pry? All she wanted to do now was say, 'Nice to see you again, Matthew – goodbye,' but she merely stood looking at him, desperately probing her mind for something to say. What else? Glad you are looking better? But he wasn't looking better. He was looking . . . not ill; he had filled out a little from that first time she'd seen him brought into the hospital. No, not exactly ill, but drawn, pulled down, despondency oozing from him because he saw no hope of any future for himself. And didn't she know why? Of course she did, and prayed to be able to put it right for him, without becoming an interfering nuisance. He wouldn't welcome her interference. His pain was private and it was obvious he intended to keep it that way.

So it took her by storm when he said, as though to himself, 'It's her photo. I was looking at her photo.'

She could have said, 'Were you?' and nearly did, but that would have been crass, false innocence. She had seen him, and he knew she had. She could have said, 'Whose photo?' but she knew whose it was, and he knew that of her as well. So she stood silent.

'There's nothing I can do,' he said in the same flat tone.

Now was the time to say something. 'What can I do?' she said simply.

He turned his eyes to her, dark with the grief that was eating him. 'I don't know.' He wasn't telling her to mind her own business, that there was nothing she could do, just that he didn't know.

'If there is anything I can do, Matthew. If you need me. I'll be here.'

She spoke few words now, not that earlier inane chatter. Words that had some meaning, she hoped. She saw relief flow into his eyes, saw him incline his head in a small gesture of acceptance and she knew they would talk again and little by little he would release into her keeping all the suppressed grief and rage and hopelessness that was within him and perhaps in this way she would lighten the burden that at this moment seemed unbearable.

Even now he was on the verge of saying something. She waited while he contemplated what he needed to say. He, who had once been unstoppable with ready quips and digs and careless laughter, must force himself to look at every word, each drowned in a mire of unspeakable memories, having to be wrung from him, and now with an added reluctance after what had been done to him by one who he had thought had stood by him.

'Maggie . . .' he said at last. 'Maggie . . . I have to see her.

287

I've got to talk to her. Somehow. If I could see her . . . There's no one, no one who'll help. They say I . . . I mustn't . . .'

Now he halted altogether, but she knew what he was trying to say. His parents' well-meaning efforts to defend him against the wife who'd caused him such hurt had resulted only in antagonising him more. They were too close in their shared grief to be of any good to him. But could she do any better?

Now wasn't the time to broach it. The least said at this moment . . .

There was movement in the house, the sound of voices, one of them high, childish. Matthew brightened immediately as a small figure came out in a rush. Margaret turned to see a small girl of around three-and-a-half pull up sharp at the sight of her, a stranger, while Margaret, relief surging over her at this timely interruption, smiled down at her. 'Hello.'

Mrs Ward stood behind her granddaughter. 'Matilda, say hello to daddy and Miss Ross.' Margaret caught the coupling of her and Matthew's names, as though she'd have liked to see them as such.

Shyly, Matilda stood her ground, her head dropping as she surveyed Margaret from under a generous dark fringe of hair. She was a beautiful child, softly rounded, sweet-faced, her eyes cornflower-blue, the rest of her hair cascading down behind her small shoulders.

Margaret glanced at Matthew. He was regarding his daughter, his eyes suddenly tender, a faraway look in them. Was he thinking of Susan? Did his daughter look like her?

She turned back to the child. 'And where have you been?' she asked.

No reply was forthcoming and the little rose-red lips began to pout in childish self-consciousness. But her grandfather, who appeared in the doorway, went to her rescue.

'We've been out, haven't we?' he said in an indulgent voice. 'We've been to Epping Forest. I came by some extra petrol so I took her out for the day. Matthew's mother stayed here for Matthew's sake. He didn't want to come along.'

'Not much point, was there?' Matthew's remark was sharp, but his father chose to ignore it, turning his attention to the child, bending towards her encouragingly.

288

'And what did we see in the woods? We saw squirrels, didn't we?'

'Squiddles,' repeated Matilda, picking up the spirit of it.

'And what else? What else did we see?'

'Squiddles.'

'And? Tell daddy what you saw. And . . . what flies in the air?'

At last she was in full command, embarrassment forgotten. 'We seed some birds and squiddles and . . .' She broke off to twist round to consult her grandfather who mouthed something at her, she in turn working at it. 'Pheasints!' she cried in triumph. 'And lots of sheeps.'

'That's really nice,' Margaret offered, bending down to be rewarded by the girl coming forward to put a small soft hand in hers. 'She's lovely.' Margaret turned to Matthew but his eyes had grown hard, not looking at any of them, so she turned hastily back to his parents, who nodded their wholehearted concurrence.

'She is,' Mrs Ward said, a little sadly. 'And very well behaved.'

'Yes.' More a sound from Matthew than a word, it was weighted with bitter incrimination leaving Margaret wondering if it had been directed at his mother, who would have insisted on good behaviour even from a three-year-old, or at his wife, whom this child obviously took after. Not a bit of Matthew could be seen in her.

'At least in that,' his mother turned on him, 'she takes after you, thank the Lord. And she has your colour hair, and . . .'

'So Susan's hair isn't dark?' he shot back at her, almost viciously. 'She takes after her in everything. *Her* eyes, *her* stature. And who does she take after for tantrums? There's only one. Well-behaved, yes, sometimes, but there are times when even you can't control her. If that's not Susan I don't know what is. Why don't you bloody-well admit to it?'

'Oh, Matthew,' his mother's exasperated voice rang out. 'Why can't you put that woman out of your mind? Why must you always bring her up?'

'Because I still love her. You can't see that. All you can see is your own damned righteousness. She was alone. She had no one. I wasn't there. I should have been. Instead I was . . . I was . . . Christ, if you'd only see how it must've been for her.

289

So she's done the dirty on me, found someone else. But you're not helping make it any bloody easier for me.'

Margaret got to her feet awkwardly, an outsider witnessing family dissension. This was a side to Matthew she had never seen. Even all that time ago when he had spoken against his mother's efforts to encourage him to go for a commission at the beginning of the war, it had not been this acrimonious, his hatred of people trying to help, the world itself. It wasn't what he was saying but the way the words were being spat out with such vehemence that was so frightening.

Matilda was looking from one to the other, her pretty face animated with anguish, nearing tears. On impulse, Margaret gathered her to her with one arm around her and the child came readily, huddling against her.

Matthew had got out of his deckchair to stand glaring at his mother, and without thinking Margaret found her voice, directing it at him.

'You're frightening your daughter, Matthew.' It amazed her how calm her voice sounded and he shot an enraged glance at her, instantly modifying it as their eyes met. He took a deep breath, a shuddering sigh, and his posture sagged a little.

'I'm sorry, Maggie, that you should hear all this.' His whole mien seemed to diminish and, appalled, Margaret let go her hold on Matilda and went towards him. He must not be diminished.

'Oh, my dear. Don't. It's not your fault. I started it.'

Of course she hadn't, but it felt like it. He was breathing hard. He began coughing, small, sharp little coughs. He looked all in, had worn down what energy he had; the disease still lurked in him. She put an arm about him, supporting him while she looked at his parents.

'I think he ought to rest,' she ordered, she the nurse in charge, and they, like admonished children, moved back before her as she went with their son into the house.

Once Matthew was installed in bed in his room, she apologised as a formality to his parents for her being here, for being a disruption to their private life. She waved away their insistence that she hadn't been, but she was still in her role of nurse, advising as she saw fit.

'I think he ought to be got to a sanatorium for a while, you know. His mind must rest as well as his body, and it's not being rested here. He's too near his wife. I think he needs a few months away, in spite of what he says.'

It was gratifying to see them nod agreement, but Mrs Ward surprised her on taking her to the door by putting a hand on her arm before opening it.

'You are of course, quite right, my dear.'

Chapter 26

There wasn't a lot he could do about it. Between them all, his parents, his doctors, Margaret Ross, whom he alternately turned to for support and backed away from, he knew that if he wanted to get better he must bow to their superior judgement, submit to being packed off to the sanatorium.

He did need to get better, to be well again to claim Susan back from that bastard who'd tempted her away. Susan was easily led. It wasn't her fault. She had this thing about sick people, but once he got himself back on his feet, all that would disappear.

The sanatorium was bright, two-storeyed, with more windows than walls, and verandas positioned to catch every vestige of sunlight. The grounds had the benefit of sea air to help with the cure, and with one of the mainstays of cure being to keep up the patients' spirits, make them feel at ease with the world, the nursing staff were attentive and cheery. He too was expected to feel at ease with the world, but he wasn't. He was an inconvenience, to be put away. He had no means of getting to Susan from here, for the sanatorium was effectively a prison too. At home he might in time have evaded his mother's eagle eye, boarded a bus for Mile End Road and burst in on Susan in the hope, vain perhaps, of getting her back. Here he could only wait to be declared fit before ever being allowed to escape and be his own man to do as he pleased.

Do as he pleased! That was a laugh. It seemed all his life he'd been in captivity. Home, the Army, prison camps, hospitals; his mother, even Margaret Ross joining the ranks of his keepers. Where had all that free spirit gone he'd dreamed of in his youth? At twenty-eight he felt every bit an old man. There had been such thoughts before the war of one day leaving home to soar free as a bird. He had left, but merely to swap one form of imprisonment for another, and there was no way he would ever be free. Only with Susan had he been free, tasting a tiny morsel, enough to reveal the golden glory of it, before it had all been snatched away.

Stuck here in this place, this morning watching his parents' cautious approach like that of people about to confront a time bomb, he wondered what was the point of all the efforts to make him well while inside memories both wonderful and evil entwined in a form of torture until he could no longer tell them apart. These memories could not be shared with anyone because no one understood what it was like to love and have it snatched away, to be strong and have that snatched away, to ache for beauty and see only misery and privation and degradation and betrayal, to contrast the wife he had loved and trusted with the truth he had come home to face. Only one sure way to be free remained. This he contemplated with strange detachment as he sat watching his parents' progress along the clean, bright ward towards him, and when they had each kissed him and asked how he was, he answered with a sort of perverse wish to witness their horrified reaction, a despondent need to gain their attention.

'Tell the truth, I've just about had enough of everything. What's the point of it all? I'd be better off finishing it and being no more worry to anyone.'

His remark was ignored.

'It's time you started thinking what you're going to do about Susan.' He turned his face away from his mother's probing eyes. 'All this hoping for miracles, it's just ludicrous, Matthew. She wants a divorce and she's not particular how she gets it.'

His eyes remained averted. No point responding when she got on this track, leaping on it the moment she arrived, and Dad putting his oar in as well.

'If you think she'll ever come back now, Matthew, you're just banging your head against a brick wall, son.'

'If she did come back,' his mother's tone sounded righteously adamant, 'I for one wouldn't give her the smell of my dish rag, much less house room . . .'

But she wasn't in love with Susan. At times his chest felt as if it was being torn out. Even his father no longer took his side. Matthew felt totally alienated seeing his father nodding at every word his mother said.

'We've spoken to a solicitor, Matthew. He has written to her on our behalf advising her to get one of her own in this matter, and she's done that now.' All this had been done without once consulting him. 'They both agree that the marriage is unsalvageable. Susan is quite happy to be cited as the guilty party.' She was as eager as that? Something inside Matthew plummeted. 'Apparently this Crawley fellow has no objections to being cited as her lover. His wife is apparently thinking in terms of divorcing him anyway. Pity it all has to take so long, and meantime the solicitor is running up a nice fat fee.'

Was that all they cared about, costs? He kept his face turned away.

'It's up to you, Matthew. How much longer are you going to let things drag on? There's nothing you can do. She's made up her mind, the slut.'

Now he turned. 'Don't say that!'

'I will say that, Matthew. Because that's what she is. How can you feel anything for her after what she's done to you, you a prisoner of war, all you went through, while she enjoyed herself playing fast and loose.'

How could he, even if he wished, tell them what he'd gone through and how it had been Susan alone who had kept him going? He still believed that, fervently, still believed she *had* thought of him, willed him to live. This adultery had come later. It didn't matter what they said, there had been a time, at first, when she had willed him to live, prayed for his safe return, cried for him. If everyone would only stop interfering, he and she could come together again. He would forgive her everything. The war had done this to them, had taken all good things out of their hands. And he could, would forgive her. If only she would come back to him.

'There's nothing you can do about it, Matthew.' This from his father, his tone pleading. 'It's gone too far. Gone on too long. You've got to file for a divorce, son. There's nothing more you can do.'

What did they bloody know? He looked at each of them, his

eyes ice-hard, but there were no words he could say and he turned away again. Let them get on with it. They would, no matter what he said. But once he was out of here, then they would see a different Matthew. No longer did he contemplate suicide. He'd fight for what was his – once he was strong again.

'I just feel I'm being buried here, Maggie, bit by bit.'

The words seemed to come from deep inside his soul and Margaret fancied she felt every iota of his pain as if it were her own. She counted the days to each visit, coming to see him whenever she could get time off from her work.

There had been a wild idea when he'd gone off to the sanatorium to give up her present post and follow him, but in time he would leave there and come home for good. It was always a fool's game following others around the country. They always moved on, leaving behind a void much as before. Not only that, here she was a visitor, a friend, a confidante. As a nurse she would have become an overseer, an official figure, not to be trusted. Things were better as they stood.

She sat now beside him on the veranda that caught the slanting, fast-diminishing warmth of an October sun. He was in a wickerwork easy chair, a cardigan about his shoulders, she on a hard chair that made her back seem unacceptably rigid. She would rather have been allowed to recline a little, to look more at ease. This way he had to look up at her which didn't help an easy relationship. Though mostly he stared at the tiled floor as he emptied out his heart to her.

'If I could only go to see her.' He seldom mentioned Susan by name. By this time they all knew who *her* referred to. 'I know I could sort things out. But no one agrees, they keep telling me it'll put my health in jeopardy, but that's an excuse. They don't want me to try getting her back. They hate her so I must hate her too.' He let his voice trail off and they sat on in silence for a while, then suddenly he looked up at Margaret, his eyes brightened by new hope.

'But you could go.'

'Me?' She was startled, lost for words. How could she go to his wife, trying to convey to her what was in someone else's heart? It was impossible.

He was looking at her from under his brow, his eyes slewing

sideways towards her. She hurried on. 'It wouldn't be right for me to pay her a visit on your behalf. What could I say to her?'

'No one has ever bothered to talk to her,' he said bitterly. 'Except to condemn her.'

She waited. He had dropped his gaze and she could see his face working very slightly, could almost see the thoughts going through his head, the pain, the longing, the hope and the hopelessness that seethed there. And memories too, memories that would never die. All he'd suffered these past years would be with him always. But none of it, looking at him now with grief and emptiness showing on every part of his face, had scarred him as Susan had.

Margaret could foster only contempt for the girl which instinctively she knew she must smother for his sake. If she did consent to being his errand boy, she would have to be sweet and understanding to gain Susan's confidence. It smacked of an unsavoury business because subterfuge did not come easily to her. But wasn't she resorting to subterfuge at this very moment, visiting him in the guise of a friend, when her whole being cried out to touch his hand in love, to kiss his lips and be kissed in return, the way he had kissed her before he'd gone away and it had all gone cold for her when he had met Susan?

'Please, Matthew, don't ask me to do that,' she pleaded. But for his sake, for the sake of the love she had for him, if he pressed the point . . .

As well she had been looking at him or she'd have missed the hand half-raised in a small poignant gesture of defeat, of humiliated pride, an effort not to recognise that he must rely on her to do his work for him. He needed help yet felt belittled by that need. Innocently she *was* belittling him. He would not ask her again, that she knew. She knew too that their friendship was being placed in jeopardy, that he would never trust her again. She needed his trust as much as he needed hers. It was a kind of love in its way.

'I'll have to see,' she added lamely; not a promise nor a denial, neither one thing or the other, a way of avoiding the total commitment she knew she was in danger of being held to. To escape it, she got up to gather up her coat and handbag, preparing to murmur some sort of farewell, when, only halfway out of her seat, she was taken by surprise as his hand closed about her wrist.

'You will see her, Maggie? You promise.'

'I haven't . . .' The commitment was already being made for her. Blackmail, trading on the affection she had for him, the thought shot through her head. He knew, he must know, how she felt about him, and was using it. That was unkind, cruel. For a second Margaret was aghast at the anger that swept through her. But the eyes staring up into hers were filled with pleading, not craftiness, were sunken with desolation, dark with pain, and though that in itself was a form of blackmail, how could she refuse him?

Yet still she hesitated. He was asking too much of her love. And she had expected him *not* to ask again, so was now taken off guard. 'What on earth could I say to her, Matthew?'

'Just that I . . . I want her to come back to me.'

'I can't tell her things like that. If you wrote a letter, I could take it to her.'

'I've written letters.'

'This time I'd be there to hand it to her, while she reads it, tell her how you are, how you feel.'

Oh God! She had walked right into it. Hope had begun to glow in his eyes. Hope was filling him as a deep hole is filled with lifegiving soil to nurture the tree with which it is about to be planted. And it was glorious to see him come suddenly alive. How could she destroy that?

'All right, Matthew. Write to her. I'll wait.'

She sat down again, put her hat and handbag aside and watched him fish a small writing case from his locker, feverishly open it and pull out the fountain pen resting inside to write his private letter to his wife.

All the while Margaret's heart was pounding against her chest wall, partly at the prospect looming before her, partly at feeling herself being used as a sacrificial lamb, partly with the same emotion he himself suffered – love that tore at the very being but which the sufferer knew to be quite futile no matter what they did.

The feeling of being made a sacrificial lamb still lingering, she reluctantly prepared herself to visit Susan.

She made three calls that week, during break times from the London Chest Hospital, none of them successful. She received no reply to her knock and had no way to tell whether they were out or merely pretending to be. Each time it had rained, not heavily but with miserable persistence that carried all the odours of the East End with it, and after her three separate attempts, standing on the doorstep wet and fed up and growing more and more annoyed, she gave up. There was only so much one could do. Besides, it was all pointless anyway. Susan would never go back to the man she had rejected. Obviously happy with her lover, what did she want with a sick man? Which Matthew still was.

In a way it was a relief not seeing Susan, loathing the girl as she did for the way she'd behaved. But more than that, a tiny spark kept leaping into her mind that the longer Susan stayed away from Matthew, the more chance there was of his coming to terms with it. Would he one day see the futility of chasing after her and turn to someone else – herself perhaps? His friend all these years, always there for him, he was fast becoming dependent on her. Could that one day lead to love?

The thought made her laugh. Little hope of that. But a week from now she'd have to confront him with her admission of failure, see his face. She found herself putting it off and on that Saturday decided to postpone seeing him until another of her days off. Instead she'd try to see Susan one last time, have something she could tell him. But that morning it rained again . . .

It was his mother who forced her hand that very morning. It came as a shock to open the door and find his mother standing there, an umbrella above her head. Mrs Ward demeaning herself to come across in the rain to a lesser neighbour's door revealed the extent to which some of her high-necked values had taken a nose-dive since the war.

She looked almost supplicant, the weight of her son's plight making her a wholly different woman from the one who'd once lorded it over others. Her principles, however, had not slipped to the extent of agreeing to Mrs Ross's invitation to come inside.

'It's Margaret I wish to speak to,' she said, her voice as sharp as it ever was, and turning to Margaret she asked directly, 'When do you next hope to be visiting Matthew?'

'I was thinking of perhaps going this afternoon,' Margaret lied, trying hard not to sound reluctant.

'That's what I thought.' Mrs Ward compressed her lips in a manner natural to her. 'We'll be seeing him too today, as soon as Mr Ward gets the car out. You can come with us. Save your train fare. Could you be ready in, say, half an hour?'

Still some of the old Mrs Ward there. Assuming everyone would fall in with her plans came as naturally to her as breathing. Margaret chewed on her lip. She and Mumsy had planned on a quiet afternoon together, but it could probably be put aside. They'd have all evening. And part of her did want to see Matthew very much, despite her trepidation at what she had to tell him.

'Yes, I could be.' His parents being there might soften his reaction.

Mrs Ward inclined her head in a small gesture of acknowledgement. 'He often asks after you, Margaret,' she said, but broke off abruptly as though that information had embarrassed her in some way.

This woman would never let her high standards slip entirely no matter what the circumstances, but Margaret had detected more than once, as she did now, a ring of suppressed hope in Mrs Ward's voice that she might one day see her as part of the family. A daughter-in-law perhaps? Vain hope, that, but she smiled as Mrs Ward added a little too briskly, 'Well, we'll pick you up in half an hour then,' before turning and going down the steps and back along the road to her own house.

Matthew was in the day room, it being too wet to go outside. October, nearly at its end, already heralded a bad winter, and the room buzzed with families and patients. Margaret prayed he wouldn't ask her what she had achieved.

She sat by while his parents put their offerings of fruit and a bar of Fry's chocolate from their sweet ration before him, asked him how he was and began on all the trivialities of their lives since last seeing him. He murmured his thanks for the gifts, after a while turning aside from what they were telling him, his attention wandering while he muttered occasional comments in whatever seemed the appropriate place.

Several times Margaret saw his eyes come to rest on her, saw the query in their depths. She smiled weakly, knowing he would wait for a moment when they were alone. As if he had planned it, his father went out on to the veranda to smoke his pipe; his mother joined her husband, leaving Margaret to hold the fort. It was a moment she had been dreading.

The second they were out of hearing, his question came direct. 'What did she say?'

'Your wife?' She stalled, trying to remember how she'd rehearsed this moment. He said nothing, but the look in his dark eyes said, 'Who else?'

Margaret steeled herself. 'I went there several times, Matthew, but there was never any answer to my knock.'

He sat silent for a moment, then said, 'You didn't speak to her.'

'I tried. Oh, Matthew, I did try so hard.'

'I expect you did.' His tone was soft but full of condemnation. 'It was unfair of me to ask that of you.'

'No, it was right.'

He shook his head, throwing off the failure. 'I've let myself down. The only one to go and see her is me. Can't ask things like that of you. My fault, expecting too much.'

'No, Matthew. I understand how you feel.'

He looked directly at her. 'Do you?' The look made her squirm, a look one would give one's executioner, defiant yet resigned.

'I want to.' That she'd let him down she felt keenly. 'I want to help.'

'You're putting yourself in a high place, aren't you, Maggie, thinking you can do anything for me? I could tell you all of what's inside me. I could tell you for a hundred years, you still wouldn't know.'

'I feel so useless.'

'Then how the bloody hell do you think I feel?' His voice had risen, bringing all heads turning in his direction. 'You all think you know how people like me feel. Trotting out your damned platitudes. "It's all behind you now – forget it – we'll make it better – tell you some jokes – snap you out of it. It doesn't matter that you wake up in a cold sweat, crying out for the friends who died while you stayed alive, feeling bloody

300

guilty for surviving, feeling that you'd trodden on them to stay alive while they died. Why d'you keep crying for the girl whose picture you kept inside your head through all those years, who you thought was waiting for you to come back home, to find it was only a dream? You must get over it." Well I can't get over it. And all your bloody understanding, Maggie, isn't going to help me get over it.'

He stopped as suddenly as he'd begun. Now he stood up, staring around him at the faces turned to him in stunned silence. His parents had come back in to gaze at him in alarm. For a moment he regarded them, then with all those in the day room watching him open-mouthed in the manner of people who feel unable to pinpoint any reason for odd behaviour, he strode from the room.

No one, not even his parents, moved, but Margaret was already on her way, hurrying after him. Thus when she caught him up they were alone. Just one other person could be seen in the corridor, a porter at the far end going about his business.

Taking Matthew by the arm she swung him round to face her and pulled him to her, gathered him in her arms. He came without protest, his head turned so that his cheek rested on her shoulder, allowing his face to bury itself in the hollow of her neck.

Cradling him, she could feel his body being shaken by quiet sobs. She heard herself crooning soft, half-formed words as a mother might do to a hurt child. 'No, no, dear, no. It's all right. It's all right.' Silly words to a grown man but they afforded the comfort of understanding and shared feelings.

But he was right. How could she share what went on in his mind? Who had any idea what it had really been like for men like him, only from what papers and newsreels showed? She had seen a Nazi concentration camp after its liberation and had been horrified. But by the time accounts of the experiences of the freed emaciated British lads had reached the papers, too much coverage had been devoted to those newsreels of Nazi atrocities for much more to be given to the horrors of Japanese prison camps. The inmates had been too far away. Also they'd been British and American and Australian, men who surely hadn't succumbed to such barbaric treatment as had those Jews of the concentration camps, their skeletal corpses piled high in ditches for the public to see on cinema screens and the front pages of newspapers. No one saw the thousands of crosses lying deep in the jungle, too deep for photographers to penetrate with their cameras. Why bother? They had the groups of smiling if skeletal freed prisoners to snap. Brits, Yanks, Aussies, Kiwis, with bottles of beer in their hands given them by their rescuers, all doing thumbs-up for the cameraman as they held each other up on matchstick legs, bony arms around each other's necks. They were all right. They weren't lying in obvious piles of dead. They were coming back, all of them looking cheerful and victorious as though they'd won a war, and no one saw the horror that lay behind those smiles, the dead comrades who'd forever haunt their dreams. Margaret's arms tightened about Matthew, imagining the pain for some like him whose wife or sweetheart hadn't waited for them.

'It's all right,' she murmured again, her face buried in his dark hair that smelled of him, spicy, and of shampoo. 'Just let me be here for you.'

Suddenly she too was crying. 'I love you, Matthew. You're all the world to me. You've always been all the world to me. That's why I've never got married. I hoped . . . I never gave up hope of you coming home. I kept it alive because I . . .'

She realised all at once what she had been saying. His body had grown calm and he lifted his head, his dark eyes still shining with moisture, looking into hers. Flustered, Margaret dropped her eyes from the gaze that seemed to bore into her. Then she heard his voice, hoarse from grieving for the woman that was his no longer. 'Maggie, I didn't know.'

Still looking down, she shrugged dismissively, no longer in command of herself, embarrassed by having her adoration revealed.

'It's a private thing,' she managed to say. 'It doesn't matter.'
'It does.'

He was looking down upon the crown of her still-bent head, she could feel it. 'I don't deserve you, Maggie. If only . . .'

She looked up as he broke off, but he was moving back from her, putting her from him. She took a deep, fortifying breath and gathered herself up. 'I'm sorry I let you down, Matthew. I did try hard.'

'I know.'

Footsteps hurrying along the corridor invaded the private moment. Voices broke in, at once irate and concerned. 'Matthew! What on earth's going on? What upset you? You'll do yourself no good getting so upset. Margaret, what upset him?' As though he couldn't talk for himself.

Margaret looked at him and a mutual spark passed silently between them. He was aware now of her feelings, but he had to bow to the stronger obsession that drew him, and she accepted that he felt tenderness towards her, a caring love which couldn't match that which was destroying him.

'I have to do this myself,' he said, mouthing the words so that only she heard them as his parents reached him. Wondering at the words he'd mouthed at her, she had a vision of a man walking knowingly to his doom. He would let Susan destroy him because he wanted her to and there was nothing anyone could do about it.

Chapter 27

'When do you think you'll be bringing Mattie to see me again?'

The last time he'd seen her had been August. It was now November. His daughter would be left with the woman who cleaned for his mother a couple of days a week with a few shillings extra to keep an eye on Mattie when they visited.

He'd liked to have said, 'ordain to bring her', his mother having the final say in things concerning him, even whether he saw his own daughter or not. Matthew felt bitterness run through him like a trickle of acid as his parents sat looking awkward and concerned. His mother frowned.

'It's too cold these days.'

'It's warm enough in here.' Weak as the autumn sun filtering through the conservatory roof was, it was enough to warm up the place considerably apart from a constant draught from the obligatory ever-open top set of windows. Used to so-called healthy draughts, it felt warm enough to him, but his mother had another ready excuse up her sleeve.

'During the summer, Matthew, she could play in the open, but with winter coming on, it's boring for her cooped up inside. It would be for any child her age. She'd get on the other patients' nerves. It's not fair on them or her.'

And besides, he finished in silent sarcasm, a sanatorium's no place for a child. True, it wasn't, but he missed her; missed Susan; felt rebellious.

'She's my child.' His and Susan's, so like Susan, even at four. He'd feast his eyes on her, still filled with wonder at this his daughter, a surge of love for her twisting inside him so that he wanted to hug her to him. Of course as yet he dared not. TB was catching, not so much from him now, as because all patients came here to this out-of-quarantine visiting area. Visitors were safe at arm's length, but Mattie had to be discouraged from approaching too near, for her own sake.

Not that she ever came that near to him. To her he was a stranger still, a man she had been told to call Daddy. As a child who had never known one and was still only four years old, she hadn't any real idea what a daddy was meant to be. His father she called Grandad, his mother Grandma, and she had experienced the feel of that, but him, he was Daddy in name only. How he longed to clasp her to him and show her what it meant. But if he did, she might ease away from him, his hug unfamiliar, maybe even a little alarming. And that was another reason why he did not try to embrace her.

The weak sun had disappeared without anyone seeing it go. A pale fog moving in from the estuary had begun licking cold white tongues against the glass, promising to rime the lawns outside with frost before morning. His father noticed it and looked at his watch.

'Nearly four o'clock. We best be getting along, son. You'll be coming home soon. By the New Year. They're pleased with your progress. You'll be with Mattie then, for all the hours you you want.'

'Do call her Matilda, dear,' interjected his mother, but Matthew hardly heard her.

Five weeks and he'd be home, to do what he liked. And he knew exactly what he would do. But that he would save for later. Five more weeks cut off from outside contact, seeing only the other patients, their visitors, the staff, and occasionally Margaret when she could get time off from her work. He had no letters to read, except from Louise, who was married and in Canada now. There seemed little point in anyone else sending letters when they came each Sunday.

Nor did Margaret write. What would she write about? Work, her life, his health, hers? She knew better than to resort to all that rubbish. His heart lifted at the thought of her. Since that unexpected episode a few Saturdays ago he hadn't been able to get her out of his mind, the way she had folded her arms around him, drawn him to her, the way she'd whispered her love for him; seemingly it had burst out of her.

305

And him? Something had stirred in him, but the image of Susan had immediately made him push Maggie away. To feel anything like that for her would destroy the love he nurtured for Susan and he couldn't bear that. It felt like being caught up in the strangling tendrils of a vine but not wanting them ever to fall away. Yet other than the unlikely hope of any visit from Susan, he found himself waiting for Maggie's visits more than anyone else's. But she wasn't visiting so often as before. She had embarrassed herself too much that day. He wanted to see her to tell her she had no need to feel bad, that he understood. But when she did finally arrive, alone, the first Sunday in December, he said nothing, seeing his planned comment as a platitude, an insult to her feelings.

He was reading Louise's letter when she came in. Louise sounded full of her life in Canada, making it seem romantic and exciting. She and her husband were so much in love with each other. He was miserably comparing his wrecked marriage to her successful one, wishing she didn't have to be so full of it. She was promising to come over to see him when they could get the money together for the flight. She'd gone out there by sea, but swore she would never set sail on the sea again; she would use one of the new airlines opened up since the war. However they had started a family, 'at last', and she didn't think it the right thing to do in her condition. She would make it next year once the baby was born, if they could still afford it. 'You know how much money a baby takes.'

No, he didn't know. He hadn't been there when Mattie was a baby. He had just screwed up that letter in a fit of suppressed hate, against whom he wasn't sure, perhaps circumstances, perhaps himself, when Margaret came in. Thus he was not exactly in any receptive mood to see her.

Sensing it, Margaret sat awkward and self-conscious. 'I hear you'll be coming home soon,' she said for want of something better to say.

She had been to see him only once since her outrageous performance in the corridor, when his parents had caught her in the act of cuddling him. Not that they mattered. Mrs Ward had appeared highly approving. But *she* had felt a fool, them seeing her holding their son, a married man, to her bosom.

'When I come home,' Maggie became aware of a mordant edge to his tone, 'I might finally be allowed to think for myself.'

'Don't you do that now?' Immediately she saw the inanity of the remark. Here, everyone thought for him, he was powerless to do what he wanted. She knew what was in his mind. Once home he would go and find Susan with no one to stop him, probably taking her daughter with him, confronting Susan with her duties as wife and mother. It would be a disaster. Margaret could see it a mile off, the selfish, spoiled, wilful bitch throwing his pleading back in his face. And where would that leave him? Didn't he realise the harm he'd be doing himself? She wanted to tell him, warn him, but it would sound presumptuous, could even wreck their friendship, certainly any hope she fostered of anything more than that. Again she squirmed at the way she had held him to her, murmured her stupid words of love. How he had looked at her then, his eyes dark and deep. Recalling it now, had his look been one of understanding and mutual affection, or merely fear and rejection?

It was the best Christmas Susan felt she had ever spent. Just her, Geoffrey and little Trevor. She wondered how Emma Crawley was. She hadn't come nigh or by since leaving. She and Geoffrey's boys were living with her sister not far away, but she might as well have been in Timbuctoo. Geoffrey never spoke about her, though now and again he would go and pay a visit for the boys' sake. It annoyed Susan a bit, but she shrank from complaining, a little superstitious that if she did, she might lose him.

From Matthew's parents there had been no sound, other than letters from their solicitor to hers. Nothing as yet was moving regarding the divorce, with Matthew playing at delaying tactics all the time. She would have gone to tell him how useless these were, that nothing would induce her to go back to him now, but her solicitor had discouraged it, urging her to leave it all in his hands. But he was taking such a bloody long time about it. Still, he was right, no point rocking the boat. Matthew was well out of the way in that sanatorium near Southend.

She didn't wish him ill, didn't hate him or loathe him. Just the illness made her shudder to think how he must be, handsome books all gone, in their place a gaunt individual who coughed and spat blood and lay pale and vapid – she'd seen it portrayed in films, the victim wasting away, dying in the arms of a lover. She'd always hated hospitals. Even setting foot in one as a visitor made her feel sick and shaky. Having Mattie in one had been bad enough. Thank God she'd had little Trevor at home.

None of these thoughts did she impart to Geoffrey. Why spoil things? Christmas passed like a dream; they'd had a wonderful time indulging in all the goodies he'd brought home. Nineteen forty-seven waited two days off and rationing was becoming less harsh even though the winter was already proving one of the severest they'd known since the one at the beginning of the war. But settled before a bright fire whose rising heat stirred the now-dusty Christmas trimmings, Susan's whole world was lit up and life couldn't be sweeter. Matthew was just a memory, at least until the divorce came through. After the New Year the solicitors might get their silly fingers out and get things moving.

But she wouldn't think about that. She'd just think about her and Geoffrey. Little Trevor was safe asleep in bed, she and Geoffrey had the evening all to themselves. Already in a slinky black nightdress, her dressing gown open to reveal her at her best behind the lace and satin, she was beginning to feel worked up by the way he was looking at her over his glass of whisky. Both their minds were focusing on the same thing. Her insides crawled deliciously as she thought how she intended to make him really happy tonight. In fact they might not even wait to get to bed. She came over, put an enticing arm about his neck, easing herself into his lap.

He grinned at her, and, the whisky glass still in one hand, fondled her breasts with the other, easing them from their flimsy lacy covering. That he kept the glass in his hand while doing so added a certain masterful casualness, heightening her senses even more to see how far this would go before he was compelled to put down the glass. Her dressing gown fell from her shoulders, the straps of the satin nightdress also slipped from her shoulders, letting the garment slither to her waist. Geoffrey's free hand was beneath the material, fingers manipulating firmly, teasing her desire with uncontrollable force. She moaned. When would he put down that damned glass? What was she – his bondmaid to do what he liked with, arousing her until she screamed? Already urgency was rising faster than she could ever remember. She cried out to him, sobbed for him to put down the glass, for God's sake, she could take no more of this. And yet how wonderful it was – this awakening without him even entering her. What a man she had.

She was hardly aware of the glass finally being put on the sideboard, of him easing her down on the hard lino, but only of his weight on her.

From somewhere came a pounding, like iron being bashed against wood. A voice raised outside in the street came dimly to her. She heard Geoffrey swear, felt his weight ease, became suddenly aware that the street door seemed in danger of being broken down.

'What is it?' Angry, she lifted her head that a moment ago had seemed to be spinning, now completely still and filled only with disappointed anger at this untimely disruption.

The voice in the street was demanding entry, the street door rattling on its lock and hinges with a resumption of the pounding it was taking. All sorts of thoughts raced through Susan's mind. Fire? Trevor fallen out of the window? A drunk? The police – what would they want, bashing on the street door? She thought of Matthew – perhaps he was dead, her husband, and they were here to inform her. Geoffrey was on his feet, frantically buttoning his fly. Still sitting on the floor, she was equally frantically dragging on her nightdress, gathering her dressing gown about her. Even so, she hissed to him, full of fear of the unknown: 'Don't answer it.'

'I've got to. Someone might be in trouble.'

'It's not our business, Geoff.' But she was thinking again of little Trevor upstairs. Was he all right? And then she too was on her feet, trying to find her slippers as Geoffrey, now respectable, made for the hallway.

She heard him open the door, waited to hear a policeman's voice. What had he to tell them? What she heard made her clutch at her throat. All these many years since she had heard that voice, its deep timbre, yet she recognised it instantly. 'Where is she?' it demanded.

* * *

Though his parents didn't know it, he spent Christmas at the sanatorium at his own request. He felt in no hurry to celebrate it at home with them carping at him to do something about his marriage. But yesterday he'd been obliged to concede. He was due to leave anyway, now or in a week's time. Two days before New Year's Eve, with the sanatorium nursing staff stretched because of leave through the festive season, his parents thought it only right that he make it now and welcome in 1947 with them as a family.

'Start the New Year afresh. Let's hope that will be the last time you have to go into hospital. They said you're clear, at last, and so long as you look after yourself and don't fret, you can only look forward.'

His first night home had to have been the worst he had ever spent under this roof, lying awake in his room while his parents slept, their sleep sound and contented in the assumption that with their anxieties for him a little easier for the present, he must be at ease too. How could he be?

Letters were lying on the doormat as they'd come in from collecting him. His father had picked them up, sorted them out, selecting one above the rest to hand to him.

'Looks like it's from your wife's solicitors.'

Taking it, he'd put it in his jacket pocket, and saw his father's face draw together with concern.

'Aren't you going to open it? It could be important.'

'It can wait,' he'd told him and, parrying his mother's arguments that followed, refused to open it for them to see what Susan was asking. He already knew what she asked, the same request kept being trotted out – for him to divorce her, she would give him grounds enough, she was in love with . . . He couldn't even read the name without a burning rage compelling his fingers to screw each letter into a ball. He would give no answer to any of these letters until he saw her face to face. This statement he'd written repeatedly, but she (or her solicitor on her behalf) had not once acknowledged them. He might as well be crying into the wind.

But whatever it contained wasn't for others to cluck over, full of their damned advice. 'Divorce her, Matthew, and get it over with. She's no good to you. You wouldn't take her back

310

after all she's done.' No, he wouldn't give them the satisfaction of raising his voice against their demands.

The letter had stayed firmly in his pocket. Finally he opened it in the privacy of his room, hating the task and what would be written there. As he had suspected it had been the usual cry. But this time a small sealed envelope had been enclosed, the flap signed across with her small uneven signature – no, not signature, just the Christian name, Susan. She didn't even deign to include her married name, which in itself provoked anger and remorse from him.

What she'd written had taken his breath away. 'I'm tired of asking. If you can't grant me a divorce, it's no skin of my nose. I'll carry on living with Geoffrey until I die wether you like it or not. What I really want to tell you once and for all is I don't ever want to set eyes on you. It would make me sick. I wasnt never cut out to be a nurse for anyone and I'm not ready to start with you. I'm sorry if I hurt you but I don't no how plane I can make it.'

Hurt him? With a seething mind he'd risen, dressed himself, fumbling in his fury and pain at her words that seemed to so encase his brain in iron that no thought could get through but the one intent of getting to her, half killing Crawley and taking whatever came from that. He'd had sense enough to creep from his room without making any noise and waking his parents up, downstairs to where his father's car keys lay on the kitchen sideboard. The car had once been given to him as a twenty-first birthday present in the happy certainty that he would have years of pleasure from it, not knowing what had awaited him. They'd kept the car, during the war years of petrol rationing, on the gravel driveway under a tarpaulin, his father cleaning and servicing it with loving regularity. This ritual silently declared the certainty that Matthew would indeed return. 'It's yours again, Matthew,' Dad had said, but until he came home and felt well enough to drive, Dad continued to use it to keep it in running order. A way of encouraging him to get fit, Matthew supposed. Well, tonight he'd be fit, if necessary.

Muffled in an overcoat, he'd driven off almost blindly in the rage that still consumed him. It was ten thirty and people were still about. Only turning into the Mile End Road from Cambridge Health Road was his brain cooled by force as a man coming out of one of the pubs made straight across his path. The car's tyres screeched to a skidding halt, in front of the man swaying and glaring at him. 'Gerrout, y'silly sod! Watch where yer goin'. Nearly knocked me darn.'

The man had staggered on across the road, as Matthew leaned his head on the steering wheel for a moment to clear his thoughts.

Geoffrey Crawley had no notion what was in store for him. Opening the door to the frantic yelling and thumping, uttering, 'What the hell . . .' he was taken totally by surprise when a hand thrust itself against his chest with such force he was thrown back against the wall, his head connecting with solid brick with a whack that for a second sent him dizzy. He had the presence of mind at least to lunge back, enough to deny the intruder entry for a brief moment during which his attacker shouted again, 'Where is she?'

Crawley, indignant now at his home being invaded, held the man with both hands on the shoulders, countering inanely, 'Who are you? What d'you want? You can't come barging in here like this!' All of it ran together like a single sentence. The man was leaning against his efforts to hold him off.

'I said where is she?' he repeated

'Get out of here!' Frightened, Crawley felt thin fingers begin to force him from the hold he was vainly trying to retain on the man. 'Go away! Who the bloody hell are you?'

For an answer, Matthew let go of the hands trying to prevent his entrance, reached back with his right and took a swing at his wife's lover. It grazed past the man's cheekbone, making his head connect again with the passage wall though less violently than the first time. The man let go of him to clap a palm to his abused cheek.

'Godawlmighty!' he screeched. 'I'm calling the police. Sue! Sue! Get out at the back, quick, get Mr Adams next door.'

Matthew heard her voice come plaintively, quavering with fear and perturbation, from a room down the passage. 'I can't. I'm not dressed.'

Not dressed? Visions of her and this bastard naked together a moment ago assailed him. He lunged, grabbing the coward by the throat, bearing him down the passageway with the force of the rush, taking him to the floor as Susan tried to run out from the room, screaming, finding her way blocked by two grappling men at her feet.

'Matthew! Oh, God, leave him alone. You'll kill him. Leave him alone!'

Crawley was making strange choking, rasping sounds as his hands flapped about, in turn trying to break the hold on his throat or scratch his assailant's face. The choking and rasping were becoming more pronounced, the defending hands weaker, now flopping to the floor between attempts to release the grip. The face had turned puce, the eyes were beginning to stare, bulge. At first deaf and blind to all else but wreaking revenge, Matthew became aware of that dreadful colour. Sights and sounds came leaping back into his brain, as Susan screamed and beat on his shoulders, plucking at them in an effort to tear him away. Yet he couldn't let go. His fingers seemed to have locked about that neck. Meantime, the face below him was darkening rapidly. Geoffrey's eyes were closing; his mouth was falling open but no sound came from it now except for a faint and fading hiss. The hands, which had ceased to flap, lay quite still against the floor, flung out as in a posture of crucifixion. It didn't need Susan's cry, 'You've killed him!' for his own brain to cry out, 'God, I have. I've killed him.'

Standing there, knowing he must go, yet feeling utterly incapable of moving himself, Matthew heard a small sound like a tiny rasping intake of breath. He saw one of the dead man's hands stir ever so slightly, turning over until the palm lay downward instead of limply on its back. Susan heard and saw it too.

'Geoffrey!' Her scream rang through the house. At the same time a small fretful cry came from upstairs. A child had awakened. Susan's child. Hers and this man's: the man who lay in her arms, miraculously stirring.

'Geoffrey, Geoffrey,' Susan continued to shriek. She was trying to shake him awake. He had begun breathing again in pain-racked, difficult gasps. It would take a stronger grip than that of a man still weak from his years of captivity and illness to kill a man in his prime, well fed, well paid, and at ease with his world.

Matthew moved forward instinctively. 'Susan?'

313

She turned on him like a tiger, blue eyes blazing. 'Get out! *Get out*! I never want to see you again. I hate you! I hate everything to do with you.'

'Susan.'

But she was crying, her head bent over the stirring, gasping Geoffrey. Her muffled words sounded full of unhappiness now. 'I did love you, Matthew. I did love you. But you weren't here.'

'That wasn't my fault.' It was a silly thing to say but all he could find.

Crawley was trying to sit up, his hands carefully feeling his throat. Susan held him to her, her glare moderating.

'It don't matter now, Matthew. It just happened. A long time ago.'

She was trying to help Crawley to his feet. Matthew watched the manoeuvres dispassionately as though this was all happening on a screen and he, the watcher, stood apart from it all, unable now to feel any emotion as to whether the man lived, died, took his wife from him, or even sprang up to murder him on the spot. Nothing inside him seemed to care any more. Nothing mattered. What was it someone once said in the prison camp – a long-faced, miserable Aussie – does it matter if yuh die now or when yuh ninety; hundred years from now, no one'll remember yuh or care and yuh certainly won't care when it was yuh died? Nothing mattered.

So why not make it now rather than lingering on with memories of a love that had vanished? Quick. Easy. No time to think. A tall building, a few tablets sending one into endless sleep, a gas-filled room, a passing train. So many ways. And yet he knew he'd do none of those things. Like the coward he was, the coward he'd been in the prison camps, dreaming of going out in a blaze of glory taking half a dozen Japs with him but too weak-willed to do anything about it, he was weak-willed now; would live out his natural lifespan and take his memories with him to the grave. He wanted to weep. But he wouldn't let her see him weep.

He left the house, left Susan still cuddling her Geoffrey to her. In a daze he got back into the car and headed east towards his home, his parents and – an odd thought filtered into his head – Margaret Ross.

Chapter 28

'Look, you're going to have to make a decision very soon, Matthew.'

He heard her well enough but chose not to heed her. It would mean committing himself and he wasn't ready, couldn't see a time when he ever would be. Far preferable to keep his eyes closed, think instead of the sun bathing him with its heat, of sitting here enjoying his surroundings; anything but the making of decisions about signing those divorce papers.

High summer. The winter had been fierce and hard. The Big Freeze they'd called it, with everything, transport, power, everyday life, paralysed by deep snow drifts right into March, then devastating floods. Now summer was making up for it.

Maggie had become his constant companion since his return from the sanatorium; the night he'd thought he had killed that bastard Crawley seemed years ago instead of just a few months as he lolled now on a bench in Victoria Park. During that dragging eternity of waiting he met each day with hope of a letter from Susan that might contain a change of mind. Such a bloody forlorn hope. All that ever arrived was legal, concerning the divorce. He had finally capitulated, the decree nisi having been granted with what had struck him as indelicate haste. Now screeds of legal correspondence followed, designed to drag as big a fee from both parties as possible. Everyone was looking to the main chance. What did they care how he spent days, weeks, months, sick with desolation while it was all going on? Now the decree absolute loomed.

Margaret was waiting for him to answer her, but he didn't want to. She too was looking to the main chance. Why else devote her time to him? He felt no swollen pride in the fact. What the hell did she see in him? He had become a man ravaged by circumstances, churlish, his thoughts invariably centred on the past, on memories best forgotten but which still persisted, emotions that tore him still with guilt and remorse. Bob Howlett dying alone still haunted him; and the sweet face that had lived in his head all through the terrible years haunted him too. The once-loving face that had hovered had grown twisted with loathing.

'Matthew, did you hear me?'

Yes, he had heard. He kept his eyes closed, pushed away a moment of irritation at her persistence. He needed her support more than he cared to admit; at times he wasn't sure what he'd do without her. With her he felt safe. When she wasn't with him, he felt lost. She remained patient and understanding when he used her as his sounding board to beat out his bad moments on, even when he sometimes went too far. He would apologise and she would accept his apologies, kiss his cheek lightly and say it didn't matter.

But it did matter. He wasn't worthy of her love. She had told him she loved him though had never said so again after that one time. He wished he could return her love, for her sake, but that would mean rejecting the feelings he had for Susan, and lying to Maggie, who didn't deserve to be lied to. Susan had become an obsession, a part of him he could not ignore.

'Matthew.'

He opened his eyes. 'I heard you.'

'Then you can't keep putting it off. You've got to start getting on with your life. I know all about getting on with one's life, Matthew. I've done it.'

The statement sounded vehement. Was it a hint that he might one day take up his life with her? He wished she wouldn't make those sort of comments. He loved Susan. But what was love? A bonding of two like souls, each helping the other without thought of self? Or was it this overwhelming, mindless desire for someone who selfishly destroyed? One endured of course, yet the other was all-consuming. What if he were to take Maggie on and Susan came crying back? Would he have strength enough to reject the one who'd torn him apart and cling to the one who'd been steadfast all these years without hope of gain? The thought frightened him, but he wasn't contemplating proposing marriage to Maggie, was he?

'Let's leave it,' he told her almost savagely. 'Just enjoy the afternoon, shall we?'

She was equally sharp. 'Yes. Shall we? If that's what you want.'

'That's what I want,' he snapped back, faintly surprised at her tone. It wasn't like her. She was usually so mild-mannered.

He lifted his face to the sun and tried to forget it as she went quiet. Not moody, Maggie was never moody, but he could sense anger simmering inside her. This was a side of her he'd not seen before. An odd tingle of new respect for her went through him, warm as the sun on his face. He let the warmth soak in and tried not to think of Margaret or Susan or anything.

It was a sweltering summer. Temperatures had been soaring into the eighties; newspapers announced it as sizzling, with photos of eggs frying on pavements, toddlers naked by the sea, tarmac bubbling. Only the holiday-makers revelled in the heat. For himself, having known the humid sweat-bath of a Burmese jungle, this English summer could be comfortably endured lounging on a bench beside a shingle path. Victoria Park again looked beautiful, its railings restored, its lawns, where he'd been told ack-ack guns had once run up and down ploughing up the grass, once more verdant and immaculate. What had been allotments were now replanted with shrubbery and bright flowers.

It was peaceful sitting here, far from the problems the country faced. Food rationing was still going on, the government was still trying to repay America's Marshall Aid loan. Attlee talked of the country as being engaged in another Battle of Britain and the cost of cigarettes had risen to three shillings and fourpence. India, Ceylon, Pakistan and Burma all wanted to break away from British rule with resultant massacres; at home the rising cost of living plagued everyone.

It all came a poor second to his own problems, with this damned divorce business. For all his efforts trying not to think about it, he was. He felt so powerless even though he could stop it at any point. But soon it would be too late. It was as if he was being driven towards a cliff edge, unable to cry out, but he could watch the precipice drawing nearer, his life ceasing to exist. Why didn't he call a halt? He could still grab the wheel of his own fate and turn it from what they were all telling him was inevitable. Why didn't he? Because breaking this marriage *was* inevitable, if not now, then at some time. He couldn't *make* Susan love him, could never reawaken those feelings she had once had for him. But, dear God . . .

'I still love her, Maggie,' he said, and his voice broke.

Sitting beside him, Margaret knew he hadn't heeded a word she'd said. He remained lost in his own world, hoping all would come out the way *he* wanted it to come out. But it couldn't. Others were making sure this broken marriage did not mend, his parents, his solicitors, his wife.

Then there was herself – she too exerted an influence on him. She knew it from the way his face brightened when he saw her, though since that day in October he seemed to be holding her at bay. Before then their friendship had been easy. Now, when she came to his home, he would get up and go out into the garden or somewhere upstairs, anything to avoid being with her in the presence of his family. Yet he readily accepted the opportunity to be with her alone, as he was now.

'I expect you'll always feel that way about her,' she returned, studying a squirrel that had scurried down from a tree to investigate a bit of dry bread dropped by children going to feed the ducks. As it nibbled it kept one eye on the couple on the bench for a more likely morsel.

She was conscious of her voice sounding strained. 'But it'll serve you to no avail, you know. You do know, Matthew?'

She felt her heart shrink as he turned on her. 'What do you know about it?' Immediately he caught himself. 'I'm sorry, Maggie, I didn't mean that to sound like it did,' he said, then justified it by repeating himself in a different way. 'But you can't know how I feel about her.'

'Perhaps I do,' she countered softly, only to reap more bitter reaction.

'You sound like my mother.' This was accompanied by a cynical curl of his lips.

She had no reply to that. Something inside her was growing angrier by the second. Usually she curbed it, waited until he

318

calmed down and tried to vindicate his hurtfulness, but this time her patience had no power and the anger exploded before she could catch it to hold it back. She turned on him, her grey-green eyes blazing.

'That's it, Matthew. Go on feeling sorry for yourself.' At her raised voice, the squirrel dropped its piece of stale bread and scurried back up the tree, but she did not see it go. 'I've just about had it up to here, Matthew. I do try to see your point of view. I do feel sorry for what's happened to you and I know I'm being unfair, that no one who's not suffered what you have can know what it was like, for all the stories and pictures we've seen. And now this on top of everything. But I'm only flesh and blood. Now do I sound like your mother? I want to help and I feel so useless, and I love you so much, Matthew. Yes I do know *exactly* what it's like to love someone who doesn't love you, when nothing can be done about it. I know it like mad.'

Tears were springing from her eyes. They rolled down her cheeks. 'I wish I was small and dainty and had someone to be crazy over me, as you are with *her*. But I'm not the sort of girl you fancy, am I? I've never been the sort of girl you fancy. Well, if she's the sort you fancy then you're welcome to her. That's what I say. But is that supposed to alter what I feel inside? You'd rather run after someone like her and let your heart be torn out of you while you grovel at her feet, pleading for her to come back and hurt you all over again. Well, honestly, Matthew, if that's what you want, I might as well just give up. No point me being your friend forever and ever. Damn what I feel.'

He was staring at her, the expression on his thin, handsome face one of confusion. Surely he couldn't be so naive as not to have some inkling of how she felt about him? She had said too much, had revealed her heart to him when she hadn't intended to. She felt exposed, but she was too angry with him to care. And now she fought to recover her composure, savagely sweeping the tears away with the back of her hand.

'What does it matter anyway? I've got a good career in nursing and that's all right with me. I don't suppose I'll ever marry, not now. I'm not the wife type. I'd only start bossing him about, whoever he'd be. I'm the bossy kind, you said so

319

yourself. Like your mother. I suppose if I was like your wife you'd be letting me wipe the floor with you. I don't think I could ever bear that – from you.'

He was looking at her in a strange way, studying her, his dark brows drawn together. 'Maggie, I'm sorry. I didn't intend to upset you.' He was always being sorry.

She shrugged and looked away from him as he went on inadequately. 'You're the last person I'd want to hurt, you know that.'

Margaret said nothing, very much in danger of refuting the statement. He didn't seem aware of it.

'I've only been thinking of myself all this time. I never once stopped to consider how you feel in all this. Even when you said you loved me, I could think of no one else but Su . . .' he hesitated over the name, but plunged on. 'Susan. All I've ever done is abuse your friendship. Your real friendship. Using it and giving nothing back, especially knowing how you felt about me. Maggie, I wouldn't hurt you for the world. You're the only decent thing that has ever happened to me, and . . .'

As he broke off, she turned to see him still gazing at her, realised he hadn't once ceased looking at her, even though she had turned away from him. Now he put his hand out and laid it on her upper arm. She could feel the warmth of the hand penetrating the thin material of her summer dress.

He was drawing her gently towards him, his voice husky. 'I couldn't have gone on without you. I know the thought of her still consumes me, and I know I've got to fight it. But I know you're worth two of her, Maggie.'

His other hand took hold of her, he was pulling her closer to him. When his face was inches away from hers, she felt his lips touch her cheek.

No, it was too much. He had no right. He was taking it upon himself to offer comfort with a kiss on the cheek. She made to turn her face aside from the insult of that friendly peck, the sudden move causing her lips unintentionally to brush his.

All at once she found herself unable to break away as the pressure of his lips on hers became instantly firm. In that second all her love for him poured out to encompass him. With a small choking sob, Margaret let her arms wrap themselves about his neck as if they had a will of their own, and to her

320

astonishment his arms encircled her in response. The squirrel in the tree ceased scratching at the bark to look down at a young couple in a close embrace, the girl crying, the man holding her, kissing her gently now, and murmuring soft words of comfort.

'It's all right, Maggie. It's all right.'

'I'm sorry, Matthew. I shouldn't have . . .'

'No, you should. I've been damned stupid, selfish.'

'But you don't love me. You can't. You love . . .'

'I don't really know any more what love is. What I do know is I can't imagine being without you, Maggie. You've become part of my life.'

The squirrel, looking down, heard only a meaningless chatter of human sounds and went on exploring his own world, seeking food and instinctively searching for a mate with whom to procreate his own species.

Below, if Margaret was expecting the words, 'I love you, marry me?' she was doomed to disappointment. The kiss had been emotional but an accident. She knew that later he would be embarrassed at having been carried away on a wave of brief, profound affection. She knew that too. She'd ruined everything in a weak, thoughtless moment. In the meantime they would walk home together as though nothing had happened.

What she didn't know about were the new feelings she had awakened in him.

Margaret took the envelope her mother held out to her: 'It's addressed to you, dear,' and stared at the unfamiliar handwriting. She rarely received mail other than *The Nursing Journal*. Her friends were local nurses with no need to write, seeing them every day. Her first thought was that it was from one of the old group in the QAs but the postmark was local. It was the small uneven handwriting that gave her the first clue as with the edge of a thumbnail she slit open the flap to withdraw a single sheet of cheap, blue-lined notepaper. She cast her eyes to the foot of the letter, noting the name.

'Who's it from, dear?' queried her mother with interest.

'Matthew's wife. Why should she be writing to me?'

'Odd.' Mrs Ross moved to lean over her shoulder. 'She won't

be his wife for much longer. The divorce comes up in two weeks' time, so I hear.'

Margaret nodded, already reading, ignoring the misspellings:

Dear Margeret, I thought I'd write to you becaus I need some advise from you if its possible. Im ever so worried and I don't know what to do. As you know the devorce comes threw in a couple of weeks time and Geoffrey. Thats the man I am living with. Geoffrey is acting very strange. I think he's worried about the devorce but he is not as nice to me as he used to be. Im getting ever so worried. I wanted to talk to Matthew but I cant very well ask him direct after all this time and I was wandring if you could have a word with him on my behalf so as to pave the way so to speek. I know youve always been a good friend of his and perhaps you can act as a go between like. I will be waiting for your reply and hope you can help me. Thank you. Susan Ward.

'Well I never,' breathed Mrs Ross in Margaret's ear. 'That's a cheek if ever there was. You're more than friends with him nowadays from what you've told me.'

Margaret had told her about the incident in the park several weeks earlier, full of hope that in voicing it she could make love come true. What she hadn't mentioned was Matthew's reticence since then, just as she'd predicted but hadn't wanted to believe. His true feelings remained a mystery, leaving her alternately filled with hope and despair: perhaps he was battling within himself as to whom he needed most, perhaps needing to come to terms with it; or again perhaps his inane pursuit of that worthless cat dominated him still and he hadn't the heart to tell her she must forget what had happened. Maybe he'd been too taken up with the finalities of the approaching divorce to think of anything else as yet, but would once it was all over. Then again, maybe he still had hopes of the divorce never taking place and hadn't the courage to tell her that either. Time and time again a flood of anger would pour through her at the unfairness of being strung along. He was not man enough to tell her the truth and still her churning soul one way or the other.

This time she held it in, so as not to give him even more

reason to fend her off. Outwardly they behaved as they had always done, still talked about all sorts of things – everything but the one thing that mattered to her. Her pent-up emotions were doing odd things to her. One minute she saw him as weak, the next she swept the thought aside in a fit of remorse, for whatever he was, she loved him. And he wasn't weak. He wasn't. He was merely terribly confused. Once this divorce was over he'd have to forget Susan.

But now she must hand him Susan's letter, stand by and watch his reaction; felt she knew already what it would be.

These closing hot days of summer they had continued to frequent the park together. He seldom wanted to go anywhere else, but now as they sat on a bench or on the lawn watching other late-summer sun-worshippers, picnicking families, children, people walking dogs, they didn't touch. They spoke of trivial things. Matthew never spoke of his wife now or the imminent divorce. It was as though neither existed and she hadn't dared bring up the subject lest she drive him further from her.

There seemed to be a dull, flat ache in her soul as she folded Susan's letter and put it back into its envelope.

'I'd better hand it to him straight away,' she said defeatedly. It went without saying what his reaction would be. A ray of hope. Margaret would be forgotten in an instant as he embraced the marvellous knowledge that Susan at the eleventh hour wanted him to take her back. He would forgive her all she had done to him and Margaret Ross would be put aside, told of his wonderful good news, thanked for all she'd done for him, and forgotten.

'He'll be pleased,' she said simply as she slid the envelope into the pocket of her nurse's dress to hand to him on her way to work. Then she would hurry off before seeing his reaction and get on with her day, get on with her own life, as she had vowed so many times before. But this time it held all the characteristics of finality.

Chapter 29

It was Saturday night, nearly ten o'clock. Little Trevor, in his cot since eight, had waited for his father well past his bedtime, and Geoffrey's key was only now just turning in the street door lock.

She stood waiting for him, the whole of her slight, small body quivering with fury.

'What bloody time do you call this?' she attacked him as he came into the cluttered living room, still innocently pocketing his keys in the jacket he'd already taken off to drop over a nearby chair.

He looked at her astonished, his jovial, 'Hello, love,' frozen on his lips. 'You know I always see the boys on a Saturday.'

'Not until this bloody hour of the evening. And you already see them twice during the week too. You never used to. So what's so special about them now? You used to come home before eight so you could see your own son before he goes to bed.'

He glared at her now, his jacket hanging by its collar from one finger. 'They're my sons too, don't forget. I owe them some of my time.'

'Not every bloody day of the week.'

'It's not every bloody day of the week.' Angered now, he flung the coat at the chair, which it missed. It slid to the floor to lie in a crumpled heap. 'It's twice a week and once on a Saturday.'

'That makes three times,' Susan stormed, standing her ground on the rug before the empty firegrate. She had no intention of moving from the spot to welcome him or go off

324

to get him cups of tea as once she always did whenever he came in the door. This time she was going to have it out with him, one way or the other.

'I'm not putting up with this, Geoffrey. Not for much longer. Why do you have to keep going to see them three times a week? It was four times last week.'

'Four?' he blazed at her.

'Yes, *four*. What about Monday? You went there on Monday as well.'

'For an hour, that was all. You're begrudging me one hour with my own boys, now?'

'It's one hour too many, Geoffrey. What about me waiting all hours God sends for you to come home and give me a bit of your time? I mean, I'm important to you too, aren't I? You used to think so. You used to be a lot different to what you are now. I need to have you here.'

'You've got me, haven't you? Nearly all the time.' He went and threw himself down in one of the pair of sagging fireside chairs. It creaked under the sudden violent weight. 'Don't start an argument, Sue,' he sighed. 'I'm tired.'

'And *I'm* tired,' she railed on at him. 'Tired of being a doormat for you. For you to come home any old time you please. And I suppose you expect to make love to me, as always, as if nothing's happened.'

'You like it.'

'That's got nothing to do with it. You come home from *her* and your blessed sons, and clamber on top of me and make love as if you've not had it for weeks. How do I know you haven't been making love to *her* as well?'

He sat bolt-upright. 'That's not fair, darling. You know I don't have nothing to do with Emma and she don't have nothing to do with me. It's just for me to see the boys, that's all.'

'What proof have I got of that?' she continued to blaze. 'And don't darling me straight after you've seen *her*. What's going on between you two?'

Geoffrey shot out of the chair and stalked about the room, flinging irritated, disbelieving glances at her. 'This is getting bloody silly. I thought our row in the week was bad enough, and over the same bloody thing. But you're going right over the top again. Nothing's going on between Emma and me.

Can't you get that straight? She'd just the mother of my sons and they live with her. Of course I have to see her when I go there, but she don't have nothing to do with me.'

'But you wish she did.'

'Of course not, darling. I love you. I left her for you and that's not changed.' His voice had grown softer, more persuasive. 'It's you I love, Sue, and no one else.'

'Huh!' She moved at last to the window to straighten the already moderately straight gold-patterned curtains. 'Love me? You don't care anything about me, only to get your oats, that's all you care about me. It's all I'm good for.'

'Don't be silly. And don't be selfish.'

'Selfish!' The curtains received a tug, almost dislodging the pelmet they hung from. 'Me? Selfish? I should think you're the one who's selfish, leaving me alone half the week.'

'You *are* bloody selfish, Sue, sometimes.'

'I'm not. I'm not selfish.'

This was how it was lately, arguments going round and round, silly and pointless, ending up unsolved unless she gave in, threw herself at him and burst into tears. Before, he would kiss her better, take her to bed to assuage his need with her. She adored being made love to in that way, the rougher the better, with her the object of his lust, the helpless recipient. But these last couple of weeks, he hadn't made love to her after any row; he had merely extricated himself from her pleas for him to forgive her and had gone sullenly to bed; he would be asleep or apparently so by the time she came to him. Any attempts to wake him up had been met with a deep snore and a mumble of protest. Many a night she had lain awake beside him, her eyes wet with what she hated to admit were self-induced tears. Her sniffling and snuffling sounded loud enough to have disturbed the devil, but not Geoffrey, even though to her mind he must have heard but ignored the noise. The next morning he would leave for work after breakfast, through which he said little but read the morning paper that fell through the letter box at six thirty. His departing peck on the cheek seemed a condemnation of her attitude of late and left her to weep silently the rest of the morning as she got his son from his cot to feed him.

Slowly she was coming to feel that their relationship was

beginning to fall apart, that he was tiring of her. But why now? In less than a couple of weeks her marriage would come to an end. She couldn't let Geoffrey lose interest in her now, not after all that had happened. She was being silly of course. He hadn't lost interest in her. His lovemaking said as much, or had done until lately. It was her fault. She *was* being selfish. He did need to see his sons by his wife. Soon she would be his new wife when his own divorce came through. This wouldn't be for several months yet; Emma had only filed for it a little while ago.

Tomorrow she would have him all to herself, all day. She would make up for her foolish, groundless tantrum by being all sweetness and light, and on Monday would run to get him his evening tea, for that evening he'd be home at the proper time. Last Monday had been the exception, because of his middle son Percy's birthday.

Sunday passed blissfully. They made love in the afternoon, with Trevor safely asleep in his cot. She bit back the cries of ecstasy Geoffrey forced from her in case she awoke the child and put an end to the unbelievable climax to which her lover was capable of bringing her. And they made love again that night with her happy cries ringing out abandoned enough to wake the neighbours.

All Monday she went about the house, content that all was well again and waited for Geoffrey to come home from work. Five thirty came and went. Six o'clock. Seven. Susan, watching the clock, the egg and bacon she'd cooked dried up in her efforts to keep it warm for him, began to seethe afresh. There was no reason for him to have been kept at work. It was obvious he had gone round again to where Emma and the boys still lived with her sister. But there was no birthday to celebrate this Monday. And hadn't she heard from Geoffrey last week that the youngest would be at a friend's birthday party this evening and that Percy and Malcolm were going off on a school coach trip to Southend and wouldn't be home until after seven thirty? And didn't Emma's sister do evening work in some nearby pub? If Geoffrey had gone round to Emma's tonight, he'd really blotted his copybook this time.

Sick at heart, Susan waited, put Trevor to bed and waited some more. It was nearly nine before Geoffrey came in. In the ensuing row, he ducked and dived like mad. He didn't admit it for one second but Susan knew he had been with Emma, really been with Emma; there was something in the look of him that showed he had. When she accused him outright, his protests were too violent to be true, so she *knew* he had.

It was then she began to be really frightened, knowing just what she had done and how her life could go. Were he to go back to his wife, what would she have left? Geoffrey's son – that was all. Suddenly she didn't want to be left just with Geoffrey's son. She didn't want to be the spurned mistress saddled with a baby. She could see it all looming before her like a great yawning canyon. She thought voluntarily of Matthew, for the first time in months. It was then that she wrote a scribbled, frantic letter to Margaret Ross in the hope that she would speak for her to him. Margaret had always been a saviour of lame dogs and desperate souls. She would not fail this desperate soul – for once in her life, Susan waxed poetic as she wrote her letter, then sat back to await the results, which she knew could only be to her advantage. Matthew would have her back in the blink of an eye, still madly in love with her as he was.

Susan rather liked that word, desperate. She said it over and over again to herself as she sealed her letter and went to post it. Her heart, though, still ached for Geoffrey and she prayed he'd have a change of heart and carry on their relationship as though nothing had happened. Then of course there would be no need for Matthew and no harm done because from past knowledge of Margaret, the girl would be very careful how she worded her errand and might even delay it in rehearsing the words she would use to him. There would still be time enough to rescind her plea. After all, Matthew had recovered, hadn't he? He was no longer the sick and ravaged person she imagined he had been after coming home. Look how he'd belted into poor Geoffrey. Geoffrey, the apparently healthier man, had been unable to defend himself. At the time she had hated Matthew, seeing a savage, embittered, degraded man. But thinking about it, his face, at the time twisted and suffused by fury, had still retained much of that which had attracted her to him that first time. Half crouched in rage as he'd been, he still looked tall and slim, a far cry from the sick wretch she had imagined. Memories of what he had been now flooded back. In time he would become that again and perhaps they would pick up the threads of those beautiful if brief months they'd had together before he'd gone away. She hoped so. That was if her and Geoffrey's affair was over, which in her heart she hoped was untrue. All she wanted in life was a stable, loving relationship with someone, to be looked after, to be loved, to be given security.

Matthew took little notice of the ringing of the doorbell. He and Dad had not long got up; both were washed and dressed and waiting for their breakfast, the nutty fragrance of toast creeping from the kitchen. He listened idly to his mother going to answer the door. Probably the postman. A parcel perhaps?

'Matthew. It's Margaret, here to see you.'

He stood up, curious, as she came in with his mother. She seldom came here on a Wednesday, and never in the morning, never so early, her nurse's coat, spattered by light, early-morning rain, showing she was in fact on her way to the hospital. She was looking a little strained.

'Anything wrong?' His first words showed his concern.

'I can't stay. I'm on my way to work.' She sounded breathless as if she'd been running, but the breathlessness seemed to have something to do as well with the strained look on her face. She was holding an envelope, holding it out in a way that did not exactly ask for it to be taken from her. 'This arrived for me in the post, but it has to do with you rather than me. I was going to pop it through your letter box but it needs some explanation why it was sent to me and not to you.'

'Shall I take your coat?' His mother eyed the rain-spotted garment with concern for her furniture lest Matthew's visitor sit herself down. Margaret shook her head quickly.

'I can't stop.' She was looking at him, her expression apologetic in a way, her high brow furrowed with concern the way it used to furrow when she had tended him in that first hospital in England.

'What is it, Maggie?' He ignored his father, who had also stood up sociably at Margaret's entrance, and came round the table towards her. Perhaps being nearer she might hand him the letter she said so concerned him.

'This isn't possible to break to you gently, Matthew. It's from your wife. I was supposed to explain, tell you what she wants. I suppose what she is hoping me to do is to . . .' She broke off with an impatient tut. 'Well, read it yourself. I can't be . . . I don't want to be her go-between. It's nothing to do with me, anyway.'

Thrusting the letter into his hands, she turned and with a little nod and a thank-you to his mother, allowed herself to be conducted out.

Left holding the envelope, he instantly recognised Susan's laboured handwriting. By the time his mother came back, eager to see what it was all about, he had the letter open, his eyebrows drawn together in a frown.

'What is it, dear?'

'As Margaret said,' his father's deep voice was deadened by the well-furnished little breakfast room, 'it's from Matthew's wife.'

'Well, what does she say? What does she want?'

'She wants to come and see me. I shall have to see her.'

'Matthew.'

'I want to hear her say this to my face.'

'You can't. You can't see her. The divorce case . . .'

'I have to.' Screwing the letter up, he thrust it into his trouser pocket and made out of the room.

'Your breakfast,' she called after him, but received no reply.

The night he'd attacked Crawley, his first glimpse of her in years had been a fleeting, distorted one, seen through a mist of rage. Now as he opened the door to her knock, she stood before him, as he remembered she had done years before that, still with the same petite build, the same blue eyes wide and timid. Perhaps she looked a fraction more mature but still vulnerable and unsure of herself, prompting a natural reaction in others to take her under their wing.

'I got your letter telling me to come here,' she began tremulously. 'I'm glad you wanted to see me.'

He didn't smile. He dared not. He stepped back to let her in and she followed him into the sitting room like a small, subdued dog at his heels. He closed the door and they stood facing each other in the filtered light of a drab September afternoon. The room was very quiet. They were alone, his mother reluctantly and full of disapproval of his request leaving them to themselves. It occurred to him that he hadn't yet asked Susan to sit down, but to do so would be an acceptance of her and he was wary of betraying how he felt looking at her. Seeing her again had resurrected that surge of adoration the sight of her had always brought and it alarmed him.

To cover the discomposure her nearness aroused, he said stiffly: 'You said in your letter you weren't happy.'

She nodded, catching the fuller part her lower lip briefly between her small teeth, an endearing little habit that had always stirred his emotions to see. Matthew clenched his hands against them.

'So what did you want from me?'

She came forward a fraction, a small movement of appeal to that love he'd once had for her, an attempt to awaken it if it now slept. She couldn't know how easily the single movement could awaken it, for its sleep had never been total. Her eyes were glistening.

'I'm so sorry, Matthew, for everything I've done. I know I was wrong, but you were so far away and I didn't know if you was . . . oh, Matthew.'

Tears had begun trickling gently down her cheeks. He was in danger of being disarmed by them. He didn't want to look at them, so lowered his eyes, remembered all the crying he too had done; the pain remembered was becoming insufferable.

'Matthew, don't turn away. Look at me. I'm sorry. I really am.'

Now he looked up, surprised at his own reaction. What did she expect of him? That he'd take her in his arms, soothe away all the sorrow she was displaying, tell her it was all right, that he forgave her and wanted only to take her back as though nothing had happened? His whole being cried out that that was what he wanted to do. He felt his lip curl contemptuously with the knowledge of how easily he might, contempt for himself that he knew how close he was. But he had grown embittered. Her tears, they weren't for him. She wasn't hurting for him, only for herself, had always only ever thought of herself.

Rationality seemed to spear through his body, but its searing pain was his only salvation. He kept hearing Margaret saying, 'It's nothing to do with me.' But it was everything to do with her, rationality, security, trust. He could trust Margaret. He could never trust Susan – ever again.

When he did speak his voice seemed to be conveying every vestige of that agony spearing him. It was an effort to talk at all.

'I'm sorry too, Susan. I can't... I can't have you back. I know I can't. You see...' He stopped as her eyes opened wide with terror. His immediate instinct was to grab her to him to stop that awful look of desolation. Fighting it, he shut his own eyes so as not to see how she was looking at him.

'I need to trust someone,' he heard himself saying. With an effort he pulled himself together, willed himself to look at her while trying to keep the mirror of his soul closed to her. It made his stare harder than he intended. He saw her shrink back a little, the gesture almost destroying his resolve until he remembered again the agony she had caused him over the years of wanting her.

'You see,' he began again. 'It wouldn't be any good – not now.'

'Matthew, no!'

He pushed on, ignoring the cry. 'The first sign of anything not going your way, any inconvenience, any outside temptation, and you'd be off again. It's not your fault. It's how you are. When we married, I'd no idea. All I knew was I loved you, adored you, thought you could do no wrong, that you were perfect. But it wasn't enough, was it? I couldn't hold you. I'll never be able to hold you.'

She had been gazing up at him, the dawning of what he was saying growing apparent in her gaze, but her protest came in a wail of disbelief. 'I don't know what you're saying, Matthew. I know I was wrong. I *am* sorry. I'll make it up to you. I will. I still love you. I'll make everything up to you.'

He wanted to counter, 'What about Crawley?' But that would be dragging it down to the level of a slanging match. Suddenly he wanted to be rid of her. He was beginning to feel unsteady, shaky, a dull nausea in the pit of his stomach. He wanted to sit down but he dared not.

'I want you to go.' His voice sounded hoarse, strangled.

'Matthew...' Her eyes suddenly hardened, narrowed with suspicion. 'Is it someone else?' He almost laughed. 'It's that

Margaret Ross. You've fallen in love with her, haven't you? You don't want me now.'

He didn't reply. Every word she said seemed to be driving her further from him. He couldn't believe that he could ever *not* be in love with her. It would hover inside him, a small devil, to the end of his days ready to resurrect itself the second his guard was lowered. But at this moment he was merely beginning to feel sickened. That she could say Margaret's name with such contempt! Margaret could make six of her, ever willing to take on his burden of fears, his indecisions, and not complain. Yet his fear was that he'd burden her too much, more than she could stand. Not for himself, but for her. Was that true love? If it was, then Susan paled into insignificance beside it.

'I might've known.' Her words pierced through his thoughts, her tone contemptuous, covering the fear that consumed her.

He blinked. 'I think you'd better go, Susan. Back to Crawley – try to make the best of it. You can use your charm on him, Susan. You know how to do that, don't you? You're good at it. He won't be able to resist. As I once couldn't. You'll be all right. You'll always be all right.'

Bitterness rose up inside him without bidding, like some other self. He was astounded by his own words, their harshness. All at once the past had become another country. He held her look of disbelief, aware that his was arid.

She took a step or two towards him, her expression still one of abject pleading, but his arid stare remained a wall of glass. Realisation began to dawn on her and she gave a small defeated sob, turning from him like a rabbit released from a car's head-lights. She had no idea how near she had come to shattering that fragile barrier.

Making blindly for the door, her sob breaking into full-blown weeping, she pulled it open, fleeing past his mother whom he saw standing just beyond. A bitter grin twisted his lips that she had been there listening to it all.

'She's gone then?' The stiff statement reached his hearing, but he found himself incapable of answering her. What in hell's name had he done? Susan had been in his grasp and he'd thrust her away. For a moment there came an urge to run after her, but he let the moment pass.

Chapter 30

It was the dim light of October making her feel low. The days had begun rapidly to shorten, the promise of a long winter already dulling the sky. It had to be; people were usually affected by the weather. Even so, she should have felt brighter than this. After all, Matthew was now a free man.

Margaret looked across the dinner table at her mother. 'Matthew Ward's divorce came through last week, did you know?'

Mrs Ross smiled as she chewed, her fork engaged in selecting a piece of potato. 'He should feel easier now. I suppose you do too.'

Margaret's knife and fork lay idle each side of her plate, although she gripped them as though gripping a pair of lifelines. 'I suppose I do in a way.'

'You and he might spend more time with each other.'

'We already do.'

'You know what I mean.' Her mother hadn't once lifted her eyes from her plate. Margaret knew exactly what she meant. It was a pity Matthew didn't.

For days he had been moping indoors. Off duty this weekend, she'd gone over to his house yesterday, been heartily welcomed in by his parents, invited to stay for a bit of tea with them. But seeing Matthew's obdurate expression of moodiness, his apparent lack of joy at seeing her, wrapped up as he was in his own sullen grief of his lost marriage, she had felt a flush of anger at him and excused herself, saying she didn't want to leave her mother on her own on a Saturday night.

She hadn't gone across today at all. He could stew in his

own morass of misery if that was what he wanted. Of course she ached to see him but she was no longer prepared to be his whipping boy whenever he felt like it. She had made up her mind about that. He was free now. Divorced. Nothing he could do about it. It was up to him to get on with his life. But she wished she was included in that life, and still had no idea whether she was or not.

'I'm sure I don't know what he's going to do,' she said to her mother, a little sharply.

'Are you going to see him after dinner?'

A ring of the doorbell interrupted an awkward denial. Margaret leapt up from the table. 'I'll go.'

She left her mother murmuring that she couldn't think who that could be on such an overcast Sunday afternoon and hurried to the door.

For a split-second her mind wouldn't work, having a problem placing the face. But already the name had burst from her lips in disbelief.

'Ronald!'

He looked awkward, a man faintly aged since she had last seen him. 'I remembered your address,' he began. 'I was going to write, but I was in the vicinity, attending a medical seminar, and I thought before going home I'd look you up. Hope you didn't mind.'

She could only stare at him. 'Er . . . no.'

He gave her a somewhat silly grin, slightly apologetic. 'I was at a bit of a loose end.'

'Oh.'

'I'm a free agent, you see. Nothing to rush back home for. Of course there's surgery in the morning, but it only takes a few hours in the car to get back to Bath, so I thought why not look up an old friend?'

'Oh.'

'My marriage broke up,' he continued by way of explanation for his unexpected appearance.

Margaret heard her mother's voice filter faintly from the dining room. 'Who is it, dear?'

Hastily she called back over her shoulder. 'An old friend, Mumsy.'

'Well, ask her to come in, dear. Don't let her stand on the doorstep.'

Margaret ignored the invitation but any moment her mother would come to see why.

'Look,' she said quickly, lowering her voice so that Mumsy wouldn't hear. 'Can you wait outside while I get my coat?' Somehow she didn't want to go through lots of introductions and explanations to Mumsy. 'We can take a walk and you can tell me about yourself and why you're here.'

He was looking embarrassed. 'Perhaps I'd better go, Margaret. I didn't mean to . . .'

'No,' she cut in. 'I'll only be a tick. I'd like to know how you are.' After all, it was only polite. She couldn't turn him away.

She closed the door, gently so as not to seem rude, and hurried back along the hall. She felt flustered, not from renewed affection but by the fact that Matthew might have seen him at the door. Silly really – it could have been anyone. But he might see her walking with Ronald. What would he think? She felt suddenly unaccountably rebellious. What the hell did it matter what he thought?

'Didn't you ask her in, dear?' Her mother, coming from the dining room, regarded her a little bemusedly as Margaret quickly gathered her coat from the skeletal stand that held their everyday coats.

'I'm just going for a walk, Mumsy. Shan't be a tick.'

'It looks rather like rain. Silly going for a walk when you could have asked her in. I wouldn't have minded. You'd best take a brolly with you.'

To appease her, Margaret grabbed one of the two umbrellas sticking out at an angle from the guard rail around the foot of the coat stand.

'Don't be out too long, dear,' her mother's plaintive departing call followed her as she made towards the door. 'You don't want to get wet. And bring her in when you get back.'

'She has to get straight back home,' Margaret returned on the point of closing the door on her. And Ronald could go straight back too. Said he was divorced. If he had come here hoping to pick up where they had left off years ago, the cheek of it!

He was leaning on the gatepost looking somewhat

woebegone. As she reached him he straightened up, taking her arm and threading it through his as though it were his right, whether she objected or not. But it would have seemed rude to have shrugged away from him. He was only trying to be amicable and he did seem a little uncomfortable.

'It's so nice to see you again,' he was saying as he conducted her, guiding her before she realised it away from the main road from where he had obviously come. Still confused by him turning up like this out of the blue, it did not dawn on her until they had gone some way that this would not have been the route she would have consciously chosen. She took a quick glance up at Matthew's house as they passed it, but there was no sign of life. Margaret breathed a small sigh of relief.

'It's nice to see you again too,' she said.

'Well, as I was nearby.' He looked abruptly at her. 'You know, I was pretty broken up when you gave me up, Margaret. I really thought we had something going for us. I kept hoping. But I know you weren't the sort to play a chap along, so I had to decide to put it all out of my mind. I joined the Medical Corps, you know. That's where I met Penelope. We got married. We didn't see each other all that much. Then I came home unexpectedly one day and found her in bed with someone.'

'I'm sorry,' Margaret said as he paused.

'I don't know why I'm telling you all this,' he went on. 'After the divorce I began thinking about you again, wondering if you'd got married. I found out the hospital you're working in and that you were still single, and I thought there might still be a chance for you and me to, well, perhaps pick up where we'd left off. The war's over. Things are different now. Settled. I just hoped you might feel, well, perhaps a bit more ready to ... well, us to, you know, start going out together again.'

So there had been a method in his coming here.

They had gone some distance when the first tiny droplet of rain made itself felt on the back of her hand. Margaret welcomed it with a stab of utter relief.

'It's started to rain. I'd best be getting back,' she said a just a little too enthusiastically. She turned to him. 'Ronald, there is someone, you see. I'm going out with someone.'

It wasn't exactly an untruth, was it? She and Matthew.

Friends. Not lovers. No proposal. But there was always hope. 'We're more or less going steady,' she said.

Working the rest of the week, there had been no chance to see Matthew. Most of the time, Margaret's mind was centred on Ronald Whittaker and the heart-breaking disappointment that had showed on his face when she had lied to him. Yes, it had been a lie – Matthew no more wanted her than he'd wanted his divorce. She found herself dreading her next evening off duty when she would have to pop over to see him, imagining his off-handed greeting. But she couldn't avoid going. They were friends.

She'd been so sorry for Ronald as he walked her back to her gate that she had leaned towards him and given his cheek a brief consoling peck, purely on impulse. He had read its message clear enough. He had taken her by surprise in catching her to him in a gentle hug. Not knowing how to break away and further hurt his feelings, she had stood thus in an embrace, half her mind thinking unkindly that the rain was getting heavier. He must have felt her tense. When he let her go, he smiled at her, such a sad smile.

'For old times' sake,' he'd murmured, then, 'Be happy, Margaret.'

With that he had walked away, leaving her standing there with tears misting her eyes, beginning to trickle down her cheeks, the spots of rain splashing them away.

She'd felt, still felt, oddly empty after his going. It created a strange sensation knowing he had walked into her life again, briefly, and as quickly walked out of it, leaving behind reawakened memories of that part of her life which felt as though it had never happened. She wondered what his world would be like, what he would do, who he would meet eventually to continue his life with? She would never know.

'Oh, Margaret, come in. I'm so glad to see you.'

Mrs Ward's expression was at once relieved and concerned. She had become a different woman lately. Margaret could almost read her mind, an ability few were privileged to possess. It invariably registered optimism whenever Mrs Ward's eyes fell upon her. It said: My future daughter-in-law, please God,

338

as surely as if spoken aloud. This evening however, concern overrode the pleasure of seeing her as she bade Margaret to come in.

The evening was proving a busy one. For the first time since the war ended, Guy Fawkes Night was being wholeheartedly celebrated, the puny explosion of fireworks no longer conjuring recollections of wartime bombing raids.

Further down the road on a cleared-up bombsite, children had a large bonfire going. The stink of burning wood, rubber and old furniture and the acrid tang of saltpetre hung in the air. But Margaret no longer noted it, the look on Mrs Ward's face alarming her.

'Is anything wrong?' she asked as she was let in.

Mrs Ward lowered her voice, hovering with her in the spacious hallway. 'It's Matthew. Perhaps you can do something with him. He's hardly spoken two words to us and then only to snap at us. Even his father's becoming angry with him, and his father is normally a mild-mannered, understanding man. Neither of us know what to do with him.'

'What's wrong with him?' Margaret whispered back in the same conspiratorial undertone.

'We just don't know. He won't tell us. If we ask, he just snaps at us, tells us to mind our own B. business.' Mrs Ward never swore, not even in quoting. She loathed the mildest epithet in her hearing, much less her home. Margaret smiled to herself. She'd heard some ripe ones from Matthew before now; had heard some even riper ones from soldiers wounded and in pain. Mrs Ward should have been a nurse. That would have broadened her mind.

Margaret's smile, a tiny one that Mrs Ward hadn't even noticed though the hallway was brightly lit, vanished as fast as it had come and she turned her thoughts to what she was telling her.

'He's in his room. He must have seen you coming up the path. But he hasn't even come down. I just don't know what's wrong with him.'

Margaret followed her into the lounge, returning Mr Ward's nod of welcome. He sat in an armchair by a low fire lit against the growing autumn damp, though it was not cold enough yet to warrant a larger blaze. He had been reading an evening paper, now folded on his knees. At Margaret's entrance he half rose then sat back down again. With a regular visitor, there was no call to stand on ceremony. His whole mien held a defeated look about it.

'Park yourself, Margaret,' he muttered, his terminology so like his son's, a breath of fresh air compared with his wife's self-conscious articulation.

'Is Matthew coming down?' Margaret asked as she sat herself on the sofa. It was him she had come to see, not his parents. The room had an odd atmosphere to it without him, almost as though he no longer lived here. She felt uncomfortable, an interloper.

'Hope so,' his father returned. 'Call him, Lilian, say Margaret's here.'

'He knows she's here,' she snapped.

'Then tell him again,' he snapped back.

It was unlike him. Margaret could sense the tension, the anger, the bewilderment that resided here, a tendency to bicker at the slightest provocation, something they'd never have done under normal circumstances. Yes, Matthew since returning home had been hard to deal with, the careless and debonair youth gone for good, in his place an embittered man tormented by evil memories. He was bound to be edgy and perverse. But not like this.

Margaret heard his mother call up but there was no reply. 'Should I try?' she said awkwardly as Mrs Ward came back into the room, her face tight with annoyance and embarrassment.

'You can if you like. Try knocking on his door.' It was a privilege Mrs Ward allowed no caller; to explore her upper floors was not their business. There was a significance in this acceptance. 'I think he might talk to you, tell you what the matter is with him.'

The newspaper rustled on Mr Ward's knees. 'You being a nurse, Margaret. If you can't pull him round, who can?'

What could she say? She nodded and got up from the sofa, wishing she was indeed wearing her uniform. It would make this confrontation with him official. Again perhaps not – it might drive him further away with whatever was worrying him. It had to be something dire. She couldn't think what.

Leaving them in the lounge she mounted the stairs and

tapped lightly on the door his mother had indicated. His voice came muffled.

'It's open. We don't have keys to bedrooms in this house.'

Tentatively she pushed the door and came in, taking care to close it behind her, a signal that no one else would be an audience to whatever he said to her.

He was standing at the window gazing out, his back to her. With the light on and the curtains open, neither the lamplit road nor its lurid bonfire further down nor the flash of fireworks penetrated. Yet he seemed mesmerised by what was going on outside. Above that faint infiltration of wood smoke peculiar to Guy Fawkes celebrations, the room smelled slightly of cigarette smoke and she noted a nearly empty packet of cigarettes on the bedside cabinet next to a saucer acting as an ashtray with several butts in it. Margaret doubted whether there were any actual ashtrays in the whole house.

He shouldn't have been smoking; hadn't done so at least since his illness; it was detrimental to anyone recently recovered from such a condition. It spoke of rebellion, but what rebellion? She ignored the packet and sat on the foot of his bed looking at him across this rather spacious bedroom. Only the main bedroom in her house was nearly as large as this one. Hers was much smaller and the box room was exactly what it sound like, a box room.

'Your mother said I could come up,' she began.

He didn't respond. He hadn't turned round to look at her at all. No use sitting here looking at someone's back. She might as well get up and go. His back had a very straight look to it. He did look very tall standing there, but not so painfully thin as he had been. He had put on a little weight at last and his shoulders seemed to have broadened again. Seeing them, she felt a thrill of love pass through her. She got up and went across to him.

'Matthew,' she whispered. She touched his shoulder, surprised and alarmed to have him shrug the shoulder away from her as though stung.

'Good God, Matthew, what is the matter?' The profile of his face in the light from the street lamps seemed chiselled in granite, exactly as his mother's sometimes appeared when in a dilemma.

There was nothing for it but to force him to turn away from the window where he seemed to be staring out, not at the celebrating children and the lingering parents, but at something entirely disconnected from then. The look he gave her on being turned to face her was no different, as though it were not she but someone else who stood there. Then he blinked, seemed to come back to himself, recognise who it was standing beside him.

'Maggie . . . Margaret . . . I don't want it to happen to me again. I don't want to be in love with someone and find they don't want me.'

So he was frightened of ever falling in love again. A sense of deadness began to grow inside her. He had made up his mind and was letting her down gently. There was a strange expression in his dark eyes, so dark they seemed to have buried themselves in the depths of his skull. There was a look on his face she couldn't understand. A silent request for her to leave, she guessed. He seemed in pain, his brows drawn together, his lips twisted.

'So if he's the one you really want.'

What was he talking about? 'Who?' she interrupted weakly.

'The chap you were out with last week.'

Oh, God, Ronald Whittaker. Matthew had seen them together, must have watched them come back, watched their embrace. It was imperative to explain. She started to but he wasn't listening, was still talking.

'I don't blame you, Maggie. What've I got to offer someone like you?'

'It's not like that, Matthew,' she blurted, but he still wasn't listening.

'I don't love you, Maggie, I just felt – watching you . . . I don't love you. You don't have to feel bound to me if there's someone else. I don't love you, you know. I really don't . . .'

Her heart plummeted in shock and misery. He stopped suddenly, his expression like one of desperation. It confused her. It also dawned on her that he was denying just too vehemently this love he was supposed not to have for her. What was it Shakespeare wrote? 'The lady doth protest too much, methinks.' Matthew too was protesting too much. He did love her.

From its downward flight, her heart was lifting up, a soaring bird within her breast.

'Oh, darling, it was someone I knew years ago. He came looking for me. I told him I felt nothing for him. And I don't. It was over long ago. He's married.' The lie tripped easily off her tongue. All she wanted was to hear Matthew translate into words that which was contorting his features. But she must be the one to say it, she knew. She didn't hesitate a single second.

'The only person I love is you, Matthew. It's always been you.'

She saw his brow clear, his eyes become brighter, his lips lose their tightness to quiver and part in a disbelieving, hesitant smile. Seconds later she was in his arms, hearing him whispering fiercely to her.

'You don't know how I felt seeing you, down there with someone else. You'll never know. That feeling of jealousy, like a huge black insect inside me, I wanted to tear it out. That was when ...' A small ragged laugh, hardly a laugh at all but a sound, escaped him. 'That's when I knew. For the first time, I really knew.'

He didn't have to say it. She knew as well. All these years. All these wasted years. They were over. From now on she and Matthew would be able to look forward. There'd be times, of course, when sullenness overwhelmed him, old memories, old regrets maybe, the empty years of want raising their ugly heads in a dream, an unguarded moment. But she would be silent or encouraging, whichever his mood called for. There would also be the happy times, the loving moments, the quiet times.

'I love you,' she murmured, for the pair of them.

She felt him nod against her cheek before he kissed her, and knew he felt the same way about her. And it didn't matter that he did not put it into words.

Beyond the window a firework exploded in a protracted series of crackling – a jumping cracker. Perhaps in a little while she would suggest they take Mattie outside to see the fun. It would be Mattie's first time. She might be a little scared, but with a packet of hand-held sparklers Mattie could be gently coaxed into holding one to watch their fairy-like corona of sparks darting out like stars. This would soon inure her to the noise and the gleeful shouts as sky rockets whooshed up into the dark heavens.

It was in triumph that she and Matthew came downstairs and into the room where his parents waited in tense vigilance. It felt wonderful to witness their utter delight in seeing the smile on his face, his arm about her.

'We're taking Mattie out to see the fireworks,' he said simply, and for once his mother did not upbraid him for not calling his daughter Matilda.

Matilda sat half asleep in one of the armchairs, a little unnerved by the bangs and cracks outside. Margaret hadn't noticed her in the fraught moments earlier on, but now she was roused, still sleepy, and had her coat and hat put on her while Margaret made off down to a shop in Mare Street to buy the packet of sparklers. On the way she stopped off to tell her mother her news that Matthew had declared he loved her. Well, declared as much as he dared.

Matthew stood by the school railings, muffled in overcoat and scarf against the December cold, watching the children spilling out of the dim building into a sleet-spattered playground as the muffled echoes of the hand bell ringing home-time died away inside.

He thought of the night nearly four weeks ago, when he and Margaret had stood together with Mattie watching the fireworks and the bonfire, Margaret holding tightly on to her as she screamed in initial fright at the sudden noises, coaxing her to hold a sparkler by its thin stick between her small fingers until alarmed cries turned to squeals of delight.

At five years old, Mattie had suffered no fear of war. Her only trauma seemed to be the school where she had been started in September. She hadn't adjusted to it as well as she'd been expected to, and would throw herself into her grand-mother's arms on coming out, saying she hated everyone there. The children were noisy and rough, the teachers frightened her; every morning she burst into tears, fighting every inch of the way as she was taken there, sometimes saying she felt sick, until on several occasions her grandmother relented and brought her home again.

Margaret had expressed concern. 'There's something worrying her.'

'Other kids cope,' Matthew had said.

'Mattie's not other kids, Matthew. She was taken from her mother, though she was too young to understand, and it must have been unsettling. She's only been with grandparents all this time. Then suddenly she had to adjust to a total stranger she is told is her father. And now she's whipped off to a school full of strangers and expected to cope. No, Matthew, she's not like other kids.'

For a moment the old ache had welled up inside him, thinking how like her mother Mattie was, wilful, at times almost uncontrollable, quick to burst into tears. Yet she could be so charming, endearing herself to everyone at first glance. She was so much like Susan, in ways and looks, that it tore him apart to watch her. Margaret was right, he often found himself actually avoiding her so as to lessen the pain it gave him.

'She'll just have to learn to adapt. We all have to learn that,' he had said, remembering that he too had had to adapt over the years after knowing only a youth full of being molly-coddled. It had come as a shock.

But Margaret had been firm. 'A child's view of things is different to ours. We know we have to put up with what comes, or go under. We learn to fight adversity. A child doesn't even know what adversity is, only that they're unhappy and can't understand why. It makes them behave oddly, and when we get confused by them, they get even worse in sheer frustration. There's something underlying all this. Something even she doesn't remember, but it's there lurking in the back of her mind. She needs a real parent, which is what you are.'

Now he was being a real parent, waiting for Mattie to come out of school.

He was remembering how Margaret had clutched Mattie to her as a banger went off nearby. The houses around them had danced and shivered in the shadows of the lurid flames leaping high into the air from the bonfire. Margaret had given a visible shudder. 'She's had enough of this. I think I have as well.'

They had walked back down the road towards his house, Mattie walking between them, each holding her hand. She had seemed happier away from the violent fun, enjoying the fireworks from a distance. Small rockets had streaked thinly up into the sky over the rooftops, dimmed by bright street lights before which the once practically touchable moon and the pure discs of stars receded, never again to be seen in their full glory by city dwellers in the way they had been during the years of blackout.

Walking back slowly, he had thought what a wonderful mother Margaret would make. And at his gate he had proposed to her and Margaret had said yes.

Recalling it all with a light feeling inside him, he waited for his daughter to emerge from the school exit.

First came the very young, protectively shepherded by a tweed-skirted, motherly teacher into the chill afternoon already gathering into dusk. They were followed closely by exuberant older children: girls in neat hats, precisely buttoned overcoats and shiny strap shoes; boys with caps askew, blazers and coats open and flying, socks concertina'd and shoes with the mud of clogged playing fields clinging to them, laces already coming unravelled.

Taking leave of their teacher, the younger children ducked in and out of the bigger ones, seeking mothers who stood in groups with craning necks to collect their offspring.

Matthew stood a little apart from them, the only man, looking for his child. He saw her moving sedately among the others – small neat figure in her blue overcoat, her short dark curly hair peeping from under the small brim of her blue school hat. Blue suited her, as it had suited her mother.

Swallowing the lump that came into his throat, Matthew called out to her. Catching sight of him, her face lit up, but she walked across the playground and out of the gate to him with all the nonchalance of one having survived a traumatic experience and come off triumphant. The first time ever, he calculated with pride in his daughter's achievement.

She looked up at him with those great soulful blue eyes, so like her mother's. 'Are *you* taking me home today, Daddy?'

'Yes, Mattie,' he replied, love swelling within him as he gazed down at her, that love filling every dark place her mother's going had left inside him. She would fill it every day from now on. She and Maggie between them. By them he would survive. 'I'm taking you home.'

'Is Maggie going to be there?'

'Yes, she'll be there.'

Margaret had come over early. They had talked while his mother had taken Mattie to school, for once without tears with Maggie – he guessed he would always call her Maggie – promising to bring her sweeties if she didn't cry. 'And next week I'll go to school and wait for you to bring you home. Is that all right?' And Mattie had squealed that it was and had taken her grandmother's hand almost with enthusiasm. Maggie was good for her, would always be good for her.

'And you should call her Margaret, not Maggie,' he said solemnly. 'Or if you like, you could call her Mummy.'

Mattie thought for a moment, regarding him steadily. 'I like Mummy, it's easier.'

Matthew felt a small pang for her. She had never truly known her real mother, had she?

She was looking up at him, her mind gone entirely off names. 'Can we go home now, Daddy? I'm cold.'

Home. He held her hand as he led her to the car, which was warmer than having to walk in this weather. Home. By Christmas it would be a new home, his and Maggie's home, paid for from the trust money he'd been given on his twenty-first birthday, put away to accrue interest through the years, once intended for him and Susan. That was in the past now. The rest of the money would go to resuscitating the partnership – his father's wedding present to him, saying he himself was too old to manage alone any more. From now on the past would be put aside, only the future of importance.

He held out a hand and felt the soft fragility of Mattie's small fingers twine around his, trusting, possessive, confident of both present and future.

What of the future, he mused as they went towards the waiting car. Two weeks from now he would be married. In two weeks' time he would begin his life anew, perhaps regain a small part of what he had lost, after all those promises so carelessly made so long ago, so lightly taken for granted. He knew better now. He would make new promises to himself now; would never again take them all for granted, but he knew it would never again be quite the same.

Guiding his daughter to the car, he opened the rear door for her to scramble gratefully in. Then he went around the front, slid into the driver's seat, started the engine and pressed down on the accelerator with a force that made the thing roar wildly into life, driving off sharply enough to toss Mattie back into her seat with a delighted giggle.